Counselors-at-Law

Books by
JEROME WEIDMAN

JEROME WEIDMAN

Counselors-at-Law

A NOVEL

1980
DOUBLEDAY & COMPANY, INC.
GARDEN CITY, NEW YORK

ISBN 0-385-12880-0
Library of Congress Catalog Card Number 78-14712

For

Lila and John
"Of Counsel"

"They have no lawyers among them, for they consider them as a sort of people whose profession it is to disguise matters."

UTOPIA, Sir Thomas More

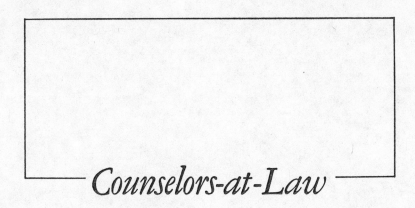

Counselors-at-Law

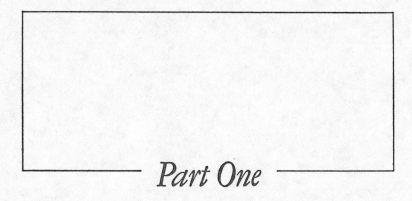

Part One

"If at first you don't succeed, try looking in the waste basket for the directions."

MAX D. STEUER

"Where you calling from?"

"Brooklyn," Ira Bodmer said into the phone.

"Grantham Estates 1977 federal return?" his boss said.

"Yes, sir," Ira Bodmer said. "I just filed it."

"Hold on a minute, son," Mr. Tessitore said. "I got a mouthful of toothpaste."

Getting rid of it clearly involved more than a spit and a rinse. Ira had never been inside his boss's home. The sounds that came roaring along the telephone wire, however, all the way from Riverside Drive and Eighty-sixth Street to the lobby of the Tillary Street Federal Building in Brooklyn, were easy to interpret. Mr. Tessitore at 6:00 A.M. in his bathroom was removing the toothpaste foam from his mouth the way he did everything in his office on Madison Avenue from 8:00 A.M. until God alone knew when Mr. Tessitore went home at night: as though he were working against a contractual deadline with a punishing default clause that allowed for no second chances. The roaring noises ceased. Mr. Tessitore came back on the wire.

"Okay, son," he said. "What time you got?"

Ira's wristwatch was on the hand with which he was holding the receiver to his ear. He looked out the glass door of the phone booth at the electric clock on the wall of the lobby.

"Ten minutes after six," he said.

"That's what I've got," Mr. Tessitore said. "Now I happen to be acquainted with that Tillary Street IRS facility. Been out there many times. It doesn't open to the public until eight-thirty."

"No, sir," Ira Bodmer said patiently.

Meeting Mr. Tessitore's challenge was as much a part of his job as was doing the task the performance of which Mr. Tessitore was challenging.

"There's an armed guard on duty around the clock in the lobby," Ira said. "He answers the night bell, and he's got a logbook for early birds like me. The Grantham Estates return is officially clocked in, sir. I've got the receipt in my hand."

"Good boy," Mr. Tessitore said.

A stranger might have drawn from Mr. Tessitore's sharp interrogation the inference that he felt Ira could have been lying about getting the Grantham Estates tax return into the hands of the federal government on the day it was due. Ira Bodmer was not a stranger. He had been one half of Mr. Tessitore's two-man staff for almost eight months. He was beginning to grasp how parts of Mr. Tessitore's mind worked.

The part that dealt with Mr. Tessitore's pride in being the managing clerk of one of New York's most prestigious law firms told Mr. Tessitore he could not himself physically perform every one of the almost innumerable functions his job demanded. Common sense told him he had to rely on a couple of youngsters like Ira Bodmer and Salvatore Giudice. A lifetime in the service of first-rate legal minds, many of them distinguished trial lawyers, had taught Mr. Tessitore how to trap the truth out of even an honest man. He would have tolerated no other kind in his service.

Being himself by nature a dishonest man, Mr. Tessitore could not afford to be served by underlings of the same stripe. By documenting the truth of something it would have been pointless for Ira Bodmer to lie about, Ira had set one fragment of Mr. Tessitore's endlessly restless mind at rest. The Grantham Estates federal return for 1977 was where it would have been if Mr. Tessitore had been physically able to place it there himself. Next!

"We're a little tight this morning," Mr. Tessitore said from his bathroom on Eighty-sixth Street. "I gave Sal the papers last night for a real estate closing Mr. Kelly's got in Jamaica this morning, so Sal will have to stick around out there until Mr. Kelly shows. He's driving in from Quogue and he's doing it in the Bentley because he has to leave it at Iggulden's, something about the steering, so God knows how long Sal will be hung up. That knocks half my team out of the box for most of the morning, which means you're all I'll have to work with till maybe eleven or twelve. You better head in."

"In" was the three-floor office complex occupied by Isham, Truitt, Kelly, Shreve, Merz, Uchitel and Condomine at 635 Madison. About this firm, with a roster of 116 lawyers and at last count almost two hundred outriders, Mr. Tessitore felt the way Chauntecler felt about the sun. It got under way every morning only because he gave the signal. Mr. Tessitore gave the signal at eight sharp, by which time he expected his two assistants to be at their posts in his office, ready for the day's assignments. Unless he had given them assignments the night before that had to be discharged early in the morning before they headed in to 635.

On this morning when Sal Giudice was out in Jamaica waiting for Mr. Kelly, Ira realized he had beaten his boss to the office. When he got out of the elevator on the twenty-ninth floor the night light was still glowing in the hall. Ira's watch showed five minutes after seven. Mr. Tessitore was a 7:45 on-the-button type.

Ira knew, from an illegal sneak look at the recitation check marks in the margin of the administrative office attendance chart, that Professor Pike would call on him that night in his Real Property II class at Alexander Hamilton Law School. Ira was not worried but he was pleased by this early morning windfall: a clear half hour that lay ahead for a review of the two assigned cases. Professor Pike was generally considered a bumbling old darling. On occasion, however, he could be a razor-tongued son of a bitch. Ira Bodmer had one more year at Hamilton before he was eligible for the Bar exam, and he wanted to participate in as little boat-rocking on Astor Place as possible.

He shifted the attaché case to his left hand, worked the door lock with his key, and let himself into the dimly lighted reception room. Ira flipped the light switch and set off down the long central corridor toward Mr. Tessitore's command post. About halfway along the spongy ribbon of thick taupe carpet Ira's ear picked up a sound he had never heard in this or any other office, and Ira Bodmer had done time in several. He stopped and listened.

The sound was repeated behind him. Ira turned and moved back slowly. The third repetition came from the right, or non-Madison Avenue side, of the corridor. That meant it was coming from one of the double cells inhabited by associates. Junior partners occupied the left, or Madison Avenue, side of the corridor where all the offices had windows and outer chambers for private secretaries. The fourth repetition of the sound nailed it down to the door a step away. Ira took the step and read the names in the slots above the knob: "J. C. Taunton" and under it "T. L. Lichine, Jr."

Having located the sound, Ira Bodmer stood there wondering what to do with it. He knew both Taunton and Lichine but neither very well. They were recent additions to what Mr. Tessitore called the Isham Truitt stable of junior geniuses. Both were law review: Taunton, Columbia; Lichine, Harvard. Both had been recruited by Mr. Merz on his last annual sweep of the Ivy League campuses. And to Ira Bodmer both were assholes, meaning objects of contempt and sources of envy.

Contempt because Ira had been with Isham Truitt almost three months longer than these two rich jerks, so he knew more of the office ropes than they did. Envy because they had been able to pick up their law degrees while lolling for three years on the water beds of parental tuition checks. And not at evening-session law schools, either, but at the Ivy League institutions from which you didn't sally forth to look for a job. You came back to your quarters after the graduation ceremonies, hung up your cap and gown, and sat down to sort out the offers from the best the world of Ira Bodmer's dreams had to offer: the two or three dozen top New York law firms.

The sounds, however, that had brought Ira Bodmer to the door marked "J. C. Taunton" and "T. L. Lichine, Jr." had nothing to do with contempt or envy. The sounds could have been made by somebody or anybody for whom Ira Bodmer felt neither. He put his hand on the knob and twisted. The door did not move. It was locked from the inside.

Ira covered the last third of the taupe corridor carpeting on the run. He tossed the attaché case on his small corner desk, sat down at Mr. Tessitore's big desk in the middle of the room, and dialed the number he had dialed an hour ago from the lobby of the Tillary Street IRS facility in Brooklyn. A woman's voice came on the wire.

"Hello?"

"This Mrs. Tessitore?" Ira said.

"Yes?"

"Mr. Tessitore still there, please?"

"Who's this?"

"Ira Bodmer? At the office?"

"One second, please." Mrs. Tessitore's voice rose an octave or two. "It's one of your boys, Tony!"

Ira Bodmer's mind recorded a moment of irrelevant surprise. Even though the managing clerk's given name was Anthony, Mr. Tessitore was known to everybody in the Isham Truitt offices, except Ira Bodmer and Sal Giudice, of course, as Tessie. To Ira it came as a surprise to hear his boss addressed as Tony.

"Yes, hello?"

"Mr. Tessitore?"

"Yes, hi. What's up, son?"

Ira Bodmer explained about the sounds coming from behind the "J. C. Taunton" and "T. L. Lichine, Jr." door. He added his decision to investigate. And he closed the report with his discovery that the door was locked.

"It's not Lichine in there," Mr. Tessitore said. "That's for sure."

"It's not?"

Ira meant how do you know it's not? Mr. Tessitore knew what Ira meant.

"Lichine's down in Alabama on that pro bono shit," the managing clerk said.

He spoke with the satisfaction of a man who enjoys being right before he starts tackling the not always enjoyable consequences of what he is right about. Mr. Tessitore viewed with distaste any services rendered to the outside world by Isham Truitt that were not reflected in the firm's billings. In the corridors of 635 Mr. Tessitore paid lip service to the valuable P.R. aspects of pro bono work. With his own team the managing clerk minced no words: "It's all crap. Money going out instead of coming in."

"I had a long-distance SOS yesterday from Alabama asking me to goose Gil Cutter in Accounting into hurrying up an expense voucher for Lichine for another two weeks," Mr. Tessitore said. "He's not due back until a week from next Thursday. That leaves his cell mate, Taunton."

Pause. Ira Bodmer could almost hear the little clock wheels of Mr. Tessitore's mind clicking away.

"Uh-uh," the managing clerk grunted. "No. This Taunton is a great one for putting on a good act how hard he works, always spreading it around he was in the office till two-thirty the night before, but it's now what?"

"Eight minutes after seven, sir," Ira said.

"That's what I've got," Mr. Tessitore said. There was a pause during which the managing clerk apparently examined what he had. Finally he came up with: "On the other hand for once Taunton could have worked that late and then fallen asleep, but—"

Mr. Tessitore was clearly unimpressed with the direction his out-loud thinking had taken. He stopped it with: "Why the hell would he lock the door from the inside?"

"That's what I thought, sir," Ira said.

"You say it sounded like a guy snoring?" Mr. Tessitore said.

"At first, yes," Ira Bodmer said.

"Then?" the managing clerk said.

"Then, well, I don't know how to say this," Ira said.

"Try," Mr. Tessitore said.

"It, well, it sounded like a guy moaning," Ira Bodmer said. "Like he's been hurt or something."

"Oh, Jesus," the managing clerk said. "Listen, son."

"Yes, sir?" Ira said.

"Don't do anything," Mr. Tessitore said. "Just wait for me. I'll grab a cab. I'm heading in."

"How'd you get into the room?" Salvatore Giudice said.

"Tessie," Ira Bodmer said. "He's got a key to every office in the place."

"What did he say?" Sal said. "Lichine?"

"At first nothing," Ira said. "You know his room?"

"Sure," Sal said. "Why?"

"The way the two desks face opposite walls?" Ira said. "With against the wall in between there's the couch facing the door?"

"Sure, yes," Sal said. "Under the picture of Chief Justice Taft."

"Right, well," Ira said, "Tessie pushes the door open, with me right behind him. The lights are off in the room but there's enough light from the corridor so you can see him lying on the couch."

"Lichine," Sal said.

"Yes, of course," Ira said. "I just told you it was him."

"I mean only Tessie was wrong, then," Sal said. "About the guy being down in Alabama."

"At seven-thirty this morning Mr. Lichine was not down in Alabama," Ira Bodmer said. "He was zonked out on the couch in his office a hundred feet down the hall from here."

"Then it was snoring after all?" Sal said.

"Mr. Giudice," Ira Bodmer said. "What is the thrust of your examination?"

"Knock it off," Sal said. "You just told me when you called Tessie at home you said first you thought what you'd heard behind that locked door was snoring, then you thought it was maybe moaning, like a guy who'd been beaten up."

"Well, yes," Ira Bodmer said. "The minute the light from the corridor hit him, Lichine started to come awake. I mean he stopped snoring. Then Tessie hit the switch, and the lights went on in the room, and Lichine sat up, rubbing his eyes. He looked terrible."

"Like a guy who'd been beaten up?" Sal Giudice said.

Ira Bodmer hesitated. He was torn between the truth and the desire to minimize what he had just begun to grasp must have been the touch of panic that had driven him to make that call to Mr. Tessitore at home early in the morning.

"Yes and no," Ira said.

"You just try to get away with that answer in my Evidence class," Sal said.

"Oh, well, Brooklyn Union Law School," Ira said.

"Oh, well, Brooklyn Union Law School my ass," Sal Giudice said. "Even in a schlock school like Hamilton with an answer like that what you'd earn is a swift shaft from His Honor. So let's cut the incidental music and have a replay of the facts. When you and Tessie opened the door of that office did Mr. Lichine look like a man who'd been beaten up or didn't he?"

"Yes, he did," Ira Bodmer said. "And all those cracks about Hamilton won't raise the status of Brooklyn Union from distinctly second-rate to just possibly adequate."

"All I want out of Brooklyn Union is a little piece of paper that says Salvatore Giudice is eligible to sit for the New York Bar exams," Sal said. "Now you just tell me did Mr. Lichine look like a guy who'd been beat up?"

"You know what a dude he is," Ira Bodmer said. "In a sort of subtle conservative-type way? Slightly on the old-fashioned side but also that with-it touch? Blue blazer? Button-down white oxford shirt? Cordovan slip-ons? Plus a twenty-bucks-a-throw golden hair-stylist job? All this tossed together on one hundred and eighty tennis-trimmed pounds of muscle?"

"You are describing my girl friend's idol," Sal Giudice said. "Arnold Schwarzenegger with a Kennedy accent."

"No," Ira Bodmer said. "I'm giving you a Polaroid shot of

T. L. Lichine, Jr. Late of Harvard Law, more recently of Isham Truitt, and early this morning sole inhabitant of the two-desk cell down the hall where Tessie and I found him at seven-twenty A.M. What he looked like, kidding aside, he looked like he'd been caught in an alley up in the South Bronx during a drug bust in which he'd absorbed a thorough working-over by the narcotics squad."

"You mean really bad?" Sal Giudice said.

"Well, I didn't have time to check for broken bones," Ira Bodmer said. "All I could do was look. What I saw was the beginnings of an impressive shiner and a few blood smears. The blue blazer was torn, the collar of his shirt was ripped open, and he was breathing in a way that sounded like, you know how a car with a bum battery trying to get under way sounds on a winter morning?"

"How the hell did the poor son of a bitch ever manage to crawl all the way from Hiroshima to six-three-five Madison?" Sal Giudice said. "And manage to lock the door of his office behind him, yet too?"

"That's what Tessie wanted to know," Ira Bodmer said.

"I suppose Mr. Lichine was too beat-up to provide a coherent answer," Sal Giudice said.

"A Brooklyn Union man would suppose that," Ira Bodmer said. "Mr. Lichine is Harvard. He informed our managing clerk that there had been an unexpected break in the pro bono case he'd been sent down to Alabama to work on. He'd flown back without warning to pick up some important papers. He'd come direct to the office because the papers were in his desk. Since he had a couple of hours before his flight back to Alabama he'd locked his door and hit the couch for some desperately needed sack time. Who the hell did we think we were busting in on him like that? Don't answer. Just get the hell out of here, both of you."

"Did you?" Sal Giudice said.

"Tessie did," Ira Bodmer said. "I hadn't really got in to begin with. I was still standing out in the hall, on the threshold, looking in across our boss's shoulder, when the eviction notice was slammed in our faces."

"Jesus Christ," Sal Giudice said.

"At Alexander Hamilton it's *oy vay*," Ira Bodmer said.

"At Isham Truitt it's nine thirty-five," Sal Giudice said. "What happened here in the dugout while I was waiting out in Jamaica for Mr. Kelly to arrive from Quogue in his Bentley?"

"I don't know," Ira Bodmer said. "Except Tessie told me to hold down the fort."

"Where'd he go?" Sal Giudice said.

"He didn't brief me," Ira Bodmer said. "All he told me was how to keep your nose to the grindstone when you show up. I'm in charge until Tessie gets back and I want no lip from Brooklyn Union Law School night students."

The door of Mr. Tessitore's command post opened. A handsome young man came in. His custom-made navy-blue blazer was beautifully pressed. His white oxford button-down shirt was freshly laundered. A black knitted tie was held neatly against his flat belly by an unobtrusively massive solid-gold safety pin. His cordovan slip-ons gleamed like mirrors. His golden hair was not exactly combed, but every strand lay with dutiful precision exactly where it had been skillfully tumbled.

"I was looking for Mr. Tessitore," the young man said.

"He's not here at the moment," Ira Bodmer said.

"I can see that," Mr. Lichine said. "When will he be back?"

"He didn't say," Ira Bodmer said. "Anything we can do?"

"No," Mr. Lichine said. Then, after a thoughtful but totally unhesitant pause: "Yes."

He looked carefully at Ira, then at Sal. His glance came back to Ira.

"You were with Mr. Tessitore this morning," he said.

"Yes," Ira said.

"I seem to have mislaid my key case," Mr. Lichine said. "You haven't seen it, have you?"

"No," Ira said.

"Mr. Tessitore?" Mr. Lichine said.

"I don't know but I think he would have mentioned it," Ira Bodmer said. "I'll tell him when he comes back. In the meantime Sal and I will spread the word around the office for people to keep their eyes open, and Mr. Tessitore will probably want to do what he always does in lost and found cases, put a notice on the bulletin board."

Mr. Lichine's glance moved again.

"You're Sal?" he said.

"Yes," Sal said. "Short for Salvatore."

Mr. Lichine's eyes came back to Ira.

"No, don't do that," he said.

"Do what?" Ira said.

"Spread the word around," Mr. Lichine said. "Or put it on the bulletin board. It's not that important. I may have left the case at home. If it shows up in the office it will probably be brought here to Mr. Tessitore, anyway, won't it?"

"Yes, that happens a lot," Ira Bodmer said. "Sometimes people take things to Mr. Cutter, the office manager. Probably not with everything, but quite a few things that people lose in the office."

"It's alligator, with gold corners," Mr. Lichine said. "My initials are on the inside."

"We'll keep our eyes open," Ira Bodmer said.

"Thanks," Mr. Lichine said.

After the door closed behind him Ira Bodmer became aware of the soft whistling noise Sal Giudice was making through his teeth.

"This the same guy you and Tessie walked in on down the hall at seven-thirty this morning?" Sal said.

"Seven-twenty," Ira Bodmer said.

"I'd say either your description of his condition was a bit on the faulty side," Sal Giudice said. "Or somebody has done a honey of a repair job in a very short space of time."

"Alexander Hamilton concedes that Mr. Lichine at nine thirty-five certainly does not look like a guy who had the shit kicked out of him in the small hours of this recent night," Ira Bodmer said.

"Brooklyn Union would like to point out, however," Sal Giudice said, "that the evidence would seem to justify drawing an inference."

"Such as?" Ira Bodmer said.

"That some time during those same small hours," Sal Giudice

said, "Mr. Lichine did some shit kicking of his own on a person or persons unknown."

"What evidence?" Ira Bodmer said.

"The knuckles on Mr. Lichine's right hand," Sal Giudice said. "They are covered with two fresh Band-Aids."

3

The phone rang. Judy Cline picked it up.

"Hello?"

"Judy?"

The grating voice of Mr. Kelly's ancient secretary had been readily identifiable to her for a full year, ever since, direct from Harvard, Judy Cline had joined Isham, Truitt, Kelly, Shreve, Merz, Uchitel and Condomine as a young associate.

"Yes, Mrs. Campion," Judy said.

"I just had a call from Mr. Kelly," Mrs. Campion said. "He's at Iggulden's. He's leaving the Bentley for repairs and then he's taking a taxi to the office. He called to check on whether you were in. I told him not yet but I knew where to reach you. He told me to do that and make sure you're here in the office when he arrives. Got that?"

"Did he say what it's about?" Judy said.

"Mr. Kelly does not pay me to tell people more than he tells me to tell them," Mrs. Campion said. "So you just better make tracks, honey."

Hugh F. X. Kelly, Jr., by his own assertion, would never have become a lawyer if his father had not been a famous Irish tenor.

"I was raised on mother's milk and father's denunciations of Caruso's morals," he once said in a speech at an Isham Truitt annual dinner in the University Club. "When I grew old enough to read the papers and learned what Caruso thought of my father's morals, I determined that when I reached man's estate and was forced to earn my own bread, I would do it in a manner as far removed from the world of tenors as I could get. It may not be the best reason in the world for choosing the law as a profession, but at an age when my father, God rest his soul, could no longer get through 'Danny Boy' and was reduced to inventing scurrilous insults about John McCormack, I can still earn six-figure fees for writing into a lease a few grace notes about metes and bounds that make the loveliest music this side of heaven. It is played, of course, on the cash register."

The reason why Hugh Kelly had played it so long and so successfully did not get into his after-dinner speeches. It was, however, a staple in the gossip of the blue-chip Bar. It was called "the Catholic Connection."

In the taxi that carried her downtown Judy Cline took from her briefcase and rechecked her Xerox of the memorandum she had prepared for Mr. Kelly to carry into this morning's closing in Jamaica. It dealt with a corner property in Kew Gardens Hills that Cardinal Cooke had set his heart on having for his new city-wide day-nursery-school program.

Ever since Mr. Merz had recruited her out of Harvard Law, Judy had been working pretty much under Mr. Kelly's wing. This was all right with her. Judy liked him, perhaps because it was so clear that he liked her. In the main, however, Judy liked working for Mr. Kelly because when it came to New York real estate Hugh F. X. Kelly, Jr., knew, as Judy's playwright father used to put it on the New York stage, his onions.

She had learned that at a closing Mr. Kelly liked to give the impression that he was personally physically familiar with the property. Judy had discovered soon enough that he rarely was. The impression of familiarity was the same, however, whether Mr. Kelly had trod the ground daily since early youth, or whether he had never laid eyes on it. The trick was his combination of a fruity brogue, plus careful staff briefing.

For this morning's closing in Jamaica, in order to make sure Mr. Kelly would be able to handle the matter with the complete authority he liked to display in all matters but especially where he was representing the Church, Judy had made a special effort in her briefing. The result, in a swift but careful taxi review, seemed to hold up. She could find nothing that might have precipitated Mr. Kelly's urgent summons by phone from Iggulden's. The small tremor in her gut upset Judy. It was the way she used to feel, she recalled with embarrassment, when as a child she had been sent by her mother into her father's presence for a bawling-out she did not doubt she had earned but did not yet know how.

"Bankers' hours?" Miss Marvin said from the reception desk when Judy came into the office.

Miss Marvin's tone was expected. The undeniably decorative feature of the Isham Truitt reception room, Cheryl Marvin, as Miss South Dakota, had been a semifinalist in one of the Miss America beauty contests of the late sixties or early seventies. The beauty contest had opened the traditional doors, apparently not all of them to bedrooms. Miss Marvin's employment trail, preserved in a Florentine-tooled leather scrapbook kept in the bottom drawer of her reception-room desk, had led briefly to Hollywood, even more briefly to modeling in New York, and briefest of all to chorus work on Broadway, where Mr. Kreel had found her.

Kenneth Kreel was the Isham Truitt junior partner who knew the theater and the allied motion picture and TV worlds the way Hugh Kelly knew New York real estate. There the resemblance stopped, or at any rate paused. Hugh Kelly was a relentlessly dedicated family man with eleven living children and, at last count, twenty-nine grandchildren and fourteen great-grandchildren. Ken Kreel was a relentlessly dedicated skirt chaser with two monthly alimony checks and a small black book with loose-leaf pages.

It was a not implausible office rumor that Tessie, finding his usual ample resources depleted when asked on short notice to supply a date for an out-of-town client, always called upon Mr. Kreel and his little black book. Ken Kreel was always glad to oblige. So, the rumor went, was his protégé Cheryl Marvin.

Judy ignored her as she moved across the reception room and pushed through into the corridor.

"Close," Mrs. Campion said with a glance at her watch when Judy erupted into Mr. Kelly's outer office. "But no cigar, honey."

"That Judy out there?"

"Yes, Mr. Kelly!" Judy called back, and, disregarding Mrs. Campion's glare, she marched firmly across the secretary's room and into what was known at Isham Truitt as "the Chapel."

To Mr. Kelly a wall was obviously a space to be concealed by pictures. With the walls of his own private office he had almost succeeded. They were hung with large, handsomely framed, warmly inscribed studio portraits of the last three popes, every cardinal of the New York Archdiocese since the time of Mr. Kelly's birth, and a couple of dozen other church dignitaries. Among these Judy had early on recognized only Fulton J. Sheen because once, when she was still at Dalton, he had come to dinner at her parents' apartment at 1010 Fifth Avenue.

The wall space in Mr. Kelly's office that was not blotted out by the Church was covered by the Kelly family. Arranged like stamps in an album, led by black-bordered pictures of the three Kelly boys who had been killed in the war, Kellys of all ages, shapes, and sizes stared down on the founding father: wives, husbands, children, grand- and great-grandchildren, diluted here and there with nannies, gardeners, butlers, cooks, tweenies, and an occasional chauffeur at the wheel of a station wagon overflowing with small fry on the grounds of the family summer place in Quogue.

Dominating this impressive array of photography, however, were two decorations that caught the eye as soon as the door opened. One was an enormous portrait of King Alfonso of Spain, inscribed to Mr. Kelly's father. The other, in the corner between the Madison Avenue windows on the right and the Fifty-ninth Street windows on the left, was a bronze statue of St. Patrick. He was depicted with a shamrock leaf, banishing the serpents. The statue came to Judy's shoulder.

"Come in, child, come in," Mr. Kelly called from behind his desk.

"Good morning, sir," Judy said. "I'm sorry to be late."

"You must abandon forevermore that apology from your speech," Mr. Kelly said. "If you don't you are doomed to waste many good hours of your life making it in vain because, as my father used to say, a sight that gladdens the eye can never be anything but late in arriving. Come sit here, child."

He patted the chair beside his desk. Moving into it, Judy realized there was a reason even stronger than the decorations of
Mr. Kelly's office for calling it the Chapel. There was Mr. Kelly
himself.

He was a large, shapeless, untidy bundle of man who nevertheless had the sharp, clean, clearly defined outlines of a child's
battered but beloved toy animal. His clothes, which were made
by Gieve & Hawkes on Saville Row, looked as though they had
been tossed at his body piece by piece until enough of the pieces
had stuck to his frame to make him decently presentable for
public view. The fringe of gray hair around the edges of his
shiny bald scalp, which was clipped weekly by a barber who
came up from the shop in the lobby, looked as though it had just
come through a bare-headed ferryboat crossing in a gale. And
there was, of course, the face. Large, dewlapped, a mass of wal-
nut shell creases out of which gleamed the sharp ice-blue eyes
and the strong straight teeth. Set in the surroundings he had chosen for his office, Hugh F. X. Kelly, Jr., looked not unlike a monk
so happily and busily absorbed in his devotional duties that he
had no time to worry about the condition of his tonsure or the ti-
diness of his cassock.

"I hope the closing went well, sir," Judy said.

"If it had gone any better," Mr. Kelly said, "I do believe they
would have thrown in the property across the street as a bonus.
Your memorandum made it possible for me to feel the people at
the other side of the table believed they were dealing with a
man who knew some real estate law. What I admired particularly was the photographs. It was the crowning touch. What
made you think of doing that, child?"

"The unpaid water bill," Judy said. "I didn't see how a structure that size could tolerate that much water pouring through its
normal facilities without causing visible damage. So I went out
with my Polaroid last Sunday, when I knew nobody would be
there, and I walked around the place. There was a depression in
the backyard cement that looked suspiciously like a concealed
cave-in, and by tracking a couple of rivulets that were slowly
working their way to low ground I found on the Seventy-eighth
Avenue side what looked like major sewer damage beginning to

surface from the building line out into the middle of the street. I
hope the pictures were okay. Photography is not one of my
strong points."

"Real estate law is, my dear," Mr. Kelly said. "A lovely job,
child, lovely. I am very pleased with you."

Judy could not, however, stop the small uneasy feeling in her
stomach that she had carried downtown with her from the moment she had received Mrs. Campion's phone call.

"Thank you, sir," Judy said.

She hesitated, waiting for Mr. Kelly to say more, but all at
once he seemed utterly absorbed by the manner in which St. Patrick was hustling the snakes out of Ireland in the corner of the
room.

"Then if there's nothing more, sir?" Judy said.

The ice-blue eyes abandoned St. Patrick and came back to
Judy Cline.

"What?" Mr. Kelly said. Then: "Oh, on this? Oh, no. We
may consider this one wrapped up, I think. No. Not this. No. I
asked Mrs. Campion to call you because something troubling has
happened, and I'm not quite sure what to do about it. I thought
you might be able to help me."

"If I can, sir," Judy said.

The small uneasy feeling vanished. In its place came something to which in recent months she had begun to look forward.
The small glow of pleasure that was part of doing more than her
job: something extra that was earmarked if only in her mind for
him.

"While I was out there in Jamaica this morning," Mr. Kelly
said. "In this lawyer's office where one of Tessie's boys had delivered the papers to me. We hadn't got under way yet, and I
was studying your memorandum, when one of the secretaries
came in and said there was a long-distance call for me from Alabama."

"Alabama?" Judy said.

Abruptly the temperature of her warm glow dropped several
degrees.

"Yes, Montgomery," Mr. Kelly said. "It was from an old friend
of mine, Father Danaher. Terence Danaher. We were at Ford-

ham Law School together, which gives you some idea how far back we go. Terence took his law degree and went into the Church, where he's been very active in legal work, especially in the South. Over the years, when we've assigned some of our young people from the office here to pro bono work, I've always seen to it that in addition to what we do in the New York area, we give Father Danaher a hand with whatever he's up to down there in Confederate territory. It's always something worthy, you can be sure. I haven't kept close track of it, frankly, aside from seeing to it that the word gets out here at Isham Truitt that I want Father Danaher to have a bit of a lift. I didn't know until Terence called me this morning that about two weeks ago one of our young men from the office here was assigned to Father Danaher in Montgomery for a month. Now yesterday it was, Terence said on the phone, yesterday something unusual happened down there in Alabama and our young man disappeared."

"Disappeared?" Judy said.

"Disappeared," Mr. Kelly said. "Father Danaher was calling to find out if he'd come back to New York. I didn't even know the young man was working for us, but Terence said he was new, less than a year with us, and we'd got him from Harvard. That meant he'd been recruited by Manny Merz, of course, so I told Father Danaher I'd call him back, and I hung up and from out there in Jamaica I called Mr. Merz here at home. He said yes, he knew the young man very well, he'd been working exclusively for Ken Kreel on his theater and TV things since he joined us, and it was because Ken Kreel had suggested him for this pro bono assignment that the young man had been sent down for a month to help Father Danaher in Montgomery. Aside from that, Mr. Merz said, he knew nothing about the young man, except that his record at Harvard had been superb, but Mr. Merz did know somebody who could probably tell me all about him, so I called Mrs. Campion and asked her to call you."

"What's the young man's name?" Judy said.

"Litch something," Mr. Kelly said. "Like those things they give you for dessert in Chinese restaurants. Lichee nuts are they not called?"

Judy laughed.

"Lichine," she said.

"That's it," Mr. Kelly said. "Manny Merz said you and Mr. Lichine were at Harvard Law together."

"Tom Lichine and I go further back than that," Judy said.

"How far back is further?" Mr. Kelly said.

"We met on a sunny morning in Central Park in 1953," Judy Cline said. "We were occupying adjoining prams. It was established later that I was not quite three months old at the time, and Tom was not quite five months old. A difference of seven weeks and three days."

Mr. Kelly laughed. It was a sound Judy had come to like. It reminded her of billiard balls rolling slowly across a table and only occasionally touching.

"Lord love us, child," he said. "You do go back a long way."

"Longer actually than that," Judy said.

The skin around the eyes in the pink face tightened.

"That's a bit of a riddle, now, isn't it, child?" Mr. Kelly said.

"I came along because my mother wanted to catch up with Tom's mother," Judy said. "Tom's mother was an actress named Amelia Troy. She became a star when she had the lead in one of my father's plays. At the same time she and my mother became great friends. They were so close they practically lived together when Miss Troy was not on stage. When Amelia Troy had a baby my mother decided she had to have one, too."

"That must have taken a bit of doing," Mr. Kelly said with a chuckle. "Since young Tom, I think you said his name was, he was a mere eight weeks older than you were when you met."

"Actually it was quite easy," Judy said. "My parents were incapable of having children. I was adopted."

"I see," Mr. Kelly said.

Judy had a feeling that in recent months had become quite common when they were alone together. It was a feeling that Mr. Kelly saw more than, from the information she had supplied, she had given him reason to see.

"Tell me something, child," he said. "You say your father wrote plays. Would he by any chance happen to be a gentleman named Clifford Cline?"

"He would," Judy said.

The billiard balls went rumbling across the table again.

"Would you believe this now, child?" Mr. Kelly said. "My father used to take me to see your father's plays. It was one of them, in fact, I don't remember the name, but it was a courtroom drama, and it was from the day I saw that play that I date my discovery of a way to get as far away as possible from the world of tenors and I reached my youthful determination to embrace the law as a way of life."

"The coincidence will please my father," Judy said.

"If it's coincidences from which he draws his pleasure," Mr. Kelly said, "I give you another one to carry to him as a gift. On our thirtieth anniversary, in 1959, Mrs. Kelly and I celebrated three happy decades of married life by attending a musical play written by your father. I have never forgotten the title."

"*I Am Dying, Little Egypt,*" Judy said. "The play was a big hit, and my father won a Tony Award for it."

"I see," Mr. Kelly said.

Again Judy had the feeling he was seeing more than she was.

"Tell me something," Mr. Kelly said. "Or perhaps you won't want to, in which case no matter, child. It's a personal thing, you see?"

"I can't imagine you asking me anything I wouldn't want to answer," Judy said.

It was true, but until this moment she had not realized it was true, and had been for some time. Judy could hear the echo of the intensity in her own voice as she had spoken the words. Her face grew hot.

"You are very kind to say that," Mr. Kelly said. "I was wondering, child, are you by any chance a Catholic girl?"

"I don't know," Judy said.

The pink skin tightened again at the corners of the ice-blue eyes.

"I don't think I understand," Mr. Kelly said. "Indeed, I'm sure I do not."

"My mother and father had very advanced ideas, I think was the way they put it at that time," Judy said. "They made it a condition of the adoption that they would not be informed what the religion of the child's parents was."

Mr. Kelly's face seemed to light up from within. It was as though his head contained a concealed chandelier and it had just been switched on. The result was as close to a look of pure pleasure as Judy Cline had ever seen on a human face.

"Then you could indeed be a Catholic girl?" Mr. Kelly said. "Could you not, child?"

"Very easily," Judy said.

"And would you as shall we say a putative Catholic girl lend a helping hand to a troubled nonputative Catholic man old enough to be your father?" Mr. Kelly said.

"Of course," Judy Cline said.

"There seems to be some confusion about what happened in Alabama yesterday," Mr. Kelly said. "When he spoke to me on the phone this morning I know Terence Danaher was telling me the truth. The truth, that is, as he saw it. The lie is not in the man. I feel the same way about Tessie."

"Mr. Tessitore?" Judy said.

"Yes," Mr. Kelly said.

"What's he got to do with this?" Judy said.

"At seven-thirty this morning Tessie found Mr. Lichine asleep in his office down the hall," Mr. Kelly said. "According to Tessie, the young man seemed upset, the condition of his clothes seemed to indicate he had been involved in some sort of very bad fight, and he very rudely ordered Tessie to get out of his room."

"I wish I could say what I've heard you say so often at a moment like this," Judy said.

"And what is that, child?" Mr. Kelly said.

"Quote I see unquote," Judy said.

For a couple of moments Mr. Kelly rumbled the billiard balls down the table.

"But you do not?" he said.

"No, sir," Judy said.

"If you were me what would you then do at this point?" Mr. Kelly said.

"I'd call in Mr. Lichine and ask him what happened in Alabama," Judy said.

"That is precisely what I want to do," Mr. Kelly said.

A straight man in one of her father's plays could not have fed her more directly the cue to the line that was now demanded of Judy Cline.

"Why don't you?" she said.

"When Mr. Lichine answers my question," Mr. Kelly said, "I'd like somebody to be in the room with me."

"Your memorandum drafter?" Judy said.

"Yes, child, if you will," Mr. Kelly said.

"Of course I will, if you want me to," Judy said. "I must say, though, I don't know what I can contribute."

"A yardstick," Mr. Kelly said. "Manny Merz told me you and Mr. Lichine are friends. You have just told me how old that friendship is. I have known you now for almost a year. I do not believe a friend of yours, a true friend, child, would in your presence tell anything but the truth."

Judy felt tears come up in her eyes. Fortunately Mr. Kelly had turned to the call box on the table back of his desk.

"Mrs. Campion," he said into it. "Ask Mr. Dent if he'd be good enough to come along now."

4

Howard Dent believed that, for a lawyer, the process of growing old presented only two hazards: falling down in the park, and joining a firm as "of counsel." It was because at eighty-eight he had suffered the first that Howard Dent had agreed to take on the second.

On his eighty-ninth birthday, when the hip had healed sufficiently so that with a single cane he could get about almost spryly, he accepted Walter Isham's invitation to join Isham, Truitt, Kelly, Shreve, Merz, Uchitel and Condomine as "of counsel." The decision made the front page of the *Times*. Howard Dent was not surprised. He had been on it for years.

First, as FDR's special prosecutor in the Wall Street investigation of SEC bribery that had brought Howard Dent to national attention as "the man who put the midget on J. P. Morgan's lap." Then as the Undersecretary of State who at Potsdam was denounced publicly by Joseph Stalin as "Harry Truman's Colonel House." And finally, for turning down Lyndon Johnson's Supreme Court appointment because the quid pro quo demanded by the President, spelled out clearly in a letter that Howard Dent made public, was a cessation of his public attacks on the legality of the Gulf of Tonkin Resolution.

"A long and honorable career as a public servant comes to an end," the *Times* had said in its front-page story announcing Howard Dent's retirement from the practice of law at the age of eighty-seven. "This man of high purpose and inexhaustible energy who has experienced everything the stage of our tumultuous century has to offer."

Not quite everything, as it turned out. Howard Dent had never experienced inactivity. When he did, it almost killed him. For eighty-seven years he had never had to walk in the park to keep busy. He called Walter Isham from his hospital bed.

"Is that offer still open?"

"I'll tell Gil Cutter to get an office ready for you at once," Walter Isham said.

"You can skip the window on Madison Avenue and provide me instead with a pretty secretary to look at," Howard Dent said.

"I'll order Ken Kreel to start flipping the pages of his little black book immediately," Walter Isham said. "When can I tell the welcoming committee to expect you?"

"As soon as I can make it from the Plaza with a single cane," Howard Dent said.

He had lived in the same hotel suite for half a century.

"We'll be glad to have the office limo pick you up and take you back every day," Walter Isham said.

"Save it for your fat Catholic partner," Howard Dent said. "I've always walked to work."

He still did. And on the way in he still paused at the reception desk to exchange with Cheryl Marvin what he still called a pleasantry. A lifelong bachelor, his taste in women still ran not to intelligence but to the number four cup. And he still enjoyed the very special pleasure of the secretly conceited man who is honored by the world for his public modesty.

At ninety-one Howard Dent had been old for so long that it was no longer a novelty. It had become a seasoned experience. From it he had learned there were no pleasures that came with old age. You had to invent them yourself. Howard Dent had invented a beauty. He called it "the Prism View."

He had learned when he was still young that looking at life through the same lens soon became a bore. It was like reading a favorite book over and over again. The process might provide a small pleasure. Howard Dent, however, had never found that it provided very much in the way of profit. When he became old he found it intolerable.

A minimum of experimentation with the lens that had served him in youth and middle age produced a surprising revelation. As with the interpretation of a restrictive clause in a contract or a statute, a difference of degree tended to become a difference in kind. It was all a matter of angle. By tipping the lens he was able to produce the effect of a prism.

Looking at the world through it, Howard Dent was able to see what everybody saw: the witless admiration of the young for the old for no reason other than the fact that the old were still on their feet, and the acceptance of this admiration by the old the way the infant mewling and puking in his crib accepts the bottle —as a natural right. In addition, because he was now looking at life through a prism, Howard Dent was able to see also what, so far as he was aware, nobody but Howard Dent had ever seen before: the endless slapstick provided by a simultaneous study in action of both these piously fraudulent points of view. The joke was on everybody, except the man with his eye to the prism. It was almost worth getting old for. Howard Dent kept the discovery to himself. At ninety-one the time of sharing was over. Greed was the watchword for whatever time was left.

Filling the time, if it was done through a prism, made every day at least interesting, some fascinating, and not infrequently one came along that was pure pleasure. A day such as this one, for example. It had begun with a number of inquiries set in motion by a call for help from Hugh Kelly out in Jamaica. The inquiries had been interesting. The accumulated revelations had become fascinating. There was every reason to expect, if Howard Dent did not jar the prism out of focus, that the meeting in Hugh Kelly's office to which he had just been summoned would result in one of those days of pure pleasure. Who could tell? Certainly not Mrs. Campion.

"Go right in, Mr. Dent," she said. "Mr. Kelly is expecting you."

Howard Dent—six-three, bacon-rind lean, ramrod straight— produced one of his courtly, gentleman-of-the-old-school bows. What the audience wanted, the audience got.

"Thank you, Mrs. Campion."

Crossing the outer office to the Chapel, through the prism Howard Dent could already hear Mrs. Campion to her chum Mrs. Bethune, the head of Stenographic, across the cups at their coffee break: "And the amazing thing, Merle, is that he never, but absolutely never, forgets my name!"

Hugh Kelly came out from behind the desk with hand outstretched as though St. Patrick himself had come down from the bronze plinth in the corner of the room to share a late-morning snort from the bottle in Hugh Kelly's bottom desk drawer.

"Good of you to join us, Howard," he said.

"Not at all," Howard Dent said.

He gave it just a touch of the "With the President's party" manner. Hugh Kelly would expect that. It was the very least he and his partners could expect for what it cost them to provide free office space and a full-time secretary for "A Living Legend." Howard Dent added to the letterhead of a New York law firm the sort of touch that the never-used office in the old State Department Building in Washington had provided for decades to the incumbent senior cabinet member: the gold-lettered sign on the door had read "General John J. Pershing."

"I'm not sure you know these young members of our staff," Hugh Kelly said. "There are so many of them these days I hardly know many of them even by sight. First, the pretty one here, that's Judy Cline. The child keeps me from falling off the sled at real estate closings by briefing me in advance the way you used to brief Harry Truman."

"With, I hope, happier results," Howard Dent said.

"Disregard our distinguished of counsel's modesty," Hugh Kelly said. "Just say hello to a great man, child."

"I'm pleased to meet you, sir," the girl said.

Howard Dent smiled. Lovely breasts. Neat little ass. Cute nose. Charming smile. Directed, Howard Dent noted, not at him but at Hugh Kelly. The prism recorded the discovery of another one of Hugh Kelly's father-image victims. This one, fortunately, looked bright as well as lovely. With luck she would discover the fraud beneath the blarney and come back to her senses before any serious damage was done. Howard Dent wondered if it might not be fun to take a hand in the freeing of Miss Cline from the Hugh Kelly spell. Hmmm.

"And this is Tom Lichine," Hugh Kelly said.

"How do you do, sir?" Mr. Lichine said.

Howard Dent nodded to the young man in the blue blazer. A son of a bitch, clearly. But the girls wouldn't care about that. Most of them wouldn't even notice. They would see only the killingly handsome male animal. The prism saw more. It picked up the sharp intelligence. The shrewdly distrustful eyes. The concealed but not totally concealed sensitivity that would have to be reached if you wanted to hurt him. The prism's verdict: the boy could be hurt.

"Howard, will you sit here?" Hugh Kelly said.

"Certainly not," Howard Dent said. "You know my anti-Catholic bias. I can manage to hold it in check when I'm in the presence of an old and valued friend, but not if at the same time I must stare at St. Patrick doing his vaudeville turn with the snakes. Young lady, you sit here."

Howard Dent took Miss Cline's hand and helped her to her feet.

"It's undoubtedly the most comfortable chair in the room," he said, "and Hugh obviously wants me to have it because I am the oldest person in the room, but it belongs to you because you are the prettiest person in the room."

Howard Dent led her to the chair Hugh Kelly had wanted him to have and helped her into it. Then Howard Dent went back to the chair in which Miss Cline had been sitting. Settling himself into it, his prism recorded that the small performance had made an impression. Something had crossed Miss Cline's polite, mechanical smile of witless admiration for an old fart who was still managing to remain on his feet. It was a flick of interest in another human being. Howard Dent settled himself in the chair with a small feeling of anticipation. This could very easily turn out to be one of those days.

"For a man my size this chair is much better," he said.

It was also much better for the prism. In this chair Howard Dent's back was not only to St. Patrick and his vaudeville turn. In this chair Howard Dent's back was also to the Madison Avenue windows. The sun, falling across his shoulders, lighted up every inch of what he had come to this preposterous room to watch: young Mr. Lichine's face.

"Howard, let me explain the background," Hugh Kelly said.

He had explained it thoroughly in his phone call to Howard Dent from Jamaica four hours ago. The statement indicated, therefore, that Hugh Kelly, who did not always keep his promises, had kept this one: not to say a word to young Mr. Lichine until he could bring Howard Dent into the room to hear him. Hugh Kelly had said nothing in his phone call about also bringing Miss Cline into the room. Perhaps Miss Cline had been a later thought. Hugh Kelly's talents as a lawyer, aside from having been born a Catholic, were not unlike those of Irving Berlin as a composer: he played it by ear. On the other hand perhaps Miss Cline had been a calculated participant in this meeting from the beginning. A point to be noted. No more than that.

"As you know, Howard, like most large firms nowadays we have for a long time now contributed the services of a certain number of our associates to pro bono work for limited periods of time each year," Hugh Kelly said. "I like to see to it that at least some of our contribution each year goes to my old friend and Fordham classmate Father Terence Danaher down in Alabama. I had a phone call from Terence in Montgomery this morning. He told me for two weeks he had been defending an impoverished man in a murder trial with the help of our Mr. Lichine. Terence told me he had found Mr. Lichine's help invaluable. That was the word Father Danaher used. Invaluable. He went on to say that the case went to the jury yesterday afternoon. As of this moment the jury is still out. At any rate when Terence called me at eight this morning the jurors were still at the motel near the courthouse where they had spent the night. Last night Terence tried to call Mr. Lichine at the hotel where he was staying but he was not in. Terence left his number but Mr. Lichine did not return the call. This morning, shortly before eight, Terence called Mr. Lichine again. He was told Mr. Lichine had not spent the night in the hotel. He had not checked out. His suitcase and personal belongings were still in the room. Terence was calling me because he was worried. He hoped nothing had happened to Mr. Lichine. He asked if I knew his whereabouts or what had happened to him. I said I did not. Father Danaher asked if I would make an effort to find out and call him back. That's all Father Danaher told me."

It was not all Hugh Kelly had told Howard Dent, who happened to be watching Miss Cline. Her expression indicated that Hugh Kelly's last statement was not true. Quite clearly it was not all he had told Miss Cline, either.

"All right, then, Mr. Lichine," Hugh Kelly said. "You've heard now what I heard from Father Danaher on the phone this morning. I must ease his troubled mind by calling him back in Montgomery to say you are here in the office alive and well."

"You mean, sir, you haven't called him back yet?"

Howard Dent doubted that the polite question could have been asked in a manner more classically correct for conveying the deference of youth for a respected elder. The prism had no such doubts. What young Mr. Lichine had just done was land a great big fat squishy pie of contempt full in the face of Hugh F. X. Kelly, Jr. Howard Dent noted that, through the ludicrous dripping of invisible custard down his pink dewlaps, the skin tightened around Hugh Kelly's ice-blue eyes.

"And what, if I may ask, boy, is the import of that question?" he said.

"Concern for Father Danaher's state of mind," Mr. Lichine said.

His tone was so calculatedly neutral that, in the slight pause that followed, Howard Dent could hear, and he did not doubt Hugh Kelly could also hear, the unspoken addition: *you stupid horse's ass!*

"You said, sir, he was upset about what had happened to me and he asked you to call him back as soon as you found out where I was," Mr. Lichine continued. "Tessie found me asleep in my office down the hall at seven-thirty this morning. It seems unlikely that our managing clerk would keep the discovery secret for very long. It is now"—the prism recorded the skillful extension of contempt from the invisibly flung pie to the casual elegance with which Mr. Lichine flicked his wristwatch into view—"six minutes short of noon."

"Father Danaher sounded upset on the phone," Hugh Kelly said. "In such a situation people don't always report with accuracy. I wanted to have your account of what happened in Alabama yesterday before I called him back." Clearly with relief for a just-under-the-wire afterthought, Hugh Kelly added, "Besides, Terence said he would be in court all morning sweating out the jury's verdict."

Howard Dent admired the restraint with which young Mr. Lichine refrained from pointing out that lawyers in court are constantly having telephone-message slips poked under their noses even when court is in session and they are working at counsels' table.

"In any case, Mr. Lichine, I would like to hear your account of what happened in Montgomery yesterday," Hugh Kelly said.

Howard Dent felt only a simpleton would have been fooled by the hint of mollification implied in the way Hugh Kelly's voice returned to the croupy rumbling roll of his professional Irish manner.

"That is, boy, if you don't mind telling me?" he added.

"Not at all, sir," Mr. Lichine said. No simpleton, he. The smile was in his voice, not on his face, as he made his own addition. "I will, of course, be telling it to Mr. Dent and Miss Cline as well."

The pink skin gathered again, more quickly this time, to frame the ice-blue eyes.

"You object?" Hugh Kelly said.

"I've just come from two weeks in a courtroom helping with the defense of an accused murderer," Mr. Lichine said. "I may be a bit hypersensitive about the difference between participating in a whispered conference at the bench with his honor and opposing counsel, and giving sworn testimony from the witness chair."

In his best that-will-be-enough-of-that-young-man manner Hugh Kelly said, "Just tell us what happened, boy."

"I seem to have stepped on Father Danaher's toes," Mr. Lichine said.

"In what way?" Hugh Kelly said.

"When Mr. Kreel told me he was recommending me for this pro bono assignment," Mr. Lichine said, "I asked who I would be working for. He said he didn't know the man personally, but Mr. Merz had told him he was a law school classmate of yours and a very good lawyer."

"That Terence is," Hugh Kelly said.

"I found only the first half of the statement correct," Mr. Lichine said.

"Explain that," Hugh Kelly said.

"Your classmate, sir, is not a very good lawyer," Mr. Lichine said.

"In your opinion, boy," Hugh Kelly said.

"I could give you no other, sir," Mr. Lichine said.

"You can give me an explanation," Hugh Kelly said.

"The defendant is a fifteen-year-old black boy," Mr. Lichine said. "There is no doubt about his guilt. There is even less doubt that he will be convicted. Now that the Supreme Court has ruled each state can make its own decision about using the death penalty, everybody in that courtroom knew what's going to happen to this boy. In Alabama the penalty for first-degree murder is the electric chair, and Alabama is right in the middle of what they call down there 'the death belt.' There was absolutely no way to get this boy free. The best we could hope for was to keep him alive. We agreed the only thing we could do was work for a life sentence."

"I am sure Terence Danaher was in complete agreement," Hugh Kelly said.

"On everything except method," Mr. Lichine said. "He put his faith in God. I felt something more was needed. I'd made friends with a young black lawyer who was monitoring the trial. We talked it over. I had an idea and asked him to do some research for me. Yesterday, after Father Danaher finished his summation and appeal to the jury, I asked the court if I could have a few moments. If Father Danaher had no objection, the judge said, it was all right with him. Father Danaher had no objection. I went up to the jury box and showed those twelve men and women a picture."

"A picture?" Hugh Kelly said.

"Of an electric chair," Mr. Lichine said. "A real one. An electric chair that had seen service. Very few people have seen one.

To most people it's just a phrase. They think all that's involved is throwing a switch. A nice clean process for disposing of an ugly chore. I learned from my young black lawyer friend that this is not so. It's a shocking process. What happens to an electric chair after it has been used, for example, can never be cleaned away. A single illustration will do. In one of the pictures my black lawyer friend had given me, a large area of the chair is stained by the burned flesh of a victim. The human flesh is seared right into the leather. It's a shocking sight. I told the jury I wanted them to understand what they'd be doing to that fifteen-year-old boy if they sentenced him to the electric chair. I showed them a picture of a convicted man before he had been electrocuted. Then I showed them a picture of the electric chair after he had been killed in it."

"What happened?" Hugh Kelly said.

"Several screams," Mr. Lichine said. "A good deal of gasping. Two women jurors vomited. One man fainted. The judge called a recess and asked Father Danaher to meet him in chambers. I left the courthouse and went back to my hotel."

"Why?" Hugh Kelly said.

"During the two weeks of our association," Mr. Lichine said, "I had come to know Father Danaher quite well. I had a pretty good idea what was going to happen."

"Did it?" Hugh Kelly said.

"Yes, sir," Mr. Lichine said.

"Tell us," Hugh Kelly said.

The "us," Howard Dent felt, was a mistake. The prism recorded that the mistake was not lost on Mr. Lichine.

"In chambers the judge bawled the hell out of Father Danaher for my disgraceful conduct in a civilized courtroom," Mr. Lichine said. "After the recess the judge charged the jury. In the charge he ordered them to disregard the disgraceful conduct of junior counsel for the defense, and he sent them off to deliberate. Court was dismissed and Father Danaher came storming around the corner to my hotel. He was in a rage that I do not think it is inaccurate to describe as almost hysterical. He said I had ruined all the good work he had done in trying to save the life of that boy. He said he'd had the jury in the palm of his hand with his appeal to their religious consciences. The judge had agreed. By my act of willful insubordination to him as senior counsel, he said, I had enraged the jury. The judge agreed. He said I had signed that boy's death warrant. The judge agreed. Father Danaher ordered me out of town. I went."

"Not home, however," Hugh Kelly said.

"The first plane I could get out of Montgomery left at nine o'clock last night," Mr. Lichine said. "It was not a direct flight. I had to lay over in Atlanta for three hours. I got to La Guardia at three-thirty in the morning. In the taxi I discovered that somehow in the confusion of the last hours I had lost my keys. I didn't want to hammer on any doors at that hour of the night. My wife is terrified about living in New York. It would have frightened her to death. I had the taxi take me here. The night watchman on duty let me into the office."

In Mr. Lichine's smooth, graceful movements as he brought his large body into standing position there was the suggestion of a man fastidiously patting the dust from his fingertips to indicate the completion of a distasteful chore. The sound of the door closing behind him seemed to prod Hugh Kelly out of what was clearly a moment of shock.

"Well, Howard?" he said.

Howard Dent had been watching Mr. Lichine. The prism had kept tabs on Miss Cline. She had listened with composure to Mr. Lichine's report. Only once had her nose done that odd bit of attractive wrinkling. When Mr. Lichine had mentioned his wife. Howard Dent was suddenly aware of an old, familiar excitement. This was going to be one of those days.

"Howard, I asked what do you think?" Hugh Kelly said.

"The boy is obviously telling the truth," Howard Dent said. "What do you think?"

"He's lying in his teeth," Hugh Kelly said. "What do you think, child?"

"I don't know," Judy Cline said.

5

Ezra Cooper did. He knew everything. Everything, his wife, Jessica, used to say bitterly, except how to make partner at Isham Truitt.

She didn't say it anymore. Ezra remembered the day she had stopped. He remembered it the way a reformed cigarette smoker never forgets the moment he quit. Ezra Cooper never put his key into the lock of their front door without wishing Jessica had not quit. Soon after Jessica stopped nagging him about not being rewarded for his brilliant work at Isham Truitt, Ezra Cooper began to understand that the engine room of their marriage had also stopped. It was as though Jessica's mind, accepting at last with weary resignation what to both of them had for so many years been unacceptable, had turned with relief to a new preoccupation. It was total.

The day it happened was not planned that way. The day was supposed to be memorable for a couple of totally different reasons. It was Ezra's forty-fifth birthday, and it was his twentieth anniversary with Isham Truitt.

Jessica had seen to it that Walter Isham was aware of the coincidence. She was certain from his response that Mr. Isham and his partners had chosen that day for the moment to which she and Ezra had looked forward since 1950 when Mr. Merz had drafted Ezra out of the Columbia graduating class as an Isham Truitt associate. Since 1950 Ezra Cooper's partnership had been earned several times over. And several times over Ezra Cooper had been passed over for lesser men. This time, on this day in

1970, it would happen at last. Jessica was sure of it. Ezra's horoscope, and hers, both of them had been sending the unmistakable signal for a month.

What happened instead made the day equally memorable, but for another reason. It was the day Artie Steinberg called from Harkness with the report by the brain surgeon Artie had brought in the week before to check out Dr. Steinberg's troubled diagnosis of Jessica's persistent headaches.

"I'm home, Jess," Ezra Cooper called as he pulled his key from the lock.

She did not answer. She never did. Ezra Cooper had long ago ceased to expect an answer. He paused as he always did just inside the closed door and listened. He could hear the exercise machine going upstairs. From the spacing of the clicks he could tell Jessica was on the hamstrings. The quadriceps came next. He glanced at his wristwatch. Six forty-five. She always came down for Cronkite. It was always a nice quarter hour for Ezra Cooper.

He walked across to the bar. It was built in. Pouring his drink, Ezra Cooper found himself smiling at a recollection. Should they or shouldn't they? Not many people in New York were building things into their walls in those days. Not many people Jessica and Ezra Cooper knew, anyway. Not many people they knew were buying brownstones on Sixty-second Street, either. Jessica and Ezra Cooper had never thought of it until it happened.

It happened because anything could happen on that extraordinary day in 1950. The day Mr. Merz had tapped him for Isham Truitt and, to celebrate, Jessica and Ezra Cooper had taxied downtown to get a marriage license. They had walked all the way back uptown and suddenly there it was, a beat-up old wreck on Sixty-second Street near the Third Avenue corner, with a "For Sale" sign inside the glass door at the top of the high sandstone stoop. Except that it had not been a beat-up old wreck to Jessica and Ezra Cooper. They didn't see it the way the people who had put up the "For Sale" sign saw it. They saw it the way it was going to look when they finished remodeling it.

Which wouldn't take too long because, even though they didn't have a You Know What to do You Know What in, Ezra had his bright and shiny brand-new job with the hottest firm in the business. And since the hottest firm in the business had the hottest young man to come out of Columbia Law since Nicholas Murray Butler was a pup, how long would it be before the Pullman-car name of the hottest firm in the business would be stretched an inch or so to include the name of Ezra Kingsley Cooper, owner of that magnificent town house on Sixty-second?

"Good evening."

The voice of Walter Cronkite. That meant Jessica had come down and turned on the set. Ezra remained at the bar, as he always did, staring down into his glass, until Cronkite was well into his first of the day's disasters. That always gave Jessica time to settle herself in the chair to the right of the set, which had never gotten itself built in, although there had been much discussion about it, because by that time Jessica and Ezra were the parents of two enchanting children, a boy named Stephen and a girl named Ruth. Even unenchanting children got first crack at daddy's paycheck, which was not exactly small, but never seemed large enough, so that not as much remodeling was getting done on Sixty-second Street as Jessica and Ezra had contemplated on that wonderful day in 1950. In fact, not much decorating was getting done, either, except for basic things like beds, and chairs, and cribs, and little toideys. The whole concept of building things in had died a-borning with the bar from which every night, when he came home from the office, Ezra Cooper poured himself the scotch and water that helped him get through the wait. The wait until Jessica had come down and settled herself carefully in the chair she always sat in for Cronkite, so that when Ezra Cooper crossed the room to greet her he would be exposed only to the good side of his wife's face.

"Hi, Jess," Ezra said as he dipped down and kissed her undamaged cheek.

"—with this man from Vienna," Jessica was saying in perfectly reasonable tones. "He'd been trained by the great Dr. Stieghoffer, who was killed by the Nazis during the war, and Dr. Quentin wrote in his last letter from Johns Hopkins that if I could get to him, if only for a consultation, it would change the whole direction of my treatment. So I wrote back to Dr. Quentin and asked if he could give me some idea of what the whole thing would cost because—"

Eight years ago, very soon after Artie Steinberg's man had successfully removed Jessica's tumor, and these interminable monologues had started, Ezra Cooper used to wonder if they went on during the day while he was at the office, or if she turned them on as soon as she heard his key in the lock. Several times Ezra had been tempted to ask the children, but eight years ago Stephen was just starting at Collegiate and Ruth was only one semester into Dalton. They had their own problems, with which it seemed to Ezra they were coping at least adequately. They were certainly doing well in school. Remembering his own school days, Ezra Cooper remembered his total absorption in the school world. He was not much interested in the world outside, which had meant everything beyond the schoolyard, including his home. It had seemed more sensible to keep the kids out of it. Now that they were at Hamilton and Radcliffe, it seemed just as sensible to keep them as uninvolved as possible. Ezra Cooper saw Jessica as his problem and his alone.

If he had succeeded instead of failed. If he had received what he still believed he had earned just as firmly as for twenty years Jessica had believed it. If he had made partner at Isham Truitt when in his youth in the normal course of events a brilliant young man expected to make it and did. If, if, if. If the if had not chosen to single him out, Jessica would not have become sick. Artie Steinberg told him to knock it off. People did not develop brain tumors because their husbands went unrewarded at the office. Once, long ago, when he and Artie were kids in P.S. 72, Ezra Cooper would have believed that. Not anymore.

Even if he wanted to believe that Jessica's tumor had not been caused by the failure of his career, Ezra Cooper would not persuade himself that the consequences were traceable to anything but his failure. He had lived with those consequences for eight years. The gap between what had been and what was now could not be overlooked. The measuring point was that day in 1950 when hand in hand they had walked back uptown from the marriage-license bureau and bought with nothing more than hope and the confidence of youth what was to be their magnificent castle.

To put Jessica's face back to what it had been on that day required money. A fifty-three-year-old Isham Truitt associate who years ago should have left to try his luck elsewhere did not have that kind of money. Now that he was too old to leave, he was also too deeply in debt to borrow. Keeping two kids in college at today's rates had also kept the beat-up old wreck on Sixty-second Street pretty much what it had been when he and Jessica had taken it to their hearts. Nothing had changed. Nothing except Ezra Cooper's high hopes and the girl he had loved. Both were gone.

"—so I said to Artie, all right," Jessica said reasonably to Walter Cronkite, whose words were not registering on either of these two members of his nightly dedicated audience. "Let's look at it practically, Artie, I said. Let's forget brain tumors and their consequences. Let's think of it as a problem in carpentry. Suppose we had this perfectly good piece of wood, a board we want to use in making let us say a table. Unfortunately it has an unsightly knot right smack in the middle. If we cut out that knot we can use the board, if we don't we will have to throw the board away. So we get the appropriate tools, and we cut out that unsightly knot. The tumor, or what you medical people, Artie, call a wart on the brain, is successfully removed but, in the process, some crucial nerves have to be severed. Unfortunately, these nerves control the facial muscles. As a result, while the human being comes out of the operation as sound as the board did, one side of her face is paralyzed. So I say to you, Artie, as I've been saying for eight years, I say why can't we rethink the whole thing, go back to the operating room eight years ago, retrace our steps and see if there isn't something we've overlooked.

"For the first time in years I could see I had Artie's complete attention. He was clearly seeing that what I said makes sense. I mean he was just beginning to listen, really listen, when that damned nurse of his, I can't think of her name, she's the one I dislike so much, she comes barging in and says Mr. Kreel is here.

Whereupon Artie gets up and says, 'Jessica, would you be good enough to wait outside for a few minutes, this is an emergency.' Before I could say anything the door opens, and Ken Kreel comes in with his arm in a sling and a bandage around his head and—"

Ezra Cooper's mind tumbled back into the room.

"Who?" he said.

"—and you know what I think of that son of a bitch," Jessica said. "The idea of asking me to wait because Ken Kreel has come in—"

"Jessica!"

He rapped out the name. She turned, away from Cronkite, toward her husband.

"What?"

"Did you just say you saw Ken Kreel in Artie Steinberg's office today?" Ezra Cooper said.

"Yes, of course," Jessica said. "I was with Artie, talking to him, and as I said he was listening, when this—"

She caught herself. Quickly, she turned her head back to Cronkite. The damaged side of her face was back out of her husband's line of vision.

"You couldn't have seen Ken Kreel today," Ezra Cooper said. "Ken Kreel is in London on the Paramount deal."

"I don't know who you're talking about," Jessica said. "The man I'm talking about is the son of a bitch Ken Kreel who eight years ago got the Isham Truitt junior partnership that belonged to you."

"That's the man I'm talking about," Ezra Cooper said. "He couldn't have been in Artie's office this afternoon. He's in London."

"How do you know?" Jessica said.

"I talked to him less than an hour ago," Ezra Cooper said. "He called me from the Savoy for some figures I've been getting up for him on the merger aspects of the Columbia involvement."

Jessica stood up and walked to the table near the couch. She picked up the phone and dialed a number.

"Dr. Steinberg, please," she said. "Oh, hello, Betty, this is Jessica Cooper. Yes, please." Pause. "Artie? Jessica. Would you hold a moment, Artie? I have somebody with me who wants to talk to you."

Jessica Cooper held out the phone to her husband.

6

In 1950, when Ezra Cooper came to Isham Truitt, he was assigned to what was then known as a "two-zee": the small double offices without windows shared by associates. Ezra's office mate was a jock named Albert Rhodes. He was known, of course, as Dusty.

"It's like sharing a locker when you're trying out for the team," he said. "You come in one day and find the other guy's stuff is gone. He's either been scrubbed or he's made the varsity. I hope I get out of here before you do."

He did, during Ezra's third year at Isham Truitt and Dusty's fifth. He didn't make partner. He resigned.

"I took a look at my new paycheck," Dusty said to Ezra as he was cleaning out his desk. "The guy I came in with from Cornell five years ago, he went from $19,500 to $22,500. I went from $19,500 to $19,500. I got the message. I called a friend at Falk Prudhomme. It's a small firm but they can use a guy my size."

In Ezra Cooper's twenty-eight years at Isham Truitt many office mates had replaced Dusty Rhodes. All of them, as they cleaned out the desk at the other side of the small room, had given Ezra Cooper some bad moments. Only one of them had earned his hatred. Ken Kreel had been tapped for his junior partnership on the day in 1970 when Artie Steinberg had called from Harkness with the report from the brain surgeon. Ezra was aware that the hatred was irrational.

Even more irrational was the extension of the hatred to Miss Gowdy. If things had gone on that day in 1970 the way for a month Jessica's horoscope had been signaling loud and clear, Miss Gowdy for the last eight years would have been not Ken Kreel's but Ezra Cooper's secretary. She obviously considered she'd had a narrow escape. Even on the phone her voice rarely approached ordinary civility.

"Mr. Cooper?"

"Yes?" Ezra said.

"Nancy Gowdy."

"I know," he said.

"I'm sending somebody around to see you."

"No you're not," Ezra said.

"What?"

It was not exactly a gasp. It was not Miss Gowdy's normal tone of unconcealed contempt, either.

"Is it your normal practice to call lawyers in this office and tell them you're sending somebody around to see them without first asking if they're free to see anybody?"

Pause. It helped, but not enough.

"Well," Miss Gowdy said, "I assumed you were free."

"I suggest you abandon making assumptions and stick to the facts," Ezra Cooper said. "Now what's this all about?"

"Mr. Tortora is here," Miss Gowdy said icily.

"Who is he?" Ezra said.

"Mr. Saxe Tortora is the eminent stage director," Miss Gowdy said. "He is a client of this office."

"Offer him my congratulations," Ezra Cooper said. "He's in good hands."

He hung up and looked at his wristwatch. Five seconds? It took six. He picked up on the fourth ring.

"Yes?"

"Mr. Cooper, would you mind telling me what's got into you today?"

"I would mind, yes," Ezra Cooper said. "Now what do you want?"

"Mr. Tortora has just come into the office," Miss Gowdy said. "He has a ten o'clock appointment with Mr. Kreel."

"I don't know how good a director he is," Ezra said, "but I see by my watch that he's prompt."

"Mr. Kreel is unable to see him," Miss Gowdy said. "I'd like you to see him."

"Does Mr. Kreel want me to see him?" Ezra said.

"Mr. Kreel is unavailable at the moment," Miss Gowdy said.

"I would suggest you tell Mr. Tortora to come back when Mr. Kreel is available," Ezra said.

"I can't do that," Miss Gowdy said.

"Why not?" Ezra said.

"Mr. Tortora is flying to the Coast at one o'clock," Miss Gowdy said.

"Does Mr. Tortora know who I am?" Ezra Cooper said.

"I told him you are one of our associates and you work closely with Mr. Kreel," Miss Gowdy said.

"Did that satisfy Mr. Tortora?" Ezra said.

"How do you mean?" Miss Gowdy said.

"Did Mr. Tortora ask how closely?" Ezra Cooper said. "Did he inquire about my status here at Isham Truitt? Did he perhaps, being a man of the theater, did he ask does this guy know his ass from a hot rock?"

Another pause. Then:

"Mr. Cooper?"

"Yes?"

"Will you please see Mr. Tortora?"

"That's better," Ezra said. "I'll come around."

"No, no, not here," Miss Gowdy said.

"Why not?" Ezra said.

"Mr. Kreel's office is not available," Miss Gowdy said.

"Get your act together," Ezra Cooper said. "Mr. Kreel called me from London late yesterday. Remember?"

He hung up, went out to the private circular staircase, climbed to the thirtieth floor, and walked down the corridor to Ken Kreel's suite. The two people in Kreel's outer office looked up at the newcomer. Miss Gowdy with the murder in her heart leaking freely from her hard eyes. The slender, balding man in blue jeans and a red Izod tennis chemise with annoyed curiosity.

"Mr. Tortora," Miss Gowdy said. "This is our Mr. Cooper."

The slender man stood up and took Ezra Cooper's hand.

"How do you do, sir," Mr. Tortora said.

"Come this way, please," Ezra said.

He led the way past Miss Gowdy's glare into Ken Kreel's private office and pushed the door shut.

"Please sit down," Ezra Cooper said.

He walked around Ken Kreel's desk. It was impossible for Ezra to walk around his own desk. The desks in associates' twozees were set against the facing walls. The office mates worked with their backs to each other. Dropping into the big leather chair, Ezra noted that Ken Kreel, presumably when he was not skirt chasing, worked with his back to a view of a corner of the Plaza and a sliver of Central Park.

"I'm sorry about the mix-up in your appointment," Ezra Cooper said. "I'll do my best to fill the gap if I can. What can I do for you, Mr. Tortora?"

The eminent stage director did not have to hunt for words. He had obviously been rehearsing a handful for a long time. They came spitting out across the room on a squeal of indignation.

"You can tell me who the fuck you lawyers think you are!"

Ezra Cooper gave himself a few moments to shift gears.

"I can't speak for all lawyers," he said. "Speaking for myself, I think I'm a man who has been trained and licensed to help the layman conduct his affairs in such a way that he gets as much financial return out of those affairs as the law allows, without at the same time running afoul of the law in such a way that he will suffer financial or physical penalties."

Ezra saw that he could have been reciting the multiplication table. Saxe Tortora had merely been marking time. As soon as Ezra's voice stopped, Mr. Tortora's interrupted explosion took off again. It was as though the slender, balding man was a bottle of soda pop that had been shaken violently, then capped temporarily by a thumb, which he was now free to remove.

"It's getting so you can't unload an off-center fart without consulting a legal beagle," Saxe Tortora said. "Everywhere a guy turns, what you used to turn into was air to breathe, but what you turn into now is a lawyer with one hand up like a traffic cop and the other hand holding out a bill. This used to be a free country. Now it's Russia with lawyers instead of commissars.

How did you guys manage to put the lock on a whole civilization while the honest citizens were watching TV?"

Ezra Cooper shifted gears again.

"We bored from within," he said.

Nope. Saxe Tortora's face, which had a Levantine provenance, slid into a thumbs-down scowl.

"Cut it out," he said. "I've got to live with you guys. Also, I've got a plane to catch."

"If you tell me what your problem is," Ezra Cooper said, "I'll do what I can to see that you don't miss it."

"You can give me my contract," Saxe Tortora said.

"What contract?" Ezra Cooper said.

"Seven weeks ago, sitting in this chair," Saxe Tortora said, "I explained the whole thing to Ken Kreel at his rates which seven weeks ago were still showing up on my bills as one hundred and fifty bucks an hour. Now, because he's off somewhere on his usual prowl for nookie, I'm asked to explain the whole goddamn thing again at how much do you show up for on my bills?"

"Seventy-five dollars an hour," Ezra Cooper said. "I'm not a partner."

"You never will be," Tortora said. "You look honest."

"It's cost you about eight dollars already just to tell me what you think of lawyers," Ezra Cooper said. "For another eight you might get your problem solved. We're not like psychoanalysts. We don't bill you for the whole hour even if the patient is in a sullen, noncommunicative mood. We bill only for the actual fraction of the hour consumed. Miss Gowdy out there punched the timer as soon as you and I walked through that door. Also, unlike shrinks, we never doze off during a consultation."

"Neither do dentists," Saxe Tortora said. "The day I came in to see Ken Kreel about this contract I also had every tooth in my head yanked. What do you think of these?"

The director bared his teeth as though in a pantomime he had been assigned to do an imitation of Theodore Roosevelt's famous smile.

"A beautiful job," Ezra Cooper said.

"I had them done by the same guy does all of Lew Wasserman's work," Saxe Tortora said. "Name dentists don't come cheap, but these things, which are in my head and working, cost me less than I've already been billed by Ken Kreel for this goddamn contract I still haven't got. And because I haven't got it to carry out to the Coast with me at one o'clock, I may not only lose a frigging fortune but because in order to keep up with Ken Kreel's bills I haven't been able to pay Lew Wasserman's dentist, the son of a bitch may repossess these choppers."

"Tell me about your contract," Ezra Cooper said. "If you lose your teeth I'll file an action for repossession at no extra charge."

"No wonder you're still an associate and not a partner," Saxe Tortora said. "All right, like this. Some time ago I found an old novel called *Praying for Rain.* It was written by a guy who used to sit around in coffee houses with Samuel Johnson, so it's pretty safely in the public domain. I think it will make a great musical show. I lined up a producer. I found my book writer. I got the composer and lyricist. I even tied in a real hot choreographer. All I need is a star, and I got her on the hook because she likes the package, but she's big in pictures and her people won't let her sign until there's a script. They gave me a memorandum of what they wanted, which is one hundred and eleven and three quarters per cent of the weekly gross and all the profits, and of course my left arm and right nut. They didn't ask for my teeth because when we worked out this very fair and equitable verbal arrangement I still had my old ones in place, and they didn't look like they'd bring much on a trade-in. Anyway, the way these deals are going these days this is considered a deal a guy can live with, because as I'm sure it comes as no surprise to you, for every talent in the package there's a Ken Kreel and his billing computer involved. All clear?"

"Up to this point, yes," Ezra Cooper said.

"All these facts, everything I just told you," Saxe Tortora said, "I gave the whole shmeer to Ken Kreel seven weeks ago. The seven-weeks time limit was set by the star. She's got commitments up to here. Her lawyers won't let her sign until they see that script. The book writer said he could finish the script in a month. That would give me three weeks for the star to read it and decide yes or no. We all shook hands, the writer started to write, and I went to the dentist. Four weeks later, that's three weeks ago, exactly as promised, the writer delivered the script."

"Is it satisfactory?" Ezra Cooper said.

"How should I know?" Saxe Tortora said.

"I don't understand," Ezra said.

"Mr. Cooper, make like you're a partner," Saxe Tortora said. "Use your head. Maybe in the old days, say when this guy who used to sit around in the coffee houses with Sam Johnson wrote this *Praying for Rain*, maybe in those days a writer delivered his script to his producer. Today? Are you kidding? Today a writer delivers his script to his lawyer. My writer did, three weeks ago, and for three solid weeks that's where that script has been. Sitting on his lawyer's desk, because the lawyer will not release the script until he has in his hot little hand his client's signed contract. His client's signed contract for my *Praying for Rain* project is floating around somewhere in this office, or it's still a dream sequence in Ken Kreel's head, or more likely it's in the kip somewhere with one of his doxies. For three solid weeks I have called Ken Kreel every single day, sometimes two, three, and seventy-four times a day, because my deadline to present that goddamn script to that goddamn star has been running out. And every single day, sometimes two, three, or seventy-four times a day, Ken Kreel or that girl out there who talks for him when he can't or doesn't want to, they say the contract will be ready tomorrow. Well, here we are on the last day of my deadline. My meeting with the star and her people is scheduled for tonight in the Polo Lounge of the Beverly Hills Hotel. I have a one o'clock plane ticket in my pocket. And the script is still sitting on the desk of the writer's lawyer, where it's probably running up bills for him at whatever lawyers charge by the hour down at 120 Broadway for letting a script sit around on a lawyer's desk. To top it all off, I come here to keep a preflight meeting with Ken Kreel in a state of what it's taking every ounce of the strength I inherited from my Lebanese ancestors to refrain from describing as hysteria, and what happens?"

"Nothing," Ezra Cooper said.

"You know something?" Saxe Tortora said. "I'm beginning to like you."

"I've been fond of you from the moment we met," Ezra Cooper said.

"Then help me, for God's sake," Saxe Tortora said. "Why should it take seven weeks to write a contract? Correction. Why should it take seven weeks not to write a contract? It didn't take seven weeks to write the Treaty of Ghent, for Christ's sake. These contracts today they're as thick as the Bronx telephone book. They weigh in at three and four pounds without the brass clips or blue binders or wax seals. Why? Because nine tenths of the alphabet soup is nothing but boiler plate. A mass of great big fat clauses that have grown up over the years and are standard for these contracts the way ear muffs are standard for skiing. They get lifted from contract to contract without a word or a comma changed, like checkers moved around on a board. There's no writing involved. There's not even any typing involved. Most of it is the standard Dramatists Guild Minimum Basic Agreement, which is a printed document they hand out free like Green Stamps and just gets stapled into each new contract. The only contract writing that's involved is a handful of numbers. The amount of the royalties for each person involved, and the percentages for the split-up of the extra rights. Even that the lawyer doesn't have to write. I gave all that to Ken Kreel on the initialed memorandum I brought back from the Coast seven weeks ago. So now tell me please what am I going to do when I get off that plane in California tonight?"

"There's only one person who can tell you that," Ezra Cooper said.

"Who?" Saxe Tortora said.

"Ken Kreel," Ezra Cooper said.

"But his girl, that Miss Gowdy out there," Saxe Tortora said, "she swears up and down she doesn't know where he is."

"I do," Ezra Cooper said.

7

So far as the general public was concerned Isham Truitt could have been the name of a baseball player or a British novelist. To the blue-chip Bar, however, it meant "David Fillmore's firm." For people who earned their daily caviar by sending out bills for legal services, it would have been as difficult to think of Isham Truitt without thinking of the Fillmore National as it would have been to think of White and Case without U.S. Steel or Milbank Tweed without Chase Manhattan. And yet one of the nice things about working for Isham Truitt was that it was not a one-client firm.

It had come into existence in 1908 when Leander Fillmore founded the Fillmore National Bank and chose as his legal team two Stanford classmates: Franklin Salsford and Harold S. Isham. Salsford died without issue and, after thirty years of honoring his memory by overcrowding the shingle, his name was dropped. The present senior partner, Howard Isham, was a grandson of the founding Isham, and David Fillmore, the present chairman of the Fillmore National, was a grandson of the founder of the bank. It was generally believed that what had kept the relationship going so successfully for seventy years was not only the law firm's expertise, which was widely accepted to be among the best in the country. More important, the two families had always been close. They summered together at Seal Harbor and they intermarried like Egyptian Pharaohs.

"As long as there is a living Isham on the firm's shingle, and a living Fillmore on the board of the bank," Westbrook Pegler had once written in a famous column, "this unholy alliance of financial pirates will walk hand in hand into the republic's sunset lining their pockets as they go with a slice of every dollar you and I and our descendants will ever earn."

The harsh words had neither ruffled the feelings of the then living Ishams and Fillmores, nor had it diminished their pocket-lining activities. Fillmore National accounted for 8 to 10 per cent of the Isham Truitt annual billings.

Of the remaining 90 per cent more than half was generated by business enterprises under the financial wing of Fillmore National. People who do business with banks are rarely inattentive to a bank's suggestion about choice of counsel.

The rest of the client roster was spread among what was known to the staff as the "fun spots." This meant that, like Fillmore National and its satellites, they not only paid fat fees to Isham Truitt; they also functioned in areas that, increasingly, the young people in the firm found more interesting than banking. The theater, motion pictures, and TV, for example. Franchise Foods, Inc., for another example.

The gratitude of the fast-food conglomerate to Isham Truitt for legal services was expressed in two ways. First, by shelling out $500 an hour for the tax skills of Paul Truitt; $150 an hour for the services of quite a few junior partners; and $75 an hour for the help of, on occasion, as many as a couple of dozen associates. The second way of expressing its corporate gratitude was what made the company a favorite with the Isham Truitt staff: an endless supply of Cola One ("The One Calorie Per Bottle" soft drink) and Chomps ("The No Calorie Candy Bar"). These were distributed like confetti in all corners as well as crevices of the known world. Nowhere, however, were they more popular than in ITCH.

The word was an acronym invented by a Harvard associate who had written the Hasty Pudding Show before he moved on to make history at the *Law Review* with an article titled "The Assault On the Citadel of Privity Has Proceeded Apace Enough Already." ITCH was short for "Isham Truitt Coffee Hutch."

It was a large airy room on the Fifty-ninth Street side of the building, just beyond Stenographic and to the left of the file

room. It was equipped with Formica-topped tables for four.
Most of the action went to the racks of free Chomps and the no-
coins-required Cola One dispensers. The latter had reduced the
water cooler almost to obsolescence. It was now used almost exclusively for popping aspirin and other chemicals of a presumably medicinal nature. In the vicinity of the water cooler, for example, jokes about the Pill were leaden, of course, but
undeniably and tediously frequent. For those who preferred an
old-fashioned cup of coffee, the great nickel urn was kept going
around the clock. As an encouragement to associates who
worked late to drink deep at this Pierian spring, even at out-of-
sight inflated prices only the finest brands were brewed at
ITCH.

Among the steady consumers were Mrs. Edwina Campion,
Hugh Kelly's secretary, and her chum Mrs. Merle Bethune, the
head of Stenographic. In addition to preferring coffee to Cola
One, these ladies were ostentatious spurners of Chomps. Both
were large meaty women of a certain age. In the long war
against girth they had achieved a deep distrust for phrases like
"The No Calorie Candy Bar." Both carried saccharin dispensers
in their purses.

"And the amazing thing, Merle," Mrs. Campion was saying as
she dropped a pellet into her cup, "is that he never, but absolutely never, forgets my name!"

"Why should he, Edwina?" said Mrs. Bethune. "Seeing as how
you are practically an Isham Truitt institution, but I know what
you mean. I had an uncle lived to be ninety-one, but he wasn't
going to an office at that age, believe me. The truth is the last
ten years of his life he was a pain in the neck to the whole family. By the way, what was Mr. Dent going in to see Mr. Kelly
about?"

Mrs. Campion sent a quick glance to left and right, then
leaned her massive bosom forward over the table.

"Some mess it looks like to me this Lichine boy got himself
into down there in Alabama," she said in a low voice.

"Lichine?" Mrs. Bethune said with a frown, and then her face
cleared. "Oh, I know. He's that handsome snotty-sort-of-looking
kid from Harvard he's the son of Amelia Troy?"

"That's how he got the job, between you and me," Mrs. Campion said. "Not that his record at Harvard was bad. I understand, in fact, he was near the top of his class, but if you want something like say a job for your son at Isham Truitt, it doesn't hurt to be an old girl friend of David Fillmore."

"Amelia Troy isn't all that old," Mrs. Bethune said. "And if you mean old the way I think you mean old when you say she's an old girl friend of David Fillmore, I think you'd be surprised, Edwina."

"No kidding?" Mrs. Campion said. "You mean it's still going on?"

"On and off," Mrs. Bethune said. Then she caught up with the joke she had not intentionally placed in her own words when she uttered them, and she laughed. "And that's exactly what I do mean, Edwina, if you know what I mean."

"Well, I'll be damned," Mrs. Campion said. "I thought all that stopped when Amelia Troy married this Lichine. He's an actor, too, isn't he, as I remember?"

"You've got a good memory," Mrs. Bethune said. "He was an actor is more like it, Edwina. He was her leading man in that big hit musical with the funny name, it had Egypt in the title, I think?"

"*I Am Dying, Little Egypt,*" Mrs. Campion said. "I got the tickets for Mr. Kelly and his wife, he took her to see it on their thirtieth wedding anniversary, and they liked it so much Mr. Kelly gave me two tickets for my birthday."

"You work for a lovely man, Edwina, you really do," Mrs. Bethune said. "That's the play they were both in. Amelia Troy and he had the male lead, Lichine, and they fell in love and got married while the play was running, as I remember. Anyway, everybody thinks that was the end of her and David Fillmore. Maybe it was for a while, till she had her child, this boy now working here at Isham Truitt."

"But it's on again, you mean?" Mrs. Campion said.

"With David Fillmore it's never off is what I mean," Mrs. Bethune said. "He's as bad as Ken Kreel, really he is, except that with the chairman of the Fillmore National it's on a different financial level, naturally, so it doesn't get around in the corridors the way Ken Kreel's goings-on do."

"Merle, how do you know these things?" Mrs. Campion said.

"The head of Stenographic sees a lot of correspondence," Mrs. Bethune said. "A lot of it is confidential and a lot of the Fillmore National correspondence doesn't always deal with banking matters."

"Does Lichine know?" Mrs. Campion said. "Not the boy working here. I mean the father, Amelia Troy's husband?"

"If he does," Mrs. Bethune said, "I don't suppose he cares. You know these theater people. Besides, he hasn't had a job I don't think since that Egypt play, but there they are, Mr. and Mrs. Thomas Lichine, the former Amelia Troy, living all these years at the Waldorf Towers, and who do you suppose is paying for that, Edwina?"

"You'd think at least as a mother she'd have some spark of decency," Mrs. Campion said. "After all, children have a sixth sense about these things, and if it's been going on all these years, why, Merle, that boy is twenty-five if he's a day. A boy as bright as that, he must have known something was going on."

"If he did," Mrs. Bethune said, "I don't think he'd care. He's sort of arrogant, if you've had anything to do with him. The way he comes into the file room and asks for things, I mean. Thinks he's better than the rest of the world, and look what he married."

"The boy who works here?" Mrs. Campion said. "I didn't know he was married. You know her?"

"No, but what I do know is she's an actress, too, like his mother," Mrs. Bethune said. "Not a star or anything like that, she's just been in some Off-Broadway things, and she's still just a kid, I'm told, but that's never stopped Ken Kreel."

"Merle Bethune!" Mrs. Campion said. "Saints alive, what are you saying?"

"Use your noodle, Edwina," Mrs. Bethune said. "Why do you suppose Ken Kreel has taken this Lichine boy under his wing?"

"I don't know," Mrs. Campion said. "I assumed because of the boy's background. Amelia Troy's son and all, in an office like this he'd sort of naturally gravitate you might say to the partner who handles that sort of work. I mean theater and movies and TV."

"So how come the partner who handles our theater and movie and TV work," Mrs. Bethune said, "all of a sudden he sticks his nose into Mr. Merz's pro bono schedule and he recommends this Lichine boy should be sent all the way down to Alabama for a month to help out with a murder trial?"

"That is a funny one, isn't it, Merle?" Mrs. Campion said.

"Not if this boy's wife is the sex pot I hear she is," Mrs. Bethune said. "Practically a nymphomaniac, I've heard tell. I've known Ken Kreel to go to greater lengths than getting a husband assigned out of town for a while, and from what I've seen of some of them he's done it for a lot less."

"Careful, Merle," Mrs. Campion said. "Here comes one of Tessie's smart alecks."

She pulled her massive bosom back upright.

"Excuse me, Mrs. Campion," Ira Bodmer said. "I don't mean to interrupt, but I was just on my way to your office and I stopped in for a Cola and—"

"—and decided whatever you were on your way to my office for could wait," Mrs. Campion said.

"Oh, no," Ira Bodmer said, and then he smirked. "I mean what I mean I guess is oh, yes. The truth is it's not very important, Mrs. Campion."

"And these Cola Ones are free," Mrs. Bethune said.

Ira Bodmer gave her a piece of the smirk, but he continued to direct his remarks at the secretary of name partner Hugh F. X. Kelly, Jr.

"It's a lost-and-found thing," he said. "Mr. Lichine reported this morning he lost his key case, and somebody just turned it in. Mr. Tessitore told me to take it around to him, which I did, but he wasn't in his office and Mr. Taunton, that's his office mate, he said he doesn't have any idea where Mr. Lichine is but the only person who might know would be you because the last he saw of Mr. Lichine was yesterday and he was heading for a meeting in your office with Mr. Kelly, so Mr. Tessitore said to take the thing up to you and would you be good enough to give it to Mr. Lichine when you see him?"

Ira Bodmer placed on the table a small, handsome alligator case with gold corners.

"If I see him," Mrs. Campion said.

"Oh, yes, well," Ira Bodmer said.

He put out his hand to retrieve the case. Before he could touch it Mrs. Campion reached out and picked it up.

"No, that's all right, Ira," she said. "I'll take it."

"Thanks, Mrs. Campion," Ira Bodmer said. "His initials are on the inside." He bobbed his head to Mrs. Bethune. "Sorry to interrupt," he said. "And thanks again."

Both women watched as Ira moved toward the door, weaving in and out around tables and taking swigs from his Cola One bottle as he went.

"Edwina."

"Yes, Merle?"

"What's this mess this Lichine kid got into down there in Alabama?" Mrs. Bethune said.

"I don't know," Mrs. Campion said.

"Edwina!"

"Well, I didn't take the call," Mrs. Campion said defensively. "It's this idiot friend Mr. Kelly's got down there, this Father Danaher he's so crazy about, God knows why. He's sort of tricky, I've found. This call, for instance, he didn't go through the office switchboard. He made the call from Alabama early in the morning out to Jamaica where he seemed to know, God knows how, that Mr. Kelly had a closing, so the first thing I knew something was rotten in the state of Denmark was when Mr. Kelly called me from Iggulden's where he'd driven the Bentley for some steering trouble, and he asked me to track down this Cline girl and make sure she was in the office when he got there."

"Cline?" Mrs. Bethune said.

"Judy Cline," Mrs. Campion said. "An associate, no less. You know. The pretty one."

"Oh, yes, if you like the type," Mrs. Bethune said.

"I don't," Mrs. Campion said. "But fair is fair, Merle. This Judy Cline is a very pretty girl."

"What's she got to do with all this?" Mrs. Bethune said.

"Only God knows," Mrs. Campion said.

"On our letterhead that means 'of counsel,'" Mrs. Bethune said. "Which explains why they sent for Howard Dent."

8

Emanuel Merz, known in the trade as Mandamus Manny, came to the law the way Saul of Tarsus came to Christianity. He had a vision.

"The geography was somewhat different, of course," he told the reporter for *People* who did the Merz cover story after Mandamus Manny won his nickname. "It happened to Saul on the road to Damascus. I got mine on the I.R.T. It was in 1932, I was just out of high school, pushing a hand truck on the streets of the garment center for twelve dollars a week, and considering myself lucky to have a job, when my luck ran out. The firm I was working for went bankrupt. The receiver's audit revealed that, in order to obtain credit with the piece-goods manufacturers, the owner of the firm had issued a false financial statement to his bank. Many people were doing that in those days, but my boss did it in a particularly stupid way. Instead of walking the few blocks down Seventh Avenue to deliver the statement to the National City, he had put a postage stamp on it. By mailing that piece of paper he had committed a federal offense. He had used the U.S. mails to defraud. The receiver turned the matter over to the federal prosecutor here in the Southern District of New York. For the record, his name was George Z. Medalie, and his chief assistant who handled the case was a kid named Thomas E. Dewey.

"The receiver's team had done its audit on the premises of the bankrupt, and they had kept me on salary as what was then becoming known as a gofor. I went out for coffee whenever they needed it and did other errands during the week it took them to get up the figures. When the receiver's lawyer went into court to support the federal prosecutor he needed the books and records to present his case. In those days before computers books and records included great big fat ledgers the size and weight of paving blocks. This lawyer was an elderly gentleman and a rather frail physical specimen. He kept me on salary to carry the books to court for him every day and carry them back to his office at the end of the day.

"One day, on the way back from Foley Square to his office on Forty-second Street, while we were on the West Side Highway, the taxi burst into flames. The taxi driver slammed on the brakes, jumped out, and ran. So did the lawyer. I followed, but not very far. It occurred to me that I was being paid to take care of those books and records, and if they burned up I might be held responsible. So, without too much thinking about it I ran back, hauled open the rear door of that burning taxi, grabbed the two bundles of books, and dragged them to the place a couple of hundred feet down the highway where the driver and my boss were watching that taxi go up in smoke. In a few minutes there were police cars, and cops squirting some sort of white foam out of fire extinguishers, and a small crowd, and the taxi driver answering questions the cops were asking. Finally, my boss hailed another taxi and climbed in. Carrying the two bundles of books, I followed and we continued our trip back to his office on Forty-second Street.

"The next morning, on my way down from the Bronx to Forty-second Street in the subway for the day's work, I picked up a discarded copy of the *Daily News*. I was working my way through to the sports section when I was astonished to stumble into a story about the taxi fire. It wasn't much of a story, but after I recovered from my astonishment at finding reported in the press an event in which I had participated, I found something else. Hanging onto a strap in that crowded subway car I was having an experience that I later realized was not unlike the experience Saul of Tarsus had on the road to Damascus.

"In my mind I had a clear picture of the event as it had happened the day before. Now, the next day, I was holding in my hand a newspaper report of the event. It described what had happened to the taxi and gave the name of the driver. It described the passenger in the taxi, gave his name, his profession, and the nature of the case with which he was helping the public prosecutor in court that day. It described with admiration the dedication to his profession that had sent this lawyer back into that seething inferno at the risk of his life to save the evidence. To the newspaper reader there had been only one passenger in that taxi.

"The nature of the revelation that was working its way through me in that subway car had nothing to do with the unfairness of the story to me, or with its total falsity. Like all true revelations this one was not wasting time with irrelevant matters. It was concerned solely with carrying the truth to the revealee. As it had succeeded with Saul of Tarsus on the road to Damascus, it succeeded on that day with Emanuel Merz in the I.R.T. The truth invaded my soul and took up permanent residence. The lesson was clear. People who carry heavy ledgers, even if they risk their lives in the process, are not news. Lawyers, no matter what they do or do not do, get their names in the papers. I had found my life's work."

The way he did it was not universally admired, but it was widely envied. Manny Merz did his work on his feet.

"People say I make up the law as I go along," he said. "That's sheer balls. What I do is find the law I want to use as I go along. The secret of being an effective lawyer is not to try to be something nature never intended you to be. I was not cut out to be a scholar. I don't function well in the library. I think of a lawyer the way I think of a pitcher. Nature fashioned him to work in a ball park. Nature fashioned me to work in a courtroom. To work well I must, of course, go into the courtroom with as much ammunition as I can pick up. I've learned about myself that I don't pick it up at certain times or in special places. I pick it up all the time, the way I pick up the air I breathe, without conscious effort, no matter where I am. Once I pick it up it's mine forever, lying there in my head, waiting for the appropriate moment to be used. I don't have to rehearse. I don't have to train. I don't even need what a pitcher needs, a three-day rest between games.

All I have to know is what the battle is about and the address of the arena. Once I walk in and they sound the bell, I'm on my feet and the right ammunition starts sliding out of the drawers in my head and into whatever artillery piece is appropriate to the action in hand. That's what's made me one of the best litigators in the business."

It was also what had made him a senior partner at Isham Truitt. Emanuel Merz was the only name on the shingle that had not served the firm in a lesser capacity. He had not worked his way up through the ranks of associates. After his triumph in *Clairouin* v. *New York* he had received an offer from Walter Isham.

"I accepted because I was beginning to understand that by running my own firm I was violating my basic principle," Emanuel Merz said. "I was doing something nature had never intended me to be. A housekeeper. I disbanded Merz & Dietmar, gave Buck Dietmar everything including the kitchen sink and my best wishes, and I went over to Isham Truitt with nothing but what I had when I came out of that revelation on the I.R.T in 1932. My self-confidence."

Quite a few people called it gall. Publicity hound, his detractors said, was closer to the truth. No matter what it was called there was little disagreement that it had taken a brilliant if off-beat concept of the laws of inheritance to spring on the sitting judge in *Clairouin* v. *New York* the demand that he slap on himself a writ of Mandamus calling for the performance of his duty as a former executor of the Clairouin estate. It won for Emanuel Merz not only a spectacularly fat fee and his Isham Truitt partnership, but also the nickname by which he was known with a certain amount of affection even to his bitterest courtroom enemies. On one point about Emanuel Merz the entire blue-chip Bar could be said to be in complete or almost complete agreement. Mandamus Manny was a man it was impossible not to like. It was this quality that had given Ezra Cooper the courage, as soon as he got rid of Mr. Saxe Tortora, to pick up the phone in Ken Kreel's private office, call Mr. Merz's secretary, and ask for an appointment.

"Come in, come in, come in," Merz boomed across his large

office at Ezra, who already was in. "Put it there, kid, and take a load off. Long time no see, Ezra."

Merz was a man who prided himself on being with it. When wide ties were in, he hung away his collection of narrow neckwear. He was probably the only lawyer in New York, certainly of his age, who was admitted regularly, indeed welcomed without a screening at the door, to Studio 54. When he got in he did not waltz. Emanuel Merz frugged. The only thing he had not kept up with was the speech patterns of the day. He seemed to be unaware that he still spoke, even though with the vigor he gave to every other activity, the slang of the day he'd had his revelation on the I.R.T.

"Too long," Ezra Cooper said.

He sat down in the chair beside the desk and crossed one leg over the other in an almost ludicrously leisurely fashion. The statement and the gesture were calculatedly uncharacteristic of Ezra Cooper's usual conduct in the senior partner's presence. He noted that the sharp-eyed courtroom performer behind the desk had noted both.

"How are they treating you, kid?" Merz said.

"Abominably," Ezra Cooper said. "And they have been for twenty-eight years, Mr. Merz, as you well know."

The courtroom performer made an invisible adjustment to his gear box. The jovial man it was impossible not to like vanished from the room as totally as if he had been dropped through a trap door. The vested suit behind the desk was refilled instantly by a fighter crouched low on his toes, gloves cocked, bouncing gently on the tightly stretched canvas floor of the ring, waiting with careful confidence for his opponent's attack.

"What's on your mind, Ezra?"

"I want to know who's going to be made partner this year," Ezra Cooper said.

"We haven't had our meeting yet," Mr. Merz said.

"Then I've come here in plenty of time," Ezra Cooper said.

"For what?" Merz said.

"To make a case for myself," Ezra Cooper said.

"You made the case for yourself a long time ago," Merz said. "The jury was not convinced."

"I'm demanding a new trial," Ezra Cooper said.

"Not a chance, Ezra," Merz said. "You'll never make partner at Isham Truitt."

"Why not?" Ezra Cooper said.

"You're a failure who's stayed too long," Merz said.

Not quietly. Not bluntly. The words were uttered with a neutrality of sound and emphasis that carried their own brutality.

"You never told me I was a failure," Ezra Cooper said.

"We sent you all the signals," Merz said. "You disregarded them."

"I had to," Ezra Cooper said. "I have a sick wife."

"That's not our problem," Merz said. "You could have solved it by taking our repeated hints and your considerable talents and going out to try your luck elsewhere while you still had time. You didn't, Ezra, so there's no point in going on with this argument. It can only become more unpleasant. I will simply state the facts. You know them as well as I do, but either you don't or you refuse to face them. Here they are. After twenty-eight years you've mastered a degree of expertise in a specific area that makes you valuable to us as an employee at a certain figure and no more. You've reached that figure. We will keep you on at that figure as long as you choose to remain here. You will never become a partner. Surely you were aware of this, Ezra, before you asked for this appointment. I don't understand what you expect to get from it except further humiliation."

"When you drafted me out of Columbia in 1950 I think I had the right to believe you felt you picked a winner," Ezra Cooper said. "Was I mistaken?"

"Not in 1950," Merz said. "Back then I felt that way. This is 1978. I now know what you don't seem to know. I was wrong about the young man I drafted out of Columbia."

"In what way?" Ezra Cooper said.

"Ezra, I ask you again to abandon this line of questioning," Merz said. "It will change nothing."

"Perhaps not for you," Ezra Cooper said.

For a moment the man even his enemies agreed it was impossible not to like reappeared in the three-piece suit, but only for a moment. It was Mandamus Manny who said:

"Ezra, what you've never grasped is the enormous difference between the world of law school smarts and the world of paying clients. The essence of law school brilliance is grasping and exploring like a ballet dancer the multiplicity of the law. Seeing what lesser intelligences miss. The endlessly various ways to go. The holes in the watertight. The on-the-one-hands, and the on-the-other-hands. The essence of brilliance in the world of paying clients, however, is just the opposite. Not letting them see the on-the-one-hands and the on-the-other-hands. Clients come to a lawyer the way they go to an engineer. Where shall I cut my canal? Through this swamp or that? The engineer they trust is the man who says firmly and without hemming and hawing—cut your canal through that swamp. No ifs, ands, or buts. No maybe it will be better this way, but on the other hand it might be better that way. No hesitation. No alternatives. Firmness, more firmness, firmness all the way.

"The same with a lawyer. The client comes to him because the client wants to get an answer he believes in our society only a lawyer can give him. That belief must never be shaken. On the contrary. It must be bolstered all the way down the track. It's what the client pays for. The client says I need ten million dollars to expand my widget plant. How can I get the money fast, cheap, and safely? The lawyer either explores all the possibilities or he knows them already, but he keeps the exploration to himself. The lawyer who lays out for the client all the possibilities that the lawyer must explore before he gives him the definite answer will lose that client. The lawyer must answer firmly. A federal subsidy. A bond issue. A merger with Company X. A national lottery, for God's sake, or even a bank robbery is a better answer if it's the only answer than an on-the-one-hand and an on-the-other-hand answer.

"What turned on your professors at Columbia, Ezra, is exactly what has consistently turned off the Isham Truitt clients who have dealt with you directly. You're an on-the-one-hander and on-the-other-hander. You never seem to be able to make up your mind. We saw that fast and started sending you the hints to try elsewhere. It's possible you've never seen that about yourself. It occurs to me now that maybe that's why you've stayed on here so long after everybody else could see your position was hope-less. Maybe even on the subject of your future at Isham Truitt you've spent twenty-eight years writing so brilliant an on-the-one-hand and on-the-other-hand law review article that you've used up your future without noticing it go by."

When his voice stopped, Mr. Merz seemed surprised by the si-lence he had himself created. He took a stab at a small smile, as though trying after the brutal assessment to retrieve a sliver of his reputation as a man it was impossible not to like. Ezra Coo-per wasn't having any.

"Anything else?" he said.

The face of Manny Merz was washed by a swift little wave of incredulity. It was as though the seasoned fighter, having deliv-ered a series of savage blows that his experience had taught him should finish off this stumble bum, sees the groggy opponent staggering back to his feet for more punishment.

"As a matter of fact there is," Mandamus Manny said. "Look at that tie you're wearing."

Ezra Cooper did not obey the order.

"What's wrong with the tie I'm wearing?" he said.

"It matches your personality," Mr. Merz said. "Which is Early American Bring Down. Neither belongs in an office where an im-portant part of a man's job is spending time with clients."

"The last client I spent time with was a few minutes before I came into this room," Ezra Cooper said. "He was wearing blue jeans and a red tennis shirt."

"Maybe if you did the same it would help clients react to you in a positive rather than a negative way," Mandamus Manny said. "The way I remember you in 1950 when we first met at Co-lumbia, you were a snappy dresser. You were an 'up' sort of per-son. Frankly, I took to you because in addition to your legal talent I sensed you were my sort of guy. I could see you making it with the girls, dancing up a storm in a night spot, charming the pants off clients. That's why I became your rabbi here in the office. I'd found you, and I was convinced you were going places. I wanted to keep you under my wing. I didn't want any-body else horning in, taking the credit for what I felt you were going to accomplish here. Instead of that I've had twenty-eight years of taking the blame. In this thoroughly unpleasant meeting, which I did not seek but you insisted on, it is now my turn to ask—anything else?"

"Yes, one thing," Ezra Cooper said.

"Let's have it," Mandamus Manny said.

"When you and your partners have that meeting," Ezra Cooper said, "I want you to put my name on the table, and I want you to see to it that they vote with you. Don't walk out of that room until you are able to continue walking down the hall to my room, where you will put your arm on my shoulder in the traditional manner and say Ezra, you've finally made it, at long last you can go home and tell the little woman you are an Isham Truitt partner."

If Ezra Cooper had been asked to characterize the expression that took over the face of Emanuel Merz he would have said, "The son of a bitch looked at me as though he thought I'd gone nuts." After a few moments Mandamus Manny seemed to adjust to what he clearly felt was the statement of a mind that had gone round the bend.

"Ezra," he said quietly, "you haven't heard a word I've said, have you?"

"On the contrary," Ezra Cooper said. "I heard every one, and they're all engraved on my heart, but they are no longer relevant. You seem to be unaware that during the past twenty-four hours there has been a major shift in the Isham Truitt power base."

"Tell me about it," Mandamus Manny said.

His body did not move, but there was in his voice and manner the feel of a man who had just leaned back in his chair and crossed his hands on his noticeable but not unsightly pot belly: a man settling himself to listen in comfort to a child's account of some misadventure at school.

"Through the work I do for Ken Kreel," Ezra Cooper said, "I have come to know one of our newest young associates, a boy named Lichine. Mr. Kreel has clearly done for Mr. Lichine what you once did for me. He has appointed himself Mr. Lichine's rabbi here at Isham Truitt. He came to you recently and asked you to put Lichine on your pro bono schedule, did he not?"

"He did," Mr. Merz said.

"Two weeks ago the boy went off to Alabama for what was supposed to be a month's stay," Ezra Cooper said. "Two days ago he came home unexpectedly in the middle of the night and found Ken Kreel in bed with his wife. Young Mr. Lichine was not pleased. He expressed his displeasure by beating the shit out of Ken Kreel. Mr. Lichine left Kreel with a bad concussion, several unsightly face lacerations, two beautiful shiners, and a broken wrist. He's such a mess that he hasn't dared show up here in the office. Kreel and his secretary have cooked up a story that he had to fly to London unexpectedly on the Paramount deal. To make the story seem plausible, Kreel called me from his hideout yesterday, pretended he was calling from London, and asked me to get up some figures for him on the Columbia involvement. Playing the game, I got up the figures and, a few minutes before I came in here to see you, I sent the figures over to Ken Kreel's hideout, which is Suite 2909 in the Park Lane Hotel. My messenger is an Isham Truitt client named Saxe Tortora. He thinks he's carrying to Kreel the draft of a contract he must take with him on a one o'clock flight to California today for a crucial meeting in Beverly Hills."

Ezra Cooper paused and looked at his wristwatch. He did it the way he came into the room and he had crossed his legs.

"In a few minutes," he said, "I think both Mr. Tortora and Ken Kreel will be shocked into a mutual surprise that is going to have some pretty drastic repercussions here at Isham Truitt."

Mr. Merz nodded affably.

"Anything else?" he said.

"For the time being," Ezra Cooper said, "I think that's enough."

"So do I," Mandamus Manny said. "These repercussions you speak of, they will include of course the dismissal of Ken Kreel as an Isham Truitt junior partner and your election as his replacement."

"I leave the details in your hands," Ezra Cooper said.

He stood up and started to walk out. Mr. Merz allowed him to get halfway to the door. Then Mandamus Manny took over.

"Ezra," he said.

Ezra Cooper stopped and turned.

"Yes?" he said.

"I wouldn't want you to leave this room without under-
standing just how capable are the hands in which you've left
those details," Mandamus Manny said. "After twenty-eight years
I finally understand the real reason why you never made partner.
You clearly have the same grasp of the realities of how a firm
like Isham Truitt functions as you have of the effect on a client
of that tie you are wearing. When you leave this room, Ezra, you
might as well carry with you a few of the hard facts of life. One,
associates are expendable. Two, junior partners with a client following are not. Mr. Lichine was fired this morning. Ken Kreel
will continue to handle his client list from Suite 2909 at the Park
Lane. Gil Cutter, our office manager, booked the suite for him at
my instructions. When Dr. Arthur Steinberg decides that Ken
Kreel is cosmetically presentable, he will move from the Park
Lane back into his office here."

Mr. Merz picked up the phone.

"Miss Overby, get me Mr. Cutter, please," he said. "No, I'll
wait." Pause. "Hello, Gil," Mr. Merz said. "You know Ezra Cooper, of course? Yes. Well, I wanted you to know that Mr. Cooper
will be clearing out his desk today. Yes. Please adjust your payroll records accordingly. Thank you, Gil."

Mandamus Manny put down the phone. It was Mr. Merz who
spoke to the man standing halfway between the desk and the
door.

"Ezra," he said, "you should have driven me to do this a quarter of a century ago."

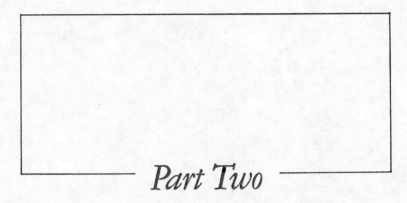

Part Two

"The law is the true embodiment
of everything that's excellent."

W. S. GILBERT

9

A quarter of a century ago Amelia Troy was what *Variety* called a "money star" and was by *Time* identified as "David Fillmore's Great and Good Friend." Then she got married and had a baby. *Variety* stopped calling Amelia Troy anything, and *Time,* on the few occasions when her name appeared in the magazine, referred to her as "David Fillmore's Former Great and Good Friend."

The change was not caused by a falling off in Amelia Troy's talent or popularity. It was just a run of bad luck. She had four flops in a row, and lost her nerve. She found it increasingly difficult to come out on a stage. Clifford Cline tried to help. He stopped work on his new musical and wrote a special vehicle for her: a courtroom drama in which Amelia Troy was supposed to play a modern Portia. She collapsed during the first day of rehearsals. The play was abandoned and she stopped trying. Now her name rarely appeared in the press, never in connection with a new play. Amelia Troy was not exactly forgotten, but at least by the public she was remembered infrequently.

All through this difficult time her husband was kind, her therapist was ineffective, and David Fillmore stood by. Or rather, he sat by.

In a reversal of the customary meaning of the term, David Fillmore, the youngest of the clan, was the legendary Fillmore. Leander, the founder of the Fillmore National, had shunned publicity. His son and the four oldest of the son's five sons shared an almost pathological passion for privacy. Their only appearance in the press was on the crossword puzzle page. Reading 46 Down: "One of Leander Fillmore's grandsons," and seeing that what was required was more than the five letters for David, even a seasoned crossword fan knew enough to work around number 46.

It was an office joke at Isham Truitt that, if a Fillmore signature was needed on a document, you had to check with Mr. Isham personally or with his secretary for the correct spelling of the given name, and it was wiser to place the task of obtaining the signature not in Tony Tessitore's normally capable hands, but hire a detective agency. If, however, it was the signature of David Fillmore that was required, "Spell it as in Goliath and, to find out where he is at any given moment, just look at the front page of that day's New York *Times*."

This was not strictly true, of course. There was enough truth in the exaggeration, however, to fuel a whole catalogue of jokes. Not the smallest category in the catalogue dealt with David Fillmore's sexual proclivities. They were allegedly insatiable. In the jokes, anyway.

Amelia Troy knew more about this than the fabricators of the jokes but she could speak only for herself. Understandably, her audience for this kind of speech was limited. In fact, it consisted of one person. Amelia Troy's chum, bosom pal, inseparable companion, and confederate during the entire quarter century of Amelia's retirement from the stage: Nellie Cline. She was an integral part of Amelia's quarter-century relationship with David Fillmore, but even Nellie Cline was privy to nothing but the arrangements. Not a word about Amelia Troy's sex life had ever crossed Amelia Troy's lips except under prodding from her gynecologist or her therapist. With both of these she limited herself primly to answering questions only with the technically appropriate medical terms.

"The secret of Miss Troy's enormous appeal," Wolcott Gibbs wrote when she made her New York debut, "lies in a sort of filtered view. While she sends across the footlights an effluvium that signals unmistakably there is no seething lubricity of which she is incapable and indeed is yours for the asking, the message comes through a filter of ladylike propriety that gives the impression that she would be incapable of uttering the classic scatological expletive if she had a mouthful of it. It is a combination no man can withstand, and indeed what fool would try?"

Not David Fillmore, even on a day as crowded as this one. The first signal for Nellie Cline came as always at the beginning of the first of the several phone calls she and Amelia Troy exchanged daily. The words of the signal were always the same.

"What are you doing around noon?" Amelia Troy said.

"Let me think," Nellie Cline said. "Don't we have a shopping date?"

"That's right," Amelia Troy said. "I'll pick you up at eleven sharp."

No matter what the rest of the conversation was about, the important point had been made. Even if Clifford Cline happened to be listening on the extension in his study, and both his wife and her chum were aware he was a shameless eavesdropper, he would not know what the girls knew: an assignation had been asked for and granted. At eleven sharp Emmett rang from the lobby.

"The car is here, Mrs. Cline."

"Thank you, Emmett," Nellie said. "I'll be right down.".

The car was an absolutely enchanting little custom-built black Mercedes with red upholstery that had set somebody back in the neighborhood of forty thousand dollars. Even though Nellie Cline knew it was Amelia Troy's birthday gift from David Fillmore, their talk about it had been limited to oohing and ahing about the vehicle's beauty. About the perquisites of her relationship with David Fillmore, Amelia Troy was as reticent as she was about her sex life. So was her husband. Tom Lichine had accepted the brand-new car as he had accepted the quarter century of continued plush living in the Waldorf Towers: a result of the brilliant investments her former Great and Good Friend David Fillmore had made for Amelia before she met and married Tom. Sliding in beside Amelia on the front seat, Nellie Cline said, "Anything special?"

Sometimes, when she got the coded signal over the telephone from what was known in the David Fillmore joke catalogue as "The Chairman of the Board's Nookie Secretary," Amelia Troy would also get a piece of gossip that kept her and Nellie Cline busy during the run down to Forty-third Street. Today, of course, Amelia had more than a piece of gossip, but she was not yet ready to share it with Nellie. Not until she had a talk with David Fillmore.

"No, nothing special," Amelia Troy said as she put the car in gear and sent it down toward Madison. "Has Judy said anything to you about the office?"

"I haven't talked to the lady lawyer for over a week," Nellie Cline said. "Why do you ask?"

"Nothing special," Amelia Troy said. She gave her attention to beating the light across Madison, then said, "I was wondering about Tom."

"He's got two more weeks in Alabama, hasn't he?" Nellie Cline said.

"I think so," Amelia Troy said. "I don't like to ask too many questions. One gets a little weary of the 'Mother, I Am Twenty-five Years Old' ploy."

"Daughters are worse," Nellie Cline said. "Sons, even the worst of them, have some slivers of residual chivalry, even when they're letting you have it, but daughters? Yich. The most casual inquiry about the weather and whammo, that was your head that just got chopped off." She was silent while Amelia Troy turned right, then said, "Come on, honey, you've got something on your mind. I can tell."

Amelia Troy hesitated, then said, "Bianca."

"Fortunately," Nellie Cline said, "I've had no personal experience with daughters-in-law. My scars have been earned in honorable combat with a daughter. What has Tom's darling little child bride done to you now?"

"Nothing," Amelia Troy said.

"You should be counting your blessings," Nellie Cline said. "Not glaring at that taxi driver as though you're planning to skewer him."

"I called the apartment yesterday," Amelia Troy said. "She was out, so I left a message with the service. I called again later in the afternoon and left another message. This morning when I called right after talking to you, even the service didn't answer. It seems to be turned off."

"Why, honey, you may be sitting on a potential lucky break of staggering proportions," Nellie Cline said. "Maybe all those pins we've been sticking into that cute wax figure we made of her have finally buckled down and done their job. If it's suicide, how would you like her to have done it?"

Amelia Troy concentrated on working the beautiful little automobile through the hell outside Bloomingdale's.

"I wasn't trying to reach Bianca," she said. "I wanted to talk with Tom."

"Why didn't you call him in Alabama?" Nellie Cline said.

"I did," Amelia Troy said. "He wasn't in."

"As I understand the pro bono work these boys are tossed out like seed at sowing time all over the country to do," Nellie Cline said, "they do it in courtrooms not hotel rooms."

"Not at midnight," Amelia Troy said.

"The bright side we should be looking at gets brighter and brighter," Nellie Cline said. "Maybe Tom has grown tired faster than most of his predecessors of the kinky sex that Bianca Bean is noted for distributing up and down the length and breadth of Off- as well as Off-Off-Broadway. Maybe my godson has come to his senses. It could be Tom just went out and picked up an authentic Mason-Dixon-line hooker."

The silence that greeted this elaborate sally was sobering. Nellie Cline was proud of her humor the way Grandma Moses was proud of her painting. Both were constructed with painstaking, time-consuming care. One of the things that had kept the two women so close for so many years was that Amelia Troy enjoyed Nellie Cline's complicated jokes. Silence was not Amelia's way of expressing enjoyment. And in the midst of the Lexington Avenue insanity the Mercedes had just emerged into one of those islands of inexplicably normal traffic that were practically designed for a bit of relaxed laughter. Amelia Troy had not delivered. She was glaring ahead with deadly concentration.

"Listen, honey," Nellie Cline said.

"Can't now," Amelia Troy said.

She made a right and started maneuvering for the strip of unblocked curb in front of 25 West Forty-third. The big office building was a Fillmore property, but not even the tenants were aware of this. It was one of David Fillmore's favorite possessions. He had never set foot on any of the upper floors. It was the lobby that got his business. It ran straight through from Forty-third Street to Forty-fourth. The tenants, as well as many nontenants in the area who knew the lobby, found it a great convenience. If you worked on Forty-third and you had a lunch date at, say, the Algonquin on Forty-fourth, it was an easy way to get there without having to circle all the way west on Sixth Avenue or south on Fifth, especially on a rainy day. The weather didn't matter to David Fillmore. For twenty-five years it hadn't mattered to Amelia Troy. She brought the car to a stop in the cleared space against the curb, shifted to neutral, but did not cut the ignition.

"Same time?" Nellie Cline said.

"Yes," Amelia Troy said. "He's got a two o'clock meeting at the UN."

"I'll be here," Nellie Cline said.

She leaned over and pecked a kiss at Amelia Troy's cheek. After a quick backward glance down the street, Amelia opened the door and stepped out into the gutter. She slammed the door and came around the front of the car to the curb. Nellie Cline slid across the front seat and settled herself behind the wheel. She waved to Amelia Troy and put the car in gear. Amelia Troy waved back and crossed the sidewalk. When she walked into the lobby of 25 West, her chum Nellie Cline was on her way in the Mercedes up Forty-third to Sixth Avenue.

Amelia Troy walked briskly down the long marble tunnel to the rectangle of sunlight at the far end. When she stepped out onto the Forty-fourth Street sidewalk the big black limousine was waiting at the curb. The rear door opened and Amelia Troy came across the sidewalk. She stepped in and sat down beside David Fillmore. As the door slammed shut and the car got under way he said, "Hello, sweetie."

One of the scraps of the David Fillmore legend was that at sixty he had started calling all his girls sweetie because he could no longer keep all their names straight. Amelia Troy doubted that this was true. There were very few things David Fillmore could not keep straight. Nevertheless, she preferred to be called sweetie. Even though Amelia and David Fillmore had never been seen in public together since her marriage to Tom Lichine, she spent an awful lot of time with Fillmore in the family limousines, and she had never lost a lingering uneasiness about the drivers. Fillmore had no such qualms, of course, but that meant nothing. If you were a Fillmore, Amelia had learned long ago, or at any rate if you were David Fillmore, you did not have qualms about anything.

"There's nothing to worry about, sweetie," he was thoughtful enough to remember to reassure Amelia every couple of months or so. "These cars are all part of the family fleet. We've got them completely rigged for total privacy. The windows are all one-way glass, so while you can see what's going on outside, nobody outside can see what's going on here inside. Not even the driver, who also can't hear anything we don't want to tell him on the intercom, and we do a better job of vetting our drivers for security than the CIA does. You're safer here than you'd be in a sealed-off hotel suite, sweetie, so you just relax and enjoy yourself."

Amelia always did. Or nearly always. There were times when even David Fillmore had something else on his mind, but those times were rare. He was an extraordinarily well-organized man, with a passion for promptness that made it possible for him to give complete attention to whatever it was that appeared at any time of day or night on his complicated schedule, including sex. While he lived within the framework of the law, the boundaries of which were set and guarded for him by what seemed on occasion almost half the Isham Truitt staff, within those boundaries David Fillmore made his own rules.

"Lunch with men, dine with women," he said. "Scotch at noon, Bourbon after sundown. As for sex," he added, "horizontal at night, vertical by sunlight."

Amelia Troy was David Fillmore's most satisfying sunlight mistress. After thirty years she knew he was genuinely fond of her. Most of the time Amelia was equally certain she was fond of him. She was certain of this certainty only when he was out of sight. When they met for an assignation, however, her first task was a quick reassessment. It never took long. A single glance was enough.

Settling herself beside him in the moving car, Amelia Troy gave David Fillmore that quick glance. It showed what the endless newspaper and magazine photographs showed: a handsome, vigorous man about whom quite a few people, including Amelia Troy, grew weary of hearing other people, usually women, say with more than the terminal exclamation point in their voices, "My God, he certainly doesn't look his age!"

David Fillmore's age was sixty-six, and to Amelia Troy, who had known him intimately for thirty of those years, he looked every month, every day, and every hour of those sixty-six years. Not because the accumulated numbers had made him less attractive, but because it was Amelia Troy's firm belief that everybody, including fifty-one-year-old ex-actresses, looked their age. The trick was not to look as old as every other fifty-one-year-old actress looked. The answer to whether or not Amelia Troy had swung the trick she was content to leave to a simple statistic. In spite of the wide distribution of his favors in other areas, there had been no falling off in the frequency with which David Fillmore's Secretary in Charge of Nookie called Amelia Troy to arrange these vertical sunlight meetings. The answer to whether or not David Fillmore had swung the trick could be heard in the echoes of all those exclamation-pointed female voices. He had, yes. In spades. But, as Amelia Troy could see in this swift preliminary survey, David Fillmore had swung it at a price of which he seemed totally unaware.

He had started life with, of course, the Fillmore Face. It was the sort of face that made a puzzle of the relentless struggle for anonymity waged by the other members of the family. Any neophyte in a beginner's class in painting would have grasped after the first lesson that what the Fillmores struggled so hard to achieve they had actually been granted by nature at birth. The Fillmore Face was forgettable.

It was clean, harmless, and totally devoid of character. It displayed just enough intelligence to indicate that its owner could be trusted to find his way to the advertising agency that was looking for something recognizably human, but no more than that, to put under the smear of shaving cream on the newly designed Barbasol can.

At twenty-one Amelia Troy had taken a second look at it only because one of the girls in the cast pointed out to her that the face, which was carried by the man who kept knocking so persistently at her dressing-room door, belonged to a Fillmore. Even at twenty-one Amelia Troy knew what that meant.

Now, at fifty-one, from her swift survey of David Fillmore's face, she knew something else. Something that perhaps explained why his four brothers, like their father and grandfather, had so relentlessly avoided the public gaze. The uses of great wealth could be coarsening.

David Fillmore's forgettable face had gradually taken on an unforgettable quality. At sixty-six he looked like an undersea creature. Clean because it lived in an element that eliminated the necessity for scrubbing. Supremely confident because of its size and strength. Compelling because of what it had the power to do. Arrogant because of the shivery sexual chords it was aware it plucked. Smiling always, not with pleasure but with a baring-of-the-teeth warning to the world not to be foolish enough to resist the irresistible.

"Okay, sweetie," he said. "Do I get a passing grade?"

Startled, Amelia Troy managed to say, "In what?"

"Whenever we meet," David Fillmore said, "I've begun to notice recently you always start by putting me through an FBI check-out."

"It's unavoidable," Amelia Troy said. "I'm always surprised by how young you look."

"That's two compliments from you in one day," David Fillmore said.

"What was the first?" Amelia Troy said.

"Your asking to see me," David Fillmore said. "It's always the other way around."

"Do you mind?" Amelia Troy said.

He laughed, leaned down, and kissed her.

"I mean I know how busy you are," she said.

"Nonsense," David Fillmore said. "I moved the UN back an hour."

He put his arm around her.

"David."

The arm tensed.

"Something's wrong," he said.

It was not a question.

"They've fired Tom," Amelia Troy said.

"Tom?" David Fillmore said. Then: "Oh, Tom. I didn't know he'd gone back on the stage."

"Not that Tom," Amelia Troy said. "Tom Junior."

The teeth-baring smile slid smoothly back into place.

"I'm never surprised by how young you look," David Fillmore said. "I'm always surprised when I'm reminded that you have a son old enough to be fired from something. Who fired him?"

"Isham Truitt," Amelia Troy said.

The sea-creature face did not take well to surprise.

"My lawyers?" David Fillmore said.

"Oh, David," Amelia Troy said with a sigh. "A year ago? I told you Tom was finishing up at Harvard Law School? He was law review and fourth in his class? He'd had offers from several New York firms?"

"There's only one New York firm," David Fillmore said. "I'll talk to Walter Isham."

"You did," Amelia Troy said. "A year ago. That's how Tom got the job."

The sea-creature smile slid back into place.

"From which you tell me he's just been fired," David Fillmore said.

"Yes," Amelia Troy said.

"Why?" David Fillmore said.

"I don't know," Amelia Troy said.

"Didn't the boy tell you?" David Fillmore said.

"I haven't talked to him," Amelia Troy said.

"Then how do you know he's been fired?" David Fillmore said.

"David, please listen," Amelia Troy said. "I called him at his apartment twice yesterday and left messages. He did not call back. Last night I called him in Alabama."

"Why?" David Fillmore said.

"He'd been assigned to help with a murder case down there," Amelia Troy said. "I left a message at his hotel but he didn't call back. This morning, after I tried him at home once more—"

"If the boy is in Alabama," David Fillmore said, "why do you keep trying him at home here in New York?"

"I expected his wife to answer," Amelia Troy said.

"I didn't know the boy is married," David Fillmore said.

"It happened only three months ago," Amelia Troy said.

"If he's got a wife," David Fillmore said, "I don't think it's too much to expect her to answer the phone."

"Nor do I," Amelia Troy said. "That's what upset me."

"I knew you were upset," David Fillmore said. "I could tell the moment I put my arm around you."

"So I called the Isham Truitt office," Amelia Troy said. "I asked to speak to Tom. I've done it many times this past year. There was some fuss at the other end. Finally the girl at the switchboard came back on the wire. She said she was sorry but Mr. Lichine didn't work there anymore."

"Did she say why?" David Fillmore said.

"No, of course not," Amelia Troy said.

"Didn't you ask?" David Fillmore said.

"David," Amelia Troy said, "I was talking to a switchboard operator."

"You should have asked her to put you through to Walter Isham," David Fillmore said. "He'd have told you."

"I don't know Walter Isham," Amelia Troy said. "He doesn't know me."

"You could have told him you're a friend of mine," David Fillmore said.

"I thought the claim should more properly come from you," Amelia Troy said.

For a moment the look of surprise again disfigured the smooth sea-creature look. But only for a moment.

"Quite right," David Fillmore said. "I'll call him from the UN."

Amelia Troy leaned over to the taboret between the facing seats and picked up the phone.

"Why don't you call him now?" she said.

David Fillmore glanced out the one-way window. The car was moving up the West Side Highway.

"It would throw me off schedule," he said.

He took the phone from her, leaned forward, and replaced the instrument on the taboret.

"Don't worry," David Fillmore said as he put his arm around Amelia Troy. "I'll call Walter Isham this afternoon and straighten this whole thing out. That's a promise."

"Thank you, David," Amelia Troy said. She kissed him and murmured, "You are a darling."

"So are you," David Fillmore said, easing himself into position. "Watch the zipper, sweetie," he said. "Remember what happened last time."

10

"In slicing the profits pie,
Walter Slidell Isham,
How does he rate?
Why, without hue or cry
He gets the slice with jam,
Because Walter Slidell Isham
Carries all of the dead weight."

These lyrics were part of a show presented at one of the Isham Truitt annual University Club dinners in which the firm's younger lawyers satirized their seniors. It brought down the house. It also caused Walter Isham to stalk out. He was aware of the nickname nobody in the office would have dared use to his face: "the Pallbearer."

Walter Isham was also known, again not to his face, of course, as a stuffy square who had no sense of humor about himself. The evidence indicated that the characterization was probably accurate, but these were the qualities that enabled him to render a service to the firm nobody else was eager to perform. Walter Isham represented Isham Truitt at all the firm's important funerals.

Hugh Kelly did not consider any funeral important unless it was held in St. Patrick's. He could see, as the office limousine edged its way into the traffic jammed around the Madison Avenue entrance to Campbell's, that a larger number of people than Hugh Kelly would have suspected considered it important to put in an appearance at the services for Sosthenes DeKalb. Hugh Kelly was surprised. It was true that Southern Shoals Asbestos, of which DeKalb had for years been chief executive officer, was a Fillmore National Bank satellite. So, however, were a hundred other corporations scattered all over the country that did not rate this sort of display at the death of a David Fillmore puppet.

"Tim, you better drop me here," Hugh Kelly said to the driver. "You'll not be getting any closer before sundown, and you're likely to lose your hubcaps in the process."

"Yes, sir," the driver said. He pulled into a clear space at the curb near the Eighty-second Street corner in front of the public school at the other side of Madison. "Will you be wanting me to wait, Mr. Kelly?"

"Yes, Tim, if you please," Hugh Kelly said. "And see you do it in the car and not in front of a slab of pie à la mode and a chocolate milkshake in that drugstore over there. You're getting as fat as a parish priest."

"On that, sir, you are in agreement with the wife," the driver said. "I'll sit behind the wheel here, Mr. Kelly, and say a prayer for the soul of the departed."

"He can use it," Hugh Kelly said. "There are people who believe Sosthenes DeKalb never had a soul."

Kelly crossed the street and shouldered his burly body through the human clusters that thickened into larger clumps as he approached the Eighty-first Street corner. Hugh Kelly collected a number of dirty looks but he got to Campbell's Madison Avenue entrance ahead of a great many people who had been trying to make it for some time. In the entrance hall he sent a quick glance through the arch down into the chapel, which was almost full, and turned toward the mahogany door on the right. In his path appeared the man in the black suit with the shaved skull and the enormous black cavalry mustache that curved upward like the horns of a miniature fighting bull.

"Are you a member of the family, sir?"

"Certainly not," Hugh Kelly said. "Do I look like a DeKalb?"

"I'm sorry, sir," the man said. "Only family are admitted to this room."

"Don't talk nonsense," Hugh Kelly said. "My partner Walter

Isham is in there, and he's not a member of the family. Now you fetch him out here fast, or I'm going in there much faster."

"Oh, I beg your pardon, sir," the man said. "If it's Mr. Isham, of course, sir. I'll tell him you're out here. Mr. Kelly is it?"

"It is, and it's urgent," Hugh Kelly said.

Walter Isham appeared as though the man with the shaved head had disappeared into a revolving door in which Isham had been standing in one of the inside wedges waiting for the door to be set in motion.

"Walter, you know your way around Campbell's the way Jimmy Walker, God rest his soul, used to know his way around the Central Park Casino," Hugh Kelly said. "They must have an office in this place where we can have a talk, and after all the business you've shepherded through this boneyard over the years, surely the firm of Campbell's would not find it in their heart to deny you the use of it, would they?"

Before Walter Isham could open his mouth the man with the shaved head said, "This way, gentlemen."

Hugh Kelly was not surprised by the swift even servile response. He had known Walter Isham since the days toward the end of the war when, as a couple of j.g.'s, they had been assigned by Secretary Forrestal's office to help Fiorello La Guardia straighten out some of the UNRRA legal problems. It had been obvious to Hugh Kelly soon enough that this handsome young WASP, who wore his whites as though he were Admiral Jellicoe reviewing the fleet before sending it into action at Jutland, had many talents. These did not include a flip lip.

Walter Isham never opened his mouth to release words until he had selected with care the ones he believed appropriate to the occasion, and had arranged them in a manner he considered most effective for the desired result. This had been mistaken for stupidity by many of the UNRRA staff members. Hugh Kelly was not one of them. Himself a loose flowing talker who used words not as instruments of precision but as showering sprays of charm, he appreciated a talent he did not possess or lust after. Not personally, anyway. As an ingredient in the character of a law partner, however, especially in a man with a talent for green goods, Hugh Kelly set his cap for it.

As it turned out, the admiration was mutual, and because of the Isham family connection with the Fillmores of the Fillmore National, it was Walter Isham who captured Hugh Kelly for the family firm before Hugh Kelly could set his verbose charms in motion to make the tag for a planned firm of his own. It had been a profitable relationship, and on the whole a happy one in spite of Walter Isham's appearance. It was forbidding.

He still looked like Jellicoe on the bridge, but the coloration was different. The close-cropped black hair was now snow white, but it was still all in place and still parted in the middle. The Charlie Chaplin mustache, however, was still shoe-polish black. Walter Isham was no longer as stuffy as he had seemed in a roomful of young smart aleck wartime naval officers, but he still had no sense of humor about himself. He still believed the client was entitled to his money's worth, and the way to give it to him was what Walter Isham still called burning the midnight oil. He was known to the young associates as a pain in the ass. To the junior partners he was rated a greedy man with a profit-sharing point. And to the Bar Association, ever anxious for an available illustration to brighten an image that in the public eye had a tendency to acquire tarnish like a brass candlestick on a windy hill, Walter Isham was known as quote the soul of integrity unquote.

"Will this be all right, gentlemen?" said the man with the shaved skull.

"If you see that nobody interrupts us," said Walter Isham.

"I guarantee it, sir," the man said.

"Thank you very much," Walter Isham said.

The man went out and closed the office door.

"Sit down, Walter," Hugh Kelly said.

"I am attending a funeral," Walter Isham said. "I would prefer to do it on my feet."

"Then I will sit," Hugh Kelly said. "I am, after all, your guest, and while I may not carry as much weight as you do with David Fillmore, it is with regret that I must say I carry a good deal more in the neighborhood of my tail."

He moved his bulk into the inadequate chair behind the small desk.

"I'm sorry to bring you up here in the middle of a proceeding for which I know you have no affection unless the auspices are Catholic," Walter Isham said. "But needs must when the devil drives. A few minutes after I got here, indeed I had just paid my respects to the widow, I was summoned to that very telephone in front of which you are now sitting. It was David Fillmore."

"When, in the life of an Isham, is it not?" Hugh Kelly said.

"Levity about David Fillmore comes ill from a senior partner in our firm," Walter Isham said. "If David Fillmore should take it into his head to carry his legal work elsewhere, Hugh, you would soon not be driving to the office from Quogue in a Bentley."

"Would that I could hasten the day," Hugh Kelly said. "The damned thing spends more time in Iggulden's running up repair bills than it does under my rear end carrying me to work. What did Fillmore want?"

"Your head," Walter Isham said.

"For the man who has everything it seems a paltry prize," Hugh Kelly said. "I am, however, a loyal Isham Truitt partner. When does he want it, and how?"

"I understand the young people in the office believe I have no sense of humor about myself," Walter Isham said. "I have never understood what they meant. If it means the sort of quip you have just uttered, I take comfort in my deficiency."

"All right," Hugh Kelly said. "This is not a confessional. Tell me why the sedulous fornicator who keeps me in defective Bentleys wants my head?"

"He has not asked for it by name," Walter Isham said. "David told me he had just learned we had fired a young associate named Thomas Lichine, Jr. If this was so, David said, he wanted the young man rehired immediately and the man who fired him kicked out and I quote super pronto unquote."

"David Fillmore, I regret to say, is not the successor to Chauncey Depew as a phrasemaker for whom the New York Bar has been waiting hopefully lo! these many years," Hugh Kelly said. "Is he serious about this?"

"He called from a meeting at the UN," Walter Isham said.

"I do not consider that answer responsive," Hugh Kelly said.

"My feelings about the UN, however, are a matter of public record."

"Too public, perhaps," Walter Isham said. "If it turns out that yours is indeed the head David Fillmore has asked for, your attitude toward his favorite charity will earn you no Brownie points."

"I gather that even though my head has not yet been ticketed by name for shipment to him," Hugh Kelly said, "you have identified me as the culprit."

"I called Ernestine from that phone in front of you and held on while she had Gil Cutter check his payroll records. They indicated that you had ordered young Lichine fired yesterday. I asked Ernestine to find you and ask you to come up here at once. Thank you for doing so."

"Not at all, Walter, not at all," Hugh Kelly said. "Your word is my command."

"A bit less of the blarney, Hugh, if you can restrain yourself," Walter Isham said. "As our British colleagues at UNRRA used to say in our green years, just put me in the picture."

He listened with his usual look of courteous, noncommittal attention. When Hugh Kelly finished, Walter Isham ran a forefinger across one side of the shoe-polish-black mustache and blew out his breath in a weary sigh.

"None of this would have happened, Hugh, if we hadn't gone along with all the pro bono nonsense," Walter Isham said. "I think Tony Tessitore has the only honest evaluation of these programs. It's all crap, Tony says, if you will forgive the expression. Money going out, he says, instead of coming in. Why do we do it, Hugh?"

"Walter, we have to," Hugh Kelly said. "If we don't we'll never bring into the fold the good young people to succeed us and keep the firm alive. My father never stopped bitching about why had the world decided to go crazy during his lifetime? Why could it not wait to change its drawers until he was gone? It's a sad truth to face, Walter, but the world never stops changing, and our lifetimes are seeing their full share. When you and I were young the world of the law was Oliver Wendell Holmes' mustache, and the Brandeis Brief, and J. P. Morgan's wisecracks about when he wants a lawyer he doesn't choose the man who tells him what he can't do, he tells Elihu Root what he wants to do and Mr. Root tells him how to do it. Would that it were still so, Walter, would that it were. Unfortunately, it's not. Why, when Essie and I were in Palm Beach last winter, I picked up the morning paper and there was an ad large as life. A couple of young whippersnappers offering their services in no-fault divorce cases at fifty dollars a shot, and willing to meet the price of the competition if anybody in town could show they'd do it for less. Right there in the morning paper, Walter, along with the ads for pest-control services and hemorrhoid remedies.

"At the other end of the pole," Hugh Kelly went on, "we've got the serious youngsters. It grieves me to keep rediscovering what I keep discovering all the time, and when I had my lunch with the Cardinal last week, His Eminence surprised me by mentioning it as a very good thing, so perhaps my grief is misplaced in the way so many of our young people are no longer interested in just making money. Manny Merz tells me in his scouting trips to the important campuses he finds more and more that the law review kids don't ask how much will we start them at, but what kind of work do we have to offer them.

"Manny got me a darling girl from Harvard this year," Hugh Kelly said. "A born lawyer, with a head for figures, and a completely fresh approach even to such a thing as a real estate closing. She's made me feel that in time, Walter, I could with a clear conscience go to my rest knowing that the real estate affairs of the Church are in good hands, but to keep her at my side I have to let Manny Merz include her in his schedule for service in the Bedford-Stuyvesant Community Legal Services Corporation out in Brooklyn. If I want to hold on to her I have to let her do it, and I want to hold on to her. This Lichine boy, Walter, Manny told me the kid was the first he'd seen in years who had a green-goods thumb that would someday put him in the class to know the glory of working all night to get out a registration statement as good as the kind Walter Isham is famous for. So what happens? He agrees to come with us only if we let him do things like go to Alabama to defend poverty-stricken black kids against murder charges. How was I to know it would turn out the way it did? I didn't even know the boy had been sent down to Alabama. I'd never had anything to do with him. He's been working almost exclusively under Ken Kreel's wing. There are those who will say I'm getting to be a forgetful old fool for telling this on myself, but do you know, Walter, until Father Danaher called me from Alabama two mornings ago, I didn't even know we had a lad by that name working for us."

"Yet a few hours later you ordered him fired," Walter Isham said.

"Lord love us, Walter," Hugh Kelly said, "I ask you, man, what would you have done?"

"I would have waited until the jury came back with its verdict," Walter Isham said.

"Would you, now?" Hugh Kelly said. "And why, may I ask?"

"I don't know Father Danaher," Walter Isham said. "Hearsay is always questionable. More so when the man reporting it is a total stranger. In your case Father Danaher is not a total stranger, of course, but his call to you seems a bit odd. The timing of it, is what I mean. He and young Lichine were trying to save the boy from the electric chair. They fought for a life sentence. When Father Danaher called you with his complaint about Lichine's conduct, the jury was still out. It still is, I gather. If the jury comes in with the verdict he and Lichine fought for, his complaint about Lichine's conduct makes Father Danaher seem a bit silly, do you not agree?"

"No, I do not," Hugh Kelly said.

"Think of the man who made that long-distance call to you as a Baptist or a Jew or a cigar-store Indian," Walter Isham said. "Now answer the question."

Hugh Kelly's rumbling, croupy laugh filled the small office.

"I don't have to," he said.

"Why not?" Walter Isham said.

"The jury is still out," Hugh Kelly said.

The phone rang. Hugh Kelly looked at it as though he could not understand why it should have done such an outrageous thing.

"The Campbell's staff knows we're both in here," Walter

Isham said. "Somebody is trying to reach one of us. It won't be me. Ernestine never relays calls to me when I'm at a funeral."

"Except from David Fillmore, of course," Hugh Kelly said dryly.

"Of course," Walter Isham said.

Hugh Kelly picked up the phone.

"Hello?" he said. "Yes, Edwina."

As he listened the baggy skin around the ice-blue eyes tightened.

"All right, Edwina," he said finally. "Thank you."

He hung up.

"Father Danaher called from Alabama," Hugh Kelly said. "The jury just came in with its verdict."

"And it is?" Walter Isham said.

"Life," Hugh Kelly said.

"I can now call David Fillmore, can I not," Walter Isham said, "and tell him it was all a mistake and the Lichine boy is being rehired?"

"I don't think that would be wise," Hugh Kelly said.

"Why not?" Walter Isham said.

"The prosecutor's office down there has issued a warrant for Lichine's arrest," Hugh Kelly said.

"What's the charge?" Walter Isham said.

"Jury tampering," Hugh Kelly said.

11

The Takashaki Garden, on the south side of Fifty-ninth Street between Park and Madison, was famous for its mizutaki and the large round table in the southwest corner of the dimly lighted room. The fame of the mizutaki was not a one-meal-a-day affair. People who liked Japanese food, especially this particular chicken dish, came to the Takashaki Garden for lunch, for dinner, for after-theater supper, and for gluttonous between-meal stokings.

The fame of the round table was more circumscribed. It was limited to the girls on the Isham Truitt staff who were known as "the paratroops." The Takashaki Garden was their luncheon hangout. Coming into the restaurant a few minutes after one, Phoebe Pember could see she was late.

"You're late," said Sandra Behr, of late a nailer-down of hard fact.

"I'm also furious," Phoebe Pember said.

She sat down, propped her shoulder bag against the leg of her chair, reached for the menu, and stopped.

"You know something?" she said.

"More than I can handle," Sandra Behr said. "But go ahead."

"I'm sick of mizutaki," Phoebe Pember said. "Hey, Yuki!"

"Yes, moddom?" the Japanese waiter said.

"Not today, Yuki, if you don't mind," Phoebe Pember said. "I'm bushed."

"But you summoned me, moddom," the waiter said.

"For a vodka martini, standing up, about this high, without an

olive, minus a twist, and devoid of even the hint of a joke,"
Phoebe Pember said. "You catch?"

"*Madame est servie,*" Yuki said and went off.

"Should you be drinking at this time of day?" Sandra Behr
said.

"Of course not," Phoebe Pember said. "Shouldn't you?"

"Not for another nine months," Sandra Behr said.

Dipping down for the Kleenex in her bag, Phoebe Pember's
body stopped moving. Frozen into immobility, she peered at her
friend across the tabletop like a masked prowler in a comic strip
peering out of the night across a windowsill into a brightly
lighted bedroom stuffed with portable valuables.

"You're sure?" she said.

"Dr. Krafft is," Sandra Behr said.

Phoebe Pember came up straight in her chair, did things to
her nose with the Kleenex, then stuffed the wad back down into
her purse.

"All right," she said. "I'll talk to Tessie as soon as we get back
to the office."

"About what?" Sandra Behr said.

"Sandy, dear," Phoebe Pember said. "Tony Tessitore and his
Katzenjammer Kids have been known to serve a subpoena on the
wrong defendant, true. And on a now legendary occasion, when
the chief executive officer of Southern Shoals Asbestos was up
from Alabama for the night to attend a Fillmore National board
meeting, and Tony Tessitore was asked on short notice to get
him a ticket to the hottest thing in town for that evening, what
knocked on the Plaza-suite door of Mr. Sosthenes DeKalb at
seven-thirty was not a Western Union boy with two down in
front for *South Pacific,* but a one-hundred-dollar-a-night hooker.
Aside from that, however, on one thing Tessie has never stubbed
his toe. He can summon the services of the best abortionist in
town at the drop of a hat."

"I gave up hats after my confirmation," Sandra Behr said.

Phoebe hesitated, even though hesitation was not her style.
She had been known to her Smith classmates as "Nat." A con-
densation of the given name of the author of the classic injunc-

tion to "Git thar fustest with the mostest": General Nathan Bedford Forrest.

"How about Bob?" Phoebe Pember said finally, with a touch of uncharacteristic caution.

"Bob hasn't owned any headgear since he turned in his Princeton football helmet," Sandra Behr said.

"Forget the hat metaphor," Phoebe Pember said. "I'll start again. With the classic directness that is common to the openings of the great English ballads. Ready? Okay. Does Bob Coffey know he's knocked you up?"

"If he doesn't," Sandra Behr said, "I chose the wrong junior genius at Milbank Tweed to be the father of my child."

"You mean this thing was deliberate?" Phoebe Pember said. Not without astonishment. Not, however, without the sound in her voice of a raised eyebrow, either.

"Nat, do be your age," Sandra Behr said. "Have you heard of anybody since those Fannie Hurst heroines who's got herself pregnant by accident?"

"My mother's cleaning woman out in Westport does it regularly," Phoebe Pember said.

"She can afford it," Sandra Behr said. "She earns more than you and I do at Isham Truitt."

"That's what we get for being neither fish nor fowl nor good red herring," Phoebe Pember said. "Smart girls like this Judy Cline went to law school and got snatched out of her cap and gown as an Isham Truitt associate. Smart girls like Phoebe Pember and Sandra Behr spent the same amount of time on getting their masters in applied psychology, then decided they didn't like the stuff and were lucky after graduation to land the jobs we have at Isham Truitt. Something between the honest plodding of a secretary and the lucrative glamour of an associate. Meaning we handle the office garbage and get called paralegals and earn forty bucks a week less than the secretaries and about half what Judy Cline started at. The window dressing for this shameless exploitation is that we are marking time while we try to make up our minds whether we want to go into the law as a career. Meaning back to the halls of academe for three years in law school or, if you can't stand the sight of another classroom by sunlight, four years at night like Ira Bodmer and Sal Giudice. It's almost as bad as being pregnant and not knowing who done it."

"At least I do," Sandra Behr said.

"Now that you've flogged the poor guy into accomplishing his mission," Phoebe Pember said, "what does Bob have to say for himself?"

"He wants us to get married at once," Sandra Behr said.

"I always said he belongs back there in a Clarence Budington Kelland story," Phoebe Pember said. "Now I say he's a scholar and a gentleman, and I'd be drinking to that if Yuki hadn't got himself mired somewhere in a vat of mizutaki."

"Here we are, moddom," the waiter said, setting down the drink.

"Thanks, Yuki," Phoebe Pember said. "And now could you send out for a Big Mac and a small order of french fries?"

"I could," the waiter said. "But we now do it better in our own kitchen, moddom. We just stole the chef from the McDonald's on Lexington."

He moved off. Phoebe Pember took a sip of her martini.

"You choose the date," she said. "I'll arrange the office shower."

"Don't bother," Sandra Behr said. "There will be no wedding."

"Didn't you just tell me Bob proposed?" Phoebe Pember said.

"I didn't tell you I turned him down," Sandra Behr said.

"Did you?" Phoebe Pember said.

"He's done his job," Sandra Behr said. "He can now go flitting off to service other beehives."

Phoebe Pember had another tremor of hesitation. It was becoming irritating. She stared across her martini at the pale, thin girl she had come to know in college. Or thought she had come to know. Since they had been at Isham Truitt there had been a slow, almost imperceptible easing away, a sort of going out of focus, a blurring at the edges. Phoebe had assumed it was due to her friend's involvement with Bob Coffey. Just because he was not her type Phoebe Pember was sensible enough to realize it didn't mean Sandra Behr couldn't be madly in love with him. Confronted now with the fact that Sandra was not, or had just clearly indicated she was not, Phoebe Pember was confronted with a puzzling question. What was Sandra Behr up to?

Phoebe couldn't tell from Sandra's new hard manner, the nailing-down-of-facts conversation that sounded like the recital of endless grocery lists. These were intended to convey, Phoebe Pember was certain, a certainty about her existence that Sandra Behr was struggling with mounting desperation to achieve. In a small shock of unexpected revelation it came to Phoebe that Sandra Behr was not making it.

"And while Bob Coffey is off on his mission of servicing beehives," Phoebe Pember said, "I'd like to know what you'll be doing?"

"What I should have been doing while I was wasting two years of my precious youth getting that goddamn master's in comparative psychology," Sandra Behr said. "What I should have been doing is what that Cline girl was doing. Nailing down a career. I'm going to have this baby. With all this crap about parenthood out of the way, I'm going to park him, her, or it with my parents, who keep making many noises about my getting married so they can live to enjoy their grandchildren. While they're enjoying the first of their grandchildren, I will be going to law school. When the first of their grandchildren is being toilet-trained, I will be back at Isham Truitt or another of these New York law factories not as a member of the paratroops but as a full-fledged associate, and I will be on my way."

"Where?" Phoebe Pember said.

"To a full-fledged big-time career at the Bar and beyond," Sandra Behr said. "Like Helen Buttenwieser, for one. With a full-fledged big-time son or daughter at my side, and none of this malarkey about being a helpmeet to my husband by making a suitable frame for the success of my spouse. I've watched my mother make a suitable frame for her spouse. If that's the road a woman has to take through life, I'm getting off here and now. In a word, Nat dear, fuck the whole institution of husbands."

"That's six words," Phoebe Pember said. "And I don't see why

you can't do all that while Bob Coffey makes an honest woman
out of you and a legitimate son or daughter out of what at the
moment is no more than a slight rearrangement of some cell
structures in your gut."

"You don't see it because you've never questioned the world
you were born into," Sandra Behr said. "When you came in here
I said you were late, and you said you were also furious. Why?"

"That bitch Mrs. Merle Bethune," Phoebe Pember said. "She
called me at twelve-thirty and said would I give them a hand in
Stenographic. She was in a jam, and it would only take a half
hour. I said I was sorry, but I had a lunch date and I was on my
way out this minute. She said young lady, my instructions from
our office manager Mr. Cutter are that, when I need help at a
peak load period, I am free to call in the executive assistants, or
legal assistants, or paralegals, or paraprofessionals, or whatever
you call yourselves, because that's what they are paid for. To
help out in all areas when, as, and if needed. Mr. Cutter said you
had just finished a testimony digest for Mr. Taunton, and you
were free to do a rush proofreading job for me. This afternoon
when he arrives from Washington, I have to put a brief that has
just come from the printer on Mr. Condomine's desk. Choose any
title you please, executive assistant, legal assistant, paraprofes-
sional, or paralegal, but you get your cute little tail up here and
do this proofreading job, or I will have a talk with Mr. Cutter,
and that cute little tail will be out on the sidewalk before dismissal bell, sweetie."

"And all that did was make you furious?" Sandra Behr said.

"No, of course not," Phoebe Pember said. "All that did was
make me laugh. It's part of my silly job just as it's part of yours.
If I didn't want to be ordered around like a janitor at Isham
Truitt by troglodytes like Mrs. Bethune, instead of wasting my
old man's hard-earned tuition money on a master's in applied
psychology, I should have taken a stenographic course at some
good commercial school or gone to Yale Law, and ended up an
honest-to-God secretary like Nancy Gowdy or an honest-to-God
white-haired girl to Hugh F. X. Kelly, Jr., like Judy Cline. I
didn't, and so here I am, at Mrs. Bethune's beck, and a dozen

other troglodytes' call. I don't believe in going backward and re-tracing steps in the great land of illusion known as 'If Only.' I got myself stuck here at Isham Truitt, and here at Isham Truitt I will stay until the right guy comes along. Which means someone who wants me to be his helpmeet and make a suitable frame for his career as the best, the most elegant, the handsomest and the highest-priced goddamn surgeon currently carving up our wealthier citizenry at New York Hospital."

"You sound as though he's come along already," Sandra Behr said.

"He sure has, honeychile," Phoebe Pember said. "And if you won't let me organize an office shower for you, I'm going to dragoon you into organizing one for me. At the conclusion of this ceremony I intend to swing my heavily shod foot good and hard against the most celebrated target in the world, an impres-sively large specimen of which is lugged around by Mrs. Merle Bethune."

For a few terrified moments Phoebe thought her friend was going to burst into tears. All at once swellings of moisture were undeniably visible in Sandra Behr's eyes, and the thin, pale lips quivered in an upsettingly uncontrolled way. Neither, however, got out of hand.

"I'm jealous," she said. "I really am, Nat."

"You don't have to be," Phoebe Pember said. "I happen to know a male chauvinist pig named Bob Coffey who would like to hear your voice at the other end of the phone uttering the sin-gle affirmative syllable that has kept the human race in business since the Garden of Eden."

Sandra Behr's smile of friendly envy eased away into what for the past few months had become for Phoebe Pember a slow going out of focus, a blurring at the edges of a once clearly defined human being she liked very much.

"You stay out of my private life," Sandra said. "You stick to telling me why you came in here and said you were furious."

"The talk up in Stenographic," Phoebe Pember said. "While I was doing the proofreading job at one of those small side desks to which they chain the visiting serfs for special duty, the chatter of stenographic voices was louder than the expensive hum of those forty-four IBM Selectrics."

"Chatter about what?" Sandra Behr said.

"You know that nice Lichine boy?" Phoebe Pember said.

"I do not," Sandra Behr said. "I know a stuck-up bastard named Lichine who shares an office with a nice boy named Taunton."

"I know nothing about Taunton except this testimony digest I just did for him," Phoebe Pember said. "I do know Tom Lichine is neither stuck-up nor a bastard. He's a very handsome young man, not quite as handsome as a certain young surgeon at New York Hospital, but he's in the same league. He's shy, especially with girls, and as a result the less perceptive ones think he's stuck-up. Not a bit. Stuck-up bastards don't volunteer for pro bono work in the heart of the southern death belt defending penniless black kids on trumped-up murder charges."

"What are you talking about?" Sandra Behr said.

"I'm not sure," Phoebe Pember said. "It was hard to make sense of the whole business because there was so much chatter, and a good deal of the detail was conflicting and unclear."

"Tell me what was sufficiently unconflicting and not unclear enough to make you furious," Sandra Behr said.

"It seems Lichine was sent down to Alabama to help defend a black boy on a murder charge," Phoebe Pember said. "He did it so well that the boy was acquitted. This got the prosecution so mad that the D.A. assembled a grand jury fast and they handed down an indictment charging Lichine with jury tampering. When they came to serve him at his hotel, the sheriff was accompanied by several of his friends. The kind who wear white robes with pointed hoods and burn crosses on lawns when other people are lighting Christmas candles. They served the subpoena southern style, meaning they jumped our hero. Jumping a Harvard quarterback is apparently not as easy as what they usually get to jump down there. Lichine fought back and did some damage. Nobody in Stenographic knew what kind or how much. Enough, however, to clear a path to the airport, apparently. Lichine skipped town. The charge of jury tampering has been changed to second-degree murder and those southern fried chickens are trying to get that attractive, darling, sexy, shy young man extradited to Alabama to stand trial."

"What's stopping them?" Sandra Behr said.

"Tom Lichine has disappeared," Phoebe Pember said. "Nobody knows where he is."

12

"I do," Howard Dent said.

"Where?" Judy Cline said.

"I won't tell you," Howard Dent said.

"Why not?" Judy said.

"You would call it contumacity," Howard Dent said.

"Not until I know what the word means," Judy said.

"What David Lilienthal used to call the ignoble pleasure of pigheadedness," Howard Dent said. "I won't tell you where I know young Mr. Lichine is hiding out because nobody knows I know, not counting my just telling you that I do. I want to be fair to all the parties concerned, including myself, because I'm not sure I'm doing the right thing by sticking my nose into this thing. I intend, therefore, to tell nobody and that means not even you."

Not for the first time since she had met him in Mr. Kelly's office two days ago, Judy Cline found herself comparing this formidable, dried asparagus stalk of a ninety-one-year-old man with the relaxed, shapeless teddy bear of her father's age under whose wing she had been working so happily at Isham Truitt for almost a year. The comparison added nothing but a few more combustible chips to the small fire of uncertainty that had been kindled at that first meeting.

"I don't see what's fair about that," Judy said.

"You would if you shared my impartiality in this matter," Howard Dent said.

Judy decided to let that go. She was struggling with her own definition of impartiality. To help her with the struggle she shifted gears to something concrete but irrelevant. Mr. Dent's bow tie. Sitting in the V of his stiff white collar and the vest of his charcoal-gray suit, it had the effect of a Hawaiian sports shirt on a minister in the pulpit. In a man who could have stepped down out of one of those old Underwood & Underwood group portraits of, say, Woodrow Wilson's Supreme Court, the red, green, and gold lightning stripes zigging and zagging across the scrap of pale-blue satin under his chin was a clownish touch. Judy wondered if it was a lapse in taste or a deliberate shock tactic.

"Who's that?" she said.

"Which one?" Howard Dent said.

"On the left," Judy said.

"See for yourself," Howard Dent said.

Judy got up, crossed the sitting room, and stopped in front of the secretary. It stood between the two tall windows that looked north across the stunning view of Central Park to 110th Street. The two pictures flanking the secretary were Bachrach cabinet photographs in expensive frames. The one on the right showed FDR, in a non-uptilted jaunty cigarette-holder pose, staring gravely into the camera lens over the words "For Howard with Every Best Wish from Franklin." The picture on the left was more interesting. To Judy Cline, at any rate. She had seen many pictures of FDR. New to her, however, was the plump, button-chinned, chipmunk-cheeked, semibald, middle-aged scowler in the picture on the right. Judy leaned close and read in the corner of the mat "To Howard with Admiration for Beating the Pants Off the Barefoot Boy from Wall Street and Giving to the People to Whom It Belongs the Glory of TVA. As Always, Harold."

"Harold who?" Judy said.

"Harold L. Ickes," Howard Dent said. "L for LeClaire. Secretary of the Interior, head of the PWA, and one of the only two truly great men I have ever known."

"Who was the other?" Judy said.

"Paderewski," Howard Dent said.

"The pianist?" Judy said.

"Among other things," Howard Dent said.

"What made them great?" Judy said.

"They had fervor," Howard Dent said.

"Would either of them have asked me to come to his apartment for lunch to tell me he knows where a friend of mine who is in trouble is hiding out, and then say he has no intention of telling me where?"

"Under similar circumstances, yes," Howard Dent said. He turned toward the discreet tap on the door. "Yes, come in."

The door opened.

"Good afternoon, sir."

"Hello, Raoul," Howard Dent said.

"Over here, sir?"

"Yes, fine," Howard Dent said. He turned back to Judy. "Come back and sit down. Raoul will be clattering silver and china for a while, and I want to hear what you say to me."

It occurred to Judy, coming back to her chair, that she did not know what suites at the Plaza went for at annual rates, but the sitting room of Howard Dent's quarters was as large as the one in which Judy had been raised at 1010 Fifth. If the bedroom was commensurately spacious, the old man behind the wild bow tie could hardly be living from hand to mouth. Judy's knowledge of the legends about the early New Dealers had been picked up at the knee of an enthusiastic contemporary: her father. She could recall nothing from Clifford Cline's accounts of their protean talents for improving the lot of the man in the street that included an intimacy with the financial dexterity required to feather a personal penthouse nest. Judy sat down.

"What do you want me to say?" she said.

"What you think about this Lichine thing," Howard Dent said.

"I thought we all made ourselves clear two days ago in Mr. Kelly's office," Judy said. "After Tom finished telling us what had happened in Montgomery and he left the room, you said you felt he had told the truth, Mr. Kelly said he felt Tom was quote lying in his teeth, and I said I didn't know."

"I am certain I was right," Howard Dent said. "I am equally certain Hugh Kelly has very sound reasons for saying what he said. I am not sure those reasons would stand up under cross examination, and I doubt if Hugh were confessing to his priest that he would have said any such thing. That leaves only you."

"I said I don't know," Judy said.

"I know what you said," Howard Dent said. "I'm trying to find out what you believe."

"I still don't know," Judy said.

"Hugh Kelly gave me the details of your background," Howard Dent said. "About your two families, growing up with young Lichine, all that. You've just confirmed Hugh's statement that you and Lichine have been friends since childhood. Do you still say you don't know what happened in Montgomery?"

"Yes," Judy said.

"Doesn't that make you uncomfortable?" Howard Dent said.

"Why should it?" Judy Cline said.

"It could be construed as disloyalty to a friend," Howard Dent said.

"Not by a lawyer," Judy said. "I was not there. I don't know of my own knowledge what happened in Montgomery. To my knowledge Tom Lichine has never been a liar. More accurately, he has never lied to me. Again to my knowledge. I hope he was telling us the truth about what happened in Montgomery. If I were asked to make a bet I would come down on the side that he was telling the truth. As a sitting judge, as a member of a jury, I would have to disregard betting odds. I would have to consider only the evidence. Tom's account of what happened in Montgomery is a self-serving declaration and therefore not admissible as evidence in a court of law."

"We were not sitting in a court of law," Howard Dent said.

"Nor was Tom Lichine under oath," Judy Cline said.

The thumb and forefinger of Howard Dent's right hand tugged slowly at the point of his long chin. He stared thoughtfully across the room. Even though Judy was in the direct path of the stare she was not at all sure the old man had her in his sights.

"Shouldn't a man of honor tell the truth under all circumstances?" Howard Dent said. "Even when he is not under oath?"

"Would you?" Judy Cline said.

Howard Dent released his chin. As though seeking alternate

employment, the long bony fingers took a flick at one end of the bow tie. The fingers apparently found this an unsatisfactory substitute. With a touch of impatience the tall, thin figure turned.

"I think, Raoul, that's enough wind-up," Howard Dent said. "Serve it forth."

He stood up and gestured Judy Cline to her feet.

"To save time I ordered for both of us," he said. "I hope you like rare steak, green salad, and chocolate ice cream."

"I love all three," Judy said.

"I thought you would," Howard Dent said.

He helped her into her chair without touching or hovering or interfering. Again, it was no more than a gesture, a courtly wave that framed the invitation to join him at table. When Judy was seated Howard Dent walked around the table and took the chair the waiter was holding for him. Then he watched in silence while Raoul served.

"Everything all right, sir?" the waiter said.

"If you close the door quietly it will be perfect," Howard Dent said.

"Yes, sir," the waiter said.

He closed the door almost noiselessly.

"Start please," Howard Dent said. "While it's hot."

It was far from that, but it was a good piece of meat, and it was warm enough. Judy was chewing away when the old man at the other side of the table stopped a slice of speared rare from completing the journey to his mouth.

"You've heard of course that he's been indicted for second-degree murder," Howard Dent said. "And the Montgomery prosecutor has announced plans to extradite him for trial in Alabama."

"Yes, but I don't know what it means," Judy said.

"You know what second-degree murder means," Howard Dent said.

"I also know what extradition means," Judy Cline said. "What I don't know are the details that brought about the indictment."

"Hugh Kelly hasn't told you?" Howard Dent said.

"No," Judy said.

"Odd," Howard Dent said.

He sent the slice of rare back on its journey to his mouth. Watching him chew, Judy listened for the giveaway clicks. She heard none. Several times, when there was a rush on something Judy was doing for Mr. Kelly, they had shared a sandwich at his desk so they could work through the lunch hour without interruption. Judy had enjoyed the feeling of intimacy, even though her concentration was broken at frequent intervals by the clacking of what must have been one of the more expensive sets of dentures turned out by Dr. Carey McDonough. "Mack the Bite," as he was known in New York's moneyed Catholic community, was not shy about letting it be known that he "handled the cardinal's teeth." Judy was pleased to note that her Plaza host, who was Hugh Kelly's senior by at least two decades, was disposing of his steak as noiselessly as Raoul had closed the door. Mr. Dent was clearly doing it with his own teeth. Judy's pleasure in the performance was followed immediately by a twinge of betrayal.

"What's odd about it?" she said.

"Hugh Kelly told me how much he admires and depends on you," Howard Dent said. "He told me he thought of you as a member of his own family. I gathered that you felt Hugh Kelly is your friend as well as your employer. He knew you and young Lichine have been friends since childhood. I assume you know that after our session the other day in his office it was Hugh Kelly who ordered Lichine sacked."

Trying to underscore her words with a note of shock she did not feel, Judy Cline said, "No, I didn't know that."

Howard Dent stopped cutting his meat. He gave her a sharp look. Judy had no trouble translating it into words. The old man did not believe her.

"If I have let any cats out of the bag," Howard Dent said, putting his knife and fork back into motion, "I am not going to scamper about trying to retrieve them and stuff them back into the bag. I am sure it was not an oversight on Hugh's part. I am equally sure he has his reasons for not telling you. It is even possible that one of those reasons is a desire not to hurt you. Nonetheless, I am shocked."

"Why?" Judy Cline said.

"I haven't known you as long as Hugh Kelly has known you,"

Howard Dent said. "We have just met. We are not yet friends, even though I hope we will be. Knowing what I know about you and young Mr. Lichine, if it was my duty or even my inclination to fire him from the Isham Truitt staff, I would not do it without advising you."

"You think that would make me feel better?" Judy said.

"I don't know what would or would not make you feel better," Howard Dent said. "Not in this matter at any rate. I can't judge a person on the minimal knowledge I have about you. I can only guess. I am going to leave guesswork out of this for the same reason I am leaving out my knowledge of young Mr. Lichine's whereabouts. I would not have fired Lichine without advising you because it would make not you but me feel better to tell you about it in advance."

"I'm glad to hear it," Judy Cline said.

"You are not," Howard Dent said. "You are contemptuous. Who cares, you are thinking, what this old gaffer feels about it? What difference does that make? It makes this difference. Because Hugh Kelly has acted badly, I feel free to do what I was not sure I had the right to do when I asked you to come here to lunch."

"I think you're going to have to start by telling me what it was you were not sure you had the right to do when you ordered up these steaks," Judy Cline said.

"That would be the wrong place to start," Howard Dent said. "Also, your ice cream is melting. Eat it while I start at the right place."

"All right," Judy Cline said.

She put down her knife and fork and picked up a spoon.

"When Manny Merz recruited you at Harvard Law," Howard Dent said. "Did he tell you that Isham Truitt is at its core the legal arm of the Fillmore National Bank?"

"He didn't have to," Judy Cline said. "Everybody in the class knew that."

"Did you also know that Southern Shoals Asbestos is one of David Fillmore's more profitable satellites?"

"No," Judy Cline said. "I've known the name Southern Shoals Asbestos since I was a kid. Who hasn't? It's like Pepsi-Cola and

Chevrolet and Macy's. It wasn't until I came with Isham Truitt, however, that I started hearing the name around the office and caught up with the fact that Southern Shoals is one of our big clients. That's why in the *Times,* yesterday I think it was, my eye caught the obituary for that man with the funny name."

"Sosthenes DeKalb," Howard Dent said.

"Yes," Judy Cline said. "Once you become aware of a name, you begin noticing it when it appears in the papers or when you hear people mention it. That's all I mean. I still don't know very much about Southern Shoals Asbestos. Except, of course, that the company makes asbestos."

"I know a good deal more," Howard Dent said. "Not because I appear on the Isham Truitt letterhead as 'of counsel,' but because I am older than you are. Back in the mid-thirties, after FDR moved into the White House, Harold Ickes over there on the wall asked me to help with the establishment of the Tennessee Valley Authority. It was not easy and it was not an overnight job. You couldn't spend much time in that part of the country without becoming aware of Southern Shoals Asbestos in the same way that in those days you couldn't spend much time in India without becoming aware of the British raj. They owned the place. They were the team to beat. Mahatma Gandhi and his team beat the British. Harold Ickes and his team beat Southern Shoals Asbestos. There is, however, this difference. India to the British is a memory. To Southern Shoals Asbestos that part of our country is still a formidably profitable private fiefdom. They run it the way the Afrikaners run South Africa. A lot of lip service is paid to things called civil rights. None of it interferes with the steady inflow of profits. The government of South Africa sees to that for the Afrikaners. Isham Truitt renders a similar service to Southern Shoals Asbestos. Would you like some more ice cream?"

"Thank you, no," Judy Cline said.

"Here, have mine," Howard Dent said. "I haven't touched it."

"No, please," Judy said. "I'm sure you ordered it for both of us because you like it, too."

"I do," Howard Dent said. "When I'm trying to make a point, however, things I like get in the way of my thinking."

"Then I will take it," Judy said. He reached the silver cup across the table. She took it and said, "It doesn't get in the way of my grasping a point."

"The point to grasp here is that the South African Government's control over its native population is an ongoing international news story," Howard Dent said. "The control of Southern Shoals Asbestos over the native population of its fiefdom gets into the headlines only when somebody upsets the invisible apparatus that keeps in balance Southern Shoals' delicate control over the area and its people. Without the interference of chocolate ice cream I feel confident I have made that point clear."

"Yes," Judy Cline said. "What you have not made clear is what Tom Lichine has to do with it."

"The same thing that last year caused Steve Biko to die under mysterious circumstances in a Johannesburg prison while in custody of the police," Howard Dent said. "Tom Lichine has upset the invisible apparatus by which Southern Shoals Asbestos maintains its delicate control over a large piece of our country."

In a voice so calm that it surprised her, Judy Cline said, "If Tom Lichine is extradited to Alabama he may die under mysterious circumstances in a Montgomery prison?"

"Not if I am on hand to defend him," Howard Dent said.

Judy gave herself a couple of moments. When her heart finally gave up on what had felt like a major effort to hammer itself out of her chest, she drew a deep breath.

"Are you going to defend him?" Judy said.

"I haven't asked him yet," Howard Dent said.

"Why not?" Judy said.

"From what I saw of that young man two days ago in Hugh Kelly's office," Howard Dent said, "I think Mr. Lichine would tell me to take my offer and put it where the monkey put the nuts."

Catching on at last, Judy Cline wished she hadn't.

"You want me to ask him for you," she said.

"Yes," Howard Dent said.

"You're inferring I know where he's hiding out," Judy said.

"I would never infer when I mean imply," Howard Dent said.

13

"How about some Band-Aids?" Mr. Metzger said.

"No, thanks," Judy Cline said.

"I got a special on those Curads you bought the other morning," the druggist said.

"I've still got every single one of them," Judy said. "Just the shaving cream and the, let's see, Atra razor?" She studied the list. "Is that what I want?"

"Everybody else does," Mr. Metzger said. "It's this new Gillette with the twin blades and the flexible head. A, t, r, a. Very popular. Anything else?"

"A Benzedrex Inhaler, two boxes of Kleenex, and that does it," Judy said.

It didn't. It helped, however, to be firm about something, even if what she was being firm about was irrelevant. Coming around the corner from Columbus Avenue into Eighty-second Street, nothing seemed more irrelevant than the pleasure Judy Cline had been taking in this block between Columbus and Central Park West since she had moved into it soon after she was hired by Isham Truitt.

It was a piece of urban renewal that had worked. Judy could imagine the statisticians being a trifle embarrassed by the reason: on this West Side block lived a dozen or more employees of the New York *Times* who worked in the paper's editorial and arts sections. In an unobtrusive way they were able to bring to bear on the appropriate city departments a certain amount of clout unavailable to citizens who were not part of the media. As a result, while the condition of neighboring blocks kept pace with the steady disintegration of the West Side, Judy's block steadily grew more attractive.

The gutter had been repaved and the sidewalks resurfaced. Two rows of butternut trees marched steadily, healthily, and, for Judy Cline, dazzlingly down the block in front of the handsomely remodeled brownstones. The street cleaners obviously paid so many more, and more thorough, visits than they paid to other streets in the area that the suspicion of discreet nudging from somewhere could probably have been documented. Assuming that anybody in a position to do so would have been politically foolhardy enough to try. Most dramatic of all was the street lighting. It was supplied by a dozen of the high-arching floods that had previously cast their shadowless blue-white gleams only in the parks and on the highways leading into and out of the city. When photographs of the new lighting had appeared in the press a spokesman for the Department of Parks had stated it was a test installation.

"If it succeeds in lowering the crime rate on West Eighty-second Street," he said on the front page of the *Times*, "the Commissioner plans to urge on the Mayor a program of more widespread installations, especially in the city's high-crime areas."

Judy Cline had never checked the statistics. She assumed, however, that they were working in favor of West Eighty-second Street. During the year she had lived there she had heard of no crimes on the block. She was pleased to remember this at the end of her uneasy day. Her house was a brownstone that had been cut up into small apartments. She shared the stoop floor with a couple of married schoolteachers who had the front apartment.

Walking through to her door at the back, Judy could hear her neighbors' TV set. Cronkite. It was not obtrusive but it was enough to mute her doorbell. She gave it the agreed-upon two longs and two shorts. No answer. Puzzled, Judy tried again. More annoyed than worried, she shifted the parcels to her left arm and dug the key from her purse. The moment she came into the apartment she knew something was wrong. After two days of a bulging presence she could feel the sudden emptiness.

"Tom?"

No answer. Judy walked across the living room to the bedroom. Nobody. She looked into the kitchen. Scattered on the drainboard were an unrinsed glass that had contained milk, and the debris of a not very skillfully constructed sandwich. Judy set down her packages and walked out into the living room for a more careful second look. The note was on the coffee table.

> Dear Jude: Sorry to pull out without waiting to say good-bye. No time. Many thanks for all your help. Also for letting me borrow your brown carry-on without permission. I'll return it in good shape or replace it with a substitute stuffed with emeralds. L. & K.   T.

The scrape of a key in the lock brought Judy's head up. The door opened. Tom Lichine started to come in, saw Judy, and stopped short. The brown carryall did not. It kept moving. After an inch or two it banged against his thigh.

"Shit," Tom Lichine said.

"Is that how you greet your wife when you come home from a long, hard day at the office?" Judy said.

"Once in a while," Tom Lichine said. "Bianca is fond of preparing little surprises."

"I'm not," Judy said.

"Then why did you?" Tom Lichine said.

"I did not," Judy said.

"Yes, you did," Tom Lichine said.

"How?" Judy said.

"By being here," Tom Lichine said.

"Where else would I be?" Judy said. "It's my apartment."

"I know it's your apartment," Tom Lichine said. "It's just I didn't expect you'd be in it."

"Forget something?" Judy said.

"Yes, but I didn't realize it until I got to Central Park West, so I ran back," Tom Lichine said. "I was sure I could get in and out before you came home."

"What did you forget?" Judy said.

"You're holding it," Tom Lichine said.

"This?" Judy said, waving the note.

"Yes," Tom Lichine said.

"You want it back?" Judy said.

"No," Tom Lichine said.

"Because I've read it?" Judy said.

"Of course not," Tom Lichine said. "Why the hell do you think I left it if not to be read?"

"The way this game has been going since you showed up on my doorstep at eight in the morning two days ago," Judy said, "I think your part does not involve asking questions but answering them. What did you come back for?"

"I wanted to add something to that note," Tom Lichine said.

"Here," Judy said, holding out the piece of paper. "Got your own writing implements, or shall I get you a pencil?"

"You can get me a drink," Tom Lichine said. "And stop being so smart-ass."

"You can make your own drink," Judy said. "I see by the condition of the kitchen you've discovered where the ingredients are kept."

Tom Lichine shoved the door shut with his foot, dropped the carryall, and glared his way out into the kitchen.

"Make one for me, too," Judy called. "I've earned a little house-guest service."

She dropped into the couch, pulled her legs up under her, and told herself severely if she burst into tears she would never talk to herself again. Tom Lichine came back with the drinks. When he leaned down to give one to Judy he said, "I'm sorry. I'm all worked up."

"Sit over there and unwind," Judy said.

He took the chair facing her, but Tom Lichine did not face her. He stared down into his drink.

"Maybe this is better," he said.

"What is?" Judy said.

"That I did find you here," Tom Lichine said. "If I tried to write it in the note it wouldn't come out the way I want it."

"If it was the truth," Judy said, "I wouldn't be fussy about the syntax."

"How's my credibility gap?" Tom Lichine said.

"From birth up to February 8, 1978, on a scale of one to ten, it was ten plus," Judy said. "From February 8, 1978, to this minute, same scale, it's minus zero."

"Then why did you do all these things for me these last two days?" Tom Lichine said.

"Why don't you drop dead?" Judy said.

He started to come up out of his chair.

"Stay where you are and finish that addition to your note," Judy said.

Tom Lichine dropped back into the chair.

"You're a hard woman," he said.

"I've had some recent lessons from a master," Judy said.

"What makes February 8, 1978, such a decisive watershed?" Tom Lichine said.

"On that night, almost exactly four months ago, you and I were supposed to attend the opening night of the Equity Library Theatre revival of father's *I Am Dying, Little Egypt*," Judy said.

"And I showed up with a new girl," Tom Lichine said.

"A month after that, almost exactly three months ago, on March 9, 1978, you married her," Judy Cline said.

"Why do you suppose a man would do a thing like that?" Tom Lichine said.

"I assume the answer to that question is what you just came back to add to your note," Judy said.

"I'd like to," Tom Lichine said. "You know I'd like to."

"I don't know any such thing," Judy said.

"Then surely you know this," Tom Lichine said. "If I haven't made any explanation for what I've done, it's because the explanation would hurt someone."

"Who?" Judy said. "You?"

"Nasty, but deserved," Tom Lichine said. "No, not me. If it was myself I was trying to protect, would I borrow your carryall to head back to the place where they've got a warrant out for my arrest?"

"Alabama?" Judy said.

"I can't answer that unless you promise not to repeat my answer," Tom Lichine said.

"After the lies you've had me telling for you all over town these last few days," Judy Cline said, "I'm not likely to suffer an attack of honesty on that one."

"Yes," Tom Lichine said, "I'm going back to Alabama."

"Why?" Judy said.

"To finish what I started on February 8, 1978," Tom Lichine said. "The night I stood you up at the opening of the Equity Library Theatre revival of *I Am Dying, Little Egypt*."

"Is it dangerous?" Judy said.

"Not if you keep your trap shut," Tom Lichine said.

"Is your bride keeping her trap shut?" Judy said.

"She doesn't have to," Tom Lichine said.

"Why not?" Judy said.

"Bianca doesn't know what you know," Tom Lichine said.

"I don't know a goddamn thing," Judy said. "That's our trouble."

"No," Tom Lichine said. "That's our salvation."

"After you finish making this addition to your note," Judy said, "what am I supposed to do?"

"Exactly what you've been doing since February 8, 1978," Tom Lichine said.

"You know what I've been doing since February 8, 1978?" Judy said.

"I can guess," Tom Lichine said.

"Guess," Judy said.

"Hating my guts," Tom Lichine said.

"It doesn't seem to have upset you," Judy said.

"Because for a long time there wasn't anything I could do about it," Tom Lichine said.

"Now there is?" Judy said.

"I think so," Tom Lichine said.

"When will you know?" Judy said.

"When I come back from Alabama," Tom Lichine said.

Judy saw him take the remainder of his drink in a single swallow. She saw him stand up. She saw him set down his glass. She saw him bend down to pick up the carryall. She saw him reach out to open the door. Only after she heard it shut behind him did she realize that somewhere in between he had kissed her.

Judy Cline was still stroking her cheek when she heard the bell. She was certain it was not the first ring. The sound reached her on the echo of a predecessor. She went to the door and put her eye to the peephole. The young man in the hall looked so familiar that Judy had the silly feeling she saw him every day. A moment later, as the young man pressed the bell again, Judy realized the feeling was not silly at all. She did see this young man every day. Judy opened the door.

"Mr. Taunton, for heaven's sake," she said.

"Not really," he said. "Just Jack Taunton for his own sake." Getting no response from Judy, Mr. Taunton inserted a nervous laugh of his own and added, "I can see from your face Tom didn't warn you I was coming."

An astonished "Tom who?" escaped before Judy put it together. Facing the fact that she was facing J. C. Taunton, the associate who shared Tom Lichine's double cell at Isham Truitt, she repeated with what she hoped was more conviction, "Tom who?"

It was Taunton's turn to look astonished. He came through, but without a scrap of conviction. He was clearly what Judy's father called "an acting actor." You could see the wheels going around inside his head, instructing him severely: "Register astonishment, for Christ's sake!"

"Tom Lichine," he said. "My cell mate. He called me at the office late this afternoon and asked me to bring up any personal stuff he may have left behind when he cleaned out his desk yesterday. He was sort of upset about being fired. Tom thought he may have left something, and if he had he wondered if I'd be a good scout and drop it off here on my way home. I'm a good scout. One of the best. Eagle, as a matter of fact. Here's what I found."

From his jacket pocket he pulled a handsome alligator key case with gold corners. It had been Judy Cline's present to Tom Lichine when they graduated from Harvard Law. She had last seen it that morning. Before Judy went out to meet Howard Dent for lunch at the Plaza she had stopped in at Mr. Kelly's office to leave her draft of the closing memorandum on the Uhlfelder property.

"Mr. Kelly wanted to take this home with him tonight," Judy had said.

"I'll put it in his briefcase," Mrs. Campion said. "Here's something you'll want to take home with you."

From the top drawer of her desk she produced the key case.

"What is it?" Judy said.

"A key case," Mrs. Campion said. "Belongs to Mr. Lichine." She snapped the case open. "There are his initials."

With a show of deep interest Judy examined the initials she had paid five dollars extra to have placed on the case.

"How did you get it?" Judy said.

"I was having coffee with Mrs. Bethune in ITCH yesterday," Mrs. Campion said. "One of Tessie's boys came in, the one called Ira. He was getting himself a Coke on the way up here with this. When he saw me he came over and asked if I'd take it and save him the trip."

"Why was he bringing it to you?" Judy said.

"Two days ago, when Lichine showed up unexpectedly from Alabama, he reported to Tessie's office he'd lost his key case," Mrs. Campion said. "It was turned in by one of the cleaning women, and Tessie wanted to get it back to him. Tessie couldn't return it to Lichine in person because Lichine was fired yesterday, as you know. So Tessie sent it up to me because the last time anybody had seen Lichine was right here in Mr. Kelly's office when he came to that meeting with you and Mr. Kelly and Mr. Dent."

"Well," Judy Cline said, "I haven't seen him since that meeting, either."

"What should I do with this?" Mrs. Campion said.

With a twinge of regret for the classic opening that had to be disregarded, Judy said, "What makes you think I would know?"

"Mr. Kelly mentioned the fact that you and Lichine are old friends," Mrs. Campion said.

"I have a lot of friends," Judy said. "I don't always know where they are. Why don't you call Mr. Lichine at home and tell him to come and pick it up? The switchboard still has his number, I'm sure. If not, Mr. Cutter will have it on his payroll records."

"Mr. Lichine's home number has not answered for two days," Mrs. Campion said. She did not add what was clear in her frozen face: "Let's see you get out of that one, honey."

Judy complied by pretending to give the problem a few moments of scowling thought.

"I have only one suggestion," she said finally. "Mr. Lichine's parents live at the Waldorf Towers. You could put that thing in an envelope marked for them and have one of Tessie's boys drop it off next time he's in the neighborhood."

Instead, Judy realized now, standing in her own apartment doorway the day after she had made the suggestion, Mrs. Campion had turned over the key case to Mr. Taunton. Or had she? The idea suddenly seemed improbable. It occurred to Judy that so did Mr. Taunton. His face did not inspire confidence. Cherubic in outline, it was depraved in detail. Especially the lidded eyes. They seemed heavily smeared with kohl. Mr. Taunton looked like a corrupt faun.

"You say you found that thing in Mr. Lichine's desk?" Judy said.

"On the floor behind his desk," Mr. Taunton said. "It probably dropped out of his pocket while he was clearing the desk."

"I suggest you take it back to the office and turn it over to Tessie or Mr. Cutter," Judy said. "Both of them handle lost and found things, I understand."

"Wouldn't it be easier if I left it with you?" Mr. Taunton said. "Why?"

"You could give it to Tom when he comes back," Mr. Taunton said.

"Why should he come back?" Judy said. "He's never been here."

"Then why would he tell me I should drop this thing off here on my way home?" Mr. Taunton said.

The hooded eyelids flicked. A small shiver tickled its way down Judy Cline's spine. Mr. Taunton's eyes, when unlidded, were what the statisticians had in mind when they discussed the advantages of installing those bright, nonglare, blue-white park and highway lights on a residential street like West Eighty-second.

"I don't know why Tom Lichine told you to drop off that key case here," Judy said. "Neither do I know he told you any such thing. Good night, Mr. Taunton."

She started to close the door. It didn't move very far. Mr. Taunton had put his foot on the threshold.

"I think you and I better have a talk," he said.

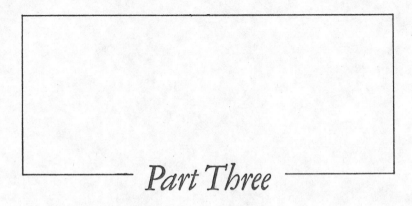

Part Three

"The law doth punish man or woman
That steals the goose from off the common,
But lets the greater felon loose
That steals the common from the goose."

ANONYMOUS

14

Mr. Coleridge was a problem. Judy Cline agreed with him on the phone that he should not be seen in New York; he agreed that Judy should not be seen with him anywhere; and besides, he had to fly right back to Alabama in a couple of hours. The sensible place for the meeting, it seemed to Judy, was the La Guardia Airport coffee shop. Unfortunately, however, Wednesday was the only day Mr. Coleridge could get away from Montgomery, and Wednesday happened to be Judy's regular day at Bedford-Stuyvesant.

"No problem," Mr. Coleridge said on the phone. "I'll take a cab from the airport and meet you in your Brooklyn office."

"I'd better tell you how to get there," Judy said. "It's sort of complicated."

"I've got the address," Mr. Coleridge said. "I'll find you."

Judy wondered. Newspaper accounts, verbal briefings, even photographic displays, none was a real preparation for Bedford-Stuyvesant. A first visit was bound to be an eye-opener. Judy had never forgotten her own first visit. Coming up out of the subway into Fulton Street was not a cheery experience, but Judy had not expected to be cheered. What had jolted her was the long block east of Nostrand Avenue.

Even at high noon on a bright sunny day it looked like a fragment out of one of those TV documentaries about Berlin after a visit from the Eighth Air Force. The abandoned buildings and the boarded-up storefronts were so depressing that number 1368 came not as a pleasant surprise but as an ominous shock. In those surroundings the structure looked so unreal that it seemed vaguely threatening: a lavish but not very skillfully camouflaged booby trap. This brand-new spic and span colonial building with honest-to-God Old Williamsburg-type gas lamps burning outside, what was it doing in the middle of a holocaust?

Why, as Judy Cline now replied with some asperity to smart-aleck friends, it is the headquarters of the Bedford-Stuyvesant Restoration, an antipoverty agency founded by Robert F. Kennedy. In it functioned the Bedford-Stuyvesant Community Legal Services Corporation, staffed by high-minded and low-spirited volunteers like Judy Cline of Isham Truitt. Like all her fellow workers, Judy Cline was never quite certain whether she was more depressed by the work or the effort involved in fighting off the feeling that the work was hopeless.

"The landlord claims you renewed the lease on November first," she said.

At the other side of Judy's desk the fat black woman with the sorrowful face released a blast of nervous noise. In its relation to normal laughter the sound was not unlike the relation of this whole block east of Nostrand Avenue to the section of the Champs Élysées below the Arc de Triomphe.

"You pay attention to what the landlord says, you gonna end up in the funny farm," the fat woman said.

It seemed to Judy that was precisely where she had begun to feel she was heading.

"That's why I want to pay attention to you," she said. "Did you renew your lease on November first?"

"You a lawyer?" the fat woman said.

"Yes, of course," Judy said.

"These schools where you learned your lawyering," the woman said. "They teach you how a person can renew something they never had in the first place?"

"Are you saying you never signed a lease on that apartment?" Judy said.

"You catching on, honey," the fat woman said.

"Take a look at this," Judy said.

From the file she pushed across the desk a Xerox copy of the disputed lease.

"What is it?" the fat woman said.

"Your lease," Judy said.

"Ain't never seen this paper before," the woman said.

"Isn't that your signature?" Judy said.

"Can't be," the woman said.

She pushed the Xerox back toward Judy.

"You haven't looked at it," Judy said.

"Why waste time?" the black woman said.

"Let me ask the questions," Judy said. "You answer them. Is this your signature or isn't it?"

"A person can't write," the woman said, "how can she leave on a paper a signature?"

"You're saying this is not your signature because you can't write?" Judy said.

"You catching on, honey," the woman said.

Judy re-examined the Xerox.

"Could you tell me whose signature it is?" she said.

"Only a guess," the woman said. "On account of that fool he sign anything."

"What fool?" Judy said.

"Salmagundi," the woman said.

"Salmagundi?" Judy said.

"That's what he call himself," the black woman said.

"Who's he?" Judy said.

"The father of my three oldest," the woman said.

"Your husband?" Judy said.

"Not on your life," the fat woman said. "I don't marry no trash."

"Are you married now?" Judy said.

"Never was, never am, never will be," the woman said. "Only way to stay out of the funny farm. Don't marry nobody. You write that down and remember it."

"I will," Judy said.

"You catching on, honey," the woman said.

"You're not," Judy said. "So I'll explain it again. Please listen."

"Every time I come here," the black woman said, "I ever not listen?"

"No, I can't say that," Judy said.

"I accept your apology," the fat woman said. "My mother taught me good. Always listen, she used to say. You listen, she used to say, you always listen, and you never get into no trouble."

"You're in trouble now," Judy said. "So maybe in addition to your mother's advice about listening, you should also try to remember what you listen to."

"You catching on, honey," the woman said.

"I'm trying to get you to catch on," Judy said.

"You ain't the first that's tried," the woman said. "So I know what you're going through. If I was any good at catching on would I end up with trash like this Salmagundi leaving me with three mouths to feed?"

"It says here you have seven children," Judy said.

"Let's see," the woman said.

She squinted up at the ceiling. Her lips moved noiselessly.

"That's right," she said finally. "Three from Salmagundi. Two from his friend that came next. Two from now."

"The one from now," Judy said. "What's his name?"

"Never had time to find out," the black woman said.

"This apartment," Judy said. "On which you are now six months behind in your rent."

"Ain't my rent," the woman said. "I never signed nothing."

"This apartment," Judy said patiently. "On which the landlord claims nobody has paid rent for six months, which is why he served you with this eviction notice—"

"You gonna let him do that to a mother with seven hungry kids?" the black woman said.

"Absolutely not," Judy said. "But I can only stop him if you co-operate. I want you to take these papers I've prepared. You deliver these this morning and you won't be evicted. For the time being, anyway, until I can think of something else."

"This morning?" the woman said.

"Right now," Judy said.

"Can't do that, honey," the woman said.

"Why not?" Judy said.

"Got a hair date in half an hour," the woman said.

"Break it," Judy said. "This is important."

She pushed the envelopes across the desk. The black woman scowled at them, moving her head slowly from address to address.

"This a week's work," she said.

"Not if you concentrate," Judy said.

"Concentrate, sure," the woman said. "But somebody's still got to do the walking."

"That somebody better be you," Judy said. "Or I won't be able to hold off that landlord, which means you won't be able to come back here for help, because you and the children will be out on the street. So get up out of that chair and get going."

The black woman did, with great effort and greater reluctance. After the door slammed Judy waited a few moments before she initialed the report. She closed the file, set it aside, and took the next file from the top of the pile. Miss Gates poked her head in the door.

"Ready for another?" she said.

"Send her in," Judy said.

"It's a him," Miss Gates said. She pushed the door wider and said into the corridor, "Miss Cline will see you now."

Easing his way around Miss Gates came a young man Judy Cline had seen many times before. On TV, wearing different basketball uniforms, but always bringing to the forefront of her mind the same feeling of wonder. How had they managed to get all of him on camera?

"Miss Cline?" he said.

"Yes," she said, standing up to take his hand. "You don't look like you wrote *The Rime of the Ancient Mariner*."

Teaman Coleridge laughed.

"When we met that was Tom Lichine's opening line," he said.

"Tom and I grew up together," Judy said. "We have a whole catalogue of uni-jokes. Sit down, please."

The way Mr. Coleridge did it changed the image in Judy's mind. Teaman Coleridge sat down like a Swiss army knife folding all its many blades into a neat little pocket-size unit.

"Coleridge is a good uni-race name," he said. "I may not look like the author of *The Ancient Mariner*, but I'm just the right color for *Kubla Khan*."

He also had the right features for the black model in the background of the Bloomingdale's Men's Shop group ads.

"Any word from Tom since we talked yesterday?"

"No," Judy said. "You?"

"I wasn't expecting any," he said. "With that indictment on the books I don't think the state of Alabama is going to see much of Tom Lichine until a lot of dust settles."

"Asbestos dust?" Judy said.

The thin, black, intelligent face rearranged itself in a new group of creases.

"You've been talking to someone," Teaman Coleridge said.

"Other way around," Judy said. "Somebody's been talking to me."

"Anybody I know?" Coleridge said.

"Taunton?" Judy said. "Jack Taunton?"

"No bells ring," Coleridge said.

"Tom's office mate at Isham Truitt," Judy said.

"What's he been talking to you about?" Coleridge said.

"Montgomery and what happened to Tom down there," Judy said.

"Does he know what happened?" Teaman Coleridge said.

"He knows as much as I do," Judy said. "Anyway, that's as much as I was able to figure out from what he was saying. He was fishing for more, but he didn't get any more. Mr. Taunton is a pretty slippery customer."

"It's the one thing you can count on in anything involving Southern Shoals Asbestos," Teaman Coleridge said.

There was a tap on the door.

"Yes?" Judy called.

Miss Gates stuck her head in.

"Just made it fresh," she said.

A shoulder followed her head, and a plastic tray with two plastic coffee cups followed the shoulder.

"Miss Gates doesn't usually serve refreshments to our clients," Judy said.

"Miss Gates knows a gentleman from a client," Miss Gates said.

She set the cups on the desk.

"Thank you," Teaman Coleridge said.

He gave the black girl a smile. Judy noted that it did not go begging for a response. Miss Gates had an eye for a good-looking man.

"How'd you know about me?" Teaman Coleridge said after the door closed behind Miss Gates.

"I wondered why you didn't ask me when I called you on the phone yesterday," Judy said.

"Down in Southern Shoals territory," Teaman Coleridge said, "I find in the work I do if I ask a question on the long-distance phone I'm usually not the only one who's picking up the answer."

"Nobody is listening in now," Judy said. "I knew from Tom Lichine that he'd had help down in Montgomery from a young black lawyer who was monitoring the trial. When he cleaned out his desk at Isham Truitt three days ago Tom lost his key case. His office mate, this Taunton character, returned it to me. I gave the thing to Tom as a graduation present last year when we got out of Harvard, so I knew it had a small address-book section inside, and I thumbed the pages."

"Until you found what looked like the name of a southern black lawyer?" Teaman Coleridge said.

"No," Judy said.

She tried for a neutral tone. Working in Bedford-Stuyvesant had given her a new awareness of unexpected shadings in black sensitivity.

"All the names in the book had been lettered carefully in ink some time ago," Judy said. "Probably when Tom got the thing from me. It's the sort of neat thing he would do. There were only two names in the book that obviously had been scrawled on a temporary basis because they were in pencil. Tom probably thought he'd erase them later when he was finished with whatever it was that had brought the names to his attention. It's another one of those things Tom would do. One of the names was Terence Danaher, about whom I knew, the other was Teaman Coleridge."

"How did you know about Danaher?" Coleridge said.

Judy described the scene in Mr. Kelly's office at which Tom

Lichine had explained to her and Mr. Dent what had happened in Montgomery.

"Mr. Dent felt he was telling the truth," she said. "Mr. Kelly did not."

"How about you?" Coleridge said.

"I saw no reason why Tom should lie," Judy said. She hesitated, then added, "Did he?"

"I don't know," Teaman Coleridge said. The look on Judy's face caused him to add, "I saw Tom Lichine in the courtroom four days ago, right after he showed those pictures of the electric chair to the jury. When all the fainting and screaming and vomiting took place, and the judge declared a recess. I walked back to the hotel with Tom, and said I'd see him in court in the morning, but when I got to court in the morning he wasn't there."

"Then the scene the day before between him and Father Danaher in Tom's hotel room?" Judy said. "When Father Danaher ordered him out of town? You didn't know about that?"

"First I heard of it is just now," Teaman Coleridge said.

Judy hesitated, not quite sure why, then said, "You know about the verdict, of course?"

"Oh, yes," Coleridge said. "That was two days later."

Judy hesitated again. The young lawyer seemed to understand her problem.

"Between the time the jury came in with the verdict," he said. "And the time the next day when the grand jury indicted Tom for second-degree murder. Is that what's bothering you?"

"The lack of information, yes," Judy said. "All I know is the rumor going around the office, and there are several versions of that."

"What's the rumor?" Teaman Coleridge said.

"When the marshal and his assistants came to serve Tom in his hotel room there was a fight," Judy said. "One of the marshal's assistants was shot, and Tom was indicted for the shooting."

"If Tom left Montgomery when he says he did, that would make it a day and a half, almost two days before the jury came in with its verdict," Teaman Coleridge said. "If that's what happened, Tom couldn't have had anything to do with that fight and the shooting, could he?"

"Did he?" Judy said.

"Not if at the time of the fight and the shooting," the young lawyer said, "Mr. Dent and you were sitting in this Mr. Kelly's office here in New York listening to Tom Lichine set up his alibi."

"You think that's what he was doing?" Judy said.

"You were there," Teaman Coleridge said. "You heard him."

"Then he has nothing to be afraid of, has he?" Judy said.

"'Nothing' is one of those deceptively long words," Teaman Coleridge said.

"Could you shorten it for me?" Judy said.

"I don't think you asked me to fly up here to tell you something you're smart enough to have figured out yourself," Teaman Coleridge said.

He leaned across to the desk, picked up his cup, and took a long sip.

"Good coffee," he said.

He took another sip, set the cup back on the desk, and looked at his wristwatch.

"If I'm going to make my plane back to Montgomery," he said, "I have just enough time left to tell you what you really want to know, but you'll have to ask for it. Not because I'm being difficult but because I'm not a mind reader. I know you want to help Tom Lichine. I ask you to believe me when I say so do I."

"I believe you," Judy said.

"Okay, Miss Cline, ask," Teaman Coleridge said.

"This boy who was being tried for murder," Judy Cline said. "Who did he kill?"

15

"The boy did not kill anybody," Father Danaher said. "He was the driver of the murderer's getaway vehicle. That's a lovely statue, Hugh, truly it is."

Hugh Kelly turned in his desk chair. For a few moments he seemed totally absorbed by the familiar but to him never boring spectacle of St. Patrick and the snakes in the corner of the room.

"Many people consider it the best thing Jo Davidson ever did," he said in a tired voice. "Even young Hoving has a good word to say for it. If he knew how much it cost, the good word would be accompanied by a loud scream. My father, God rest his soul, didn't realize when he commissioned the statue what in those days Jo Davidson was charging the paying customers who were not museums."

Hugh Kelly drew a deep breath. He blew it out slowly, like a man easing a suspicion of dust out of a watch movement, and turned back to his visitor.

"This is a bad business, Terence," he said. "Very bad."

"Indeed it is," Father Danaher said.

He opened his mouth to say more, hesitated as though uncertain about the words that had come to mind, then apparently decided to risk them.

"I had no idea it would come to this," the priest said. "I am truly sorry, Hugh."

"Not as sorry as I am," Hugh Kelly said. "Our long friendship has built such a warm glow in my heart for those grand old days at Fordham that I seem to have confused your talent for generating warm glows with your capacity to use your common sense."

Father Danaher's clerical collar appeared to jerk upward on his skinny neck as his shaggy white eyebrows seemed to explode to the top of his naked skull.

"Hugh, for mercy's sake," the priest managed, not very successfully, to chirp. "What are you saying, old friend?"

"What the cardinal, who has more forgiveness in his heart than your old classmate, would never say," Hugh Kelly said. "Terence, you have fucked this thing into a truly nasty heap."

"Hugh, now really," said the cleric from Alabama. "Isn't that language a bit excessive?"

"Not by comparison with the language David Fillmore will employ if this thing ever gets to his ears," Hugh Kelly said.

"God grant, then, that it doesn't," Terence Danaher said.

"In calling upon Him for help, Terence, I must point out that you have some time ago reached the classic relationship of the straw and the camel's back," Hugh Kelly said. "This mess you have created calls for more worldly attention."

"What's to be done?" Father Danaher said.

"There is only one thing to be done," Hugh Kelly said. He turned, flipped the key on his call box, and into it said, "Edwina, please ring Mrs. Shreve. If she's free, would she be kind enough to allow me to come around to her office for a few minutes with an old friend? If you can do it without making it sound like a fire alarm, Edwina, you might insert into the request the word 'urgent.' But gently, Edwina, very gently indeed. You know how Mrs. Shreve is about her time."

Everybody at Isham Truitt knew how Saphira Shreve was about her time. She measured it out with coffee spoons.

"Solid sterling, of course," said Ludwig Uchitel, the firm's rainmaker.

Ludwig Uchitel's function as an Isham Truitt partner was not unlike that of a barker at a carnival. He stood out in front and sweet-talked the passers-by into buying tickets. Uchitel had not set foot in a courtroom since the day he had taken his oath as a member of the New York Bar. His talents as a ticket salesman for his performing colleagues was so great, however, that for some years now his share of the annual profits had been equal to that of Walter Isham, grandson of the firm's founder and brother-in-law of David Fillmore. Ludwig Uchitel's greatest triumph was adding Saphira Shreve's name to the shingle.

In his family-commissioned biography of Leander Fillmore, founder of the Fillmore National Bank, Harold Nicolson wrote of Ludwig Uchitel's achievement, "It may be compared with the success Stanley Baldwin might have claimed if, after the royal infatuation palled, he had succeeded in bringing the Duke of Windsor back to the British throne."

Saphira Shreve was of the blood royal: the youngest daughter of the oldest son of Leander Fillmore. In 1938, when Saphira at twenty married a song writer named Sammy Shreve, her father cut her out of his will and had her name removed from all the family trusts. The youthful Mrs. Shreve scarcely noticed the vindictive acts. Her husband was one of the nation's three most successful composers of popular songs.

In 1948, when Sammy Shreve died in a plane crash, he left his devoted wife with three small daughters and a surprisingly modest ASCAP rating. Saphira Shreve added up her resources, then divided them in two. With one half she subsidized a live-in nurse for her children. With the other half she paid her way through Columbia Law School. She graduated at the head of her class but she skipped the commencement exercises because they were held in the afternoon. Saphira did not want to miss part of her first day as an associate in the offices of Sullivan and Cromwell.

Her field was wills and trusts. She had not yet done any plowing in the field when she joined Sullivan and Cromwell, but it had always been a firm with vision. Saphira Shreve's lineage was no secret. Soon, neither were her methods. She moved in on her relatives. She had always been popular with her cousins, nieces, and nephews. The latter particularly: they were all Sammy Shreve fans. By the time Saphira became a junior partner at Sullivan and Cromwell all the younger Fillmores were her clients and, soon after her partnership was official, she added to her list three of her uncles. Including the David who was not yet legendary and not yet chairman of the board of Fillmore National but clearly on his way to both. He effected a reconciliation between Saphira and her father. She set out at once on the complex task of rewriting all the Fillmore wills, including her father's, and installing the widow of Sammy Shreve as executor in all the family trusts.

When Saphira's father died Ludwig Uchitel accompanied Walter Isham to Campbell's. After the service he took Saphira into one of the small side rooms for a talk. When they emerged the only point that had not been settled was the position of her name on the Isham Truitt shingle.

"I left that up to her because during the negotiations I had come to know something about the lady," Ludwig Uchitel said later. "She is not a shrinking violet like her grandfather and father and three of her uncles. Neither, however, is she a media person like her uncle David. Saphira Shreve has something that's rare in women. A sense of balance. Because she knows precisely what she is, she sees no point in wasting time reminding people about it. Bringing into the firm as she did every square inch of the huge Fillmore and Isham family trust business, a lesser woman might have insisted on having her name come first. Not Saphira. Mr. Isham is her godfather. Mr. Truitt and Mr. Kelly are her seniors. Manny Merz and the rest of us are her juniors. Saphira decided the spot between Hugh Kelly and Manny Merz was just about right. There were no dissenting votes."

Not about the sequence of names on the Isham Truitt shingle, anyway. About Saphira Shreve's character there were many. She was a perfectionist who expected from her peers, her staff, her friends, acquaintances, and the world at large no more than she expected from herself and regularly delivered. It was more than most people were able to supply. In the case of many who had the ability, it was more than they cared to make the effort required for delivery.

"If the army wasn't male chauvinist to the core, Saphira Shreve would make the best superintendent West Point ever had," Ludwig Uchitel said. "Coming into her office is like stepping out on the parade ground during June Week. You feel you must remember to brace."

Father Danaher didn't, which was understandable. He had never met Saphira Shreve. Hugh Kelly, however, crossing her threshold, could feel his sagging gut moving in and up to his backbone. Acting out of habit, completely on its own, his chin began tucking itself painfully against his Adam's apple. By the time Hugh Kelly reached his partner's desk Judy Cline would not have recognized her boss. Hugh Kelly looked ten years younger.

"Saphira, it's grand of you to let me break in on you this way," he said. "I wouldn't do it if it wasn't something important."

"My secretary gathered from Mrs. Campion that it's also something urgent," Saphira Shreve said. "Will it take long?"

She sounded perfectly relaxed. But Saphira Shreve always sounded perfectly relaxed. Just as she always sat at her desk the way she was sitting at it now. As though her weight, which could not have come to very much more than one hundred pounds, was not resting on a chair with a supporting back. Saphira Shreve's posture always suggested she was sitting in a saddle, controlling a spirited mount with her knees, guiding the horse with gentle but firm precision toward an approaching jump.

Hugh Kelly turned and said, "Terence, will it take long?" Then: "Oh, I'm sorry, Saphira. This is my old friend Father Danaher. We were at Fordham Law School together. He's just flown up from Alabama."

"How do you do?" Saphira Shreve said. "Not Montgomery, Alabama, by any chance?"

"As a matter of fact, yes," Father Danaher said.

"Do sit down," Saphira Shreve said.

There was no reason why Father Danaher should believe he had heard anything but an innocuously polite phrase. Hugh Kelly could see from Danaher's face that his old friend believed precisely that. Hugh Kelly, however, could tell that Saphira Shreve had made a small decision. Her face was dominated by her lips. They were not large but seemed large because her face was so small. She kept her lips pursed always, perhaps to minimize their size. As a result, to Hugh Kelly she always seemed on the verge of breaking into a whistle. Saphira Shreve never did, but a change in the arrangement of her lips, Hugh Kelly had learned, signaled a change in the direction of what at the moment was going through her mind. The change from keeping her visitors standing to inviting them to be seated was the result, Hugh Kelly was sure, of Terence Danaher's announcement that he had just flown up from Montgomery.

"If you don't mind, Saphira, I'll sit down, too," Hugh Kelly said. "What I've come to see you about, I don't think I can listen to it again on my feet."

"Please do," Saphira Shreve said.

Hugh Kelly gestured Father Danaher to one of the two chairs in front of Saphira Shreve's desk. Dropping into the other, Hugh Kelly noticed what he realized he might have noticed as soon as he came into the room. Might have noticed, but not necessarily should have noticed: Saphira Shreve was wearing her hat. Not that she always wore her hat in her office. When she did, however, it was intended as a sign to those who dropped in that, while they would not be asked rudely to leave, it might come to that if they were not brief, because Mrs. Shreve had an imminent appointment outside the office.

The hats, like Saphira Shreve's custom-made suits, were more expensive than anybody but an expert would have noticed. Also they all looked alike. Mainly, it was said by people like Hugh Kelly's wife Essie, because Saphira Shreve had never gotten over her schoolgirl crush on FDR's Secretary of Labor, Frances Perkins. It was believed that Saphira Shreve had, in fact, modeled her career on that of Mrs. Perkins. There was no doubt about the model for Saphira Shreve's hats. They were all copies of Mrs. Perkins' famous tricorne.

"For a number of years Terence has been actively engaged as a volunteer in the legal arm of the Southern Poverty Relief Legal Assistance Association," Hugh Kelly said. "Over the years I have made it a point to see that Isham Truitt gives him a hand by nudging Ludwig Uchitel, who handles our pro bono schedule, into not overlooking SPRLAA. With that short introduction, Saphira, I turn the floor over to Father Danaher."

"Thank you, Hugh," the priest said. "About three weeks ago Mr. Uchitel was good enough to send down one of your young associates named Lichine to help me with a murder case. I don't want to bore you, Mrs. Shreve, with a long, detailed recital of the facts, but—"

"You don't have to," Saphira Shreve said. "I am aware of all the facts."

Astonished, Hugh Kelly said, "You are?"

Saphira Shreve disregarded the interruption. Keeping the front point of her tricorne trained directly on Father Danaher, the severely straight-backed little horsewoman astride the invisible mount behind the desk said, "You are referring to the fifteen-year-old black boy named Virgil Pridemore. Who four days ago was sentenced in Montgomery to life imprisonment. For driving the pickup truck in which his father, Ansel Pridemore, at two-thirty one morning last June left an all-night pizza restaurant. Where in the course of an armed robbery he had just shot and killed the owner. Is that correct?"

"Why, yes," Father Danaher said. He sounded dazed. "Hugh, here, Mr. Kelly, that is, he didn't tell me—"

"He couldn't tell you what he doesn't know," Saphira Shreve said. In appearance calm and unhurried, but in her voice the beat of a ticker clicking out a news tape, she said, "Behind your back, Father Danaher, our Mr. Lichine sought the help of a young black lawyer in Montgomery named Teaman Coleridge. Mr. Coleridge's help was responsible for the jury coming in with a verdict directing a sentence of life imprisonment. Without Mr. Coleridge's help the boy would undoubtedly have been sentenced to the electric chair. Is that correct?"

"Well, now, Mrs. Shreve," the priest said. "I don't know about that word 'undoubtedly.'"

"I do," Saphira Shreve said. "During your seven years with SPRLAA in the Montgomery area, Father Danaher, you have defended eleven blacks under circumstances not too dissimilar. All eleven were sentenced to die in the electric chair."

"They are all, however, still alive," Terence Danaher said.

"Not because of your skills as a defense attorney," Saphira Shreve said. "They are still alive because of the Supreme Court's skill at dithering. Now that the Court has stopped dithering, and has tossed the problem of capital punishment back into the laps of the fifty states, Alabama may still send all eleven of those blacks to the electric chair. Given the economic forces at work in the area, the betting odds are that they will. You have done your work well, Father Danaher."

"Almighty God, Saphira, what are you saying?" Hugh Kelly said.

"I am saying, Hugh, that if in my youth I had suffered the accident of being this man's classmate," Saphira Shreve said, "I would not go around bragging about it today."

The neat little splinter of female contempt disengaged herself from the invisible stirrups, slipped out of the unseen saddle, and came out from behind the desk. Saphira Shreve looked like a figure in one of those religious paintings of the Last Supper who has just arrived with a crucial message for the guest of honor.

"Saphira," Hugh Kelly said, "I brought Father Danaher in here because the problem in Alabama is moving in a direction that could be damaging to this firm. You are closer to Southern Shoals than anybody else in the office. I did not come to you for an insulting tirade against Father Danaher. I want your advice."

"Here it is," Saphira Shreve said. "Send Father Danaher on a long holiday to the Holy Land. That will leave you and me free from amateurish interference as we divide up the work of heading off disaster."

"Tell me the part you want me to do," Hugh Kelly said.

"Find this young Mr. Lichine before Alabama starts extradition proceedings against him," Saphira Shreve said.

"And you?" Hugh Kelly said.

"I'm due in David Fillmore's office in ten minutes," Saphira Shreve said. "The board must discuss the choice of a successor to Sosthenes DeKalb."

"Who?" Hugh Kelly said.

"I don't know yet," Saphira Shreve said. "You can be sure, however, it will be someone who has enough brains not to hire people like your friend Father Danaher to do his dirty work."

16

"Miss Pember?"

"Speaking," Phoebe said into the phone.

"Judith Cline."

"Oh," Phoebe Pember said. The small eruption of surprise did not get into the telephone mouthpiece. It sounded noiselessly inside Phoebe Pember's head. She laughed and said, "Our Miss Judith Cline?"

"Isham Truitt's Judith Cline, yes," the voice at the other end said with a laugh. The laugh almost matched Phoebe's. Almost but not quite. The not quite was Phoebe Pember's second surprise. She had never actually met the associate for whom Mr. Kelly had set himself up as office rabbi, but Phoebe had seen Miss Cline around. A pretty girl, with good clothes, and a cool in-charge manner.

Phoebe did not like Mr. Kelly's protégé, but there was nothing personal in the dislike. If you were an Isham Truitt paratrooper you were supposed to dislike female associates the way, if you were a Jew, you were supposed to dislike Arabs. It had never occurred to Phoebe Pember that there was anything wrong with disliking Arabs or female associates. Now, unexpectedly, she found her mind invaded by doubt. She gave it a moment of thought and decided it was because of the way Miss Cline had returned Phoebe's laugh. The sound lacked the in-charge quality of Miss Cline's appearance. Phoebe Pember found this distressing. It was like seeing a beautiful horse come into the stretch with a comfortable lead and then, within sight of the finish line, unexpectedly stagger. Phoebe did not like cool people to lose their cool. It was the core of her worry about her friend Sandra Behr.

"What can I do for you, Miss Cline?" Phoebe said.

"You can let me pick your brains, if I may," Judith Cline said.

"On office time," Phoebe said, "you'll have to clear it with Mr. Cutter or Mrs. Bethune."

"How about on your own time?" Judy Cline said.

"You'll have to let me buy you a drink," Phoebe Pember said.

This time the laugh was in the area where Phoebe felt it belonged.

"Okay," Judy Cline said. "If you let me buy you the lunch that follows."

"How about the Takashaki Garden?" Phoebe Pember said.

"Won't the other paratroops open fire as soon as they catch sight of the enemy?" Judy Cline said.

"Not if we avoid the command post in the southwest corner," Phoebe Pember said. "When?"

"How about now?" Judy Cline said. "It's twelve twenty-five."

"I'll race you," Phoebe Pember said.

She lost. When Phoebe came into the restaurant Yuki was giving Miss Cline his full Arthur Treacher treatment at one of the small, usually reserved, booths in the northwest corner.

"You didn't tell me you're a double agent," Phoebe said as she shook hands with Judy Cline. "I'll have to put this in my next report to Graham Greene. You know what I want, Yuki."

"*Oui, madame,*" the waiter said.

He held the table clear so Phoebe could get her knees in place, then went off to the bar.

"That boy is getting to be a character's character," Phoebe said. "I assume you ordered?"

"I didn't have to," Judy Cline said. "When I told him I was waiting for you he said he'd bring me what you always have."

"You should have told me you're a regular," Phoebe Pember said. "It's part of the paratroop honor code."

"I'm not a regular," Judy Cline said. "I've been here only once before, and that was more than a year ago."

"You sure made an impression on Yuki," Phoebe said. "Or it

could have been your date. Yuki is a snob about his countrymen. Unless they appear regularly with all their teeth in those big Come-Do-Business-with-Japan magazine layouts he bars Japanese at the door. Who were you with? The president of Seiko Watches?"

"No," Judith Cline said. "Mandamus Manny."

"But you said it was over a year ago, and you've been with Isham Truitt less than—"

Phoebe Pember stopped and giggled.

"I know," she said. "He'd been up there at Harvard on one of his campus recruiting sweeps, and because you're a pretty girl as well as law review, he offered you not only the going rate of thirty thousand to start, but he also invited you to come down to New York for lunch and have a look at the show."

Judy Cline laughed. Phoebe Pember had been admiring the Hermes alligator clutch the other girl had set on the table at her elbow. Phoebe now decided she also wanted Judy Cline's laugh.

"I see why Graham Greene recruited you," Miss Cline said. "You missed on only one point. Mr. Merz did not refer to Isham Truitt as the show. He asked me to come down to New York for lunch and have a look at the shop. Would it upset you if I ask a personal question?"

"Probably, but they're the only kind that don't bore me," Phoebe Pember said. "Okay, I'm dug in. Go."

"How does a girl like you find herself doing paratroop work?" Judy Cline said.

Phoebe Pember decided she was in love.

"It's like this," she said.

When she finished her condensed version of the Pember-Behr-Applied Psychology-Masters-at-Smith saga, Yuki appeared with the drinks. He set a vodka martini in front of each girl, placed menus beside both glasses, and stepped back.

"Order now, ladies?" he said.

"Good idea," Phoebe Pember said. "Yuki's performance tends to run down, and as the applause diminishes he begins to pout and goes off in search of a more appreciative audience."

"I seem to have done very well by following your lead on the drink," Judy Cline said. She picked up her glass. "I'll do the same on the food. Here's to what?"

"Brain picking," Phoebe Pember said.

The glasses touched across the menus. Both girls sipped.

"Following me on the food may not be as good as on the booze," Phoebe Pember said. "What did you have on your first visit?"

"Mr. Merz recommended the mizutaki," Judy Cline said.

"Did you follow the recommendation?" Phoebe Pember said.

"I did," Judy Cline said.

She took another sip.

"Bum steer?" Phoebe Pember said.

"I don't remember," Judy Cline said. "My mind was not on food."

"Then you won't feel deprived if I lead you in a more sensible direction," Phoebe Pember said. "How do you like your hamburger?"

"Medium rare," Judy Cline said. "If there's a way to say that in Japanese."

"There isn't but in this place it's the only way they know how to make them," Phoebe Pember said. "Two hamburgers medium rare, Yuki, and two orders of french fries."

"*Oui, madame,*" the waiter said.

He collected the menus and left.

"It's the best hamburger in town," Phoebe Pember said. "It has been ever since they hijacked the chef from the McDonald's on Lexington. Now that you know how I got to be a paratrooper, would you think I'm driving a hard bargain if in exchange I asked you a personal question?"

"That depends on how you phrase it," Judy Cline said. "But it wouldn't affect your right to ask it."

"We're the same age," Phoebe Pember said. "Don't deny it. I looked you up. We're the same scholastic level. I looked that up, too. Everything else, I'd say, checks out in pretty much the same way. So how come I'm a paratrooper and you're an associate?"

"Easy," Judy Cline said. "You didn't have Clifford Cline for a father."

"The man who wrote all those plays?" Phoebe Pember said.

"You must have looked that up, too," Judy Cline said. "He hasn't written any plays since you were old enough to read the ABC ads in the *Times*."

"I didn't look that up," Phoebe Pember said. "Sandra Behr did. We divvy up the work, then swap information. If you and I are the same age that means you never read about any of your father's plays in the ABC ads, either."

"No, but I grew up on the author reading them aloud to me," Judy Cline said. "When other little girls went to the park to ride the carrousel and watch little boys sail their boats around the pond, I went to my father's study and watched him act out his big successes. I had a much better time than all those other little girls. My father's big hits were almost all courtroom dramas and he must have written the prosecutors and the defense attorneys with himself in mind. He was a very good actor. Not professionally, but he did direct some of his own plays, and in his study he put on a very thrilling show. For a little girl, anyway. The determination to become a lawyer was planted in me when I was so young that I can't remember when it wasn't part of me. I was halfway through law school, and loving every minute of it, before I realized that I may have had the desire to be one of my father's characters but my talents such as they were belonged not in the courtroom but in the library. I grew up wanting to be Perry Mason but I ended up preparing closing memoranda on corner properties for Hugh F. X. Kelly, Jr."

"It pays better than preparing testimony digests for J. C. Taunton," Phoebe Pember said. Then: "I've said something wrong."

"No," Judy said. She completed the interrupted attempt to take a sip of her drink, and set down the glass. "He's what I want to pick your brains about."

"What's a nice girl like you doing with a creature like J. C. Taunton?" Phoebe Pember said.

"I could ask you the same question," Judy Cline said. "At least I can say in my case he came around to see me."

"No excuses, please," Phoebe Pember said. "You could have slammed the door in his face. Better yet, you could have kicked him out on his ear. After all, aren't you an Isham Truitt associate? And don't you have a senior partner for a rabbi? But me? A lowly paratrooper? I have to do what I'm asked to do even if it's things like J. C. Taunton who do the asking."

"Is that how it happened?" Judy Cline said.

"How what happened?" Phoebe Pember said.

"The testimony digest on *Pridemore* v. *Southern Shoals Asbestos*," Judy Cline said. "Jack Taunton came and asked you to do it?"

"A nice girl like you, a contemporary I envy, admire, and intend to emulate," Phoebe Pember said, "I hate to hear you call him Jack. It implies a degree of respect, even intimacy, that I deplore. Please withdraw it at once or the brains-picking act is finished before it starts."

"I withdraw it," Judy Cline said. "I also apologize. A slip of the tongue, believe me. That's how he introduced himself to me. 'I'm Jack Taunton,' he said. I'm now willing to pretend I never heard the introduction."

"That's a pretense in which I will happily join you," Phoebe Pember said.

"Just the same, if we're going to get anywhere with this conversation," Judy Cline said, "I think we're going to have to settle on something. We can't just call him it, and I refuse to call anybody X. Taunton, maybe?"

"Too human," Phoebe Pember said. "How about J.C.?"

"My rabbi is a Catholic," Judy Cline said. "In view of all the things he's done for me at Isham Truitt, I'd feel disloyal to Mr. Kelly if we used the initials of the headman of his club for—"

"Don't say it," Phoebe Pember said.

"Sorry," Judy Cline said.

"I don't mean J.C. as in the Gospels," Phoebe Pember said. "I mean J.C. as in Just Crud."

"I like that," Judy Cline said.

"Good," Phoebe Pember said. "Now, what has he done to you?"

"He hasn't done it yet," Judy Cline said. "He barged in on me late yesterday and started talking. By the time I got rid of him I realized he'd left something behind."

"A threat?" Phoebe Pember said.

"How did you know?" Judy Cline said.

"That's what he left me with," Phoebe Pember said.

"After you finished the testimony digest?" Judy Cline said.

"No, after I cracked him across the face and gave him a piece of advice," Phoebe Pember said.

"About what?" Judy Cline said.

"His hands," Phoebe Pember said. "If in the future he didn't keep them to himself, I told him, I'd turn my fiancé loose on him with the tools of his trade."

"Which is what?" Judy Cline said.

"Orthopedic surgeon," Phoebe Pember said.

"I don't have anybody as effective as that in my corner," Judy Cline said.

"You have Phoebe Pember," Phoebe Pember said.

"Thank you," Judy Cline said.

"Set me in motion," Phoebe Pember said.

"After Just Crud left," Judy Cline said, "I went over in my mind what he'd laid out on my plate. All of it seemed to flow from an Alabama indemnification case our hero kept calling *Pridemore* v. *Southern Shoals Asbestos.* I called Mrs. Hoag in the library and asked her to look it up for me in the Alabama *Reports.* She called back and said it was listed in the index but the volume in which the case appeared had been checked out to you last Thursday because you were doing a testimony digest on it for Mr. Taunton. I knew nothing about you but after my session with J.C. I felt I knew quite a lot about Mr. Taunton, so it seemed more sensible to take a shot at you. I did, and here we are."

"About to tackle a McDonald's hamburger under Japanese auspices," Phoebe Pember said.

"*Très chaud, mesdames,*" Yuki said. He set down the plates and picked up the empty glasses. "*Un autre?*"

"Not for me," Judy Cline said.

"Thanks, no, Yuki," Phoebe Pember said.

The waiter bowed and went away.

"Would you happen to have a copy of the digest you made for J.C.?" Judy Cline said as she picked up her fork.

"No, but we paratroops have a pretty good infiltration network," Phoebe Pember said. "It would be no trick at all for me to sneak a Xerox out of Stenographic." Picking up her fork, Phoebe Pember added, "In fact, considering my personal feelings about Mrs. Merle Bethune, it would give me a great deal of pleasure."

"That's great," Judy Cline said. "It would be helpful in the meantime if you could give me a sort of verbal digest of the digest."

"If you don't mind a nonprofessional's sketchy recollections?" Phoebe Pember said.

"That would be fine," Judy Cline said.

"This Mr. Pridemore," Phoebe Pember said. "He went to work for Southern Shoals Asbestos in Montgomery during the war, back in 1945. Thirty years later, that's today, more accurately three years ago in 1975, he came down with a disease called, I think, mesothelioma. It could be a form of lung cancer, but I'm not sure. Anyway, it's one of the terrible things you come down with if you're dumb enough to hang around asbestos for thirty years. Or even less, I gather, but this Mr. Pridemore was in the thirty-year bracket. Leaving aside the spelling of what he had, it seems to be pretty rough stuff. The company doctor said they couldn't do anything for him, so Mr. Pridemore went to a private doctor. He couldn't do anything for Mr. Pridemore, either, but he told him it was the thirty years of working with asbestos that had made him sick, and the doctor felt Mr. Pridemore should get some help from his employers. Southern Shoals did not agree, so Mr. Pridemore went to a lawyer.

"The lawyer brought suit against Southern Shoals," Phoebe Pember continued. "The case was thrown out of court. Down in Alabama, the testimony indicated, most cases against Southern Shoals get thrown out of court. The lawyer was not surprised. He appealed. By the time the appeal came up for trial Mr. Pridemore was living on oxygen. All this oxygen was costing a lot of money. Mr. Pridemore didn't have a lot. He was suing Southern Shoals for enough to stay alive on. I forget how much, but it's in the digest, and that's about all I remember, except that the court of appeals sustained the lower court. Mr. Pridemore got no money. Until I can get the Xerox to you, I hope that helps."

"It does," Judy Cline said. "I wish there was something I could do for you in exchange."

"There is," Phoebe Pember said.

"Tell me," Judy Cline said.

"Not for me, actually," Phoebe Pember said. "It's for my friend Sandra Behr."

17

"And that's the way it is," Walter Cronkite said. "On this Friday night, August 11, 1978."

The commercial came on, and Ezra Cooper became aware of the doorbell. He turned toward Jessica. She was facing the TV screen. The damaged side of her face was turned away from Ezra. She was, as always, unaware of the commercial. She may have been unaware of Cronkite. She frequently was. Jessica was certainly unaware of the doorbell. It rang again. Ezra Cooper stood up and went out to the foyer. Behind him he could hear his wife. She was speaking quietly, relentlessly, sanely, as always.

"—this man from Vienna," Jessica was saying. She could have been reading a letter aloud to herself. "The one who had been trained by the great Dr. Stieghoffer before the Nazis killed him. He's finally been located in Zurich by a man from Johns Hopkins. Dr. Quentin writes that he knows the clinic in Zurich, and he's pretty sure that the work this man has been doing there for about ten years has been on cases so similar to mine that Dr. Quentin feels it's well worth the financial risk of a trip to Switzerland, even if it means—"

Ezra Cooper slid aside the brass cap and put his eye to the peephole. The man on the stoop looked familiar. Ezra slid back the bolt and opened the door.

"Mr. Cooper?"

"Yes," Ezra said.

"Jack Taunton. No reason why you should remember me, but—"

"Of course," Ezra said. "Forgive me. We've been watching the news and I forgot to take off my glasses."

He did so now.

"Of course I remember you," Ezra said. "You shared an office down the hall from me with that Harvard boy. Lichine?"

"That's right," Jack Taunton said. "Tom Lichine."

"Come in," Ezra said. He pulled the door wide, stopped, and said with a laugh, "I assume you want to come in?"

"If you don't mind," Jack Taunton said.

His responding laugh had an odd quality. As though Ezra's pleasantry had reminded Taunton it was generally regarded as a matter of politeness to respond in kind, but because of infrequent use he had gone rusty in the process.

"We don't get many drop-in callers," Ezra Cooper said as Taunton stepped into the foyer. Sliding the bolt back into place, Ezra added, "My wife is an invalid."

"I'm sorry," Taunton said.

More easily this time, but still with the faint creaks involved in getting a more or less forgotten piece of machinery under way again. An odd thought cut swiftly across Ezra Cooper's mind: what sort of people did this boy spend his time with?

"I hope I'm not intruding?" Taunton said.

"No, of course not," Ezra said. "Let's go into the study."

Following Ezra across the rear of the living room, Mr. Taunton sent a quick look at Jessica. She hadn't moved, of course. The damaged side of her face was still averted. She was still staring at the TV screen, and she was still inaudibly reading aloud from the invisible letter. She did not turn to look at Ezra or the visitor.

"My wife is deaf," Ezra said.

This was not true. Not technically, anyway. Ezra had found, however, it was a convenient way to eliminate a lot of awkward q. and a. from plumbers and TV repairmen.

"You don't think I'm upsetting her by dropping in like this?" Taunton said.

Perfectly normal delivery at last. He must have been raised in a civilized society, Ezra concluded. Maybe he'd been kidnaped by Gypsies while still very young and only recently returned to a society where people used handkerchiefs and forks. Ezra chuckled inwardly at his small joke. It was pleasant to feel pleasant again.

"I assure you you're not upsetting her at all," Ezra Cooper said. "She's completely unaware of us. With this door closed she won't know we're in the house."

He closed the door.

"Nice place you've got here," Jack Taunton said.

His empty politeness repertoire was obviously no better stocked than that of most people, including his host. Ezra Cooper felt, however, that only a fool, which he doubted Mr. Taunton was, or a man totally disinterested in the effect of the words he was using, would have chosen the five Jack Taunton had just released. The nice place Ezra Cooper had here was what had once been, in the days when Ezra Cooper's beat-up old brownstone was the apple of an original owner's eye, a butler's pantry. On that great day in 1950 when Jessica and Ezra found the place and began putting together their remodeling plans, the beat-up old butler's pantry had been earmarked for conversion into a brilliant young lawyer's study.

During the intervening twenty-eight years not quite nothing had been done to implement the plan, but not much had been done, either. The shelves and cupboards designed originally for china and glassware were now crammed with books and magazines and old newspapers. The two serving counters had been torn out and replaced with a couch and a desk. Both had been purchased second-hand because the plan called for them to be discarded when the remodeling process gave way to the redecoration plan. Both the desk and the couch were still second-hand. Ezra Cooper gestured toward the couch.

"Try that end," he said. "Some of the springs over there are still working."

"Thanks," Jack Taunton said, peeling off his trench coat.

"Here," Ezra Cooper said. "Let me take that."

While Mr. Taunton settled himself over the springs that still worked Ezra dropped the trench coat at the other end of the couch. He then pulled the typewriter chair away from the desk and swung it around to face the couch. Ezra paused before sitting down to face Taunton.

"Can I get you something to drink?"

"Thanks, no," Jack Taunton said. "I'm a teetotaler."

Ezra Cooper was not surprised. The vague look of the Christer lurked somewhere in Mr. Taunton's slippery features. Somehow it seemed appropriate for this odd little young man, in politely refusing a drink, to make of the refusal a statement about a way of life. Ezra sat down and realized it was only on second glance that Mr. Taunton began to look really creepy.

Heavily lidded eyes set in deep black sockets were not common in Ezra Cooper's experience. They were not, however, unknown, either. For years he had been seeing pictures of Theda Bara in the photography exhibits at the Museum of Modern Art. What Ezra had never before seen, certainly not in what his tiny study made an almost knee-to-knee situation, was a face it seemed to him Mr. Taunton had picked up somewhere on his way over here. Ezra had certainly never seen it during the innumerable times he had passed Taunton in the Isham Truitt corridors.

In the primitively converted old butler's pantry on Sixty-second and Third, Jack Taunton was wearing a face borrowed from newspaper photographs of any one of a hundred or more survivors of the mass suicide at the Jim Jones cult in Guyana.

"I owe you an apology for dropping in on you like this without warning," he said.

Ezra supposed Mr. Taunton did, but it seemed an odd way to put it, so he said, "We're in the phone book, of course."

The effect was not exactly what he had expected, but close enough: a contraction of Mr. Taunton's facial muscles. He could have been gathering his words to phrase the apology he felt he owed, or restraining himself from throwing a punch at the perpetrator of an insult.

"I didn't know how to say it on the phone," he said.

"Say what?" Ezra said.

"I just learned in the office today by sheer accident you were no longer with us," Jack Taunton said.

The flicking of the dark eyelids added to the impression that

Mr. Taunton had learned it when he had been asked if he planned to attend the funeral of the departed.

"I was fired two days ago," Ezra said. "I wasn't in much of a mood for parading around the office on a farewell tour saying good-bye to people."

"Especially to people you'd never had anything to do with," Jack Taunton said.

A touch of bitterness? Perhaps. Yet could the statement have been made by anybody who was not bitter?

"Not by choice," Ezra said.

"Of course not," Mr. Taunton said. "I didn't mean that."

"What did you mean?" Ezra said. "What do you mean? Why have you come to see me? What's going on, Mr. Taunton?"

"Take it easy," Mr. Taunton said. "I know exactly how you feel."

"Do you want to bet?" Ezra Cooper said.

Startled, Mr. Taunton said, "What?"

"How old are you?" Ezra Cooper said.

"Twenty-five," Jack Taunton said.

"How long with Isham Truitt?" Ezra said.

"Eight months," Taunton said.

"When you've been there twenty-eight years, and you still haven't made partner," Ezra Cooper said, "I'll believe you when you tell me you know exactly how I feel today."

"That's never going to happen to me," Mr. Taunton said.

"I hope not," Ezra Cooper said.

"I'm not counting on hope," Jack Taunton said.

"Don't count on your rabbi, either," Ezra said. "They're a fickle bunch."

"Not mine," Taunton said.

"Who is he?" Ezra Cooper said.

"My father," Jack Taunton said, and he laughed. "Don't run down the list of names. He's not with Isham Truitt."

"Who's he with?" Ezra said.

"Himself," Jack Taunton said.

"I don't understand," Ezra said.

"The name George B. Taunton mean anything to you?"

"'B' for Bruce?" Ezra Cooper said.

"The same," Jack Taunton said.

"I thought he was dead," Ezra said.

"You mean you wish he was," Taunton said.

"I didn't say that," Ezra Cooper said.

"You don't have to," Taunton said. "You postwar pinkos are all alike."

"Now, look, buster," Ezra Cooper said.

"Don't get worked up," Jack Taunton said. "I'm not. I told you I know how you feel. Maybe I know better than you know yourself. When my old man went to work for Joe McCarthy he was the same age you were when you came to work for Isham Truitt. A couple of kids just out of law school looking for careers. Who recruited you for Isham Truitt?"

"Mr. Merz," Ezra Cooper said.

"When you accepted his offer to come with Isham Truitt did you know anything about Mandamus Manny's politics?" Jack Taunton said.

"I wasn't interested," Ezra said.

"Neither was my old man interested in Joe McCarthy's politics," Taunton said. "By the time he found out, my old man had what he wanted. The experience that means the beginning of a career. He told Joe McCarthy to shove it and set up shop for himself. He's done well."

"I'm not surprised," Ezra Cooper said.

"That's why I'm here," Taunton said.

"Why?" Ezra said.

"To surprise you," Taunton said.

"In what way?" Ezra said.

"By showing you how to do something you've never known how to do at Isham Truitt," Taunton said.

"What's that?" Ezra said.

"Make partner," Taunton said.

"You're a little late," Ezra said.

"Because you were just hired by Falk Prudhomme?" Taunton said.

"How did you know that?" Ezra Cooper said.

"Remember Dusty Rhodes?" Taunton said.

"We shared an office when I first came with Isham Truitt," Ezra Cooper said.

"You didn't share it for long," Jack Taunton said. "After three years Dusty got the message you never got. He quit while he was still young enough to be negotiable and went with a smaller firm."

"They're not so small anymore," Ezra Cooper said. "They're starting me at the same salary I was getting at Isham Truitt three days ago."

"Because Dusty Rhodes is now one of their senior partners," Taunton said. "And my old man went to Cornell with Dusty. When I heard Isham Truitt had fired you I called my old man in Washington. He called Dusty Rhodes, and Dusty called you. It was Dusty who called you, not the other way around. Right?"

"Right," Ezra Cooper said. "I thanked him for the job. I suppose you came over here to tell me I should have thanked you."

"I don't want verbal thanks," Taunton said. "I want something concrete."

"If I can supply it," Ezra said, "I guess I owe it to you."

"You owe it to yourself," Jack Taunton said. "You're fifty-three years old. In the years you've got left you think you're going to have any more luck making partner at Falk Prudhomme than you had the last twenty-eight years making it at Isham Truitt?"

"I don't see what else I can do," Ezra Cooper said.

"You can wake up to something that men your age don't seem to be aware of," Taunton said. "Something all the people my age are completely aware of."

"What's that?" Ezra Cooper said.

"The law business isn't what it used to be when you were my age," Taunton said. "Things are moving faster. You no longer have to wait until you get what a bunch of old farts consider ripe before you can expect them to tap you for partner. Today you can get tapped for partner at any age. My twenty-five or your fifty-three. The years don't count anymore."

"What does?" Ezra said.

"Clout," Taunton said. "Forget seniority. Forget keeping your nose clean. Forget apple polishing. Remember only this. The notion that lawyers are infallible was invented by lawyers. It's a lot of crap. They're always leaving a scalpel in the patient's gut when they sew up the wound. Other lawyers are always covering up for them. It doesn't wash anymore. Today all a man has to do is keep his eyes open. The younger he is the more he's likely to see. When he sees a ball get dropped all he has to do is field it, set his sights, and carry the ball to the target."

"Blackmail?" Ezra Cooper said.

"If you want to call it that," Taunton said.

"I did, once," Ezra Cooper said. "That's how I got fired."

"That wasn't the reason," Taunton said.

"What are you talking about?" Ezra Cooper said.

"Ken Kreel," Jack Taunton said.

In a way Ezra Cooper felt his reaction was a small triumph. Only his gut jumped.

"What do you know about it?" he said.

"You went for the wrong target," Jack Taunton said. "Outfits like Isham Truitt don't get rocked when a junior partner gets caught in the wrong bed. You have to catch the top man."

"Is that what you're after?" Ezra Cooper said.

"Yes," Taunton said. "If I get the right help."

"From whom?" Ezra Cooper said.

"You," Jack Taunton said.

The door opened. Jessica came in.

"The Vice-President is dead," she said.

"We know," Jack Taunton said.

"You can't possibly," Jessica said. "John Chancellor just announced it on the air."

"Before I came over here," Jack Taunton said, "I had a call from Washington."

Jessica Cooper turned to her husband.

"Who is this man?" she said.

"One of my business associates," Ezra Cooper said.

"I wish you would tell me when you bring strange people into the house," Jessica said. "Now I've missed Brinkley."

She went out.

"What's this all about?" Ezra Cooper said.

"Your future and mine," Jack Taunton said. "The V.-P. was in Jerusalem heading up our delegation to the Golda Meir funeral.

When he dropped dead late this afternoon the telephones started ringing in Washington. My father had the news before Cronkite did. He called me right away."

"Why?" Ezra Cooper said.

"It's the scalpel in the patient's gut my old man and I have been waiting for," Jack Taunton said.

"And that's what brought you over here to see me?" Ezra Cooper said.

"Of course," Jack Taunton said.

"You better clarify that," Ezra Cooper said.

"When a Vice-President dies," Taunton said, "the President has to appoint a successor."

"I'm not interested in the job," Ezra Cooper said.

"No," Jack Taunton said. "But David Fillmore is."

"Why?" Ezra Cooper said.

"He's got everything else," Jack Taunton said.

"Will he get this?" Ezra said.

"Not if you and I play our cards right," Taunton said.

"You're talking about a game in which I don't have any cards," Ezra Cooper said.

"You may have," Jack Taunton said.

He pulled a batch of papers from his pocket, leaned over, and placed them in Ezra Cooper's lap. Ezra studied the caption on the top sheet: *"Pridemore v. Southern Shoals Asbestos.* Alabama Supreme Court. Testimony Digest Prepared for J. C. Taunton by P. Pember, August 1978."

"What is this?" Ezra Cooper said.

Jack Taunton stood up.

"Your homework," he said. "While you're doing it I'll get my other cards in position, and then we'll have a strategy session."

"About what?" Ezra Cooper said.

"How to destroy Isham Truitt," Jack Taunton said.

18

The Tessitore marriage was built around a central joke rooted in the banking crisis of 1933.

Anthony Tessitore was born on March 4 of that year. On that day FDR, fresh from his inaugural, invoked the World War I Trading with the Enemy Act to declare a four-day bank holiday. Sylvia Tessitore, née Caransa, was born on March 12, 1933, the day FDR in his first fireside chat announced to the nation that it was now "safer for an American citizen to put his money into a bank than into a mattress."

"That makes me the senior member of this team by eight days," Tony said with a chuckle.

He said it in 1953 to the members of both the Tessitore and Caransa families as they were herded by the photographer into Tony and Sylvia's wedding pictures.

Tony added, "The groom hereby warns the bride never to forget it."

Sylvia Tessitore heeded the warning. Not because Tony was a bad husband. On the contrary. Sylvia was the envy of her sisters. All four of them seemed incapable of making conversation about anything but illustrations of boorishness and perfidy on the part of the men to whom, all being Catholic, they were riveted until death did them part. One of the four, a crossword puzzle fan, during an afternoon visit with Sylvia once referred to Tony as uxorious. After her sister left Sylvia Tessitore got out the dictionary and looked up the word. She called her sister on the phone and told her, "You said a mouthful."

To her husband Sylvia said nothing. Tony did not understand the meaning of a compliment. He treated statements of fact as indirect orders or veiled criticism. Immediately on hearing them he set about making corrections. Tony did not, however, say he felt he had been criticized or was being pushed around. After almost a quarter century of marriage Sylvia Tessitore had learned to accept as unimportant her husband's basic dishonesty. She disregarded what he said. What Sylvia watched, in her own phrase "like a hock," was what she herself said.

If it was cold in the apartment, for example, and she was finding that pleasant, Sylvia was careful to make no comment about the temperature of their living quarters. If she did, Tony would start fussing at once with the thermostat to warm things up. If Sylvia had told Tony that her sister had called him uxorious, with his customary almost mindless efficiency he would have gone to work immediately on demonstrating he was neither excessively fond of, nor submissive to, his wife. Sylvia Tessitore did not care to speculate on where that would lead.

Once, in a moment of admiration for the zeal that had just resulted in a salary raise, she had complimented him on what she felt was the cause: the number of hours her dedicated husband devoted every day to the affairs of his employers. From that moment on Tony Tessitore never got home from the Isham Truitt office later than eight o'clock.

It was a rare evening, however, when he took less than half a dozen business calls between dinner and bedtime. Not infrequently there were physical intrusions by messengers with legal documents, and callers with information Tony had commandeered. In performing his duties as the Isham Truitt managing clerk, Tony Tessitore often had to deal with delicate matters.

"This is a matter of the utmost delicacy," Mr. Kelly had said four days ago at their closed-door meeting in the senior partner's office. "We've got to find Lichine before the police do."

"This would be a federal matter, sir, would it not?" Tony said.

"Ordinarily, yes," Mr. Kelly said. "Extradition usually is. The problem here, Tessie, is that at the moment the matter does not look ordinary. What we want to do is grab hold of it while it's still grabbable and shove it back into the ordinary category, if you know what I mean."

"Yes, sir," Tony said.

He had no idea what Mr. Kelly meant, but Tony Tessitore was not lying. As the Isham Truitt managing clerk he had a clear vision of his mandate. To keep it unclouded in his own mind Tessie had for almost a quarter century leaned on the slightly rearranged words of a man he knew nothing about but admired deeply: "Theirs not to reason why, theirs but to do or die."

"What we know is that Lichine has been indicted by an Alabama grand jury," Mr. Kelly said. "The charge is second-degree murder. We also know he has removed himself from the jurisdiction of Alabama, and the prosecutor down there has announced his intention to seek extradition. So far the prosecutor has not acted on that announcement. At any rate, to our knowledge papers have not yet been served up here in New York. Six days ago, after you found Lichine asleep in his office, I had a meeting with him here in my office. He sat in that very chair you're sitting in now. Nobody has seen him since. Nobody I have talked with, anyway. Naturally, we would like to help the boy. Not only for his own sake but also for ours. He was, after all, sent down to Alabama on this pro bono assignment under our auspices. We have a clear duty to ourselves as well as to the boy. The best way to perform that duty, we feel, is to find the boy and talk to him before anybody official does. It is far too delicate to risk a lot of dumb cops shoving and pushing their way around. Until we can get with the boy we are flying blind. We must have the facts that will enable us to set a course of action when he makes his move. We are counting on you, Tessie."

Tessie started to say "Yes, sir" but the words stopped in his throat. All at once they seemed inadequate. There was something in Mr. Kelly's voice. No, not in his voice. It was in the way Mr. Kelly, as he talked, kept turning uneasily for glimpses of the statue in the corner of the room. Yes, that was it. Mr. Kelly looked the way Tessie felt he himself looked when he brought something more than a list of routine sins into the confessional. Mr. Kelly looked scared. As he talked he sought nourishment from St. Patrick and the snakes.

For the polite "Yes, sir" he had aborted Tony Tessitore now substituted a firm "I understand, sir."

The substitution seemed to cheer Mr. Kelly. He smiled.

"I thought you would," he said.

Unexpectedly Tessie sensed the beginnings of a small, ominous rumbling in the lower area of his stomach. Mr. Kelly's words were not part of the smile. Neither was the tightening of the skin around the senior partner's ice-blue eyes. Tessie grasped what Mr. Kelly had omitted from his reply to the managing clerk's "I understand, sir." Mr. Kelly had omitted the words "Or else."

19

Nobody was expecting Ira Bodmer. That was the trouble. Mr. Tessitore had assured him the man in the tan zipper golf jacket would be waiting near the phone booth. Except for the armed guard at the desk facing the Tillary Street entrance, however, the lobby of the IRS facility was deserted.

Ira Bodmer reminded himself that, at six o'clock in the morning, it was supposed to be deserted. The large, high-ceilinged area had the same feel he remembered from his first visit. On that morning two weeks ago when he had filed the Grantham Estates 1977 federal tax return. The morning when, less than an hour later, Ira had heard Tom Lichine's rasping snores behind the locked door of his office at 635 Madison.

The armed guard at the desk looked up from his *Daily News*. Ira had an uneasy moment. It was the same man who two weeks ago had logged in the Grantham Estates tax return. He had signed the receipt Ira Bodmer carried back to Mr. Tessitore at 635.

"Help you?" the guard said.

Ira Bodmer's stomach eased back into place. There was no recognition on the guard's face or in his voice.

"I was looking for a phone booth," Ira Bodmer said.

"In that corner over there." The guard jerked his head to the left. "Back of the directory."

"Thanks," Ira Bodmer said.

He moved toward the booth from which two weeks ago he had called in his report to Mr. Tessitore in the managing clerk's

Eighty-sixth Street apartment. The guard bent back over his newspaper. When Ira was halfway across the marble tiling between the guard's desk and the concealed phone booth, a man appeared from behind the directory. Ira Bodmer's stomach went into action. The man was wearing a tan zipper golf jacket and, it seemed to Ira for a tense moment, a look of inquiry.

Then the moment was gone. So was the man. And Ira Bodmer, in spite of his uneasy stomach, was beyond the directory. He stepped into the phone booth and pulled the door shut. The receiver went up to his ear as the dime he had been holding all the way in from the sidewalk went into the slot. Ira waited for the ping and the dial tone, then at random tapped out seven digits on the push-button panel. With the pieces of his covering performance all hung into place, Ira permitted himself a casual glance through the phone-booth door. The only thing in motion was the red sweep second hand of the electric clock staring at him from the far wall.

Ira slid his hand under the small shelf that supported the Manhattan directory. He moved his fingers slowly to the right. Almost immediately, no more than a couple of inches from the starting point, his fingers touched the edge of an envelope. He took the corner between his fingers and gave it a slow, firm tug. The envelope came free with the Scotch tape fastenings. Ira pasted back on the envelope the strips of loose Scotch tape and slid the envelope into his breast pocket. He put up the receiver, came out of the phone booth, and started back across the marble tiling toward the building entrance. When he reached the desk the armed guard looked up.

"Thanks," Ira Bodmer said.

"You bet," the guard said.

Moving into the revolving door, Ira had a feeling the man was watching him, but he didn't turn back. All night, coming out of every office building and apartment house on Mr. Tessitore's list, Ira had felt the night man on duty in the lobby was watching as Ira walked back out into the street. Ira knew, however, that if he were the night man in any of those office buildings or apartment houses, he would have done the same thing. Daylight was beginning to move in over Brooklyn from somewhere beyond the buildings by which he was surrounded. Ira walked up Tillary Street to the corner. The taxi was waiting.

"Ninety-sixth Street and Fifth," Ira said to the driver. "Eleven forty-eight. The entrance is on Ninety-sixth, just in from the Fifth Avenue corner."

"I know the building," the driver said.

So did Ira. During the eight months of his service as one half of Mr. Tessitore's staff at Isham Truitt, Ira had made several deliveries to Cheryl Marvin's apartment house. Most of these had been large, thick Isham Truitt clasp envelopes that were used for legal documents. Ira Bodmer wondered at first what sort of legal documents had to be delivered to the home of a former Miss South Dakota now employed as receptionist in the Isham Truitt outer office. Then Ira learned that, like many other employees, Miss Marvin was frequently asked to witness a signature that could be obtained only at that moment because the signer happened to be in the office, and as a result it was frequently necessary for her to sign subsequent releases. On one memorable occasion the envelope Ira delivered had been a very small one. He had picked it up at the Shubert Theatre. It contained two down in front for that night's performance of *A Chorus Line.* According to Sal Giudice, who had been in Mr. Tessitore's office when Mr. Kreel came in and asked Tessie to have the tickets picked up and delivered, they were for a client who had arrived in town without warning for an overnight stay and expected Mr. Kreel to provide him with a date for the evening.

"The little old loose-leaf black notebook ran dry," Sal Giudice said. "Kreel had to call in his relief pitcher."

In the taxi carrying him to the Isham Truitt relief pitcher's apartment Ira Bodmer unzipped the small plastic bag with which Mr. Tessitore had provided him for the night's work. To the envelopes he had been picking up all over town since midnight Ira now added the envelope he had picked up on Tillary Street. The taxi stopped.

"Wait for you?" the taxi driver said.

"No, thanks," Ira Bodmer said. "This is the end of the line."

He paid off the driver and crossed to the building entrance.

Through the glass door the night man saw him coming. He pulled the door open.

"Miss Marvin?" Ira said. "Ten C?"

"Who's calling, please?" the night man said.

"Bodmer," Ira said. "Ira Bodmer."

"You're expected," the man said.

Ira went down the lobby and into the elevator. When the car stopped at ten, and the door slid open, the C door facing the elevator across the foyer was pulled wide. Miss Marvin, wearing a bright-red velour bathrobe, appeared in the doorway. Ira handed over the small plastic bag.

"Mission accomplished," he said.

"I'll bet you could use some sleep," Miss Marvin said.

"I'll have to catch up in my Bills and Notes class tonight," Ira said. "In less than an hour Tessie will be expecting me in the office to fire the starting gun."

"A hard man, Tessie," Cheryl Marvin said.

"But a big heart," Ira said.

"One of the biggest," she said.

There was a pause. Ira Bodmer knew all the office gossip about Cheryl Marvin. For eight months he had grown accustomed to seeing her and talking to her every day, often many times a day, on his way through the reception room. He had never, however, seen Cheryl Marvin in a bathrobe. At this hour of the morning. Inches away from an open door that could be closed behind them both as easily as she had opened it for him. The possibility that would have seemed preposterous in the office during business hours seemed far from preposterous in this open apartment doorway at this hour of the morning. Ira Bodmer felt a familiar tremor in his groin. Why should what Mr. Kreel and other men had achieved be beyond Ira Bodmer's grasp? If he had the guts, if he made a move—

Cheryl Marvin made it for him. She smiled, as though she had read his mind and she was flattered by what she had read, but not flattered enough to give this kid something he would later be able to brag about to his friends. Still smiling with a touch of mockery, but in a friendly way, Cheryl Marvin eased the door shut as she said, "See you in the office."

When Ira came out of the elevator into the lobby, Sal Giudice came up out of a deep chair under a potted aspidistra.

"What the hell are you doing here?" Ira said.

"Same thing you just did," Sal Giudice said. "Except I did it twenty minutes ago and I've been waiting for you. Let's get some breakfast."

They walked down Ninety-sixth Street to Madison and into an all-night coffeepot. For a few minutes their only conversation was directed at the waitress. When she went away Sal Giudice lit a cigarette.

"Want one?" he said.

"The surgeon general says it's bad for my health," Ira Bodmer said.

"Not as bad as what Tessie has had us doing all night," Sal Giudice said. "We have been collecting unmarked, untraceable money. By doing this our boss has rigged a great big high sling in which you and I may find before too long that our asses have been caught."

"How do you figure that?" Ira Bodmer said.

"For two weeks," Sal Giudice said, "ever since that Lichine guy was fired, the entire machinery of Isham Truitt, including the time and energy of practically every senior partner, has been devoted to one thing—locating this Lichine guy. This includes the Alabama cops, the Department of Justice, and Tessie's private eyes, who are currently named Womack and Povey. What they have all come up with may be described in one short word of two curt syllables—zero. Until last night, when the missing young Mr. Lichine showed up alone, without warning, of his own free will, in the apartment of our Mr. Paul Truitt at the Waldorf Towers."

"How do you know that?" Ira Bodmer said.

"There's a girl sits next to me at Brooklyn Union Law School," Sal Giudice said. "She works in the bookkeeping department at Waldorf Towers. It turns out that's not only where Mr. Truitt lives, but this Lichine boy's parents, she used to be an actress named Amelia Troy as well as a girl friend of David Fillmore, she and her husband they also live in the Waldorf Towers."

"Why would Lichine turn himself in?" Ira Bodmer said.

"He's obviously decided to stop running," Sal Giudice said.

"By coming to Mr. Truitt he's dumped himself and his problem, whatever it is, squarely in the collective Isham Truitt lap. It looks to a Brooklyn Union man like the boys at Isham Truitt don't like this, but they can't help themselves. They've got to save Lichine's ass, and he turned himself over to them because he knows that they know—it's his ass or theirs. To save his as well as theirs, they can't use for bail any of the money at their command, which includes everything they and David Fillmore have tucked away in their mattresses and tax shelters and Swiss bank accounts as well as the Fillmore National vaults. They have to put their hands on money that can't be traced. You and I did that for them tonight. I'd feel better if we hadn't, but in our innocence we did. Now we've got to join the party and do what they're all doing."

"Which is what?" Ira Bodmer said.

"Save our ass," Sal Giudice said.

"How?" Ira Bodmer said.

"That depends," Sal Giudice said.

"On what?" Ira Bodmer said.

"Who this Lichine picks to defend him at that extradition hearing," Sal Giudice said.

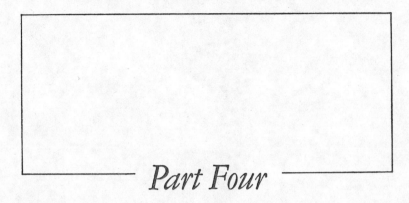

Part Four

"The law is a mouse-trap: easy to
enter but not easy to get out of."

LORD BALFOUR

20

"If Your Honor please," Judy Cline said, "I would like with your kind indulgence to make a short opening statement about why I have asked for this hearing under Section Five-seven-o of the Criminal Procedure Law of the State of New York."

Judy looked up from the words she had written on the yellow foolscap pad. They had seemed fine when she wrote them.

"If Your Honor please," she said, "I think I'd better take another crack at this."

Judy took a sip from her coffee cup, did some work with her pencil, then looked up again.

"Okay, Your Honor," she said. "We'll skip the kind indulgence, and never mind Section Five-seven-o of the Criminal Procedure Law of the State of New York. I'm going to stick to what I'm trying to say. Just the facts and no window dressing. Okay, Your Honor? . . . Thank you, sir."

She cleared her throat, sneaked a glancing look at herself in the mirror over her dressing table, and went back to the corrected words on the foolscap pad.

"In my opening statement, Your Honor," Judy said, "I would like to make clear—"

The doorbuzzer rasped. Judy looked at her watch. Six forty-two. "In the morning," she muttered. She pushed herself away from the dressing table, pulled the terry-cloth robe close, and put a more secure knot into the belt. Then she walked out of the bedroom, crossed to the front door, and slid aside the peephole cover.

"Oh, no," Judy said softly.

She undid the chain. She released the bar of the Fox lock. She shot the bolt of the Unwin Super Guard. And she returned to the "Off" position the switch of the Grinker electronic monitor. It had been recommended, and bought at a New York *Times* Group Discount rate, from the Eighty-second Street Tenants Association. Judy now twisted the knob and tugged the door. Nothing happened.

"Have you got an Unwin Super Guard in there?"

"Yes," Judy called through the locked door. "Why?"

"You've done the sequence wrong," the voice called back from the other side of the door. "You'll have to start again. Turn the monitor switch back to 'On,' then move the Unwin bolt to 'Open,' and the last thing turn the monitor to 'Off.'"

"Thanks," Judy said.

She followed instructions and tried the knob again. The door came open smoothly.

"It has nothing to do with you or geography," Bianca Bean said. "I've got the same trouble at our apartment on Third Avenue. May I come in?"

"Of course," Judy said.

She pulled the door wide. Tom Lichine's wife came in. She did it as though she were entering a stage set for what she had been told was a rehearsal but, unexpectedly, the lights had come on and she realized she had walked into a paid performance. Bianca Bean faltered on the threshold.

"Oops," she said, and then, after a slow sweeping glance around the room, she recovered with "I didn't know your place was so attractive."

"How could you?" Judy said. "You've never been here."

The bitchy tone was satisfying. Not, however, for long. Judy's mathematical mind, geared to thrust automatically toward accuracy, pushed her immediately into a distinction she had never before had occasion to make.

She had seen Bianca Bean only once before: three months ago at the girl's wedding to Tom Lichine. It had been a confused half hour in Judge Rosella's chambers in the New York Supreme Court Building on Centre Street. Judy had a fuzzy recollection of familiar faces unexpectedly gone out of focus. Tom Lichine looking like an uneasy contestant on a TV quiz show. His mother doing an embarrassed imitation of Myrna Loy forgetting the brittle zinger she was supposed to hurl at William Powell in a Late Late Show rerun of *The Return of the Thin Man*. Tom's father looking the way the senior Lichine had always looked to Judy: a wax figure that had lost much of its paint and was waiting nervously for Madame Tussaud's crew to carry it out and make room for John Travolta. Clifford Cline smiling with avuncular indulgence on a scene he could have improved with a few deft lines. Judy's mother, Nellie, looking as though she had been summoned to the office of Harry Winston to receive her long-overdue due: the Hope Diamond. Only to discover Mr. Winston had summoned her merely to act as a witness to the legality of his presenting the great prize to a teen-age doxy who was about to become the latest Mrs. Rex Harrison.

Judy remembered only two unfamiliar faces in the scene: Judge Rosella, who looked like a New York *Times* picture of a distinguished jurist being arraigned for bribery before an as yet still unapprehended colleague, and Tom Lichine's bride, who looked like everything his mother and Judy's mother had been saying about Bianca Bean during the week since she had unexpectedly surfaced in their lives as Tom's prospective bride.

Now, three months later, at six forty-five in the morning in her own untidy living room on West Eighty-second Street, Judy saw that her recollection was wrong. Either that, or twelve weeks of marriage to Tom Lichine had changed Bianca Bean's appearance to an astonishing degree. Astonishing to Judy Cline, anyway. She saw that she had been wrong to treat this young actress in her mind the way Judy treated the aging bimbo who queened it over the reception desk in the Isham Truitt outer office. Judy's dislike for Cheryl Marvin was based on the receptionist's dislike for all the younger Isham Truitt female employees, especially associates. Judy's dislike for Bianca Bean was based, she suddenly grasped, on the fact that Tom Lichine's mother and Judy's mother, who was Amelia Troy's best friend, both felt Amelia Troy's son and Nellie Cline's godson had married beneath him. The moment of clarity brought with it a moment of doubt. Perhaps Tom Lichine had not married beneath him? More accurately: how did Judy Cline know he had?

"And the fact that you've never been here before is my fault," Judy said. "I can't expect you to come hammering on my door and demanding that you be admitted into a home to which you've never been invited."

The neat, bright, shiny little blond girl in the tightly belted trench coat gave Judy a quick, darting look. The surprise was genuine. So was the abrupt pink flush that swept the high cheekbones. Neither was the result of a director's nudge.

"And yet that's what I'm doing," Bianca Bean said with a halting, frightened, tentative little smile that was a revelation. Judy Cline could see that smile coming across the footlights somewhere without warning and breaking her heart. Well, somebody's heart.

Steeling herself to dispense no more than the polite, not unpleasant welcome to which even a total stranger was entitled, Judy said, "I'm glad you are. It's my fault I haven't seen you since the wedding. I could say I've been up to my ears, and it would be true, but it's no excuse. Please come in and sit here and I'll get coffee."

"Don't bother," Bianca Bean said. "I don't want to be a nuisance."

"It's no bother," Judy said. "I've got a fresh pot all made. I won't be a minute."

She wasn't much longer than that, but it was long enough for Judy to face up to the question that had hit her a few minutes ago in the doorway. How did Judy Cline know Tom Lichine had married beneath him? Answer: she didn't. Not after the events of the last two weeks.

"I take it black, so I don't ever have any cream in the house," she said as she came back into the living room with the tray. "But I do have this Half 'n' Half if you like it?"

"I don't but Tom does," Bianca Bean said. "So now I just automatically keep it in the refrigerator when he's in residence."

The pint of Half 'n' Half on the tray between them had gotten into Judy Cline's refrigerator for the same reason, but she did not volunteer the information.

"Now what can I do for you?" she said, sitting back with her cup.

"You can tell me if Tom is in prison," Bianca Bean said.

"You mean he's not at home?" Judy said.

It was the wrong thing to say, and Judy knew it, but the right thing required sorting out more facts than she had in her possession at the moment.

"You know he's not," Bianca Bean said quietly. "And he hasn't been for a month, since the office sent him down to Alabama."

"Who told you he's in prison?" Judy said.

"Mrs. Lichine," Bianca Bean said.

"You consider that a reliable source?" Judy said.

"Of course not," Bianca Bean said. "That's why I'm here now."

"You consider me a reliable source?" Judy said.

"More reliable than Mrs. Lichine," Bianca Bean said.

"Why?" Judy said.

"She's his mother," Bianca Bean said. "You're his friend."

It was like that moment at the door when Judy had been forced into an assessment of why she did not have the right to bracket this kid in her mind with the veteran at the Isham Truitt reception desk. The kid was show biz, what to Judy Cline had always meant her father and her mother and Amelia Troy and the people with whom they lived their lives like angleworms in a bottle. If Bianca Bean was not show biz, what was she doing in show biz? Not much, Judy guessed, but that guess could mean no more than not much yet. She was, Judy reminded herself, only nineteen. At nineteen Julie Andrews had knocked them dead in *My Fair Lady* and at nineteen Lauren Bacall had married Humphrey Bogart. A similar destiny could be waiting in the wings for this blond kid with the open, shiny face who was nestled on Judy Cline's couch. Until it happened, however, the kid had to be judged on the evidence available. What was available to Judy was what she saw, and what she saw had a quality of candor that demanded the sorting out of imprecise images.

"What's the difference?" Judy said.

"If a mother expects her son to marry Grace Kelly's daughter she'll hate anybody he marries who isn't," Bianca Bean said. "A friend never expects her friend to marry anybody until he does, and then she could hate the girl for doing it, but that doesn't mean she'd necessarily lie to the girl about things like is he in prison or not."

"I wouldn't lie about it for a simpler reason," Judy said.

"What's that?" Bianca Bean said.

"I'm a lawyer," Judy said.

"Is Tom in prison?" Bianca Bean said.

"No," Judy said. "He's in jail."

A look of disappointment washed across the bright, scrubbed face like a wet felt eraser sweeping across a blackboard. For a puzzled moment Judy wondered what it meant. Then the moment caught up with her and Judy Cline felt her face grow warm. The attractive youngster in the trench coat was disappointed. In guess what? Or who? Judy Cline, that's who. Bianca Bean, Judy saw, had not expected smart aleckry.

"That's not intended as a joke," Judy said, trying and she was sure failing in an effort to conceal a defensive note. She felt like a teacher in school who has fallen down in the eyes of a trusting pupil and hurries to make amends. "There's a technical difference," Judy said. "I think you should understand it."

"All right," the trusting pupil said with a flat, let's-see-if-you-can-retrieve-yourself inflection.

"I don't know what happened down in Alabama," Judy Cline said. "Hopefully we'll find out at this extradition hearing today. I do know what happened to Tom here in New York. Which is why he's not in prison but in jail. All right?"

"So far," Bianca Bean said.

"Ten days ago in Alabama a grand jury handed down an indictment against Tom for murder. Tom was no longer in Alabama. He had come back to New York. So the chief executive officer of the state of Alabama asked the chief executive officer of the state of New York to arrest Tom and send him back to Alabama to stand trial. In legal jargon that means that through the legal jargon machinery set up for such matters, the governor of New York refers the request to the district attorney of New York County. The district attorney of New York County sends out a police officer with a warrant for the arrest of Tom Lichine. The police officer takes Tom down to jail at 100 Centre Street. Tom is booked. He says I want to call my lawyer. He does so. Tom's lawyer comes hustling down to Centre Street with an application for a writ of habeas corpus. You know what that means?"

"Last year I did *Counselor at Law* for two weeks in summer stock," Bianca Bean said. "It means I demand that the court turn over to me the body of my client."

"Correct," Judy said. "Unfortunately 100 Centre Street is a busy place and there are never enough judges to handle all the work as fast as they should. This means they don't always get around to answering all the demands made on behalf of arrested clients by all the lawyers on the day they're made. Almost always the man who has been arrested has to hang around for hours until his lawyer's request is heard. Sometimes it's longer than a few hours. Sometimes the man has to wait overnight or even longer. That's what happened to Tom. He was brought to Centre Street two days ago. They didn't get around to him so he was held overnight. Yesterday Tom was arraigned. After listening to Tom's lawyer the judge ordered him to make his application for a writ of habeas corpus to the New York Supreme Court, Special Term, Part Two. The supreme court in this state is not the equivalent of the Supreme Court in Washington. In New York State the equivalent of the Washington Supreme Court is the Court of Appeals. In New York the supreme court is the supreme court of the First Judicial District, which covers the Bronx and Manhattan. Tom's lawyer did as he was told. He made his application on Tom's behalf for a writ of habeas corpus to the Civil Branch of Special Term, Part Two of the New York Supreme Court, and this morning at ten o'clock the application will be heard."

"Meaning what?" Bianca Bean said.

"The judge may be impressed with the reasons Tom's lawyer gives for demanding the writ of habeas corpus," Judy said. "In which case the judge signs the writ and Tom is set free."

"They won't send him back to Alabama?" Bianca Bean said.

"No," Judy said.

"What if the judge doesn't sign the writ?" Bianca Bean said.

"Then the extradition hearing must be held," Judy Cline said.

"In which case the judge releases Tom on bail, or in the custody of his lawyer, or on his own recognizance, so that Tom and his lawyer can prepare themselves to face the opposition of the district attorney, who will be presenting the case for Tom's extradition based on the evidence he gets from the district attorney in Alabama. That's the mechanics of the thing."

"What happens to Tom is not mechanics," Bianca Bean said. "What happens to Tom depends on what happens at that extradition hearing."

"That's right," Judy said.

"And what happens at that hearing could depend on how good a lawyer Tom has," Bianca Bean said.

"On that point," Judy Cline said, "I wouldn't worry."

"Why not?" Bianca Bean said.

"The man defending Tom is one of the greatest and most successful lawyers this country has ever known," Judy Cline said.

"Who is that?" Bianca Bean said.

"Did you ever hear of Howard Dent?" Judy Cline said.

21

"It seems to me for the last two weeks I haven't heard of anybody else," Nellie Cline said.

"No kidding?" Mrs. Kelly said.

"It's not a subject I would ordinarily consider a fruitful source of raw material for humor," Nellie Cline said.

The fat woman at the head of the table looked startled. Or as startled as the face of Mrs. Hugh F. X. Kelly, Jr., was capable of looking. It was a face that to Nellie Cline clearly showed more than every one of the seventy-eight years through which its owner had lived. It showed the way during all those years the owner had worn that face. As a shield between herself and the rest of the world. Mrs. Kelly's face had spent its life on the defensive. It was dented and bruised by not-quite-parried blows. It had lost the capacity to lean forward and peer with curiosity. It had learned to live in a leaning-back position, sunk in its own tonnage, waiting for orders. Nellie Cline still did not know why the wife of her daughter's boss had invited her to lunch, but all at once Nellie knew where the invitation had originated.

"What I mean," Mrs. Kelly said, "I mean I know Howard Dent is a famous man and all that, but not in the way like say Bob Hope or Jimmy Carter. You know?"

"I'm not quite sure that I do," Nellie Cline said.

It was as though without warning she had criticized Mrs. Kelly's dress, which was a name designer's mistake. Or mocked the fat woman's accent, which was Irish Sam Levenson. The chatelaine of this expensive dining room cringed.

"Howard Dent is of counsel," Mrs. Kelly said. "Even for a younger man that's like being put on the shelf, sort of, which in Howard's case is about time on account of he's going to be ninety-two next August the twenty-ninth."

"Ninety-two," Nellie Cline said.

With a small, lady-like exclamation point in her voice.

"Ninety-two," Mrs. Kelly said. "I know I'm right because me and Mr. Kelly, we were married on an August twenty-ninth. On our fortieth anniversary the cardinal gave us a little private party in the parish house, and he made a lovely little speech with a nice little toast, and then the other people made little speeches. Nothing fancy, you understand, but for the sentiment of the occasion, a wedding anniversary with old friends, and when it came Howard Dent's turn, guess what he said?"

"I couldn't possibly," Nellie Cline said.

"He lifted up his champagne very high, like this," Mrs. Kelly said, "and he said 'this is a happy occasion for me. Not only because I have known Maxine and Hugh Kelly all during the forty years of their married life, but also because every time Maxine and Hugh celebrate one of their anniversaries I celebrate a birthday.' That's what Howard said, so I know Howard's birthday is on August twenty-ninth. I also remember when he said it that time, the cardinal spoke up and he said 'would it be indiscreet, Mr. Dent, to inquire how many years the Heavenly Father has blessed you with on this day,' and guess what he said?

"'Not indiscreet at all, Your Eminence,' Howard said. 'I am proud to admit I am eighty-three years old today, and I still have in my head every tooth the Heavenly Father blessed me with at birth.' He was kidding around a little there, because Howard always makes jokes about Catholics. In a nice way, of course, because Howard is a real gentleman to his fingertips, but that was in 1970. Now we're in 1978, which is eight years later, so if you add eight to eighty-three you get ninety-one. It's only a matter of a few days, though, and he'll be ninety-two officially, which is pretty good, isn't it?"

"Better than that," Nellie Cline said. "I must confess Mr. Dent is the only man of ninety-one going on ninety-two whose name I've been hearing so frequently these last two weeks that I feel he's a member of my family, which of course he isn't, so I can't help wondering why."

"I can tell you the reason for that," Mrs. Kelly said.

Before she could get under way, however, the swing door at the far end of the room chunked open and the butler reappeared with the silver tray.

"You'll have some more?" Mrs. Kelly said to her guest.

"No, thank you," Nellie Cline said. "I'll wait for the dessert you praised so highly."

"Wait till you see it," Mrs. Kelly said.

"Don't tell me," Nellie Cline said. "I like to be surprised."

"You will be, honest," Mrs. Kelly said. "This new chef my husband hired, desserts are Samuel's specialty. He never tells us what it's going to be because Samuel likes it to come as a surprise. He's been with us almost two months and would you believe it, every time it comes in from the kitchen it's a knockout."

"Before it does," Nellie Cline said, "I wonder if you'd tell me why I keep hearing Howard Dent's name so often these days?"

"It's on account of the Lichine boy," Mrs. Kelly said. "What happened down in Alabama? You know about him?"

"Indeed I do," Nellie Cline said. "I'm his godmother."

"You don't mean it," Mrs. Kelly said.

"It's hardly the sort of thing one would lie about," Nellie Cline said.

"No, no, of course not," Mrs. Kelly said. "I wouldn't dream of such a thing. It's just when my husband asked I should invite you to lunch, Hugh didn't tell me that."

"What did Mr. Kelly tell you?" Nellie Cline said.

"Oh, my God," Mrs. Kelly said.

"I beg your pardon?" Nellie Cline said.

"He told me I shouldn't tell you he was the one told me to invite you to lunch," Mrs. Kelly said.

"I won't repeat it," Nellie Cline said.

"You mean it?" Mrs. Kelly said.

"Cross my heart," Nellie Cline said, and she did.

The sagging face stopped attempting the impossible: a further descent into its supporting collar of dewlaps.

"I appreciate that," Mrs. Kelly said. "I really do, because the only thing that gets my Hugh mad is if you don't follow his instructions."

"What were they?" Nellie Cline said.

"I should invite you to lunch," Mrs. Kelly said, "and I should ask your permission if we can take your daughter Judy—that's her name, isn't it?"

"Yes," Nellie Cline said. "Judith."

"Hugh wants me to ask you if we can take Judy with us as our guest all expenses paid to Rome next month?" Mrs. Kelly said.

"Rome as in Italy?" Nellie Cline said.

"Yes, Rome, you know, it's in Italy," Mrs. Kelly said. "I'm sure you saw in the papers the President just appointed Hugh his special liaison officer they call it with the Vatican."

"I certainly did," Nellie Cline said. "And I congratulate you."

"Thank you," Mrs. Kelly said. "It's a great honor, we feel, and we're going over next month for a couple of weeks. Rome is always such a pleasure for Hugh, and me, too, of course, and this time he thinks it will be an even greater pleasure, what with it's official this time, the liaison thing, if you know what I mean."

"Of course," Nellie Cline said. "It sounds terribly exciting."

"That's just the way Hugh put it," Mrs. Kelly said. "For a young girl, a trip like that, meeting His Holiness and all, Hugh said it would be terribly exciting for her. Not to mention the extra pleasure it would be for us. We've been to Rome many times, of course, Hugh and I, but we've never been with any of our children because whenever Hugh and I were going, they were always all tied up in one way or another, school or college or having babies or something, if you know what I mean."

"I can imagine," Nellie Cline said.

"And I'm sure you know how fond Hugh is of your Judy," Mrs. Kelly said.

"I do, and I'm deeply flattered," Nellie Cline said. "So is my husband."

"Hugh thinks your Judy has the best legal real estate mind he's ever come across," Mrs. Kelly said. "You know what he has planned for her?"

"What?" Nellie Cline said.

"You won't tell her?" Mrs. Kelly said.

"Cross my heart," Nellie Cline said.

For a moment she considered doing it again. Her dramatic instincts, however, had been honed by a long marriage to a playwright and an equally long friendship with an actress. Nellie Cline's dramatic instincts shook their cautionary heads at her from the wings. She desisted.

"Hugh plans to train your Judy to take over one day from him as the caretaker of all the church real estate in the archdiocese," Mrs. Kelly said. "It means a partnership, of course, which is no small thing for a young girl to be heading for, is it?"

"Not an Isham Truitt partnership," Nellie Cline said.

"Hugh feels it would be a nice thing for his plan," Mrs. Kelly said, "if he could introduce your daughter at this early stage to His Holiness as his protégé, and then when we come back from Rome take her to lunch with the cardinal. The Vatican visit will carry a lot of weight in her favor, because the cardinal has a very independent mind. He likes to get all the advice he can from all the reliable people he knows and trusts, people like Hugh, for example, but in the end His Eminence always makes up his own mind. Hugh feels the earlier he plants the seed with the cardinal about his grooming Judy to be his successor, the better, don't you agree?"

"I certainly do," Nellie Cline said. "Does Mr. Dent also agree?"

The sagging face achieved the impossible. Or seemed to. Nellie Cline would have sworn it sank noticeably deeper into the collar of dewlaps.

"Howard?" Mrs. Kelly said, staring wide-eyed across the table at the life-size white marble statue of the Virgin and Child beside the windows that faced Central Park. "What's he got to do with it?"

"I don't know," Nellie Cline said. "I thought you were explaining to me why I've been hearing Mr. Dent's name so frequently these last two weeks."

"I told you it's because of the Lichine boy," Mrs. Kelly said uneasily. "I'm sure I told you that, didn't I?"

"Yes, you did," Nellie Cline said. "But then you went on about you and Mr. Kelly wanting my permission to take Judy with you to Rome, and I felt there was some connection."

"There must be," Mrs. Kelly said.

"Don't you know?" Nellie Cline said.

"Hugh didn't tell me," Mrs. Kelly said.

"Perhaps you could ask him?" Nellie Cline said.

"Oh, no," Mrs. Kelly said.

"Why not?" Nellie Cline said.

"Hugh wouldn't like that," Mrs. Kelly said.

"I see," Nellie Cline said.

It proved to be the wrong thing to say. At the other end of the table the sagging face seemed to pull together an unsuspected network of concealed muscular underpinning. It came up out of its tonnage with a touch of truculence.

"No, you don't see," Mrs. Kelly said. "Hugh asks me to do things and I do them. I don't make connections. Hugh likes to do that himself. I do my part, and that's all, which about today is he told me what to tell you. He told me to do it at lunch, and he told me to make sure the lunch was delicious."

"It has certainly been that," Nellie Cline said.

The swing door chunked open. The butler came in. He looked stricken under the vast painting of the Descent from the Cross that guarded the entrance to the kitchen.

"Dennis, what is it?" Mrs. Kelly said.

"Samuel dropped the pie," the butler said.

Nellie Cline's mind was already at work on her telephone call to Amelia Troy. In it she was deep into fashioning this meeting into one of the witty anecdotes that for a quarter century had bound the two women to each other. Nellie's skilled mind told her she was on the brink of one of her better achievements. Her editorial instincts, however, warned that the anecdote was not yet complete. It lacked a clean, sharp finish. With relief the seasoned performer stepped fearlessly into the disaster area in quest of what was missing.

"What kind of pie is it?" Nellie Cline said.

"Apple, madame," the butler said.

"My favorite," Nellie Cline said.

She turned to her hostess with a curtain line she felt even Amelia Troy would applaud.

"Mrs. Kelly," Nellie Cline said, "I've earned my dessert by giving up my second helping of that delicious roast. Would you please ask Dennis to get a clean spoon and scoop up a generous portion of that apple pie for me?"

22

Not for the first time Judy Cline found herself wondering about the people who design courtrooms.

Judging by the arenas in which justice fought for its existence, some of these designers could have been pranksters. A few, perhaps many, must have been charlatans. The faceless group was entitled, however, to what the law granted the rest of humanity: the presumption of innocence. Looking around Special Term, Part Two of the New York Supreme Court, where Howard Dent in ten minutes was scheduled to argue his application for Tom Lichine's writ of habeas corpus, Judy wondered what a presumption of innocence in architectural design added up to.

"You look troubled."

Judy turned to the old man sitting beside her at counsels' table. Howard Dent, she noted, had decorated himself for the occasion with the jazzy bow tie he had worn when he gave her lunch in his Plaza suite two weeks ago. Judy wondered what the designer of the mahogany and sandstone cavern in which they were seated would have thought of the way the red, green, and gold stripes zigged and zagged across the scrap of pale-blue satin under the long bony chin of the man Stalin had denounced at Potsdam as "Harry Truman's Colonel House."

"Not troubled," Judy said. She was sure the lie would be accepted for what it was: a stab at professional correctness. "Just puzzled," she said.

"About what?" Howard Dent said.

"This place we're sitting in," Judy said.

The lean head moved swiftly. Left, right, up, around, and back to Judy.

"I've lived so much of my life in courtrooms," Howard Dent said, "all I ever see now when I walk into one is the judge's bench, the jury box, and the nearest exit to the men's room. What do you see that puzzles you?"

"It's what I don't see," Judy said. "The people who design courtrooms."

"Come to think of it," Howard Dent said, "I never heard the name of a courtroom designer spoken aloud. Which one did you have in mind?"

"All of them," Judy said. "I haven't been inside many courtrooms, and I've never thought much about them, but this one seems to me to be typical."

The handsome white-haired head made another darting sweep around the huge spaces by which its owner and Judy were surrounded.

"'Typical' is one of those words," Howard Dent said. "Like 'average man.' You don't remember F.P.A., of course."

"My father does," Judy said. *The Conning Tower.* "My father is always quoting him."

"In that case I'll risk quoting him now," Howard Dent said. "The average man, F.P.A. once pointed out, is not so average. The same could be true of courtrooms."

"Only in details," Judy said. "Basically they're all alike."

"In what way?" Howard Dent said.

"The tendency they have to overwhelm you," Judy said. "The last one I was in, out in Queens yesterday, you could fit the whole operation into a corner of this place, but I had that same feeling the architect had been trying to reproduce what my fine-arts text at Radcliffe called and I quote the dodecagonal chapter house of a Gothic cathedral whose corporate body numbered half a thousand canons unquote."

"What a satisfying student you must have made for some Radcliffe instructor in fine arts," Howard Dent said. "Now tell me what's wrong with reproducing as a theater for the law the dodecagonal chapter house of a Gothic cathedral?"

"It's taking unfair advantage," Judy said. "You haven't even had a chance to open your mouth. You've just walked in, and already the place is giving you that over-the-glasses look. Watch your step, kid. Mind your manners. This is no place in which to fool around. Before you put down your briefcase and slide back the zipper, your surroundings are cutting you down to size, telling you what you came here for is not as important to the rest of the world as it is to you."

"Whose side are you on?" Howard Dent said.

"Tom Lichine's, of course," Judy said.

"So am I," Howard Dent said. "The designers of courtrooms, however, are not primarily concerned with Tom Lichine. They're concerned with all the Tom Lichines who will be coming into their creations over a long period of time for a serving of the same fairness Tom Lichine is seeking here this morning."

"If you're fair to one Tom Lichine," Judy said, "I always assumed in the long run you're being fair to all the Tom Lichines who come along later."

"Your assumption is correct," Howard Dent said. "It will never be more than an assumption, however, unless it is implemented. The designers of courtrooms are part of the implementation process. Lord Hardwicke once observed that certainty is the mother of repose, and therefore the law aims at certainty. That's what the designer of this courtroom aimed at. You and I have come here today to see that justice is done to Tom Lichine. Suppose we were summoned to do our jobs in the back room of some grocery store, or a high school auditorium that happens to be unoccupied at the moment. Do you think our effort to make sure the law is fair to Tom Lichine would have as good a chance of success as it has here in this intimidating imitation of a dodecagonal chapter house?"

"I don't see why not," Judy said.

"Here comes an illustration that will help you see why not," Howard Dent said and, across Judy's head, added, "Good morning, Murray."

"Good morning, Howard," the sandy-haired man said. "I see you've brought your usual handsome claque."

"Judy, this irreverent gentleman is Murray Hyatt," Howard Dent said. "More formally, J. Murray Hyatt, a good specimen of the sort of raffish friend a man who has lived as long as I have is bound to accumulate over the years. Mr. Hyatt is not a very good lawyer, but he is a very good politician. As a result he has many friends in high as well as low office. One of these is Herman L. Hofnagel, the warden of the City Prison in the Borough of Manhattan, who is the respondent in this habeas corpus action. Mr. Hofnagel doesn't care who gets the fee for defending him, since it comes out of the public treasury, but Murray does care because he is on the district attorney's staff and it is part of his job to make the public feel he works for his salary, so we will have to endure Mr. Hyatt's company for the next few hours. Murray, this is not a claque. This is Miss Judith Cline of the Isham Truitt staff. She will be acting as my assistant here today. I know it will be difficult for you, Murray, but for the sake of our old friendship I ask you to make a special effort and mind your manners. Miss Cline is not accustomed to the low company I am accustomed to keeping."

The sandy-haired man bowed.

"This is a great pleasure, Miss Cline," he said. "Howard can always be counted on to brighten the dreariness of a courtroom by bringing along a lovely member of the fair sex to applaud his efforts, but today he has outdone himself. I regret to say that it will do you no good, however, because we have your cat all wrapped up and addressed and ready for shipment to Alabama. We will be carrying him to the post office as soon as the formalities are attended to by Judge McNally."

"Here he is now," Howard Dent said. "So will you remove yourself to the far end of the table, Murray, and try to restrain your misplaced self-confidence, meaning shut up while your betters are talking."

Mr. Hyatt smiled at Judy, bowed again, and moved off to the end of the long, heavy table. He did not sit down because the judge was in motion, crossing from the side door to the high-backed chair in the center of the bench. The uniformed attendant as well as the few spectators spread around the large chamber were all getting to their feet. Howard Dent and Judy did the same. The judge reached the center of the bench. He set down the file folder he was carrying, and looked out into the court-

room with a sudden, shy, surprisingly sweet smile, as though astonished to discover he was not alone. He bobbed his head and
said, "Be seated, please."

A look of annoyance crossed the face of the uniformed attendant to the left and slightly below the bench. He clearly felt the
judge had taken the words out of his mouth.

"Be seated, please," the attendant said in a slightly breathless
catching-up voice.

Along with Howard Dent and Mr. Hyatt and the few spectators, Judy sat down. Judge McNally fitted a rimless pince-nez to
the bridge of his nose and opened the file folder.

"Habeas corpus," he said almost inaudibly to nobody in particular. "*Thomas L. Lichine, Jr.* v. *Herman L. Hofnagel,* as warden of the City Prison, Borough of Manhattan, defendant. For
the relator, Howard—"

Again with the small, sweet, shy smile Judge McNally looked
up in surprise.

"Well, Mr. Dent," he said with an unmistakable touch of deference. "I haven't had the pleasure of seeing you for a long
time. Your hip is mended, I hope, and you're keeping well?"

Howard Dent came to his feet saying, "Yes, I think so, thank
you, Your Honor."

"Well enough to get us under way?" the judge said.

"Yes, Your Honor," Howard Dent said.

"Then please do, Mr. Dent," the judge said.

He put the tips of his fingers together to form a cage, leaned
back in the tall, leather-upholstered chair, and smiled down on
the tall, thin, white-haired figure.

"If Your Honor please," Howard Dent said. "My client,
Thomas Lichine, Jr., has been detained upon a warrant issued by
the governor of this state for extradition to the state of Alabama.
It is alleged by the district attorney of Yates County in Alabama
that Mr. Lichine committed in that jurisdiction the crime of
murder in the second degree at approximately twenty minutes
after one o'clock in the afternoon on Thursday, August 10, 1978."

Howard Dent paused to look up at the judge as though he had
come to a convenient stopping place in his reading. It was only
then that Judy Cline realized the old man had not been reading.

Howard Dent had been staring with a small frown at the toes of his gleaming Vici kid shoes as he rolled out the smooth flow of words.

"My client, Your Honor, was not in the state of Alabama on the date when the crime is alleged to have been committed," Howard Dent said. "My client seeks, therefore, to challenge the legality of his detention. He asks that his writ of habeas corpus be granted so that he may be discharged from custody. Thank you, Your Honor."

Howard Dent sat down. Judge McNally glanced briefly at his file.

"Mr. Hyatt, yes," he said, again in that scarcely audible mumble to nobody in particular. Then he looked up, adjusted his pince-nez, and said, "Do you want to add anything, Mr. Hyatt?"

"Not at the moment, Your Honor," the sandy-haired man said.

It was the usual defense counsel we're-biding-our-time reply to which even in her limited courtroom experience Judy had grown accustomed. She would have thought nothing of this one if, when the words were spoken, her glance had not been resting on Howard Dent. Her eyes recorded a darting upward flick of his long bony forefinger at one of the wings of the pale-blue satin bow tie. The movement took Judy by surprise. Also, it left a small residue of uneasiness, and caused her to send a quick glance at the far end of counsels' table. Mr. Hyatt's pouched little face was set in a smug smile.

Howard Dent looked up from his papers and said, "I will call Thomas L. Lichine, Jr., please."

The uniformed attendant came to his feet as though, after throwing leisurely for a while in the bull pen, he had at last received the signal from the manager in the dugout to come out and relieve.

"Thomas L. Lichine, Jr.," he called in a voice somewhere between an uneasy bark and an unpremeditated roar. "Come forward, please."

Judy did not exactly turn. She was not eager to display special interest. She did, however, want to see if Tom was alone. Judy compromised by leaning forward and down so that, with a forefinger, she was able to ease away the nonexistent pressure of

a perfectly comfortable shoe on her instep. The small performance gave her a casual, slanting backward glance into the courtroom behind her. Tom Lichine was not alone. Or rather, he
had not been alone before he started down the aisle in response
to the clerk's summons. Behind him, in the second seat in from
the aisle, Tom Lichine had left his wife, Bianca.

She was wearing, in addition to the trench coat in which she
had rung Judy's doorbell at six forty-five that morning, a look of
slightly open-mouthed concern delicately mixed with unmistakably affectionate pride. It was the sort of look that, when
Judy was a small girl, only one actress to her knowledge had
ever been able to achieve on the screen. Judy's father maintained
it was the look that had made Margaret Sullavan a star.

The attention the look was attracting from the few spectators
now scattered around Bianca Bean suggested to Judy that it was
the hope of catching such a glimpse that had drawn these people
to a spectacle they could not have understood very much about,
or at this inconvenient hour of a business day been especially interested in, in a chamber that could have been no more comfortable for their modern rear ends than the dodecagonal chapter
house of a Gothic cathedral had been for half a thousand seven-
teenth-century canons.

"Raise your right hand, please."

Raising it, Tom Lichine, with a touch of elegantly executed
contempt, also placed his left hand on the Bible the clerk was
holding out like a tray of hors d'oeuvres intended for inspection
only.

"Do you solemnly swear to tell the truth, the whole truth, and
nothing but the truth, so help you God?"

"I do," Tom Lichine said.

His voice surprised Judy. She had been hearing Tom Lichine's
voice ever since that famous day in Central Park when Judy's
nanny had pulled her pram alongside Tom's. This was the first
time in the intervening quarter century, however, that Judy had
heard Tom Lichine's voice in a courtroom. Her feelings for his
career went up a couple of notches. Tom Lichine did not sound
like a witness. He sounded like a prosecuting attorney who had
been appointed by the political party currently in power.

"Be seated, please," the clerk said.

Tom did it, Judy noted, the way he did everything: leaving on the commonplace act a distinctive mark of his own. Before lowering himself into it, Tom Lichine gave the witness chair a careful glance. He could have been making sure it was clean enough for his carefully pressed gray flannel slacks. Howard Dent came forward, studying as he moved a sheet of foolscap. He stopped a few feet from the witness box and glanced at his toes. He could have been checking a line marked on the floor to make sure he had reached the correct distance between himself and the witness.

"Your name, please?" Howard Dent said.

"Thomas L. Lichine, Jr."

"And you reside where, Mr. Lichine?" Howard Dent said.

"Ten seventy-five Third Avenue, New York City," Tom Lichine said.

"Do you live alone?" Howard Dent said.

"No, sir," Tom Lichine said. "I live with my wife."

"Whose name is?" Howard Dent said.

"Bianca," Tom Lichine said.

"Your age, please?" Howard Dent said.

"Twenty-five," Tom Lichine said.

"Your profession?" Howard Dent said.

"I'm a lawyer, sir," Tom Lichine said.

"Are you presently engaged in active practice?" Howard Dent said.

"Yes, sir," Tom Lichine said.

"May I ask where, Mr. Lichine?" Howard Dent said.

"Here in New York, sir," Tom Lichine said.

"You are, then, a member of the Bar of the state of New York?" Howard Dent said.

"Yes, sir," Tom Lichine said.

"And have been for how long?" Howard Dent said.

"Ten months, sir," Tom Lichine said.

"Are you self-employed?" Howard Dent said.

"No, sir," Tom Lichine said. "I work for the firm of Isham, Truitt, Kelly, Shreve, Merz, Uchitel and Condomine, six-three-five Madison Avenue, New York, one-o-o-two-two."

"Can you tell us, Mr. Lichine, where you were at twenty minutes after one o'clock in the afternoon on Thursday, August 10, 1978?" Howard Dent said.

"Yes, sir," Tom Lichine said. "I was in the private office of Mr. Hugh F. X. Kelly, Jr., a senior partner in the firm of Isham, Truitt, Kelly, Shreve, Merz, Uchitel and Condomine at six-three-five Madison Avenue, New York, one-o-o-two-two."

"Were you at the time alone with Mr. Kelly?" Howard Dent said.

"No, sir," Tom Lichine said. "Two other people were present."

"Name them, please," Howard Dent said.

"You were one, sir," Tom Lichine said. "Miss Judith Cline was the other."

"Who is Miss Judith Cline?" Howard Dent said.

"An associate on the staff of Isham, Truitt, Kelly, Shreve, Merz, Uchitel and Condomine. Miss Cline is seated behind you, sir, at counsels' table."

"For the record, Your Honor," Howard Dent said, "Miss Cline is seated at counsels' table because she is acting as my assistant at this hearing."

"I understand, Mr. Dent," Judge McNally said.

"Thank you," Howard Dent said. He turned to the sandy-haired man at the end of counsels' table. "Your witness, Mr. Hyatt."

Howard Dent sat down. The assistant district attorney rose and came forward. He did it with head bowed, eyes fixed on his toes. Remembering the small, smug smile with which a few minutes earlier Mr. Hyatt had told the judge he had at the moment nothing to add, Judy all at once found herself wondering if the assistant district attorney was in a subtle way mocking the manner in which Howard Dent had approached the witness box. A couple of moments later Judy stopped wondering.

Mr. Hyatt paused and scowled appraisingly at his toes. He took a step backward. He paused. He inched himself half a step forward. He paused again. Then, apparently satisfied, he looked up at Tom Lichine in the witness box. He did it with a smile that would have been not inappropriate on the face of Sir Edmund

Hillary as he stepped out to join Tiger Tensing on the summit of Mount Everest.

Judy sent a fast glance to her left. She was quick enough to catch the long bony forefinger flicking upward at the wing of the jazzy bow tie. Judy felt a stab of sympathy for the old man who had asked her to assist him at this hearing. With it came a surge of rage at the sandy-haired man who had created this moment of mockery. Mr. Hyatt was apparently unaware that Howard Dent had only recently discarded his cane and, favoring his not quite completely mended hip, had to walk with care. It was possible that Mr. Hyatt was unaware of this, but it did not change the way Judy Cline felt. The name of J. Murray Hyatt, like that of Abou Ben Adhem on another compilation, now led all the rest on Judy Cline's private shit list.

"Tell me, Mr. Lichine," the assistant district attorney said. "By the way, that's Thomas L., is it not?"

"It is," Tom Lichine said.

"'L' for Learned?" Mr. Hyatt said. "As in Learned Hand, I hope?"

"No," Tom Lichine said. "'L' for Louis as in Lefkowitz. My father grew up with the former attorney general of the state of New York."

It was as though just as the conqueror of Everest took his place beside Sherpa Tensing for the official photograph, Sir Edmund had felt his boots begin to slip out from under him. The smile of conquest vanished.

"An admirable man to be named after," Mr. Hyatt said, struggling to recapture his balance. "Now of counsel to Phillips, Nizer, Benjamin, Krim and Ballon, as I'm sure you know."

"Yes," Tom Lichine said. "My father told me."

"I would like you to tell me something," the assistant district attorney said.

"If I can," Tom Lichine said.

"The warrant under which you have been detained for extradition asserts that you have been indicted in Alabama for a murder committed in that state at approximately one o'clock in the afternoon on Thursday, August 10, 1978," Mr. Hyatt said. "You have just stated under oath that at that time you were here in New York City attending a meeting in the office of a senior partner in the firm by which you are employed. Is that correct?"

"It is," Tom Lichine said.

"Can you prove that?" Mr. Hyatt said.

"I can," Tom Lichine said.

"How?" the district attorney said.

"Of the three people who attended that meeting with me," Tom Lichine said, "two are present in this courtroom right now. I have no reason to doubt that, when questioned under oath, Mr. Dent and Miss Cline will both tell the truth."

"What about the third person who is alleged by you to have been present at that meeting?" Mr. Hyatt said.

"I suggest you ask him," Tom Lichine said.

"He is not present," the district attorney said.

"Mr. Kelly has been a responsible member of the New York Bar for almost half a century," Tom Lichine said. "I am certain he will respond to a subpoena."

"This hearing has surely not been a secret in the offices of Isham, Truitt, Kelly, Shreve, Merz, Uchitel and Condomine," Mr. Hyatt said. "It seems reasonable to assume that the firm's of counsel as well as the associate serving here today as his assistant were both aware of the nature of your defense, were they not?"

"They were," Tom Lichine said.

"Knowing he was a part of your defense," the district attorney said, "I ask you why a man who has been a responsible member of the New York Bar for almost half a century did not choose to attend this hearing voluntarily instead of waiting to be summoned by subpoena?"

Howard Dent leaned forward, touched Judy Cline's elbow, and nodded. She stood up.

"If it please the court," Judy said. "I can answer that."

"So can I," Tom Lichine said, keeping his glance on the district attorney. "During the recent newspaper strike most citizens of this city managed to keep up with the news by listening to TV. Apparently, Mr. Hyatt, you did not. If you had, you would have known that a few days ago the President appointed Mr. Kelly his personal representative to the Vatican. Mr. Kelly leaves for Rome next week. He was summoned late yesterday to a briefing session at the White House this morning."

Judge McNally squeaked his high-backed leather chair forward and leaned his elbows on the bench.

"Mr. Hyatt," he said.

"Yes, Your Honor?" the assistant district attorney said.

"I suggest you move on," the judge said.

"Very well," the assistant district attorney said.

He turned his back on the witness box. For a few moments, staring at the floor, he worried his lower lip with thumb and forefinger. Then, with an abrupt movement, as though he had seized an invisible object to use as a fulcrum, he spun himself around.

"Mr. Lichine," he said. "Would you please tell us what took place at that meeting in Mr. Kelly's private office on Thursday, August 10, 1978."

Tom Lichine made a small leisurely ritual out of rearranging his body in the witness chair. He crossed his legs. He adjusted the crease in his flannels across the knees. He slid his spine up a few inches against the back rest.

"By advice of counsel," he said, "under Amendment Five of the Constitution I refuse to answer on the ground that such answer might incriminate or degrade me."

On the last word Tom Lichine uncrossed his legs. The assistant district attorney stared at him for several moments, then moved his head.

"If Your Honor please," he said.

"Yes?" Judge McNally said.

"I would like—" Mr. Hyatt said, then stopped.

Judge McNally, his face distorted by a sudden grimace of concern, was staring across the district attorney's head. Mr. Hyatt turned and saw Howard Dent's assistant on her feet.

"Your Honor," Judy Cline said, "may we have a recess for a few moments? Mr. Dent is—"

"No, I'm not," the old man said, but the denial lacked conviction. The words had been addressed to the table. Howard Dent was supporting himself on the polished wood with both hands, palms down.

Judge McNally pushed himself up out of the high-backed chair. He leaned far across the bench and made a hard, quick gesture to the uniformed guard. The guard was already in motion. He reached counsels' table as Judy Cline took Howard Dent's arm.

"I've got him," the guard said, taking the other arm. He leaned down to the old man's ear. "Can you walk, sir?"

"Of course I can walk," Howard Dent said irritably, but the unlikely statement did not have to be put to the test. Another guard, pushing a wheelchair, was on the way down the aisle at a half trot. He swung the chair parallel with counsels' table. The two men eased Howard Dent into the wheelchair. Judy Cline walked along with them up the aisle, out into the corridor, and down the steps to the sidewalk. They were greeted by a wailing siren. It was followed by an ambulance that pulled up at the curb in front of the courthouse steps.

The driver and a young man in whites transferred Howard Dent from the wheelchair to a stretcher, then eased the stretcher up into the ambulance. The intern fastened the straps across the thin body, then stepped across to pull the doors shut.

"Where do you think you're going?" he said.

"Wherever you are," Judy Cline said, climbing in.

23

"Miss Pember?"

"Speaking," said the voice at the other end of the phone.

"Judith Cline."

"What's with the Miss Pember?" Phoebe Pember said.

"I'm sorry," Judy Cline said. "Phoebe?"

"That's better," Phoebe Pember said.

"I apologize for interrupting you at lunch," Judy said.

"Don't," Phoebe Pember said. "I yielded to Yuki's blandishments and canceled my hamburger for a return engagement with the mizutaki. A bad mistake, as I knew it would be. Being summoned to the phone will not only allow the stuff to get cold, which means I can send it back, but it will add a small badly needed touch-up to my status image here at the Takashaki Garden. You sound troubled."

"I am," Judy said.

"What can I do to help?" Phoebe Pember said.

"Didn't you once tell me your fiancé works at New York Hospital?" Judy said.

"They think he works there," Phoebe Pember said. "Actually he runs the place. I also told you his name is Olin. Henry Olin, but his friends call him Hank, and any friend of mine is a friend of Henry's, which means you are authorized to call him Hank. Promise?"

"Of course," Judy Cline said. "I have to meet him first, however."

"How about a drink around six?" Phoebe Pember said.

"I may not get that far," Judy said.

"Trouble?" Phoebe Pember said.

"Yes," Judy said.

"Where are you?" Phoebe Pember said.

"In a phone booth in the lobby of New York Hospital," Judy Cline said.

"This phone is not tapped," Phoebe Pember said. "Everybody at Isham Truitt knows you're down on Centre Street in Special Term, Part Two helping Mr. Dent prevent those Alabama nasties from dragging the heartthrob of six-three-five Madison back under the Mason-Dixon line to face a trumped-up murder charge. Now start again. Where are you?"

"In a phone booth in the lobby of New York Hospital," Judy Cline said.

"Oh," Phoebe Pember said. Pause. When she came back on the wire Phoebe said quietly, "All right. Forget the levity. You're in a phone booth in the lobby of New York Hospital. Why?"

Judy told her.

"When I got out of the ambulance they wouldn't let me follow the stretcher into Emergency," she said. "They wouldn't tell me anything, either. That was an hour ago. I've been all over the place, including the director's office. Correction. The outer office of the director's office. All I've got is a fat collection of no-word-yets, plus you'll have to wait, please, and a blinding headache. I stopped running around and took two Bufferin. They helped me out of the panic and into a moment of reasonably clear thinking, and what surfaced was what you once told me about your fiancé—"

"Hank," Phoebe Pember said.

"Hank," Judy said, accepting with gratitude the therapy of the quietly spoken correction. "Anyway, here I am and—"

"What's the number of that phone booth?" Phoebe Pember said.

Judy read it off.

"Hang up and stay put," Phoebe Pember said. "Either I'll call you back in a couple of minutes or, if my luck holds, you will be picked up by the handsomest surgeon in New York."

Phoebe Pember's luck held. A few minutes later there was a

tap on the glass of the telephone-booth door. Judy Cline looked out at a young man in white. He had the sort of face that had been imbedded with admiration in the American pantheon by Will Rogers.

"You're Hank Olin," Judy said as she came out of the booth.

"You're Judy Cline," he said. "Let's get some coffee."

He led her along corridors, through groups waiting for elevators, and around orderlies shoving linen carts, into a cafeteria.

"Sit here," Hank Olin said.

Judy sat down. He crossed to the steam tables. Watching Phoebe Pember's fiancé carry a tray to the coffee urns and fill the cups, Judy decided that Phoebe was probably not exaggerating, certainly not by very much, when she described Henry Olin as the handsomest surgeon in New York. Judy remembered her father, a Will Rogers admirer, saying one thing for which the cowboy star had never received full credit was the fact that, in the Ziegfeld *Follies* that had brought him to fame, he was the handsomest star on the stage of the New Amsterdam Roof. The other stars of the show had been Ed Wynn, W. C. Fields, Eddie Cantor, and Fannie Brice.

"I forgot to ask if you take cream and sugar," Hank Olin said when he came back with the tray.

"I don't," Judy said.

"That's what I thought," he said. "Phoebe doesn't, either."

He sat down, facing Judy across the cups, took a sip, and pushed back his cowlick.

"It's his heart," Hank Olin said.

"Bad?" Judy said.

"Bad enough," Hank Olin said. "He's ninety-one, and he busted a hip eight months ago."

"After he gave up the cane, though," Judy said, "he seemed to be able to do pretty much what everybody around him did."

"Except go into court," Hank Olin said.

Judy looked up from her cup.

"A mistake?" she said.

"Not if it was just part of the day's work," Hank Olin said.

"Meaning what?" Judy said.

"How much this particular case meant to him," Hank Olin said.

Judy dropped her glance back to the cup. She knew why Howard Dent had insisted on defending Tom Lichine.

"How does he stand?" Judy said.

"Let me go see," Hank Olin said.

Judy forgot to look at her watch. She didn't realize she had forgotten until Hank Olin came back. She couldn't tell by her cup, either. She had not touched her coffee.

"Bad?" she said.

"Not good," Hank Olin said.

He sat down and picked up his cup. He got it to his lips but set it back on the table untasted.

"Let me get you a cup of hot," Judy said.

She started to push her chair back, but Olin reached across the table and touched her arm.

"No, thanks," he said. "I don't want any."

"What do you want?" Judy said.

He looked troubled. Judy could see how, when he had not been onstage or in front of a camera, Will Rogers would have been considered a very handsome man.

"I want to know how much this means to you," Hank Olin said.

"He's a man I met only two weeks ago," Judy said. "He didn't have to go into court today. He did it because the man on trial is a friend of mine. We've known each other all our lives. We grew up together."

"All right," Hank Olin said. "I'll go take another look."

When he was gone Judy went across to the serving counter and brought back two cups of fresh coffee. They were still sending up wisps of steam when Hank Olin came back. He sat down and took a sip from his cup.

"Hot," he said. "Thanks."

"Well?" Judy said.

"Not good," Hank Olin said.

"Worse?" Judy said.

"Afraid so," Hank Olin said. "I think I'd better go back for another look-see."

"Don't bother," Judy said.

Hank Olin looked startled.

"What do you mean?" he said.

"The last two look-sees," Judy said. "You didn't really have to go back for them either, did you?"

Hank Olin scowled down into his cup. The way he did it gave Judy a funny little feeling in her heart.

"I'm sorry," Hank Olin said.

"That's all right," Judy said.

It wasn't, but that was not Hank Olin's fault.

"It's what Phoebe told me," he said in a troubled voice.

"What was that?" Judy said.

"She told me he meant a great deal to you," Hank Olin said. "Phoebe told me she'd gotten the feeling you thought of him sort of like your father. Phoebe said if it was bad, I shouldn't hit you with it all at once."

"You didn't," Judy said.

The troubled look that made him so attractive raked her face.

"Phoebe said I should let you down easy," Hank Olin said.

"You did," Judy said. "Thanks."

"I wish there was something more I could do," Hank Olin said.

"There is," Judy said.

"What?" Hank Olin said.

"Don't let that girl get away," Judy said. "You've got yourself a good one."

24

The size of the crowd outside Campbell's was no surprise to Judy Cline. Howard Dent's obituary had started on the front page of the New York *Times* and carried over for three inside columns.

"What I always do when I bring Mr. Isham up to one of these things," said the driver of the office limousine, "I always park across the street there, near the Eighty-second Street corner, in front of the school."

"That will be fine, Tim," Judy said. "Isn't Mr. Isham coming to the funeral?"

"He's been in the area since nine o'clock," the driver said. "It was after I dropped him, miss, that he sent me across town I should pick you up."

"That's very nice of him," Judy said. "You, too. Isn't nine o'clock pretty early for a funeral?"

"Not this one," the driver said. "Mr. Isham's secretary told me he had a call from Mrs. Truman last night. She flew in from Independence special for this. On account of Mr. Dent was with her husband at Potsdam. She's staying with her daughter down the street at the Carlyle. Mrs. Truman invited Mr. Isham to come have breakfast with her. After I drop you I'm going over to the Carlyle to pick them up. This okay?"

"Fine, yes, thanks," Judy said.

Pushing through the crowd toward the Campbell's entrance on the Eighty-first Street corner, she caught the fragment of an icy exchange between Mayor Koch and a large hat. Judging by the voice under the hat, it could have been concealing Bella Abzug. Judy did not pause to verify. She kept going. In the entrance hall the crowd was more compact. Working her way toward the arch that led down into the chapel, Judy found herself confronted by Mr. Hugh F. X. Kelly, Jr. He took her arm.

"I knew Tim would not fail me," he said.

"He told me it was Mr. Isham who sent him to pick me up," Judy said.

"I planted the idea in Walter Isham's head," Mr. Kelly said. "Here, over this way, child."

He apparently meant a man in a black suit with a shaved skull. He had an enormous black cavalry mustache that curved upward like the horns of a miniature fighting bull.

"This way, Mr. Kelly," the man said.

He moved them across to a door at the other side of the entrance hall. He pushed it open, and led them into a small office.

"Will this be all right, Mr. Kelly?"

"As I heard Mr. Isham say to you only last week," Hugh Kelly said, "if you see that nobody interrupts us."

"I guarantee it, Mr. Kelly," the man said.

"Thank you," Hugh Kelly said.

The man went out and closed the office door.

"Sit down, child," Hugh Kelly said.

"Why don't we both?" Judy said.

She pulled a small straight-backed chair across from the wall and set it next to the small desk.

"An excellent notion," Hugh Kelly said.

He moved his bulk into the inadequate chair behind the small desk. Judy sat down on the chair she had brought across the room.

"This is a sorrowful business," Hugh Kelly said. "These things always are, of course, yet in this instance it is perhaps less sorrowful than most. Howard had achieved, after all, more than his biblical allotment of three score years and ten. A fully rounded two decades more, in fact. Our sorrow, therefore, is permissibly tempered with gratitude for the length of time the Heavenly Father allowed Howard to remain in our midst and brighten our lives. Nonetheless, your feelings for Howard were I think like mine somewhat deeper than those of the average person who crossed his path. I am pleased, therefore, to be able to offer you a change of venue. It should, I think, ease the understandable sorrow. At any rate, child, Mrs. Kelly and I trust that it will."

"What's that?" Judy said.

"I had a call from the President this morning," Hugh Kelly said. "He wants me to go to Rome at once."

"What does 'at once' mean?" Judy said.

"The plane leaves at seven," Hugh Kelly said.

"Tonight?" Judy said.

"It's the earliest flight the State Department could arrange," Hugh Kelly said.

"What about Tom Lichine?" Judy said.

"I don't understand," Hugh Kelly said.

"His extradition hearing," Judy said. "We're defending him."

"Howard Dent was defending him," Hugh Kelly said.

"Mr. Dent is dead," Judy said.

"New York is full of lawyers who are not," Hugh Kelly said. "There's nothing *sui generis* about pleading a writ of habeas corpus."

"What could be more *sui generis* than the witnesses on whom the plea is based?" Judy said.

"Now, look, child," Hugh Kelly said. "I'm talking about my responsibility to the President."

"I'm talking about our responsibility to Tom Lichine," Judy said. "His defense is that at the time he is supposed to have committed that murder in Alabama he was actually attending a meeting in your office here in New York. Three people were in that office with Tom Lichine. One of them is dead. That leaves you and me. If you go to Rome without testifying, that leaves only me."

"You forget that you're going to Rome with me, child," Hugh Kelly said.

"No, I'm not," Judy said.

"Your mother told Mrs. Kelly you are," Hugh Kelly said.

"My mother told Mrs. Kelly she was flattered by your invitation," Judy said. "When my mother passed the invitation on to me, I also said I was flattered, and other things being equal I would be happy to accept. That was three days ago. Other things stopped being equal yesterday. We have an obligation to Tom Lichine. We can't walk out on it."

"You keep saying 'we,'" Hugh Kelly said. "You sound like one of the heroes of my youth. Charles Lindbergh never claimed sole responsibility for his great achievement. He gave full credit to his collaborator *The Spirit of St. Louis*. Whenever Lindbergh referred to that achievement he always said 'we.' You and I, child, our situation in this Lichine matter is entirely different. You and I are not responsible for what Tom Lichine may or may not have done down there in Alabama."

"Mr. Dent felt we were," Judy said.

"How do you know that?" Hugh Kelly said.

"He told me so," Judy said.

"When?" Hugh Kelly said.

"When Mr. Dent urged me to use my influence with Tom Lichine to get him to appoint Mr. Dent as his defense counsel," Judy said. "Mr. Dent said that Isham Truitt had sent Tom Lichine to Alabama. Whatever Tom did down there was done under our auspices as a law firm. For Tom to allow anybody but Isham Truitt to defend him would be, Mr. Dent said, a repudiation of Tom by his own firm. Mr. Dent felt this would not only jeopardize Tom's chances in court. Mr. Dent felt it would also be a reflection on the integrity of Tom's firm. I told all this to Tom."

"Why didn't you tell it to me?" Hugh Kelly said.

"I didn't think it was necessary," Judy said. "I assumed you felt the same way. It's your firm, Mr. Kelly. Even more than it was Mr. Dent's."

Hugh Kelly paused and sent his glance prowling around the small office. Judy had a feeling he was hunting for the reassuring sight of St. Patrick and the snakes.

"You are not going to be on that plane tonight with me and Mrs. Kelly?" he said finally.

"No, sir," Judy said. "Neither are you, Mr. Kelly."

The sagging skin at the corners of the ice-blue eyes came together in the two hard little knots of muscle.

"I have given my promise to the President," Hugh Kelly said.

"Howard Dent gave his promise to several Presidents," Judy

said. "That didn't stop him yesterday from giving his life for a principle."

"What principle?" Hugh Kelly said.

"I don't know," Judy said. "Maybe nobody ever knows. Or maybe everybody knows in his own way but can't put it into words that will make sense to anybody but himself. I know only this. When Mr. Dent asked to defend Tom Lichine he knew what he was doing, and what he was doing meant more to Mr. Dent than his life."

"I don't understand you," Hugh Kelly said.

"His heart was very bad," Judy said. "He was under orders from his doctor never again to set foot in a courtroom. When he decided to do it he knew what the consequences might be."

25

"How do you know?" Mr. Merz said.

"A doctor at New York Hospital told me," Judy Cline said. "He was on duty in Emergency when Mr. Dent was brought in."

"Friend of yours?" Mr. Merz said.

"Fiancé of a friend," Judy said.

"Then he must have told you more," Mr. Merz said.

"He did," Judy said. "Mr. Dent's heart was so bad that going into court to try a case was almost a suicidal act. He never got to the digitalis in his pocket. When they got him to the hospital he was D.O.A."

" 'The stars in their courses do not always merit passing grades,' " Emanuel Merz said. "Mr. Justice Holmes. *McCurrie* v. *Hensch*. Not exactly a landmark decision. Useful, though, for the litigator who runs out of words of his own. Especially when he's on his feet in front of a jury trying to explain yet another manifestation of the total incomprehensibility of human conduct."

"You think what Mr. Dent did is incomprehensible?" Judy said.

"Don't you?" Mr. Merz said.

"Yes, but I'm an outsider," Judy said.

"Outsider to what?" Mr. Merz said.

"Whatever it is in this Southern Shoals Asbestos mess to which you're an insider," Judy said.

"Insider in what way?" Emanuel Merz said.

"Isham Truitt," Judy said. "You're a senior partner."

"You're inferring Isham Truitt as a firm has a united interest in whatever it is young Lichine did down in Alabama?" Manny Merz said.

"Mr. Dent taught me never to infer when I mean imply," Judy said.

Mandamus Manny Merz stood up, came out from behind his desk, and walked to the door. He opened it, stuck his head out into his secretary's office, and said, "Jenny, hold my calls."

"Yes, Mr. Merz," Judy heard the secretary say. "Hospital posting?"

"Yes," Manny Merz said.

He closed the door, came back to his desk, and sat down.

"Hospital posting," Judy said. "What does that mean?"

"No visitors," Manny Merz said.

Judy laughed. Mr. Merz grinned.

"You like that," he said.

"I came in here wanting something," Judy said. "I now feel I'm going to get it."

"A year ago, when I recruited you up at Harvard," Emanuel Merz said, "I knew I was picking a winner. I didn't know, of course, how you were going to prove it. Even a picker as shrewd as I am has to wait for the proof to happen."

"I haven't done anything to prove it yet," Judy said.

"Before I tell Jenny to take down the 'No Visitors' sign," Mandamus Manny said, "I have a feeling you will. Okay, young lady, let's have the bill of particulars."

"One," Judy said. "At the same time you recruited me you also recruited Tom Lichine."

"I didn't ask him, however, to come down to New York and have lunch with me," Mr. Merz said.

"I attribute that to nothing more than the sex bias for which every big New York law firm is noted," Judy said.

"That ends my attempt to disrupt the itemization of the indictment," Manny Merz said. "Proceed."

"Two," Judy said. "You thought highly enough of Mr. Lichine to recommend him to Mr. Uchitel as a candidate for an important pro bono assignment in Alabama. Something unpleasant happened down in Alabama. Nobody seems to be clear about

what it is, which leads me to suspect that everybody would
rather be unclear about what it is. One thing, however, is perfectly clear. Whatever it was that happened, it proved upsetting
to Isham Truitt."

"Don't you think you want to narrow that down?" Mandamus
Manny said.

"Yes, I do," Judy said. "You don't have to help me, however.
If I didn't have this thing firmly in hand I wouldn't have come in
here, I assure you."

"I don't want assurance," Manny Merz said. "I want the architecture of your case."

"Narrowing it down, then," Judy said. "Mr. Kelly was the first
Isham Truitt partner to be upset by what happened in Alabama.
He ordered Mr. Lichine fired at once, and he was."

"Once you get them away from covenants running with the
land," Manny Merz said, "I find real estate lawyers are like TV
gunslingers who have been separated from their scripts. They
tend to shoot from the hip."

"May I go on?" Judy said.

"Please," Emanuel Merz said.

"As soon as the news of Mr. Lichine's firing worked its way
upward to the proper level," Judy said, "he was rehired so fast
and with so many apologies that only out of a sense of pride and
personal dignity was he able to fight off the offer of an accompa-
nying raise, a promotion, and conceivably a knighthood."

"A question, please," Manny Merz said.

"Of course," Judy said.

"What do you consider upward to the proper level?" Mr. Merz
said.

"David Fillmore," Judy said.

"Hmmm," Emanuel Merz hmmned.

"Upward enough?" Judy said.

"Proceed," Manny Merz said.

"Rehiring Mr. Lichine proved to be more difficult than firing
him," Judy said. "He had disappeared. His disappearance upset
Isham Truitt."

"Again, do you want to narrow that down?" Merz said.

"Mr. Kelly told Tony Tessitore to find Mr. Lichine and find him fast or else," Judy said.

"Meaning if Tony did not find Mr. Lichine like say yesterday, he could go down to Gil Cutter's office and pick up his paycheck and keep on going?" Manny Merz said.

"Yes," Judy said. "Mr. Tessitore didn't like that alternative, and he had been warned by Mr. Kelly to avoid calling on the police for help, so Tony brought in a firm of private investigators. Womack and Povey."

"Good people," Manny Merz said.

"In this instance not good enough," Judy said. "They had no luck, but Mr. Lichine had apparently made his point."

"Which was what?" Merz said.

"That he meant business," Judy said.

"What sort of business?" Manny Merz said.

"We'll touch that base in a moment," Judy said. "At the moment let me indicate only that Mr. Lichine decided to underscore his point so there would be nobody at Isham Truitt who could misunderstand him. He turned himself in to an Isham Truitt senior partner."

"Which one?" Manny Merz said.

"I ask you to cast your mind back to your opinion of the girl you recruited at Harvard a year ago," Judy said. "Then I ask you to run your last question through your mind. Do you expect your recruit to answer it?"

"No," Manny Merz said. "What did Paul Truitt do?"

"He called a meeting of the Isham Truitt senior partners," Judy said. "You are an Isham Truitt senior partner, Mr. Merz."

"Sorry," Mandamus Manny said with a grin. "The good litigator is well served by an elephant's memory, but it doesn't hurt if on the proper occasion he can seem as convincingly vague and forgetful as that lady in the George Kaufman–Marc Connelly play."

"*Dulcy*," Judy said.

"How do you know a piece of history like that?" Manny Merz said.

"My father is a piece of that history," Judy said. "He and Marc Connelly are old friends. If I may refresh your memory,

Mr. Merz, what happened at that meeting of senior partners was a unanimous decision that Isham Truitt would be well advised to go bail for Mr. Lichine, but to make absolutely certain their efforts to help him could not be traced. Shall I go into detail about how the cash was raised?"

"Spare me," Manny Merz said. "Fund raising is a tedious business, even the campaigns one stages oneself, and I staged this one. What you can do is fill in the one thing that's puzzled me since we had that meeting."

"If I can," Judy said.

Manny Merz grinned.

"If you can't," he said, "I'll drag you back to the Takashaki Garden and make you eat a double order of the mizutaki."

"I'd rather break down and tell all," Judy said.

"If all the senior partners are so smart," Emanuel Merz said, "how come we allowed Howard Dent to step in and defend Lichine?"

"You didn't," Judy said. "Mr. Kelly pleaded with Mr. Dent to stay out of it."

"What made him step in?" Manny Merz said.

"He did it for me," Judy said.

Emanuel Merz fingered the narrow Brooks Brothers black knitted tie he had hung away in his closet a decade ago until, the week before, he had decided the pendulum of fashion in men's neckwear had swung back sufficiently for him to acknowledge it publicly. As he played his fingers up and down the delicately knitted black silk like a musician fingering a clarinet, he stared hard at Judy Cline. She returned the stare calmly. Finally Mandamus Manny seemed to settle on what he wanted to say.

"Howard Dent didn't end up doing very much, did he?"

"He did more than he intended," Judy said.

"How?" Merz said.

"By not managing to reach the vial of digitalis in his pocket Mr. Dent demonstrated that what he gave his life for is worth an honest lawyer sticking his neck out for."

"His?" Manny Merz said. "Or her?"

"Both I hope," Judy said.

"In what way?" Merz said.

"At ten o'clock tomorrow morning somebody has to go back into Special Term, Part Two of the New York Supreme Court to pick up where Howard Dent left off yesterday," Judy Cline said. "I'm hoping it will be the man who is known with what I believe is good reason to be the best litigator in the business."

"Suppose he says no?" Manny Merz said.

"You know this friend who has a fiancé who works at New York Hospital and tells me things?" Judy said.

"What about her?" Merz said.

"She has a friend whose fiancé works at Milbank Tweed," Judy said. "This last year or so he has been hanging up a record that has caused people in the trade to call him the best litigator to appear on the New York legal scene since Mandamus Manny Merz came out of the New York University Evening Session Law School."

"You think you can get this kid to go to bat for Howard Dent?" Merz said.

"His fiancée has got him to promise he'll be there tomorrow morning at ten sharp," Judy said. "All she has to do is make a phone call."

"This kid," Merz said. "Would his name be Bob Coffey?"

"It would and it is," Judy said.

"Tell your friend not to waste the dime," Emanuel Merz said. "There is only one litigator in New York who can handle this. Tomorrow morning at ten o'clock Mandamus Manny Merz will give you a ride to Special Term, Part Two in our office limousine."

26

The courtroom looked different. No, Judy decided a moment later. What she meant was it felt different. It was the different feel of any second visit, whether to Mr. Metzger's drugstore, the bathroom in a friend's apartment, or a nameless architect's imitation of the dodecagonal chapter house in a Gothic cathedral designed to shelter a corporate body of half a thousand canons. It was the difference of familiarity.

"I have been here before."

"'But when or how I cannot tell,'" Mandamus Manny said. "'I know the grass beyond the door, the sweet clean smell, the sighing sound, the lights around the shore.'"

Astonished, Judy turned to the senior partner sitting beside her. He had been removing papers from his attaché case and arranging them in front of him on counsels' table. Mr. Merz did it as though he were laying out the flagstones on a walk he was building between himself and a swimming pool he wanted to be able to reach with a minimum of discomfort whenever on the spur of the moment he decided to knock off work for a quick, refreshing dip.

"You didn't know I quote poetry the way Muhammad Ali quotes his press agents," Emanuel Merz said. "You don't even have to drop a hat. All it takes to set me off is hearing a familiar line."

"What did I say that was familiar?" Judy said.

"I have been here before," Mandamus Manny said. "First line of *Sudden Light* by Dante Gabriel Rossetti, 1828–1882, founder of the Pre-Raphaelite Brotherhood and the greatest boon to the trial lawyer since Warner Brothers starred Warren William in *The Great Mouthpiece*. That little celluloid epic fired a whole generation of slum kids with the notion that the way to fame and fortune is a law degree plus a copy of Bartlett's *Familiar Quotations*."

"I didn't mean to trigger all that," Judy said. "I thought I was merely making a remark about how quickly things become familiar. This is only my second visit to Special Term, Part Two but already the place feels like my own office."

"Considering the size of the offices Isham Truitt provides for associates," Emanuel Merz said, "you've made your point with a refreshing disregard for Bartlett. Considering what is bearing down on us right now under full sail I have to make a fast decision."

"About what?" Judy said.

"Between Bartlett's two offerings," Mandamus Manny said. "'Upon more familiarity will grow more contempt' from *The Merry Wives of Windsor*, or the more blunt 'Familiarity breeds contempt' from Aesop's *The Fox and the Lion*."

Merz stopped arranging papers and showing off for Judy Cline. He stood up and took the assistant district attorney's outstretched hand.

"I wondered who would be coming in to bat for Howard," J. Murray Hyatt said. "I'm told he was just a few weeks short of ninety-two, so expressions of sorrow have to be tempered with common sense. That's easy enough to do in the case of someone like Howard Dent. He had more of that rare commodity than most people. He also had a good run. Not to mention that he went the way I wouldn't mind going myself. With his boots on, in a place where he had happily spent most of his life, a courtroom."

"Murray, you sound like a poet," Emanuel Merz said. "If you don't watch out I'll start quoting you. We understand from the doctors the end was absolutely painless, so what more can a man ask?"

"A stumblebum to replace him," Mr. Hyatt said. "So what do I draw?"

"Miss Cline," Manny Merz said, "I don't know if you've met this idle flatterer—"

"Two days ago," Judy said. "Right here. Mr. Dent introduced us. Good morning, Mr. Hyatt."

"Good morning, young lady," the sandy-haired man said. "I don't want you to think the D.A.'s office is staffed by insensitive louts. I meant every word I said about Mr. Dent. I shall miss him."

"We all will," Judy said.

"Everybody rise, please!"

Judy turned toward the bench. So did Mr. Merz and the assistant district attorney. Judge McNally was crossing from the side door to the high-backed chair. The uniformed attendant to the left and slightly below the bench was giving the courtroom a swift examination. Apparently to make sure the few spectators in the large chamber were obeying his order. Then he turned and sent a quick glance at Judge McNally. The judge was setting down his file folder. He seemed to feel the intensity of the attendant's glance. For a moment it appeared to puzzle him, then Judge McNally smiled and nodded. The attendant beamed.

"Be seated, please!" he called in a loud, clear voice. He was obviously delighted not to have been beaten to the punch this morning by His Honor.

Judy and Mr. Merz sat down. Mr. Hyatt moved to the end of counsels' table and set down his attaché case. It was not, like the receptacle in which Mr. Merz carried his papers, a name number made of ostrich hide that appeared in the Gucci ads in *The New Yorker*. The container in which Mr. Hyatt had carried his papers into Special Term, Part Two could have been the one in which as a student a quarter of a century ago he had carried his notebooks to class. From it Mr. Hyatt now drew what Judy could see was a Xerox of the document Emanuel Merz on her left had in front of him and Judge McNally had picked up from his open file on the bench.

"Mr. Hyatt," the judge said.

"Yes, sir," the assistant district attorney said.

"You have seen this copy of relator's request for substitution of counsel?" Judge McNally said.

"I have it in my hand, Your Honor," Mr. Hyatt said.

As though it were a check he had just signed and wanted to make sure the ink was dry before he passed it along, he gave the sheet of paper a short wave.

"Do you have any objection?" Judge McNally said.

"None at all, Your Honor," the assistant district attorney said. "Mr. Merz and I are old friends."

Judy found herself wondering if the canons for whom the original of this dodecagonal chapter house was built had been on terms as relaxed and casual as the contestants who in 1978 fought for justice in this copy of their arena.

"Good," Judge McNally said.

The small, shy smile swept fleetingly across the solemn face. It sat like a swiftly sketched cartoon pumpkin on the mass of black robe between the chin and the bench.

"May I say," the judge said, "that Mr. Merz and I have known each other for many years. One could wish that the occasion for this reunion were happier than it is, but the law can do no more than mark our moments of sorrow by the entries on our dockets. Mark this, please."

He held out the sheet of paper. The attendant reached up, took it, and handed it down to the stenographer.

"Your Honor," the district attorney said.

"Yes, Mr. Hyatt," Judge McNally said.

"To review for a moment, if I may, the event on which this hearing was adjourned two days ago?" Mr. Hyatt said.

"Please do," the judge said.

"Your Honor will recall that the defendant, Mr. Thomas Lichine, was in the witness chair," the district attorney said. "Mr. Lichine had just testified that the warrant under which he had been detained for extradition to the jurisdiction of the state of Alabama to face an indictment for murder states that the crime was committed in that state at approximately one o'clock in the afternoon on Thursday, August 10, 1978."

"That is correct," Judge McNally said.

"Under questioning by counsel," the district attorney continued, "then the late Mr. Howard Dent, Mr. Lichine further testified that at approximately one o'clock in the afternoon

on Thursday, August 10, 1978 he was not in the state of Alabama. Mr. Lichine stated under oath that at that time he was up
here in New York City attending a meeting in the office of Mr.
Hugh Kelly, a senior partner in the law firm by which Mr. Lichine is employed. When asked if he could produce witnesses to
this event, Mr. Lichine said he could, and he provided the names
of three people who were present in the room with Mr. Lichine
and Mr. Kelly. May I ask counsel if he will stipulate the correctness of this recital of the facts?"

"I do," Emanuel Merz said. "I have read the record and, in
addition, I have consulted my assistant, Miss Judith Cline, who
was present in this courtroom two days ago when Mr. Lichine's
testimony was taken. Miss Cline is present in this courtroom
now, serving with me as two days ago she was serving with Mr.
Dent."

"Thank you, Mr. Merz," the district attorney said. "Your
Honor, at this point Mr. Lichine was asked a question by the district attorney. I read from the record. 'Mr. Lichine, would you
please tell us what took place at that meeting in Mr. Kelly's private office on Thursday, August 10, 1978?' Is that correct, Mr.
Merz?"

"According to the record, corroborated by my assistant, Miss
Cline, who was present, it is," Emanuel Merz said.

"Thank you, Mr. Merz," the district attorney said. "I now read
from the record Mr. Lichine's reply. 'By advice of counsel,' Mr.
Lichine stated, 'under Amendment Five of the Constitution I refuse to answer on the ground that such answer might incriminate
or degrade me.' Is that correct, Mr. Merz?"

"According to the record, corroborated by my assistant, Miss
Cline, who was present, it is," Emanuel Merz said.

"Thank you, Mr. Merz," the district attorney said.

He put down the paper and stepped to the left, away from
counsels' table. Judy grasped that he wanted to make it clear by
moving his physical position that he was moving his case into a
new area of conflict.

"Your Honor," the district attorney said, "I move that the
witness be instructed by the court to answer the question or be
held in contempt."

Like a spectator in the stands following the ball at a tennis match, Judge McNally moved his head toward the place where it would bounce. Emanuel Merz was right there, on his feet, body poised for the return.

"I object, Your Honor," he said.

"On what grounds?" Judge McNally said.

"My client has been detained under Article Four, Section Two of the U. S. Constitution," Emmanuel Merz said. "This is our so-called interstate rendition law. It provides that a person who commits a crime in one state, and then flees to another state, may be brought back physically to the state in which the crime was committed in order to stand trial. To implement this section of our federal constitution, Section Eight-three-o of the Code of Criminal Procedure of the State of New York sets forth the conditions under which the governor of this state may comply with the request for such seizure by the governor of the demanding state.

"The authorities are unanimous," Manny Merz continued, "and I will cite them at the appropriate time. The authorities are unanimous, I repeat, in holding that a person cannot be a fugitive from the justice of a demanding state if in fact he was not physically present in that state when the crime charged against him is alleged to have been committed. My client, Mr. Thomas Lichine, has stated under oath and is prepared to prove that at the time the crime involved in this case was committed in Alabama he was actually physically seated at a meeting in an office here in New York City. What took place at that meeting is irrelevant to the issue my client is testing here in his writ of habeas corpus. The only relevant issue before this court is clear. Was Mr. Lichine present or was he not present in Alabama at the time of the alleged crime? If he was not present in Alabama at that time, then the writ must be signed by Your Honor and my client discharged. We are prepared to prove Mr. Lichine was not present in Alabama at that time. It is the duty of the state to prove he was. I suggest to Your Honor that the district attorney be instructed to stick to the discharge of his duty under the law."

Emanuel Merz paused, drew a deep breath, and, with the faintest echoes of a supporting trumpet in his voice, said, "I urge

Your Honor to dismiss the district attorney's motion that Mr. Lichine be held in contempt for refusing to testify about what happened at the meeting in New York."

Promptly, without hesitation, as though he had been poised on the balls of his feet for the return shot, Judge McNally said, "Motion dismissed."

"Exception, Your Honor," the district attorney said.

"You may have your exception, Mr. Hyatt," the judge said.

"Thank you, Your Honor," Mr. Hyatt said.

"You may proceed, Mr. Merz," the judge said.

"Thank you, Your Honor," Emanuel Merz said. "I will call Mr. Ira Bodmer."

Turning to look up into the well of the court, Judy Cline had a moment of surprise. Bianca Bean was seated where she had been sitting two days ago. Today, however, she was not occupying the second seat in from the aisle. Today Tom Lichine's wife was in the aisle seat. It occurred to Judy that she had not seen Tom's wife enter the courtroom. This nudged Judy's mind into recording that she could not have seen Bianca's husband come in with her. This meant Judy had not seen Tom Lichine since he had invoked the Fifth Amendment on the stand just before Howard Dent had collapsed two days ago. Wondering what that could mean, and making a mental note to find out, Judy ran into another surprise.

Ira Bodmer, coming down the aisle, did not look like one of the two members of Tony Tessitore's staff Judy had known for almost a year. He had lost the appearance of a harassed office boy who raced around town performing the managing clerk's endless errands. Coming down the aisle, Ira Bodmer looked anything but harassed. In his neat, dark suit, moving with purpose at a comfortable gait, his face set in a look of composed gravity, he could have been someone who belonged in this arena not as a casual spectator but as a crucial participant. Ira Bodmer looked as though he had already achieved what he had been working for years to become: an associate in a big New York law firm not unlike Isham Truitt.

"Do you swear to tell the truth, the whole truth, and nothing but the truth, so help you God?" the uniformed clerk said.

"I do," Ira Bodmer said.

The court clerk swung the Bible out of the way and said, "Be seated, please."

Ira Bodmer settled himself in the witness chair as though he were composing himself for a preview screening of a major movie in a private projection room: a man aware that he was the recipient of a privilege, but determined to hold his gratitude in check until he saw the picture. After all, it could be a stinker.

"Your full name, please," Emanuel Merz said.

"Ira S. Bodmer, Jr., sir."

"Your place of residence?" Merz said.

"Two-o-seven-eight Vyse Avenue," Ira Bodmer said. "The Bronx, New York City."

"Your age, Mr. Bodmer?" Mr. Merz said.

"Twenty, sir," Ira Bodmer said.

"How do you spend your time?" Emanuel Merz said.

"Like where I work, sir, you mean?" Ira Bodmer said.

"Yes, and anything else to which you devote yourself, Mr. Bodmer, if you will," Mandamus Manny said.

"Well, sir, at night I am a student at the Alexander Hamilton Law School on Astor Place," Ira Bodmer said. "I will be graduating in June, sir, when I will be taking the Bar exams, and during the day I work for Isham, Truitt, Kelly, Shreve, Merz, Uchitel and Condomine, six-three-five Madison Avenue, New York, New York one-o-o-two-two."

"Thank you, Mr. Bodmer," Emanuel Merz said. "I thought you looked familiar."

Ira Bodmer grinned. Judge McNally smiled. Mr. Hyatt barely suppressed a small look of pain. A titter washed like a rustling taffeta skirt across the large chamber behind Judy Cline. Turning to examine the source, Judy noted that the additional spectators who had appeared in the courtroom since her first examination now included Tom Lichine. He was sitting beside his wife in the aisle seat. Bianca Bean had moved over. Turning back to the bench, Judy glanced at her watch. Not quite ten-thirty. She began shaping the thought that it was not like Tom Lichine to be a half hour late for a court appearance, but Judy didn't get very far with that particular thought. To her knowledge this was Tom Lichine's first court appearance in which he was the defendant.

"Would you tell us, Mr. Bodmer, what your duties are in the firm we both have the honor to serve?" Mandamus Manny said.

"I'm an assistant to Mr. Anthony Tessitore, our managing clerk," Ira Bodmer said.

Prodded by Mandamus Manny, he said a good deal more. Spelling out in detail the events of the Thursday morning, August 10, 1978, when Ira had found Tom Lichine asleep behind the locked door of his room in the Isham Truitt office. The facts were dull. The questions in which Merz imbedded his demand for them, as well as the answers in which Ira Bodmer delivered them, were even duller. And yet both men, the seasoned lawyer and the youthful witness, brought to their exchange all the verve and excitement of a couple of actors performing during the early days of a newly opened hit play. Judy glanced at the spectators. They listened with the absorption of members of an audience who had succeeded in spite of many obstacles in putting their hands on tickets for the smash.

It occurred to Judy that, of the performing arts, the law was one of the more durable. It could be tedious, witless, slow-moving, improbable, poorly structured, unpleasant, boring, even detestable. It could not, however, be killed with a venomous epigram. The power of the law was its negative strength. It was impervious to the reviews of the aisle-sitters.

"Thank you, Mr. Bodmer," Mandamus Manny said. "No further questions." He turned to counsels' table. "Your witness, Mr. Hyatt."

Merz started back to his chair beside Judy. The district attorney came to his feet.

"No questions, Your Honor," Mr. Hyatt said.

"You may proceed, Mr. Merz," the judge said.

"Thank you, Your Honor," Mandamus Manny said, wheeling away from Judy's chair and coming back to the witness box. "I will call Mr. Anthony Tessitore."

The uniformed guard stood up and called, "Anthony Tessitore, please come forward."

Coming forward down the aisle, Tessie slowed his pace when

Ira Bodmer reached him on the way up. Without stopping, Tessie whispered something to Ira Bodmer. Also without stopping, Ira Bodmer whispered a reply and continued on up the aisle. While Tessie was being sworn in, Judy kept her eyes on Ira Bodmer, but she was actually watching Tom Lichine. He was whispering to his wife. Bianca Bean nodded solemnly, as though acknowledging some sort of instructions.

"I do," Tony Tessitore said.

Judy turned back to the witness.

"Your full name, please," Emanuel Merz said.

"Anthony Tessitore."

"Your home address?" Merz said.

"Four-nine-eight West Eighty-sixth Street, New York City," Tessie said.

"Your age, Mr. Tessitore?" Manny Merz said.

"Sixty-two, sir," Tessie said.

"Your occupation, Mr. Tessitore?" Mandamus Manny said.

"I am the managing clerk of Isham, Truitt, Kelly, Shreve, Merz, Uchitel and Condomine," Tessie said. "Six-three-five Madison Avenue, New York, New York, one-o-o-two-two."

"Mr. Tessitore, you have heard the testimony given here this morning by your assistant Ira Bodmer?" Manny Merz said.

"Yes, sir," Tony Tessitore said.

What he had to say was no wittier than what Ira Bodmer had said. Yet what he said seemed to have greater impact than what Ira had said because, in saying it, Tony Tessitore was not breaking new ground. He spoke his piece standing on the platform Ira Bodmer had built with his preceding testimony. It was not unlike, Judy thought, the railroad builder who followed the moccasined Indian scout. The spoils went not to the explorer but to the exploiter.

"No further questions, Mr. Tessitore," Manny Merz said. He turned to counsels' table. "Your witness, Mr. Hyatt."

The district attorney came to his feet.

"No questions, Your Honor," Mr. Hyatt said.

"You may proceed, Mr. Merz," Judge McNally said.

"Thank you, Your Honor," Mandamus Manny said. "I will call Mr. Salvatore Giudice."

The uniformed guard stood up.

"Mr. Salvatore Giudice, please come forward!"

In the difference between the way Sal Giudice came down the aisle and the way Ira Bodmer had done it could be read, Judy Cline felt, the difference between the schools in which they were preparing for their careers at the Bar. Alexander Hamilton was not Harvard, but it bore a name that its graduates, among them some of the nation's most widely known lawyers, were able to pronounce with a certain amount of proud defiance. Brooklyn Union, on the other hand, no matter what it was not, bore a name that sounded like a labor organization. Judy Cline had never met any of the school's graduates. It occurred to her that perhaps she had met some of them but none had chosen to volunteer the connection. Judy had a feeling they all looked the way Sal Giudice, coming down the aisle of Special Term, Part Two, looked now on his way to the witness box: as though he were checking in at a strike meeting. Placing his hand on the Bible to be sworn in, Sal Giudice could have been flashing his membership card at the door of his union meeting hall.

"Your full name, please," Emanuel Merz said.

Sal Giudice gave it the way he gave the rest of the biographical data requested by Mandamus Manny: with a slight but clearly discernible air of take-it-or-leave-it truculence.

"As an assistant to Mr. Tessitore, then, Mr. Giudice, your duties are not unlike those of Ira Bodmer," Manny Merz said. "Is that correct?"

"They are identical," Sal Giudice said.

"And where were you at nine-thirty in the morning on Thursday, August 10, 1978?" Mr. Merz said.

In telling him, Sal Giudice was unable to do very much with his role. He didn't even try. He reminded Judy of an understudy who had to cover several actors in a large cast. He had learned to walk through the spear-carrier roles, and save his fire for the ones that might lead to something. This one led to nothing more than Mr. Merz's terminal: "Thank you, Mr. Giudice, no further questions." He turned to counsels' table. "Your witness, Mr. Hyatt."

The district attorney stood up.

"No questions, Your Honor," Mr. Hyatt said.

"You may proceed, Mr. Merz," the judge said.

"Thank you, Your Honor," Manny Merz said. "I will call Mrs. Edwina Campion."

The uniformed guard stood up.

"Mrs. Edwina Campion, please come forward!"

Mr. Kelly's secretary was not a woman Judy Cline would have described as larger than life, even though Mrs. Campion was clearly in the 180–200-pound class. The frame within which Judy was accustomed to seeing Mr. Kelly's secretary, however, had given her in Judy's eyes a dimension beyond avoirdupois. The outer offices in which Isham Truitt secretaries functioned, even the secretaries of senior partners, tended to take their shape and size from whatever space had been left over after the private lair of the man the secretary served had been blueprinted by the architect and his assistant. The assistant was almost always the senior partner's wife. As a result Gil Cutter, the office manager, had once said and often repeated, "Secretaries who are unable to work in rooms where they can't swing a cat are not hired at Isham Truitt."

Mrs. Campion was more fortunate than the secretaries of most Isham Truitt partners. The reason was that Mrs. Kelly had just about as much to do with putting together her husband's private lair at 635 Madison as she had with the other details of his private life. This was, in a word, nothing. In this area Hugh F. X. Kelly, Jr., knew exactly what he wanted and how to get it: by spurning interference and giving orders.

"Just make sure all my pictures get up on the walls and see to it that the statue of St. Patrick doesn't look crowded," his order had been to the architect and decorator. "All the rest of the space you can give to Mrs. Campion."

With the result that she worked in surroundings that were known to her envious colleagues as the Botanical Garden. Mrs. Campion, who owned a sharp tongue and supported a pouter-pigeon prow, also had a green thumb. Not infrequently, when Judy came to see Mr. Kelly, she found his secretary in the outer office wearing gardener's gloves, busily transplanting with a trowel some bulbs from the window box to the planter beside her typewriter stand or vice versa. Watching Mr. Kelly's secretary come down the aisle of Special Term, Part Two, Judy was surprised therefore to realize Mrs. Campion suddenly looked tiny. A moment later Judy realized it was the surroundings. Human beings more amply proportioned than Edwina Campion had been dwarfed for centuries by the architecture of dodecagonal chapter houses.

"I do," Mrs. Campion said to the uniformed clerk.

He carried away the Bible. Emanuel Merz came forward.

"Your full name, please," he said.

"Edwina Campion," the surprisingly shrunken woman said.

Judy noticed, however, that as Mr. Merz worked Mr. Kelly's secretary through the list of biographical questions that on the stenographic record fixed her in the time and place where she was giving her testimony, the temporarily shrunken Mrs. Campion expanded noticeably. Like one of those dried Japanese bulbs dropped into a bowl of water, by the time she reached the announcement that she was employed as Mr. Kelly's private secretary, and had been for twenty-two years, Mrs. Campion seemed to have picked up twenty or thirty of her temporarily mislaid pounds.

"You have been here in court all morning?" Emanuel Merz said.

"Yes, sir," Mrs. Campion said.

"You have heard the testimony of Mr. Bodmer, Mr. Tessitore, and Mr. Giudice?" Manny Merz said.

"Yes, sir," Mrs. Campion said.

"All of it, you will have observed, dealt with their contacts with Mr. Lichine on the morning of Thursday, August 10, 1978 in the Isham Truitt offices at six-three-five Madison Avenue," Mr. Merz said.

"Yes, sir," Mrs. Campion said.

"On that morning, Thursday, August 10, 1978," Mandamus Manny said, "I ask you, Mrs. Campion, did you have any personal contact with Mr. Lichine?"

"Yes, sir, I did," Mrs. Campion said.

Her performance, like Sal Giudice's, was not inspired. Judy had the feeling the heavy woman was annoyed by the realization that she was being led down paths not only well trodden but deeply rutted. Mrs. Campion might have been more spirited, Judy guessed, if she had been Mandamus Manny's first witness of the day. The guess was proved accurate when, having listlessly established Tom Lichine's presence in her office on Thursday, August 10, 1978, Mrs. Campion started to gather her purse and herself for Mandamus Manny's verbal farewell note.

Instead, Emanuel Merz said, "One more thing, Mrs. Campion, if I may."

Perking up at once, Mrs. Campion said, "Of course."

"Would you look out into the courtroom, please, and tell us if Mr. Lichine is present?"

Mrs. Campion opened her purse, pulled out a pair of horn-rimmed spectacles, and set them carefully on her fleshy nose. She moved her head deliberately, as though she were sighting a gun, and peered across counsels' table.

"Over there," she said, lifting her hand in a ladylike gesture that was part wave and part forefinger stab.

"Where?" Mandamus Manny said, shifting his body from side to side and squinting, as though from the bridge of a battleship he were sighting a telescope into the mists of a turbulent sea.

"That horizontal sort of aisle?" Mrs. Campion said. "The walkway across the courtroom? Count four rows down from the last row. Then the aisle seat on the right, four rows down. Next to the young lady with blond hair wearing a trench coat."

"Yes, I see," Manny Merz said. "What is Mr. Lichine wearing?"

"A navy-blue blazer with gold buttons," Mrs. Campion said. "White shirt. Black knitted tie. That's him."

"Sir!" Mandamus Manny called. "In the navy-blue blazer? With the white shirt and black knitted tie? Fourth row down from the horizontal walkway? Aisle seat? Would you be good enough to stand up, sir?"

Judy Cline grinned involuntarily at the way Tom Lichine did it. With a mixture of stunned disbelief and uncertain reluctance. Like a contestant in a TV quiz show who finds it difficult to accept in the first moments of revelation the shattering truth that the spinning finger of fate has indeed singled him out for the jackpot.

"The gentleman standing up in the aisle," Mandamus Manny said. "Is that the man who was locked away in Mr. Kelly's private office with Mr. Dent, Mr. Kelly, and Miss Cline? From twelve noon to one-forty? On the afternoon of Thursday, August 10, 1978?"

"Yes, sir," Mrs. Campion said. "That's Mr. Lichine."

"Thank you, Mrs. Campion," Emanuel Merz said. "And thank you, Mr. Lichine. You may sit down, sir. No further questions, Mrs. Campion." He turned to counsels' table. "Your witness, Mr. Hyatt."

The district attorney came to his feet. This time he made of the movement a small, graceful burlesque. It was as though, by this point in the long morning's work, after the third or fourth repetition, while displaying no disrespect for the law they both served, he wanted to indicate one civilized man's awareness to another that, if only in its minor aspects, they were both engaged in the sort of ludicrous but necessary minuet that made the uninformed public leap to the erroneous conclusion that the law is an ass.

"No questions, Your Honor," Mr. Hyatt said.

"You may proceed, Mr. Merz," the judge said.

"Thank you, Your Honor," Manny Merz said. "I will call Mr. J. C. Taunton, please."

The uniformed guard stood up.

"Mr. J. C. Taunton, please come forward!"

Watching him take shape out of the far from dense but not very clearly defined mass of spectators, following with her glance his start down the aisle toward the witness box, Judy Cline was reminded of the night two weeks ago when Taunton had appeared with the alligator key case at her door on West Eighty-second Street. In the poor light of her brownstone hallway the man who shared an office with Tom Lichine had looked sinister. In the bright Centre Street sunlight now pouring down from the high windows into Special Term, Part Two, Jack Taunton still did.

"And how long have you known Mr. Lichine?" Emanuel Merz was saying.

"Since the day he moved in and took over the second desk in my office," Jack Taunton said.

"Until then the office had been yours alone?" Manny Merz said.

"Yes and no," Jack Taunton said.

The answer, Judy saw at once, did not sit well with Mr. Merz. He had fed Taunton what Judy's father would have called a throwaway line. Part of the verbal lumber needed to get an actor newly arrived on stage settled into his role. So the audience, unaware that it is being manipulated by the playwright, will know who the newcomer is and what he is doing out there in full view of the paying customers. Jack Taunton, however, like all bad actors, was not content to do what the author had arranged for him to do. Jack Taunton wanted to hold the attention of the audience a little longer. The face of Mandamus Manny did not lose its look of gently smiling Big Brother affability. Underneath the smile, however, Judy could see the formation of a subsurface hardness: the annoyed pro forced into taking time off from the serious business at hand to teach this snot-nose a lesson. Mr. Jack Taunton, Judy saw, was about to get it in the neck.

"I seem to have missed something," Mandamus Manny said. "What do you mean, Mr. Taunton, by 'yes and no'?"

"Yes, when Tom Lichine moved in with me the office had been mine alone," Jack Taunton said. "But no it hadn't really been."

"Somebody else was sharing it with you?" Manny Merz said.

"Not at that moment," Taunton said.

"The moment when Mr. Lichine moved in with you?" Emanuel Merz said.

"Yes, sir," Jack Taunton said.

"You're sure of that?" Manny Merz said.

"Sure of what, sir?" Taunton said.

"That at the moment Mr. Lichine moved in with you, Mr. Taunton, you were or were not the sole occupant of that office," Mandamus Manny said.

"I didn't say that, sir," Taunton said.

"Would the stenographer please read back the question?" Emanuel Merz said.

The neat little man at the Stenotype machine tipped up his head. He poked the glasses a bit higher on his nose. With his other hand he neatly scooped up several folds of the tape piled up behind his machine.

"Beginning where, sir?" he said.

"Beginning with the witness' answer 'yes and no,'" Manny Merz said.

His voice was as calculatedly devoid of expression as that of the caller in a Bingo game.

"Witness yes and no," the stenographer read, matching his voice so perfectly to that of Mandamus Manny that they could have been members of a seasoned vaudeville team. "Mr. Merz I seem to have missed something what do you mean Mr. Taunton by yes and no Mr. Taunton yes when Tom Lichine moved in with me the office had been mine alone but no it hadn't really been Mr. Merz somebody else was sharing it with you Mr. Taunton not at that moment Mr. Merz the moment when Mr. Lichine moved in with you Mr. Taunton yes sir Mr. Merz you're sure of that Mr. Taunton sure of what sir Mr. Merz that at the moment Mr. Lichine moved in with you Mr. Taunton you were or were not the sole occupant of that office Mr. Taunton I didn't say that sir Mr. Merz would the stenographer read back the question."

The stenographer replaced the lifted folds of tape on the pile behind the machine as though he were setting a string of pearls back in a satin box. He tapped the nose piece of his glasses and repoised his fingers over the Stenotype keyboard like Horowitz coming into working position for one of the Brandenburg concertos.

"Mr. Taunton, will you answer the question, please," Mandamus Manny said gravely.

Jack Taunton made a nervous pass at the knot in his tie.

"I think I'm a little confused, sir," he said.

"The fault is mine, I'm sure," Manny Merz said. "I apologize. Let's try again, shall we? All I want to know, Mr. Taunton, is were you or were you not the sole occupant of your office at Isham Truitt when Mr. Lichine moved in with you?"

"Yes, sir, I was, but I had been for only a few days," Jack

Taunton said with obvious relief. "My previous office mate had left about a week before to take another job."

"I thought so," Manny Merz said.

"Your Honor," the district attorney said. "I wonder if it would be amiss to ask Mr. Merz at this point if he would give us some hint as to the thrust of his examination?"

"My thrust is the thrust of all interrogation," Mandamus Manny said. "A quest for accuracy. As a senior partner in the law firm by which Mr. Lichine and Mr. Taunton are employed, I am aware of our office-space arrangements. I want the record to reflect with unchallengeable correctness, as clearly as a photograph, the place in which Mr. Taunton and Mr. Lichine came to know each other."

"Would it matter to the issue we are probing here today," the district attorney said, "if they had come to know each other in, let us say, the men's washroom, Mr. Merz?"

Judge McNally lifted his gavel and gave the bench a single, light tap.

"Gentlemen," he said. With a brief flash of the pleasant little smile, he added, "I suggest, Mr. Merz, you move on."

"Thank you, sir," Emanuel Merz said with a small bow. "Mr. Taunton, how long ago did Mr. Lichine become your office mate?"

"About a year, I think," Jack Taunton said. "A little less, probably. Ten months, I'd say."

"No matter about the exact numbers," Manny Merz said. "What I'm after is was it long enough for you to become friendly, would you say?"

"Oh, yes," Jack Taunton said. "I would certainly say that, sir."

"Do you happen to have any independent recollection of the events we have been discussing?" Merz said. "The events of Thursday, August 10, 1978, in the Isham Truitt offices?"

"Yes, sir, I have," Jack Taunton said.

"Would you be good enough to let us have them, please?" Emanuel Merz said.

"According to my desk diary I had a nine o'clock meeting that morning at Paul Weiss," Jack Taunton said. "I don't recall exactly how long it lasted, but the diary indicates I got back to my office at Isham Truitt at eleven forty-five. Tom Lichine was at his desk. I was surprised to see him because two weeks ago he'd gone down to Alabama on a pro bono assignment that I understood was to take a month. Tom said he'd flown back the night before to pick up some papers and he'd be returning to Alabama late in the day but first he had a noon meeting in Mr. Kelly's office. In fact, when I came in he was straightening some papers on his desk in preparation for that meeting, and a few minutes after I came in Tom went off to the meeting. According to my desk calendar I then had a one o'clock lunch date at Fried Frank down at one-twenty Broadway. When I got back to my own office a little after three, Tom was at his desk and he looked, well, I don't know how to describe it."

"Please try," Emanuel Merz said.

"Sort of grim," Jack Taunton said. "Yes, grim. He kept banging the drawers of his desk, which was not like him, because he's a thoughtful and considerate person. Anyway, I'd always found him so, and this disturbed me, so I asked him if anything was wrong. His answer was a surprise."

"What was his answer?" Manny Merz said.

"He said you could call it that," Jack Taunton said.

"Why did that answer surprise you?" Emanuel Merz said.

"The tone of his voice," Jack Taunton said.

"Still grim?" Manny Merz said.

"Yes, but more," Jack Taunton said. "Bitter, I'd say. Yes, that's right. He sounded bitter, which, again, I must say was not like him at all. I'd always found Tom Lichine a sort of lighthearted person. Not lacking in seriousness is what I mean. I mean that's what I don't mean. That he was lacking in seriousness. I mean only that he was a wisecracker, so to speak. You know what I mean, sir."

"Jokes?" Manny Merz said.

"Yes, sir," Jack Taunton said. "A nice guy to share an office with. Always something flip and funny, so I told him I didn't want to pry, but if there was anything I could do all he had to do was ask."

"Did he?" Manny Merz said.

"He said you can get me another job," Jack Taunton said. "So that's how I found out he'd just been fired and what he was doing, banging drawers and so on, he was clearing out his desk."

"How long did that take?" Manny Merz said.

"I can't say exactly because I don't know when he started," Jack Taunton said. "But it must have been before three-thirty that he finished and we said good-bye and he left."

"How do you nail it down that it must have been before three-thirty?" Emanuel Merz said.

"My telephone log shows I took a call at three-thirty from Walter Fried of Fried Frank, the man I'd been lunching with less than an hour earlier, and I remember clearly because of the subject matter of the call that I was alone in my office when I took it."

"Let me recap, then," Mandamus Manny said. "According to your recollection, supported by your desk diary and your telephone log, on Thursday, August 10, 1978, you saw Tom Lichine twice. First, in the morning, briefly, from eleven forty-five to noon when he told you he was on his way to a meeting in Mr. Kelly's office. Is that correct?"

"Yes, sir," Jack Taunton said.

"And then later in the day," Manny Merz said. "From approximately a few minutes after three, when you came back into your office from a downtown lunch date, to no later than three-thirty when your telephone log indicates you took a three-thirty call while you were alone in your office. Is that correct?"

"Yes, sir," Jack Taunton said.

"And what we're talking about," Merz said, "we're talking about Thursday, August 10, 1978 in the offices of Isham, Truitt, Kelly, Shreve, Merz, Uchitel and Condomine at six-three-five Madison Avenue here in New York City. Is that correct, Mr. Taunton?"

"Yes, sir," Jack Taunton said.

"Thank you, Mr. Taunton. No further questions," Mandamus Manny said. He turned to counsels' table. "Your witness, Mr. Hyatt."

The district attorney came to his feet. No funny stuff this time, Judy Cline noted. Mr. Hyatt just stood up.

"No questions, Your Honor," he said.

"You may proceed, Mr. Merz," the judge said.

"Thank you, Your Honor," Manny Merz said. He paused, looked thoughtfully down at the floor, then at his wristwatch. "Do we have time for a motion, Your Honor?"

The judge glanced up at the wall clock. So did everybody else in the courtroom, including Judy Cline. The clock showed a quarter to one.

"Unless it's lengthy," Judge McNally said.

"On the contrary, sir," Manny Merz said. "It's very short."

"Proceed, then, Mr. Merz," the judge said.

"Thank you, Your Honor," Manny Merz said. "My client, Mr. Lichine, has been detained by the governor of this state for extradition to the state of Alabama to face a charge of murder that, according to the indictment, was committed in the state of Alabama at approximately one o'clock in the afternoon on Thursday, August 10, 1978. The evidence that has been adduced here this morning, Your Honor, proves indisputably that on Thursday, August 10, 1978, between the hours of seven-thirty in the morning, when he was found asleep on the couch here in New York in his office, until approximately three-thirty in the afternoon when he said farewell to his New York office mate, my client, Mr. Thomas L. Lichine, Jr., was not in Alabama but was physically present here in New York City at the offices of his employer, Isham, Truitt, Kelly, Shreve, Merz, Uchitel and Condomine, at six-three-five Madison Avenue, New York, New York, one-o-o-two-two.

"Under Article Four, Section Two of the U. S. Constitution," Emanuel Merz continued, "implemented by Section Eight-three-o of the Code of Criminal Procedure of the State of New York, both previously cited, my client has thus met the burden of proof required to challenge in this hearing the legality of his detention by the governor of this state. My client asks, therefore, that his writ of habeas corpus be granted, and that he be discharged from custody forthwith. Thank you, Your Honor."

"Mr. Hyatt?" Judge McNally said.

The sandy-haired man glanced from the bench to Emanuel Merz, then back to the bench. He did not look troubled, but Judy Cline had now watched the assistant district attorney through two lengthy court sessions. She had learned to read his moods. Some of them, anyway. At the moment, Judy felt, Mr. Hyatt was unsure of something. The look on his face reminded Judy of her father when he was about to ask her for a loan. He was weighing his chances.

"If Your Honor please," the district attorney said, "I wonder if I could have a word in private?"

"Come to the side bar, please," the judge said.

Mr. Hyatt went up to the bench and around to one side. He leaned his chin toward Judge McNally. The judge leaned across the bench, down to the district attorney, and cupped a hand to his ear. They talked in whispers for what seemed to Judy Cline no more than a few moments. Then Judge McNally looked up.

"Mr. Merz," he called.

"Yes, Your Honor?" Manny Merz called back.

"Would you be good enough to join us?" Judge McNally said.

"If I may say so, sir," Mandamus Manny said, "I think I am entitled to a ruling on my motion without further discussion."

The small, shy smile flicked across Judge McNally's face. The eyes, however, or so it seemed to Judy Cline, pulled together into a couple of hard glints, as though they were steel marbles caught in the reflected sunlight from the high windows.

"Please come to the side bar, Mr. Merz," the judge said.

"Certainly, Your Honor," Mandamus Manny said.

He went up to the bench. With alacrity? Judy decided not. There was no joy in Mandamus Manny's gait. Only haste. He moved like a man who, supremely confident of his game, had just learned to his puzzled astonishment that, somewhere along what had seemed a careful and sensibly played line, he had missed a shot. Or thought he had. He was totally concentrated on getting to the place where he could learn what it was.

Mandamus Manny took his place beside the district attorney and leaned his chin toward the judge. The sun pouring down from the high windows caught only the heads of the three men. They seemed momentarily separated from their bodies. Judy Cline was reminded of a souvenir statuette of Mount Rushmore she had once seen.

Then the heads separated. Mandamus Manny and the district attorney walked back to counsels' table. Their faces, it seemed to

Judy, were so relentlessly expressionless that both men seemed to be in pain. It was as though in making this effort to give no physical indications of what was going through their minds they were using muscles never before called into play. Judge McNally waited until both men reached counsels' table. Then he lifted his gavel.

"Court is adjourned until ten o'clock tomorrow morning," he said.

One tap.

27

"I'm afraid I can give you only a few minutes," Mrs. Shreve said. "I'm in a hurry, as you can see."

Judy could see more than that. She saw a small, neat woman in a tweed suit out of this year's Paris showings. She wore a tricorne hat out of an early FDR newsreel. And her seat in the chair behind the desk belonged under the rump of any British monarch who ever rode sidesaddle.

"I'm sorry to be late," Judy said. "I just got back to the office. I came along as soon as I saw your message."

"I left it for you at ten-twenty this morning," Mrs. Shreve said.

It was not in the words. It was not in the tone. It was suddenly in the air. A whiff of divine right had entered the room.

"I was in court down on Centre Street," Judy said.

The eyes under the tricorne hat dropped to the clock on the desk.

"Until now?" Mrs. Shreve said.

"No," Judy said. "I had a lunch date."

"It is now twenty-six minutes after three," Mrs. Shreve said.

Judy looked at her wristwatch.

"I make it twenty-eight after," she said.

The voice chasing her did not get louder. What stabbed at Judy from behind was the sense of astonished outrage.

"Where are you going?"

Judy turned at the door.

"Back to my office," she said. "After I saw your message I felt the other things that had piled up could wait. I was wrong."

"Please forgive me."

Judy stopped pulling the door open. Holding the knob, she turned back to the anachronism behind the desk.

"All right," Judy said. "Let's start again."

"Please," Saphira Shreve said. She smiled. "Do sit down. It's true that I'm in a hurry, but it's equally true that I'm always in a hurry, as you may have heard."

Judy returned the smile and came back across the room. She sat down beside the desk of the improbable equestrienne.

"I've been at Isham Truitt for almost a full year," Judy said. "I still haven't met all the partners, but over coffee in ITCH and around the water cooler I've had volunteer character sketches dropped in my lap about pretty nearly all of them. If you've been hit with one about me it seems only fair for me to say that it wouldn't be accurate if it didn't include the fact that I'm always in a hurry, too. Mainly because I'm not very well organized, so I'm sympathetic toward someone who feels as I do that there's never really enough time to get it all done."

"I was rude," Mrs. Shreve said. "You don't owe me an explanation for the length of time you take for lunch."

Judy was not fooled by the shift in gears. It did not change the thrust of Mrs. Shreve's interest. Judy could see that the older woman realized she had made a mistake in tactics. Judy could also see that to Mrs. Shreve it was not an occasion for despair or even embarrassment. It was a mistake based on lack of knowledge about the person she had attempted to bully. As a result, for the next few minutes Mrs. Shreve was probably not going to be an obvious bully. She would, however, never stop being a demanding tyrant. Now that Judy's feathers were smoothed down she was able to note also that there might be something admirable about this ninety-five-pound martinet.

"Just the same I think you're entitled to an explanation," Judy said. "The lunch was with my father. It was not prearranged. He happened to drop into the courtroom this morning, and when it was over he asked me to have lunch with him. I don't see him very often, so I couldn't say no, and I didn't feel I could rush him. After all, he paid my way through law school."

"In a way he did the same for me," Mrs. Shreve said.

"My father?" Judy said.

Saphira Shreve laughed.

"If you are Clifford Cline's daughter, yes," she said.

"Wait a minute," Judy said. "Pieces are falling into place. Mr. Shreve was Samuel Shreve?"

"Sammy Shreve," his widow said. "Songwriters are never known as Samuel. When Sammy died in a 1948 plane crash what he left me and the children to pay the bills with was an ASCAP rating. Some of the things that contributed to it came out of a couple of scores Sammy had written in his early days for a couple of early Clifford Cline musicals. Three of the songs in those scores became standards. They still are. I used part of that ASCAP rating to underwrite my tuition at Columbia Law School, and my daughters may very well end up doing the same thing with it for my granddaughters. Lawyers used to stumble in and out of my family. Now they seem to run in it. How is your father?"

"Very much with it," Judy said. "He spent most of our lunch today analyzing this Tom Lichine extradition hearing and telling me how he thought I should proceed after this morning's adjournment."

"How odd," Saphira Shreve said. "That's what I wanted to talk to you about."

"At ten-twenty this morning?" Judy said.

The pool-cue-straight back could not have lost its stiffness. Not, Judy felt, without causing the owner to collapse like a pricked balloon. And yet, because it was the core of Saphira Shreve's image, it bore the brunt of her slightest physical change. Even when the change was invisible. Judy could not see the impact, but she knew Mrs. Shreve had been jolted by Judy's question.

"No, of course not," said the neat little woman in the tricorne hat. "I had no idea at ten-twenty what was going on down on Centre Street. I rang you because I had a call from Hugh Kelly in Rome and he asked me to talk with you."

"About what?" Judy said.

"The Uhlfelder property," Mrs. Shreve said.

"I drafted the closing memorandum for him on that two

255

weeks ago," Judy said. "I accompanied him to the closing three days before he took off for Rome. It's all buttoned up, down to the last transfer stamp. What's he doing worrying about it in Rome at ten-twenty this morning?"

"Ten-twenty this morning New York time," Mrs. Shreve said. "Mr. Kelly is not worrying about it. Cardinal Fratianni is doing the worrying."

"Who is Cardinal Fratianni?" Judy said.

"The man in charge of whatever they call the office in the Vatican that hands out decorations," Mrs. Shreve said. "The Uhlfelder property apparently extends beyond the boundaries of the Borough of Queens. When nobody was looking a large dollop of it seems to have spilled over on the Duchy of Luxembourg."

"That's news to me," Judy said.

"It seems to be news to Hugh Kelly as well," Saphira Shreve said. "That's why he called you and, when he couldn't get you, he spoke to me."

"I wasn't aware that you knew anything about the Uhlfelder property," Judy said.

"I don't," Mrs. Shreve said. "But I know Clitus Uhlfelder, the last survivor of that tight-fisted clan. I sometimes think I know him too well. I rewrite his will at least three times a year. If he's well enough in August to get up to Saratoga, it usually means four rewrites that year. Watching his horses come in last seems to inspire Clitus to the invention of newer, more complicated, and more unworkable codicils. He's more or less harmless, at least so long as he pays his bills for all this foolish work we do for him, and he has absolutely no control over the Uhlfelder property that has just been added to the Church's American real estate holdings, but Cardinal Fratianni seems to be a cautious type."

"What's he got to do with it?" Judy said.

"In one way, nothing," Mrs. Shreve said. "In another, or Hugh Kelly way, everything."

"What's the everything way?" Judy said.

"If he can satisfy Cardinal Fratianni," Mrs. Shreve said, "Hugh Kelly may come back from Rome a prince of the Church."

"I suppose if I don't ask the next question you'll think I'm backward," Judy said.

"No chance of that, I assure you," Saphira Shreve said. "But do ask it anyway."

"What have I got to do with making Mr. Kelly a prince of the Church?" Judy said.

"You can fly to Rome tonight and assure Cardinal Fratianni as one Catholic to another that the Uhlfelder spillover into Luxembourg will never, as Hugh Kelly puts it in any way, shape, form, or manner, seep back to damage the legitimacy of the Church's title to the property in the Borough of Queens."

"I'm not a Catholic," Judy said.

"I pointed that out to Hugh Kelly," Mrs. Shreve said. "I told him I knew you were Clifford Cline's daughter, and I knew also from my husband that Cline was a Jew, so it seemed most unlikely that you could be a Catholic. Hugh Kelly said you very well could be because you are an adopted daughter and it had been a condition of the adoption that the Clines should not be told the religious affiliation of your natural parents. In Vatican circles, at least in the Vatican circles where Cardinal Fratianni functions, this seemed to clinch it. Not knowing what you are, Hugh Kelly said, Cardinal Fratianni cannot imagine you doing anything but leaping at the opportunity to nail down your claim to being a Catholic."

"Do you believe that?" Judy said.

"Hugh Kelly didn't ask me to express an opinion," Saphira Shreve said. "He asked me to convey a message."

"You've done that," Judy said. "I'm now asking for your opinion."

"In matters involving other people's religious beliefs," Mrs. Shreve said, "I have no opinions."

"I'm not asking for your opinion about a religious belief," Judy said. "I'm asking your opinion as a lawyer about a matter of credibility."

"Credibility about what?" Saphira Shreve said.

"Mr. Kelly's motives," Judy said.

The pool-cue-straight back repeated its earlier performance. It did not bend, but it conveyed a message. It told Judy that Mrs. Shreve had been jolted again.

"You'd better explain that," she said.

"Last week I turned down Mr. Kelly's invitation to accompany him and Mrs. Kelly on a holiday trip to Rome," Judy said. "You can tell Mr. Kelly today I'm turning down his request to come talk to Cardinal Fratianni for the same reason."

"What was your reason?" Mrs. Shreve said.

"Howard Dent had asked me to serve as his assistant in the defense of Tom Lichine at his extradition hearing," Judy said.

"Howard Dent is dead," Saphira Shreve said.

"Tom Lichine's extradition hearing is not," Judy said.

"It's in what I believe every knowledgeable lawyer in New York would agree are capable hands," Mrs. Shreve said.

"Will the owner of those hands be in Special Term, Part Two tomorrow morning ready to go to work?" Judy said.

"I suggest you ask Mr. Merz," Saphira Shreve said.

"Mr. Merz hurried out of court today before I could get to him with the question," Judy said. "When I got back here to the office I called his secretary. She said Mr. Merz had been called out of town unexpectedly. I asked if he would be back in time to resume the conduct of Mr. Lichine's defense. She said I'd better ask you."

"Phrase your question," Mrs. Shreve said.

"Why did Mr. Merz consent to the adjournment of Mr. Lichine's extradition hearing until tomorrow morning?" Judy said.

"Before he left his office this morning for the courtroom," Saphira Shreve said, "the assistant district attorney received a crucial piece of information. Mr. Hyatt had learned that the board of directors of the Fillmore National Bank had just elected Mr. Merz to succeed the deceased Sosthenes DeKalb as executive operations officer of Southern Shoals Asbestos. Mr. Hyatt felt Judge McNally should be aware of this before he acted on Mr. Merz's motion that Mr. Lichine's writ of habeas corpus be granted."

"Why?" Judy said.

"If Judge McNally denied the motion," Saphira Shreve said,

"Mr. Hyatt felt it might leave Mr. Lichine without counsel to continue the prosecution of his writ."

"Isn't that precisely what today's adjournment has done?" Judy said.

"Neither precisely nor even remotely," Mrs. Shreve said. "It is not our custom here at Isham Truitt to abandon a staff member in time of trouble. Mr. Merz's departure to take up the reins of Southern Shoals in Alabama was preceded by the retention of substitute counsel to replace him in Special Term, Part Two tomorrow morning."

"Who?" Judy said.

"Ezra Kingsley Cooper," Saphira Shreve said.

"The man Mr. Merz fired two weeks ago from Isham Truitt for incompetence," Judy said.

"Not incompetence," Mrs. Shreve said. "Mr. Merz fired Mr. Cooper to force him into taking the chance elsewhere that Mr. Cooper in spite of his brilliance as a lawyer had somehow missed here at Isham Truitt. Mr. Merz proved to be right. Mr. Cooper was hired almost immediately by Falk, Prudhomme and Rhodes at a salary handsomely in excess of what he was earning with us plus the promise of a partnership in the imminent future. Mr. Cooper is pleased by Mr. Merz's action in hiring him as his replacement in the Lichine matter. It is, Mr. Cooper feels, a corroboration at long last of the confidence Mr. Merz had displayed when he recruited Mr. Cooper out of Columbia twenty-eight years ago."

"Was Mr. Lichine consulted about this substitution of counsel?" Judy said.

"Does it matter?" Mrs. Shreve said.

"Not to you, perhaps," Judy said. "It could matter a great deal, however, to Mr. Kelly's chances of coming back from Rome as a prince of the Church."

"I fail to see the connection," Mrs. Shreve said.

"Cardinal Fratianni won't," Judy said.

"What is the connection?" Mrs. Shreve said.

"When I got back here after lunch with my father," Judy said, "I found Mr. Lichine's wife waiting for me in my office. Bianca Bean and her husband had learned about Mr. Merz's election to succeed Sosthenes DeKalb at Southern Shoals. Mrs. Lichine told me she and her husband were in the market to find a lawyer who would succeed Mr. Merz in Special Term, Part Two tomorrow morning."

This time there was no doubt about the movement of Saphira Shreve's body. It wheeled smoothly, as though with a light tap of the spur she had touched the flank of her invisible mount. She picked up the telephone.

"Get me Gil Cutter, please," said the woman in the tricorne hat.

She replaced the phone.

"If you accept Mrs. Lichine's offer," Saphira Shreve said to Judy, "if you show up in Special Term, Part Two tomorrow morning, you need show up here at six-three-five Madison only one more time. To clear out your desk. I am about to instruct our office manager to adjust his payroll records."

The phone rang. Saphira Shreve edged the instrument neatly into place against her ear under the brim of the tricorne hat. She talked across the mouthpiece without bothering to cover it.

"What shall I tell Mr. Cutter?" Saphira Shreve said to Judy Cline.

28

"And that's the way it is," Walter Cronkite said. "On this Thursday night, August 25, 1978."

The commercial came on. Ezra Cooper became aware of the doorbell. With the sound came a moment of surprise. He had forgotten he was expecting a visitor. This had not happened since Jessica's operation. Ezra Cooper glanced at his wife. She sat, as always, facing the TV screen. The damaged side of her face was turned away from her husband. Jessica was, as always, unaware of the commercial. This meant she had not heard the doorbell. Slipping out of his chair to answer it, Ezra became aware of something else: the pleasure in his moment of surprise.

This was the first time since Jessica had come home from the hospital that there was something new in her quiet, dogged, uninflected, relentless monologue. Moving away from her, toward the foyer and the ringing doorbell, Ezra Cooper found himself responding to the new thing in Jessica's voice. It was hope.

"—this man from Vienna," she was saying. "The one who had been trained by the great Dr. Stieghoffer before the Nazis killed him. Dr. Quentin writes from Johns Hopkins that the man is working in Zurich, and the work he's been doing has been on cases so similar to mine that Dr. Quentin feels it's worth the financial risk of a trip to Switzerland. Up to now there has been no money, of course, with which to take the financial risk. Now, however, now that after all these years you have left Isham Truitt, where they never appreciated you anyway, and you have joined this new firm, the risk doesn't seem so large. Your Falk, Prudhomme and Rhodes salary should enable us to finance this trip. Not on a lavish scale, of course, but at least adequately, and if the Falk Prudhomme promise of a partnership should ever turn out to be more than a promise, I think we will look back on this decision to go to Switzerland and have this doctor take over my case as a turning point in our lives. A turning point for which we will—"

Jessica's voice receded as Ezra Cooper moved out into the foyer. He moved with a lightness that brought back memories of the day long ago when he and Jessica had walked all the way back uptown from the marriage license bureau. The day they had stumbled into the "For Sale" sign on the stoop of the beat-up old brownstone at Sixty-second and Third in which they had been imprisoned for twenty-eight years. As he slid aside the brass cap and put his eye to the peephole, the feeling of being a prisoner came back to Ezra with a small, disturbing shock.

For almost two weeks he had been wondering what it was about Jack Taunton that made him feel uneasy. Squinting out at the young lawyer on the stoop, Ezra suddenly knew. Jack Taunton looked like the sort of man who lived in places where people didn't come out into the street until after dark, and turned up their coat collars as they looked both ways before they walked off into the night. Ezra pulled open the door.

"Hope I didn't keep you waiting," he said. "We had the TV set turned up high."

"No, of course not," Jack Taunton said. "Mrs. Cooper okay?"

"Fine, yes," Ezra said. "Let's go into the study."

Crossing the rear of the living room, he noted that Jessica had not moved from the chair in front of the TV set. Turning into the study, Ezra noted that Jack Taunton had noted the same thing.

"That reminds me," Jack Taunton said as Ezra closed the study door.

"Of what?" Ezra said.

"Last time I was in this room Mrs. Cooper brought in the news the Vice-President had just dropped dead," Jack Taunton said. "On the car radio coming over here a few minutes ago the CBS man in Washington said the replacement field had narrowed down to Kissinger and David Fillmore."

"Don't you find it expensive keeping a car in New York?" Ezra said. "You were sitting over there at the end of the couch where some of the springs were still working."

"Feels like they still are," Jack Taunton said with a smile as he dropped onto the couch. "Keeping anything in New York, whether it's a car, a dog, or a mistress, is never cheap. The trick is not to avoid what costs money. The trick is to manipulate yourself closer to where the money is handed out."

"Drink?" Ezra said. Then: "No, I forgot. You're a teetotaler."

He sat down at the desk he and Jessica had bought second-hand twenty-eight years ago to tide them over until on their clearly mapped life plan they would be ready to move out of the remodeling phase into the redecorating phase.

"Still liking it at Falk Prudhomme?" Jack Taunton said.

"Very much," Ezra Cooper said.

"I happen to know the feeling is mutual," Jack Taunton said.

He said it with a movement of the heavily lidded eyes that indicated the face of the depraved faun was registering a smile. Ezra Cooper recognized the signal. He laughed.

"There are times when a man doesn't mind learning people are talking behind his back," he said. "Who's talking behind mine?"

"People who call my father in Washington," Jack Taunton said. "He calls me back and reports in detail."

"What do you report to him?" Ezra Cooper said.

"Pretty damn near everything," Jack Taunton said. "A little while ago, for instance, I told him I had a date here tonight to go over the homework I left with you on my first visit."

From the papers on his desk Ezra Cooper picked up the batch of Xeroxed sheets. He didn't like playing Pavlov's dog to this slippery kid half his age, but in looking back on his twenty-eight years at Isham Truitt one thing stood out clearly in Ezra Cooper's survey: all the kids who were half his age when he started had made it to what Jack Taunton had just called the place where the money was handed out. Ezra doubted it was fair for him to add to his observation that they all looked slippery, but the doubt did not linger. During the past twenty-eight years Ezra Cooper's interest in fairness had undergone major erosion.

"*Pridemore* v. *Southern Shoals Asbestos*," Ezra read from the top sheet. "Alabama Supreme Court. Testimony Digest Prepared for J. C. Taunton by P. B. Pember, August 1978." Ezra looked up. "What would you like to know?"

"For starters, how did the case hit you?" Jack Taunton said.

"Unless I get more of a directive than that," Ezra Cooper said, "I'm afraid all I can give you is a recital of the facts."

"I'm listening," Jack Taunton said.

Ezra Cooper put down the batch of papers.

"During the war in 1945 a man named Ansel Pridemore goes to work in one of the Southern Shoals Asbestos plants down in Montgomery, Alabama," Ezra said. "Thirty years later, in 1975, he comes down with a lung disease known as mesothelioma. He goes to the Southern Shoals employees' dispensary for treatment. The company doctors say there's nothing they can do for him. Mr. Pridemore goes to a private doctor. He says what's made Pridemore sick is thirty years of breathing asbestos on his job and he should ask for compensation from his employers at least to pay for all the oxygen Pridemore now has to buy just to keep himself alive. Southern Shoals disclaims responsibility. Pridemore goes to a lawyer. Lawyer starts suit. Case is thrown out of court."

Ezra Cooper again lifted the batch of Xeroxed pages.

"Pridemore appeals," he said. "Court of Appeals sustains the lower court." Ezra Cooper dropped the pages back on the desk. "End of recital."

"You don't sound impressed," Jack Taunton said.

"Not yet," Ezra Cooper said. "But I'm waiting."

"For what?" Jack Taunton said.

"When you were here last and you gave me this digest," Ezra Cooper said, "I think I'm quoting accurately when I say you told me here's your homework. While you're doing it, you said, I'll get my other cards in position, and then we'll have a strategy session. I wanted to know about what, and there I know I'm accurate. You said quote how to destroy Isham Truitt unquote. I assume we're having that strategy session right now."

"We are," Jack Taunton said.

"Why don't we start it with the answer to a question?" Ezra Cooper said. "How is this small-potatoes indemnification case, flowing out of a boondocks asbestos plant down in Montgomery, Alabama, going to lead to you and me destroying one of the most prestigious big-time law firms in the country?"

"Good question," Jack Taunton said. "Try one of mine. Did anything unusual happen to you today?"

"That's the glimmer of light at the end of the tunnel?" Ezra Cooper said.

"Answer the question and we'll see," Jack Taunton said.

"What happened to me today is so unusual," Ezra Cooper said, "it occurred to me immediately that's the reason you called and asked could you come over tonight."

"That's not an answer to my question," Jack Taunton said.

"All right, try this," Ezra Cooper said. "At two o'clock this afternoon the man who two weeks ago fired me from Isham Truitt asked me, because he's been unexpectedly called out of town, to take over from him as defense attorney in a case he's been trying in Special Term, Part two."

"What's the name of the case?" Jack Taunton said.

"*Thomas L. Lichine, Jr.* v. *Herman L. Hofnagel,* as warden of the City Prison, Borough of Manhattan," Ezra Cooper said.

"Do you know Herman Hofnagel?" Jack Taunton said.

"No, but I know Tom Lichine," Ezra Cooper said.

"Do you know the facts in the case?" Jack Taunton said.

"Does Napoleon know the geography of Waterloo?" Ezra Cooper said. "It's because two weeks ago I laid the facts about Tom Lichine on Mandamus Manny's desk that Mr. Merz kicked me out of Isham Truitt on my ass."

"I'll bet today he made a suitable apology," Jack Taunton said.

"It's the sort of situation in which I'm not sure I know what's suitable," Ezra Cooper said. "I do know at two o'clock this afternoon Mr. Merz said he was sorry about what happened two weeks ago. He called it a misunderstanding and said so far as he was concerned it would have a happy ending if I would say yes to his offer that I take over from him tomorrow in *Lichine* v. *Hofnagel.*"

"And you said what?" Jack Taunton said.

"My question comes first," Ezra Cooper said. He picked up the testimony digest of *Pridemore* v. *Southern Shoals Asbestos.* "How is this thing going to lead to our destroying Isham Truitt?"

"Tomorrow morning in Special Term, Part Two," Jack Taunton said, "you will find out at ten o'clock."

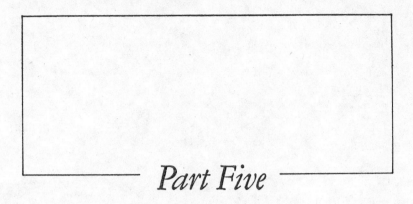

Part Five

"The law protects everybody who
can afford to hire a good lawyer."
THE HONORABLE JAMES J. WALKER

29

Actually he didn't find out until almost ten-twenty. Neither did Judy Cline. It took Judge McNally ten minutes to get to the core of the confusion, and another ten to set it straight. At the end of the fuss the judge, apparently speaking to himself, said, "Very well." He looked up from the papers in front of him. With the gavel he gave the bench a single, sharp, decisive tap. He cleared his throat.

"We have here what might be described as a superfluity of relator's requests for substitution of counsel," Judge McNally said. "We will take them one at a time. Mr. Cooper?"

"Yes, sir," Ezra Cooper said.

He could not have taken a step forward. He could not have moved at all. Ezra Cooper was already, like Judy and the assistant district attorney standing beside her, so close to the bench that his chin was almost resting on the edge. Just the same, Ezra Cooper did give the impression that he had stepped forward. It could have been, Judy felt, no more than a nervous movement. An indication, perhaps, of deference involving no physical movement at all. Or perhaps the inner reflection of a strong eagerness to please. During her year with Isham Truitt, Judy Cline had never met Ezra Cooper. She had become aware of his existence less than two weeks ago, on the day he had been fired. Now, keeping him just barely in sight out of the corner of one eye, Judy was aware of a moment of irrelevant interest.

So this, her mind recorded with an invisible raised eyebrow, is what they look like. The men and women who stayed too long without making partner and then, knowing they would never make it, stayed on because they were too old to step out on their own and try elsewhere. Judy realized for the first time she was standing cheek by jowl with one of those associates known contemptuously at Isham Truitt as permanent fixtures.

"Mr. Merz, who yesterday represented the plaintiff in this action, has been called out of town," Judge McNally said. "Relator requests that you be allowed to substitute for Mr. Merz as counsel for the plaintiff. Is that correct, Mr. Cooper?"

"Yes, Your Honor," Ezra Cooper said.

"Now, then, Miss Cline," Judge McNally said. "When this hearing started four days ago you were acting as assistant to Mr. Howard Dent, who was serving as counsel for the plaintiff. After Mr. Dent's unfortunate demise, when Mr. Merz took over yesterday as plaintiff's counsel, you continued to act as assistant to Mr. Dent's successor. Today, with Mr. Merz's unexpected departure, relator requests that you be allowed to substitute for Mr. Merz as counsel for the plaintiff. Is that correct, Miss Cline?"

"Yes, Your Honor," Judy said.

"In other words," Judge McNally said, "the relator has requested that both you and Mr. Cooper represent him?"

"I don't think so, Your Honor," Judy said.

"Your Honor," Ezra Cooper said. "May I clarify that?"

"Yes, if and when Miss Cline fails to do so," Judge McNally said. "I will then ask for your assistance. Right now I am addressing myself to Miss Cline. Please proceed, Miss Cline."

"The relator's wife, Mrs. Thomas Lichine, Jr., personally requested me to take over as her husband's counsel," Judy said. "The request was made at two o'clock yesterday afternoon in my office."

The judge nodded slowly and then created the impression that he was with difficulty wheeling himself into position to face a new situation with forthright directness. In fact, all he did was roll his eyeballs to the right.

"Now it's your turn, Mr. Cooper," the judge said. "Who asked you to take over as the plaintiff's counsel?"

"Mr. Merz, Your Honor," Ezra Cooper said.

"Not Mr. Lichine?" Judge McNally said.

"No, sir," Ezra Cooper said. "Mr. Merz called me about two o'clock yesterday afternoon. He explained the situation and asked if I would step in for him. I agreed to do so."

"How about Mrs. Lichine?" the judge said.

"I have never met Mrs. Lichine or talked with her on the phone," Ezra Cooper said.

"I said if Miss Cline failed to make the situation clear I would call for your assistance," Judge McNally said. He rolled the eyeballs to the left. "Miss Cline, do I need Mr. Cooper's assistance?"

"No, sir," Judy said. "I don't think you need mine, either, Your Honor."

"What do I need?" the judge said.

"A statement from the relator," Judy said. "Mr. Lichine is present in the courtroom right now, Your Honor."

Judge McNally looked across the heads of Ezra Cooper, Judy Cline, and the assistant district attorney as though he had just been advised that the representative of an invading enemy force had appeared at the courtroom door with a request for its immediate surrender. The uniformed attendant got the message.

"Thomas L. Lichine, Jr., please come forward," he called.

Judy turned with Ezra Cooper and the assistant district attorney. She saw Tom Lichine come to his feet from the same seat he had occupied the day before. He stepped out into the aisle and took three measured steps forward. When he stopped, Tom Lichine looked down at his shoes as though to make sure he was toeing an officially marked line.

"Yes, Your Honor," he said.

"Mr. Lichine, did you request the appearance of Miss Judith Cline as your counsel here today?" Judge McNally said.

"Yes, I did, sir," Tom Lichine said. "The request was made through my wife."

"Do you still want Miss Cline to appear here today as your counsel?" the judge said.

"Yes, I do," Tom Lichine said.

"Mr. Lichine, did you request the appearance of Mr. Cooper as your counsel here today?" Judge McNally said.

"No, I did not, sir," Tom Lichine said.

"Did your wife or anybody else acting or purporting to act on your behalf make such a request?" the judge said.

"Not to my knowledge, sir," Tom Lichine said. "And not at my behest, Your Honor."

"Thank you, Mr. Lichine," Judge McNally said. He turned to Judy. "I think you will agree, Miss Cline, that perhaps this would be a good moment for me to call on Mr. Cooper to lend a clarifying hand?"

"Yes, Your Honor, I do agree," Judy said.

"Mr. Cooper," the judge said. "Can you explain this odd situation?"

"I think so," Ezra Cooper said.

The tone of his voice made Judy turn her head for a better look. It was not the voice of a permanent fixture. It was the voice of a man annoyed, and Mr. Cooper's face matched his voice. It bore the look of a pitcher working his wad of cut plug into position inside his cheek as he wound up to put the old zip on his fast one.

"Please do," Judge McNally said.

"I have known Mr. Emanuel Merz for twenty-eight years," Ezra Cooper said. "He is an advocate of what is known in some legal circles as an excess of caution. My father would have put it differently. He would have said Mr. Merz is the sort of man who, when the welfare of a client is at issue, puts on a belt as well as a pair of suspenders to hold up his pants. In this situation I don't know if Mr. Merz considered me the belt or the suspenders, but I do know I would find neither role compatible with my legal skills such as they are, and therefore not in the best interests of Mr. Lichine. I am a lawyer with three decades of experience at the New York Bar. I am not a back-up assistant. If Your Honor please, I would like to withdraw my name as a candidate for what seems to be a contest to represent Mr. Lichine. What I will have to say to Mr. Merz for entering me in this contest is, as I am sure you understand, Your Honor, irrelevant to this record."

There was a nice ripple of laughter from the spectators.

"Thank you, Mr. Cooper," the judge said. "I do understand and I will accept the relator's request, then, that Miss Cline take over as his attorney in this matter. I hope I am correct in assuming that by so doing I will not be rendering a disservice to you, Mr. Cooper?"

"You are correct, sir," Ezra Cooper said. "I apologize to Your Honor for whatever role I may have played, unconsciously I assure you, in this morning's inconvenience to this court."

He turned and walked up the aisle like a man who clearly had only one thought in mind: how to find as quickly as possible the son of a bitch he intended to deck. For a moment Judy wondered how such a man could have permitted himself to become a permanent fixture in a firm like Isham Truitt, but the moment was brief. The assistant district attorney was addressing the court. Judy snapped to attention.

"If Your Honor please," Mr. Hyatt said. "I am beginning to feel somewhat like George Washington during the French and Indian War. I was taught at school that at the Battle of Fort Duquesne, even though his commander, General Braddock, was defeated, Washington was brought to national attention by this event because in the course of the battle he had three horses shot out from under him. In this matter of *Lichine* v. *Hofnagel* I have already had two of plaintiff's counsel shot out from under me, and I wouldn't want to tie Washington's record here in Special Term, Part Two. With Your Honor's permission, therefore, I would like to renew the motion I made four days ago, just before Mr. Dent collapsed."

Judge McNally flipped the pages of his loose-leaf notebook, stopped, turned back, and spent a few moments studying something on the page he had selected.

"You refer to Mr. Lichine's refusal on the stand to answer your question about what took place at the meeting in Mr. Kelly's private office on Thursday, August 10, 1978?" the judge said.

"I do, Your Honor," the assistant district attorney said.

"And your motion that I instruct Mr. Lichine to answer your question or be held in contempt?" Judge McNally said.

"Yes, Your Honor," Mr. Hyatt said.

"I dismissed your motion," the judge said.

"I am aware of that, sir," the assistant district attorney said.

"You asked for and I granted an exception," Judge McNally said.

"Yes, sir," Mr. Hyatt said.

"Why then do you want to renew the motion now?" the judge said.

"To save the court's time," the assistant district attorney said.

"The time of a court is saved by the repetition of matters already disposed of, Mr. Hyatt, only in courtrooms presided over by judges who are forgetful, indolent, or stupid," Judge McNally said. "Proceed, please."

"Your Honor," Judy said.

Even the head of the stenographer turned. Judy could feel her nose begin to wrinkle. Oh, God, she thought desperately, not now. By concentrating on the reason for the surprised attention her interruption had attracted she was able to suppress the attack of the cutes. The reason they were all staring, Judy realized, was that she had just uttered her first words in the courtroom not as an assistant to but as counsel for the plaintiff. It didn't seem possible to Judy that by so doing she was blazing a trail in a dodecagonal chapter house that had seen as much service as Special Term, Part Two. On the other hand, the same possibility may not have occurred to Madame Curie, either, when she first dipped her arms to the elbow in pitchblende.

"Yes, Miss Cline?" the judge said.

"I think Mr. Hyatt has his motions confused," Judy said.

"With what?" Judge McNally said.

"With the motion Mr. Merz made just before the adjournment yesterday," Judy said.

Again the judge flipped the pages of his loose-leaf notebook. He found what he wanted and studied the page briefly.

"Yes," he said. "Will the stenographer read it back, please?"

The neat little man at the Stenotype machine reached across his table to a stack of transcripts bound in blue. He picked one from the top and flipped to the last page.

"Mr. Merz," he read. "Under Article Four Section Two of the U. S. Constitution Your Honor implemented by Section Eight-o-three of the Code of Criminal Procedure of the State of New York both previously cited my client has thus met the burden of proof required to challenge in this hearing the legality of his detention by the governor of this state my client asks therefore that his writ of habeas corpus be granted and that he be discharged from custody forthwith thank you Your Honor." The stenographer looked up. "Shall I go on, sir?"

"No, thank you, that will do," Judge McNally said. "What happened after Mr. Merz made his motion was Mr. Hyatt's request for a word in private with the court. A few moments later Mr. Merz joined the conference for a while, and then court was adjourned until this morning. Is that correct, Miss Cline?"

"It is, Your Honor," Judy said. "I now move that the motion made yesterday by Mr. Merz be granted."

On Judge McNally's face the small, shy smile made a quick, reluctant appearance, as though it had taken itself by surprise, and then the smile promptly disappeared.

"If I did," the judge said, "I would be bringing Mr. Hyatt's record here in this courtroom up to that of George Washington's at Fort Duquesne."

"Your Honor would also be granting my client the relief he deserves and has brought this action to obtain," Judy said.

"That has not yet been determined to the satisfaction of the court," Judge McNally said. "Motion dismissed."

"Exception, Your Honor," Judy said.

"You may have your exception, Miss Cline," the judge said.

"Thank you, Your Honor," Judy said.

"You may proceed, Mr. Hyatt," the judge said.

"Thank you, Your Honor," the assistant district attorney said. "I will call Mr. Teaman Coleridge."

Judy's first reaction was astonishment. Watching him come down the aisle, she realized there were not enough spectators in Special Term, Part Two for her not to have noticed the only black face in the courtroom. How could she have missed him? Judy's next reaction was resentment. Judy thought she and Mr. Coleridge had hit it off rather well at their Bedford-Stuyvesant meeting the week before. Judy agreed with her annoyed self that it was possible she had missed the only black face in the courtroom for the very good reason that Mr. Coleridge may have entered the courtroom after she did, while Judy and Ezra Cooper and Mr. Hyatt were standing at the bench talking with Judge McNally. There was no doubt about another fact, however, and it came clear in Judy's mind just as Mr. Coleridge in the witness box was finishing the whole-truth-and-nothing-but-the-truth bit with the Bible. Mr. Teaman Coleridge had arrived in New York without letting Judy Cline know he was coming.

"Your full name, please," the assistant district attorney said.

"Teaman Coleridge."

"And where do you reside, sir?" Mr. Hyatt said.

"One-six-dash-ay South Bedelia Street, Montgomery, Alabama," Teaman Coleridge said.

"Your age, Mr. Coleridge?" the assistant district attorney said.

"Twenty-five," Teaman Coleridge said.

"Your profession?" Mr. Hyatt said.

"I am a member of the Bar of the state of Alabama," Teaman Coleridge said.

"Do you specialize in any particular branch of the law, Mr. Coleridge?" the assistant district attorney said.

"Not intentionally," Teaman Coleridge said. "My practice happens to fall about equally between civil and criminal work."

"Do you know an organization called the Southern Poverty Relief Legal Assistance Association?" Mr. Hyatt said.

"I do," Teaman Coleridge said.

"Are you in any way connected with the organization?" the assistant district attorney said.

"I am," Teaman Coleridge said.

"Would you be good enough to tell us something about what the organization does and what your relationship to it is?" Mr. Hyatt said.

"The Southern Poverty Relief Legal Assistance Association, as the somewhat unwieldy name indicates, is in the business of providing legal help for people who cannot afford to pay for lawyers," Teaman Coleridge said. "It is a nonprofit organization staffed by a partially paid secretariat plus mostly volunteers, as well as a few paid lawyers but also mostly volunteers. The volunteers are practicing attorneys in the area, people like myself who are part of a pool. SPRLAA calls on us as help is needed for particular cases and as members of the pool are available."

"What is known as pro bono work?" the assistant district attorney said.

"Yes, sir," Teaman Coleridge said.

"In connection with your work for the SPRLAA," Mr. Hyatt said, "are you familiar with a recent case identified as"—the assistant district attorney glanced down at a slip of paper—"*State of Alabama* v. *Prideman?*"

"Pridemore," Teaman Coleridge said.

"Sorry, Pridemore," Mr. Hyatt said. "Are you familiar with the case, Mr. Coleridge? *Alabama* v. *Pridemore?*"

"I am," Teaman Coleridge said.

"Would you tell us about it?" the assistant district attorney said. "I mean the nature of the case, your relationship to it, the work you did, what happened, as briefly or extensively as you choose, Mr. Coleridge, is what I mean. Could you, sir?"

"Certainly," Teaman Coleridge said, and he did what Judy remembered him doing in her Bedford-Stuyvesant office when Miss Gates brought in the coffee. Except that this time Mr. Coleridge was not smiling at a pretty girl. He was smiling at a not particularly ugly but certainly not outstandingly handsome sandy-haired, potbellied, middle-aged public servant who was about as glamorous as a scuffed tennis sneaker. The effect, however, was the same. Mr. Hyatt, Judy could see, was all at once very pleased with his witness.

"The defendant is a fifteen-year-old boy named Virgil Pridemore," Teaman Coleridge said. "On a Sunday morning back in February of 1978 Virgil was sitting at the wheel of a Ford pickup truck outside an all-night diner on the outskirts of Montgomery, Alabama. At two-thirty in the morning a man came running out of the diner, jumped into the pickup truck beside Virgil, and Virgil drove off. The man he drove away from that diner was Virgil's father, Ansel. It was determined later that when he came running out of that diner Ansel Pridemore had just shot and killed the short-order cook in the course of an armed holdup. Virgil and his father were both taken into custody and tried for murder in the first degree. In Alabama the penalty for conviction on a murder-one charge is death in the electric chair. Neither Ansel Pridemore nor his son could afford to hire a lawyer. The SPRLAA stepped in."

"The Southern Poverty Relief Legal Assistance Association?" the assistant district attorney said.

"Yes, sir," Teaman Coleridge said. "The SPRLAA provided counsel."

"Could you give us the name of the defense counsel they provided?" Mr. Hyatt said.

"Father Terence Danaher," Teaman Coleridge said.

"Father?" the assistant district attorney said.

"Father Danaher is an ordained Catholic priest," Teaman Coleridge said. "He was a member of the New York Bar and still is. A few years ago he also became a member of the Alabama Bar when he came down to Montgomery to take over the active direction of the SPRLAA. Father Danaher reviews all the cases the organization is asked to handle. He assigns counsel out of the available pool. He takes on many of the cases himself. Father Danaher took on the defense of Ansel Pridemore and his son Virgil."

"With what result?" Mr. Hyatt said.

"Both Ansel Pridemore and his son Virgil were found guilty," Teaman Coleridge said.

"Of murder in the first degree?" the assistant district attorney said.

"Yes, sir," Teaman Coleridge said.

"Did that end the matter?" Mr. Hyatt said.

"No, sir," Teaman Coleridge said. "Father Danaher appealed the conviction. In his appeal he petitioned the court to separate the two defendants. The petition was granted. The appeal of the boy came to trial first."

"Virgil," the assistant district attorney said.

"Yes, sir," Teaman Coleridge said.

"That's the case we are discussing," Mr. Hyatt said. "*Alabama* v. *Virgil Pridemore?*"

"Yes, sir," Teaman Coleridge said.

"Did Father Danaher try the case on appeal?" the assistant district attorney said.

"Yes, but he brought in some help," Teaman Coleridge said.

"What sort of help?" Mr. Hyatt said.

"A New York lawyer named Thomas L. Lichine, Jr.," Teaman Coleridge said.

"Under what circumstances, if you are aware of them, Mr. Coleridge, please?" the assistant district attorney said.

"There was no secret about it at SPRLAA or in the Montgomery district attorney's office," Teaman Coleridge said. "There never is. Pro bono help from New York and other parts of the country is quite common in SPRLAA cases. Mr. Lichine is an associate of Isham, Truitt, Kelly, Shreve, Merz, Uchitel and Condomine, a New York firm that provides pro bono assistants regularly for SPRLAA cases. Mr. Lichine was sent down at Father Danaher's request to serve for a month."

"In the Pridemore boy's appeal?" Mr. Hyatt said.

"Yes, sir," Teaman Coleridge said.

"Were you involved in the appeal, Mr. Coleridge?" Mr. Hyatt said.

"Only indirectly," Teaman Coleridge said.

"Would you explain that?" Mr. Hyatt said.

"I was interested in the case because of its legal aspects," Teaman Coleridge said. "I was interested, of course, in the fate of the boy on trial, but in the course of this sort of trial it is possible to learn things that can be useful as general principles in future trials. So I attended this trial purely as a spectator. On the second day, as I was walking out at the lunch break, Mr. Lichine came up and introduced himself and asked if he could join me for lunch. I said yes, and we had lunch."

"Would you tell us, Mr. Coleridge, what happened at that lunch?" the assistant district attorney said.

"Mr. Lichine shocked me," Teaman Coleridge said.

"In what way?" Mr. Hyatt said.

"He told me he was convinced he was wasting his time," Teaman Coleridge said. "Mr. Lichine believed Virgil Pridemore was going to lose his appeal."

"Did Mr. Lichine say why he believed that?" the assistant district attorney said.

"Father Danaher's ineptness," Teaman Coleridge said.

"I beg your pardon?" Mr. Hyatt said.

"Mr. Lichine told me," Teaman Coleridge said, "he was convinced young Virgil Pridemore was going to lose his appeal and would die in the electric chair because the man who was conducting his defense, Father Terence Danaher, was a stupid son of a bitch."

The murmur in the courtroom had started before Judy was fully on her feet.

"If Your Honor please," she said.

"Yes, Miss Cline?" the judge said.

"If that is a direct quotation," Judy said, "I would ask that the district attorney be instructed to set it in context at once so the record will indicate clearly the circumstances in which the statement was made."

Speaking as though he were having trouble with a lemon drop from which, he had just discovered after popping it into his mouth, he had failed to remove completely the tin-foil wrapper, Mr. Hyatt said, "Counsel has my assurance that the district attorney's office is as dedicated as she is to the creation of a record that reflects the spirit as well as the letter of the testimony adduced. Suggestions for improvement are, however, welcome from any citizen who indirectly pays the district attorney's salary, and so I thank you, Miss Cline."

Judy dropped back into her seat with two things she felt she richly deserved: a hot face and an uncontrollably wrinkling nose. She did not know if she was more furious with herself for providing Mr. Hyatt with the opening for his scrap of lumbering sarcasm, or with Judge McNally for his brief kindly smile and needlessly understated "Please proceed, Mr. Hyatt."

"Mr. Coleridge, would you explain the circumstances in which Mr. Lichine delivered this opinion of Father Danaher?" the assistant district attorney said.

"Mr. Lichine pointed out that Father Danaher's defense was based entirely on an old-fashioned sentimental appeal to the jury not to send a fifteen-year-old child to his death in the electric chair but to reduce the boy's punishment to the more humane life imprisonment," Teaman Coleridge said. "Mr. Lichine felt this sort of appeal had never been effective in the Deep South and especially in a place like Alabama, which is known as the 'death belt.' Mr. Lichine felt the only way he could justify his being on Virgil Pridemore's defense staff was to go beyond this old-fashioned sentimental appeal and come up with something fresh."

"Did he?" the assistant district attorney said.

"He certainly did," Teaman Coleridge said. "More accurately, at that first meeting Mr. Lichine told me he thought he had a fresh approach, but to put it into action he needed help from someone who knew the area, meaning Montgomery, and that was why he had asked me to lunch with him."

"Were you able to provide Mr. Lichine with the help he needed?" Mr. Hyatt said.

"The results would seem to indicate I did," Teaman Coleridge said.

"What were the results?" the assistant district attorney said.

"The jury brought in the verdict the defense had asked for," Teaman Coleridge said. "Life imprisonment. That fifteen-year-old boy will not die in the electric chair. Thanks to Mr. Lichine."

"And, I would say, to you for helping him?" Mr. Hyatt said.

"My help was not unique," Teaman Coleridge said. "Mr. Lichine's was. Any other lawyer in the area could have come up with the material Mr. Lichine was looking for. Only Mr. Lichine came up with the idea that the material was worth looking for."

"Would you tell us what Mr. Lichine's idea was?" the assistant district attorney said.

Judy came to her feet with a just-as-firm but more even-tempered "I must object, Your Honor."

"On what ground?" Judge McNally said.

"Irrelevance," Judy said. "The question at issue in this hearing remains what it was when stated by Mr. Dent and then by Mr. Merz, namely, was Mr. Lichine or was he not physically present in Alabama on the afternoon of August 10, 1978. The information Mr. Hyatt has just asked Mr. Coleridge to supply has no bearing on that question."

"Sustained," Judge McNally said.

"Exception," the assistant district attorney said.

"Exception granted," the judge said.

"Thank you, Your Honor," Mr. Hyatt said. He turned back to the witness box with "Could you tell us where you were, Mr. Coleridge, on that afternoon?"

"In a rowboat on McWhirter Creek," Teaman Coleridge said.

"Doing what, if I may ask?" the assistant district attorney said.

"Helping my nephew Worsham assemble the raw material for our regular family Sunday dinner," Teaman Coleridge said.

"Could you explain that?" Mr. Hyatt said.

"Our family is rather large," Teaman Coleridge said. "Eleven children. I'm the youngest, with six brothers and four sisters. I'm the only one still not married, so I have certain family duties the others have outgrown. One of these is to accompany my nephew Worsham when he goes out for the catfish my mother insists on having for the big Sunday dinner she cooks every week for the entire family. Worsham pitches for the high school baseball team, and he's a linebacker on the football team, and he sings in the glee club. He's involved in a number of other school activities that tend to congest his schedule. As a result the only time Worsham can work in his weekly fishing chore is on Friday after glee-club practice, which means I have to hold myself in readiness for going fishing at four o'clock every Friday afternoon. Since Worsham became the family's official Sunday-dinner catfish provider I've never missed that Friday afternoon date, but on this Friday I almost did."

"You mean Thursday, do you not, Mr. Coleridge?" the assistant district attorney said.

"No, sir," Teaman Coleridge said. "My mother would never use for Sunday dinner fish caught on Thursday. Worsham knows the earliest his grandmother will tolerate is a Friday catch. So do I."

"And on this Friday you almost missed your fishing chore with your nephew Worsham?" Mr. Hyatt said.

"Yes, sir," Teaman Coleridge said.

"Could you tell us the reason?" the assistant district attorney said.

"An SPRLAA executive board meeting," Teaman Coleridge said.

"You are a member of the Southern Poverty Relief Legal Assistance Association Executive Board?" the assistant district attorney said.

"No, sir," Teaman Coleridge said. "I'm just a member of the volunteer lawyers' pool. This was the first executive board meeting I had been asked to attend."

"Was there a reason?" Mr. Hyatt said.

"Yes," Teaman Coleridge said.

"What was it?" the assistant district attorney said.

"The verdict in *Alabama* v. *Pridemore* that the jury had come in with that morning," Teaman Coleridge said.

"Why did that cause the executive board to invite you to attend this meeting?" Mr. Hyatt said.

"Father Danaher was apparently very upset by the tactics Mr. Lichine had used," Teaman Coleridge said.

"The tactics with which you had helped?" the assistant district attorney said.

"Yes, sir," Teaman Coleridge said. "The executive board was afraid, more accurately Father Danaher was afraid, that Mr. Lichine would use the same tactics when the case of Virgil's father came up for appeal."

"They were afraid?" Mr. Hyatt said.

"Father Danaher was," Teaman Coleridge said. "He's the most powerful figure on the executive board. He runs it. He wanted to make sure Mr. Lichine's tactics were not repeated."

"The tactics that had saved the life of that fifteen-year-old boy?" the district attorney said.

"Yes, sir," Teaman Coleridge said.

"And that's why they asked you to come to the meeting?" Mr. Hyatt said.

"Yes, sir," Teaman Coleridge said.

"But you were not a member of the defense team," the assistant district attorney said. "Not officially, anyway. You had merely helped Mr. Lichine get some material he wanted. What did Mr. Lichine say at the meeting?"

"Mr. Lichine was not present," Teaman Coleridge said.

"Mr. Lichine was not present at that executive board meeting?" Mr. Hyatt said.

"No, sir," Teaman Coleridge said.

"Where was he?" the assistant district attorney said.

"Nobody seemed to know," Teaman Coleridge said. "He had apparently left town that morning, after the jury came in with the verdict."

"That morning?" Mr. Hyatt said.

"Yes, sir," Teaman Coleridge said.

"Friday, August 11, 1978?" the assistant district attorney said.

"That's right, sir," Teaman Coleridge said.

"The murder of which Mr. Lichine is accused took place on the day before?" Mr. Hyatt said. "Thursday, August 10, 1978?"

"So the indictment reads," Teaman Coleridge said.

"Did you see Mr. Lichine on that day?" the assistant district attorney said. "Thursday, August 10, 1978?"

"No, sir," Teaman Coleridge said.

"When did you last see Mr. Lichine before the murder?" Mr. Hyatt said.

"On Wednesday, August 9, 1978," Teaman Coleridge said. "I was sitting there, watching him address the jury, presenting to them the evidence based on the material I had helped him get. The evidence that resulted two days later, on Friday, August 11, 1978, in the jury coming in with the life-sentence verdict."

"So on Wednesday, August 9, 1978," the assistant district attorney said, "you saw Mr. Lichine in the courtroom, addressing the jury?"

"Yes, sir," Teaman Coleridge said.

"And you did not see Mr. Lichine the next day, Thursday, August 10, 1978?" Mr. Hyatt said.

"No, sir," Teaman Coleridge said. "I had other business to attend to, so I called Mr. Lichine at his hotel from my office, but he was not in. I left my name and called the clerk of the court. He said the jury was still out. I made several calls to the court during the day, but the jury had not yet come back. The jury did not come back until the next morning, Friday, August 11, 1978, when they brought in the life-sentence verdict."

"Were you present in the courtroom when the jury came in with that verdict?" the assistant district attorney said.

"Yes, sir, I was," Teaman Coleridge said.

"Was Mr. Lichine present?" Mr. Hyatt said.

"Yes, sir," Teaman Coleridge said. "I was sitting next to him in the courtroom."

"So on Friday morning, August 11, 1978," the assistant district attorney said, "Mr. Lichine and you were both present in the courtroom when the jury brought in its life-sentence verdict in *Alabama* v. *Pridemore?*"

"Yes, sir," Teaman Coleridge said.

"And that courtroom is located, of course, in Montgomery, Alabama?" Mr. Hyatt said.

"Of course, sir, yes," Teaman Coleridge said.

"Thank you, Mr. Coleridge, no further questions," Mr. Hyatt said. He turned to counsels' table. "Your witness, Miss Cline," the assistant district attorney said.

It was a morning to keep a girl on her toes. After Teaman Coleridge's testimony, two more surprises erupted in a quick, not untheatrical sequence.

The first surprise was the note. It consisted of three penciled words followed by two initials: "Lunch, Osprey's, Urgent. T.C." Judy found them on a folded slip of paper Scotch-taped to the top of her attaché case when she came back to counsels' table after Judge McNally granted her request for an immediate midday adjournment.

The second surprise was Ira Bodmer. He was waiting in the corridor when Judy came out of the courtroom.

"Tessie told me I should make sure I don't leave this lying around anywhere or give it to third parties to deliver to you," Ira said, holding out an envelope. "My orders were I should put it right in your hand."

"You've done it," Judy said, taking the envelope. "Did Tessie order you to get a signed receipt?"

Ira laughed. Uneasily, Judy noted. She knew, therefore, that Ira Bodmer knew the contents of the envelope. Judy didn't, but she doubted that the contents would come as a surprise to her. Saphira Shreve, laying it on the line, had left no room for ifs, ands, or buts. Judy had accepted the challenge. She could not avoid the clearly spelled-out consequences.

"On some things Tessie takes my word," Ira Bodmer said. "I got here in time, by the way, to catch the end of your act from the back of the house."

"What do you think of the show?" Judy said.

"You've got a hell of an Act One curtain," Ira Bodmer said. "In case you need any help with Act Two you can always call on me, Miss Cline. No fee involved. Strictly pro bono for a friend."

"Thanks," Judy said. "You may have to hand-wrestle Sal Giudice for the privilege. Before I left for court this morning he called me at home with the same offer."

"Isn't that just like Brooklyn Union?" Ira Bodmer said. "What can you expect from a school that specializes in turning out ambulance chasers? You stick with me and Alexander Hamilton, Miss Cline, and you'll not only get the verdict you want but also a guest shot on Merv Griffin."

"Sal Giudice offered Johnny Carson," Judy said. "Why don't you and Sal work it out between you, then stand by till I get into trouble and whistle 'Send In the Clowns'?"

"Yes, miss," the headwaiter at Osprey's said. "This way, please, miss."

He led her across the busy but not bustling restaurant.

"How did you know about this place?" Judy said after she was seated.

"Miss Gates suggested it," Teaman Coleridge said.

Judy had known, of course, that the pretty girl in the Bedford-Stuyvesant office had an eye for a handsome man. This was Judy's first hint that perhaps Miss Gates' eye was equally sensitive to the main chance.

"I'm glad to learn you didn't come to New York without an extended helping hand waiting in the wings," Judy said as she sat down in the chair the headwaiter had pulled out. "Thank you."

"Something to drink?" the headwaiter said.

"Not for me, thanks," Judy said.

"I'll have a martini," Teaman Coleridge said. "Beefeater, standing up, and stirred, not shaken, please."

"Yes, sir," the headwaiter said.

He made a note on his pad, set down two menus, and went off to the bar.

"When Hyatt called me in Montgomery yesterday and asked if I'd come up to testify he also asked if I wanted a subpoena,"

Teaman Coleridge said. "I said no, all I wanted was my expenses, and he said he'd wire the plane fare. I wanted to call you, of course, but as I think I explained at our first meeting in Bedford-Stuyvesant, down in Southern Shoals country when an SPRLAA lawyer makes a long-distance call he can never be sure he's talking only to the person he dialed. So I called Vernadine Gates instead."

"I've been working with her for almost a year and I never knew that was her name," Judy said. "We all call her Verna."

"She's a very shy girl," Teaman Coleridge said. "I think with a man, certainly a stranger, she wouldn't want to be that informal."

"If you stay in New York for a while instead of dashing back to Montgomery on the late-afternoon plane the way you did last time," Judy said, "I imagine she'll warm up a bit."

"The length of my stay depends on you," Teaman Coleridge said.

"How do you mean?" Judy said.

"As I told you when we had our first talk at Bedford-Stuyvesant last week," Teaman Coleridge said, "I'm on Tom Lichine's side."

"You couldn't prove that by your testimony this morning," Judy said.

The headwaiter arrived with the martini. He set it in front of Teaman Coleridge and said, "Have you decided?"

"Not yet," Teaman Coleridge said.

The headwaiter nodded and went away.

"Before I start thinking about food," Teaman Coleridge said, "I'd like you to explain that remark."

"Howard Dent set the strategy for this action four days ago," Judy said. "The indictment naming Tom down in Alabama states the murder he's accused of committing took place on Thursday, August 10, 1978. Mr. Dent brought the writ of habeas corpus on the ground that on Thursday, August 10, 1978, Tom was not in Alabama but up here in New York. After Mr. Dent disappeared from the picture, Mr. Merz followed the same line. This morning, when I inherited the case, I thought I was picking up where my distinguished predecessors had left off. Instead what I picked up is you."

"I can't figure out whether you're sore about my showing up in New York without warning you I was coming," Teaman Coleridge said, "or whether you're up-tight about my testimony."

"I wasn't aware that I'm what you describe as up-tight," Judy said.

"Few people are," Teaman Coleridge said. "If they were, they wouldn't be."

"The roast-beef hash looks tempting," Judy said.

"Don't be hasty," Teaman Coleridge said. "I worked my way through Yale wrestling pots and pans in the cafeteria. I learned roast-beef hash usually means what was left over from the prime-ribs special the day before."

"Thanks for the warning," Judy said. "I would have appreciated a similar advance notice about your coming up here to testify."

"I've explained why you didn't get it," Teaman Coleridge said. "If only to even things up a bit here, you might explain what difference it would have made if I had warned you. I couldn't have changed my testimony this morning. Once Hyatt called me and said he wanted me to come to New York to testify, I knew I had to do it with or without subpoena, as any member in good standing of the Alabama Bar or any other Bar in this country would have known. That's what I am and what I intend to continue being, a member in good standing of the Alabama Bar, so I obviously had to tell the truth, which I did. It might help Tom Lichine, which I assume we're both interested in doing, if you told me why my telling the truth has rubbed you the wrong way."

"Excuse me," the headwaiter said. "Have you decided yet?"

"No," Teaman Coleridge said. "But you can bring me another one of these, please."

"Yes, sir," the headwaiter said. "Miss?"

"The same, please," Judy said. "But I'd like mine on the rocks."

"Very good, miss," the headwaiter said and went away.

"Want me to wait until you've had a whack at your drink?"

Teaman Coleridge said. "Or can I expect a reasonable answer without the help of the soothing syrup?"

Judy laughed.

"Were you in court when Hyatt made his remarks about George Washington at Fort Duquesne?" she said.

"Yes," Teaman Coleridge said. "In my part of the country when a lawyer uses that gambit in court the number of horses is the same but the battle is Shiloh and the general is Beauregard."

"I've never handled this sort of thing before," Judy said. "My experience has been almost totally in the field of real estate. I still don't know why Tom Lichine wanted me to take over from Mr. Dent and then from Mr. Merz, but his wife told me he did, so I did. All I had to use as a blueprint was the strategy Mr. Dent laid out and Manny Merz indorsed and followed. Nothing could be simpler, or so it seemed. Murder in Alabama on Thursday, August 10, 1978. Bring in your witnesses to prove accused was in New York on August 10, 1978, then move that writ of habeas corpus be granted, and step aside fast not to interfere with His Honor's writing arm as he snatches pen and signs writ. Instead of that, the first thing that happens when I climb into the saddle on my third and still unpunctured horse, is a government witness who testifies it doesn't matter if Tom Lichine was in New York on Thursday, August 10, 1978, because the murder he is accused of having committed took place in Montgomery on Friday, August 11, 1978, and on that day the witness testifies he was sitting right next to Tom Lichine in that Montgomery courtroom. Courtrooms are sometimes more densely populated than at other times, but when they're functioning at any time they contain more than just two people. So if this witness testifies he saw Tom Lichine sitting next to him in Alabama on the Friday, August 11, 1978, when the murder took place, the chances are Mr. Hyatt can produce other witnesses who will testify to the same thing. Where does that leave me?"

"Have you decided yet?" the headwaiter said as he set down the drinks and picked up Teaman Coleridge's empty glass.

"What's the special today?" Teaman Coleridge said without looking at the menu.

"Baked Alaskan crab legs," the headwaiter said. "They're very nice, sir."

"Then that's what I'll have," Judy said.

"So will I," Teaman Coleridge said.

"Thank you," the headwaiter said and went away.

Teaman Coleridge picked up his glass.

"Here's to Washington's next mount," he said.

"And Beauregard's," Judy said.

They touched glasses and sipped.

"After he made his way through that bit about George Washington at Fort Duquesne," Teaman Coleridge said, "I noticed Mr. Hyatt got his knuckles rapped. Something about a motion he'd made four days ago, just before Howard Dent collapsed. What was that all about?"

"One of my current headaches," Judy said. "After Mr. Dent established that on the alleged day of the alleged murder in Alabama Tom Lichine had been in a meeting here in New York in Hugh Kelly's office, the D.A. asked Tom to describe what took place at that meeting. Tom took the Fifth and refused to answer. Mr. Hyatt moved that the judge order Tom to answer or be held in contempt. The judge denied the motion, Mr. Dent collapsed, and four days later Mr. Hyatt tried to revive the motion."

"When you and I met last week for the first time in your Bedford-Stuyvesant office," Teaman Coleridge said, "you told me what happened at that meeting. Tom described those pictures of a real electric chair in which a real human being had been burned, the pictures I had helped him dig up, and what happened in court as a result. Wasn't that the substance of the meeting?"

"Yes, the effect they had on the jury," Judy said. "How they screamed and fainted among other things, so the judge had to call a recess. Tom went back to the hotel. Father Danaher followed him, bawled the hell out of Tom for his tactics and ordered him out of town. Tom went."

"That was the late afternoon of Wednesday, August 9, 1978," Teaman Coleridge said.

"Which got Tom back to New York in plenty of time to attend

the meeting in Hugh Kelly's office the next day, Thursday, August 10, 1978," Judy said.

"What Tom told you and Mr. Dent and Mr. Kelly in that meeting in Mr. Kelly's office on Thursday, August 10, 1978," Teaman Coleridge said. "Do you see anything in those facts that would cause Tom to invoke the Fifth Amendment?"

"No, but I see something else," Judy said.

"What's that?" Teaman Coleridge said.

"Tom obviously finished giving us his account in Mr. Kelly's New York office in time to fly back to Montgomery and sit beside you in the courtroom the next morning," Judy said, "when the verdict came in on Friday, August 11, 1978."

"Which happens to be the day the murder took place in Montgomery for which Tom Lichine was indicted and for which they are now trying to extradite him back to Alabama," Teaman Coleridge said. "Is that your problem?"

"No," Judy said. "My problem is something you told me last week in my Bedford-Stuyvesant office and repeated just a few minutes ago at this table."

"What's that?" Teaman Coleridge said.

"You told me down in Southern Shoals country, when an SPRLAA lawyer makes a long-distance call, he can never be sure he's talking only to the person he dialed."

"That's my problem, not yours," Teaman Coleridge said.

"It became mine the day Howard Dent asked me to urge Tom to allow Mr. Dent to defend him," Judy said. "I didn't connect it up until you testified about the dates this morning."

"I don't see what there was to connect up," Teaman Coleridge said.

"Try this," Judy said. "Tom was indicted for a murder he's supposed to have committed on Thursday, August 10, 1978. The state of Alabama is so anxious to get him back and try him for the murder that they overlook the fact that the murder actually took place on Friday, August 11, 1978."

"That could be an accident," Teaman Coleridge said. "They do happen."

"Howard Dent told me nothing that happens in Southern Shoals country is an accident," Judy said. "Not even a long-distance call made by an SPRLAA lawyer."

"By tapping one of my long-distance calls they might pick up a piece of useful information," Teaman Coleridge said. "What can they gain by mixing up the dates on an indictment?"

"I don't know," Judy said. "Maybe Tom Lichine does."

"Maybe in this context meaning maybe that's why he took the Fifth?" Teaman Coleridge said.

"Maybe," Judy said.

"Very hot, please," the waiter said.

Judy stared at the plates as he set them down. So did Teaman Coleridge.

"This thing Judge McNally was making jokes about this morning," Teaman Coleridge said. "What he called a superfluity of relator's requests for substitution of counsel. You said your request had come from Tom's wife. In a visit to your office yesterday afternoon."

"That's right," Judy said.

"He's free on bail," Teaman Coleridge said. "He has no physical infirmities that I know of. Why didn't Tom Lichine come visit you in person?"

"His wife said Tom didn't want me to get fired," Judy said.

"Fired from what?" Teaman Coleridge said. "Your job as his defense counsel?"

"No," Judy said. "My job at Isham Truitt."

"Is there any chance of that?" Teaman Coleridge said.

From her purse Judy took the letter Ira Bodmer had given her half an hour ago.

"This was hand delivered to me in the corridor outside the courtroom on my way out to meet you here for lunch," she said. "The signature at the bottom, Gilbert Cutter, he's the Isham Truitt office manager."

Teaman Coleridge read the letter and looked up.

"Tom Lichine's strategy to save your job seems to have failed," he said.

"Maybe," Judy said.

"There's nothing 'maybe' about this letter," Teaman Coleridge said. "It's as forthright a pink slip as the one Harry Truman handed General MacArthur. It even includes a check for your severance pay."

"That's what's wrong with it," Judy said. "It's like the accident about the dates on the indictment."

"In what way?" Teaman Coleridge said.

"It's too neat," Judy said.

"Neat?" Teaman Coleridge said.

"My father is a playwright," Judy said. "He maintains when a writer confuses real life with the way he writes about real life, the French have a phrase for the result."

"*C'est littérateur,*" Teaman Coleridge said.

"How did you know?" Judy said.

"Two years of college French," Teaman Coleridge said. "Just about the same amount of time I've put in as a volunteer in the SPRLAA lawyers' pool. Putting in that much time on anything should teach a man something about the subject."

"Like what?" Judy said.

"Let's eat some of this stuff while it's hot," Teaman Coleridge said.

Judy forked up some of her baked Alaskan crab legs.

"Tepid," Teaman Coleridge said. "Good, though. They remind me of something else I remember from my college French."

"What's that?" Judy said.

"We were working our way through some of Balzac's essays," Teaman Coleridge said. "He was explaining how the mind of a novelist works. How Balzac's mind worked, anyway. He said when the novelist starts setting down his story on paper he should never know too much about it. He should be aware of only two things—the beginning and the end. Everything in between should take him by surprise, because if what happens in between does not surprise the novelist, how can he expect it to surprise his reader? Balzac compared a novel with a long train journey. When he climbs aboard the novelist should know that he's going from, say, New York to, let us say, San Francisco. Not until he begins to smell the stink of the stockyards, however, should he become aware that he had planned to stop off in Chicago."

Judy stopped chewing.

"You're beginning to smell something," she said.

"I think so," Teaman Coleridge said. "Anyway, our train is slowing down."

"Where?" Judy said.

Teaman Coleridge made the motions of a traveler wiping away a circle of dust on a window and peering out at the passing scene.

"Looks like an outpost of Southern Shoals country," he said.

"It must have a post office address," Judy said.

"Let's see," Teaman Coleridge said, squinting through the imaginary pane of glass. "Yes, I can just make it out. Six-three-five Madison Avenue, New York, New York, one-o-o-two-two."

"Sounds like Isham Truitt," Judy said.

"Not the whole piece of geography," Teaman Coleridge said. "Just a crucial corner."

"Does it have a name?" Judy said.

"The way I read the sign on the station," Teaman Coleridge said, "it says 'Ludwig Uchitel.'"

31

"Do you swear to tell the truth, the whole truth, and nothing but the truth, so help you God?" the uniformed attendant said.

"I do."

The court clerk swung the Bible out of the way and said, "Be seated, please."

The heavy man in the tight four-button suit settled himself in the witness chair. He did it with a combination of diffidence and directness that commanded attention. It was the low-key performance of a man who wanted it known that he disliked the public eye, but was aware of his responsibility to the media by which it was serviced. If his position dictated that he submit to the boredom of being photographed, very well, then, it was his duty to present his better profile to the cameras. He did his duty.

"Your full name, please," Judy said.

"Ludwig Uchitel."

"Your place of residence?" Judy said.

"Hotel Pierre," Ludwig Uchitel said. "Two East Sixty-first Street, New York City."

"What is your line of work, Mr. Uchitel?" Judy said.

Under the wide, drooping, boar's-bristle mustache the full pink lips pursed in what could have been a smile.

"I am a member of the New York Bar," Mr. Uchitel said.

It was not a smile.

"Would you give us the name of your firm, please?" Judy said.

She had not expected a smile. Not with Gil Cutter's letter stuffed in her purse on counsels' table behind her.

"Isham, Truitt, Kelly, Shreve, Merz, Uchitel and Condomine," said the man in the witness chair. He could have been made up, it seemed to Judy, to play an aging Edwardian dandy in a segment of *Upstairs, Downstairs.* "Six-three-five Madison Avenue, New York, one-o-o-two-two."

"In which you are a senior partner, sir?" Judy said.

"I am," Ludwig Uchitel said.

"Are there any areas of the law that might be described as your special province at Isham Truitt?" Judy said.

"Could you clarify that, please?" Ludwig Uchitel said.

"Your partner Mr. Hugh Kelly, for example," Judy said. "His special area at Isham Truitt is New York City real estate, is it not?"

"Yes, it is," Ludwig Uchitel said.

"In like manner, sir, is there any area in which you are considered your firm's special expert?" Judy said. "Tax law? Debentures? Wills and trusts? The entertainment field, meaning TV, movies, theater? Whatever?"

"Well, now, let me see," Mr. Uchitel said.

He seemed to feel what he wanted to see was concealed somewhere in the long strips of sunlight that fell down into the courtroom from the tall windows behind Judy. At any rate, Ludwig Uchitel squinted with obviously special concentration across her head into the glare. Judy wondered what he would pick for his answer. There was certainly plenty to choose from. Ludwig Uchitel had come to the law from a highly successful, even spectacular, youthful career as a press agent. He was credited with saving the Alaskan salmon industry from dying before it could find its feet because the public, accustomed when it opened a can of fish to see red, did not take to the Alaskan variety, which was white. Ludwig Uchitel came up with a device that turned the tide, so to speak, into a river of gold. He ordered the desperate canning tycoons to place on the label of every tin of Alaskan salmon that went to market eight words in large type: "Positively Will Not Turn Red in the Can."

Ludwig Uchitel did not take public credit for the invention, but he did take the handsome fee. With it he paid his way through law school. After he hung out his shingle he continued the dual practice of representing fledgling business enterprises that were having growing pains and, when they outgrew their pains, denying modestly that he had been responsible for their achieving financial maturity. Operating from behind the dignity of a shingle, as opposed to functioning as a raffish press agent, Ludwig Uchitel made only one change in his business life-style. He started taking his fees in the form of common stock in the companies he served. By the time he joined Isham Truitt as a senior partner he could no longer recall the difference between a misdemeanor and a tort, but he knew the first name and golf handicap of the chairman of the board of every major bank in the United States.

"Perhaps I can answer your question best, Miss Cline," he said, "not by trying to pin down any particular field in which my partners at Isham Truitt might consider me the firm's expert, but by telling you what they call me."

"What's that?" Judy said.

"They call me the firm's rainmaker," Ludwig Uchitel said.

"You are, then, the firm's bringer-in of new business," Judy said.

"Not all of the firm's new business, of course," Ludwig Uchitel said. "But enough, perhaps, to justify the sobriquet."

"Is that why you are in charge of the firm's pro bono program?" Judy said.

"I think so, yes," Ludwig Uchitel said.

"Would you explain that, please?" Judy said.

"Simple enough," Ludwig Uchitel said. "Providing people or organizations with free or pro bono legal assistance is like making campaign contributions to political candidates, or handing out perfume samples to women. Even if you do it badly you can't help earning a lot of thanks, and maybe even a grateful kiss or two. A vote of thanks here, a kiss or two there, and not infrequently they lead directly or indirectly to a new client. There are people who look down on rainmaking. Not me. I find it satisfying work."

"The people at Isham Truitt you send out on pro bono assignments," Judy said. "How do you choose them for the work they get sent out to do?"

"There is no one way," Ludwig Uchitel said. "Every request requires special handling. Sometimes an organization will ask for a specific kind of person. They want a man, or they want a woman. They tell us they want someone who's had experience in tax work, or in setting up trusts. They want someone who gets along well with ghetto types, or someone who knows how to talk to dowagers who wear seed-pearl choker collars. Sometimes they want what they want in a negative way. They will say please don't send us an active liberal, or a stiff-necked reactionary. I had a request once for an expert in naturalization law who spoke Japanese. Believe it or not we had at Isham Truitt an absolutely brilliant young woman who had written several important articles for the *Columbia Law Review* on naturalization laws. She had been born and raised in Tokyo before her parents, who were missionaries, sent her back to school in the States. She was eager for the assignment, and I felt pleased with myself for pulling what amounted to a rare rabbit out of the hat, but they refused to accept the girl I sent. It seemed they just didn't want a female lawyer. So it goes. The work is unpredictable, like life itself, but well worth doing, just as life is well worth living."

"Do you know the plaintiff in this habeas corpus action?" Judy said. "Mr. Thomas L. Lichine, Jr.?"

"Yes, I do," Ludwig Uchitel said.

"How well do you know Mr. Lichine?" Judy said.

"Let me tell you how I know him, and then you tell me how well you think that adds up to," Ludwig Uchitel said. "Okay?"

"Certainly," Judy said.

"About a year ago David Fillmore told me he'd heard of a brilliant young man up at Harvard Law who was about to graduate, and Mr. Fillmore thought Isham Truitt should grab him before anybody else did," Ludwig Uchitel said. "You know David Fillmore?"

"Not personally," Judy said. "I know who he is, of course."

"Then maybe you don't know that in all the years I've known Mr. Fillmore this was the first time I ever knew or even heard of him taking an interest in who we hired at Isham Truitt," Ludwig Uchitel said. "I got Emanuel Merz on the blower at once, and I passed the word along. A couple of weeks later Mr. Merz sent me a note saying he'd been up at Cambridge on one of his recruiting tours and he'd seen this young Mr. Lichine who had been recommended by Mr. Fillmore, and Mr. Merz reported he'd made the young man an offer. I believe that was the same trip on which Mr. Merz also made you an offer, Miss Cline, wasn't it?"

"Your Honor," Judy said, "I would like that stricken, please."

"Yes, of course," Judge McNally said. "Strike the last part of Mr. Uchitel's answer," he said to the man at the Stenotype machine, and turned back to the witness. "The plaintiff and his counsel as well as a number of the witnesses in this matter are, as you are of course aware, Mr. Uchitel, members or employees of the same law firm. For this reason it is important in the interests of clarity to keep the record free of personal references. I'm sure, Mr. Uchitel, as a senior partner in Isham Truitt you know many things about many of the people who work there. Wherever possible it would help here if you would try to screen these things out of your testimony. In this examination I ask you to bear in mind only that Miss Cline is acting as counsel for Mr. Lichine and nothing else."

"Of course, Your Honor," Ludwig Uchitel said. "I'm sorry, Miss Cline."

"Quite all right," Judy said. "You were explaining how well you know Mr. Lichine."

"All right, then, that was for starters," Ludwig Uchitel said. "A young man who gets recommended by David Fillmore personally you don't forget, if you know what I mean."

"I believe I do," Judy said.

"Then the next thing, about a month ago," Ludwig Uchitel said, "I got a call from Mr. Merz and he said to me this young man, that's Mr. Lichine, he wants to see you, you meaning me of course, about his pro bono assignment. I said what pro bono assignment? It seems when Mr. Merz talked with Mr. Lichine up at Harvard about coming to work at Isham Truitt the young man said before he signed on he wanted to be assured he would be able to spend some time on pro bono work. Mr. Merz said of course, because that's a promise we now make to all our young people if they ask for it. So I told Mr. Merz fine, send Mr.

Lichine along and I'll discuss his assignment with him. When Mr. Lichine came into my office I found there was nothing to discuss. He had made up his mind. He wanted to be assigned to this case in Montgomery, Alabama, a first-degree murder situation that was up on appeal, *Pridemore* v. *Alabama*. Mr. Lichine wanted to help fight the appeal. Nobody had ever before come to see me and told me as precisely as that, practically giving me the dates and docket numbers, what he or she wanted as a pro bono assignment. I don't think anybody would forget a young man who made that kind of request, and I certainly didn't. Now you put those two things together, the initial recommendation by David Fillmore and then this request for a specific pro bono assignment, and I ask you, Miss Cline, how well would you say I know Mr. Tom Lichine?"

"I'm afraid, Mr. Uchitel, it is my role in this proceeding to ask you that question," Judy said.

"Quite right, young lady, quite right," Ludwig Uchitel said. "Pardon me, I mean quite right, Miss Cline, quite right. And the answer is I think I know Mr. Lichine about as well as I know most Isham Truitt people who are not partners. If it kills me I'm going to stay within His Honor's guidelines and refrain from saying that, as an illustration of what I mean, I think I know Mr. Lichine better than I know you, Miss Cline."

A small laugh from the spectators. A small gavel tap from His Honor.

"Mr. Uchitel, please."

"Sorry, Your Honor," Ludwig Uchitel said.

"Did you ask Mr. Lichine why he wanted this specific pro bono assignment in Montgomery, Alabama?" Judy said.

"I did," Ludwig Uchitel said.

"What was Mr. Lichine's answer?" Judy said.

Apparently setting out in quest of inspiration for a reply in the beams of sunlight falling into the courtroom, Mr. Uchitel added a small new touch to his thoughtful stare across Judy's head. He ran a forefinger slowly from one end to the other of his long, narrow, drooping, boar's-bristle mustache. The hairs were so tough, and so clearly separated, Judy half expected that, as one by one they were bent by Mr. Uchitel's manicured fingertip, when he allowed them to snap back into place the hairs would twang.

"Mr. Lichine's reply was and I quote," Ludwig Uchitel said, "'I suggest you ask David Fillmore.'"

Out of the corner of her eye Judy could see Teaman Coleridge lean forward across counsels' table and make a note. She was not the only one, therefore, who found Mr. Uchitel's answer an attention grabber.

"Did you?" Judy said.

Ludwig Uchitel stopped fussing with his mustache. Perhaps to give his sudden smile a chance to reach without obstruction every member of his available audience, he moved his hand down to his lap.

"As Miss Doolittle once remarked in a not dissimilar situation," he said, "not bloody likely."

"Meaning what?" Judy said.

"Meaning Mr. Fillmore is a very busy man," Ludwig Uchitel said. "He is my firm's most important client. One of the duties of a senior partner at Isham Truitt is to make sure Mr. Fillmore is not bothered with junior questions."

"What did you do?" Judy said.

"I initialed Mr. Lichine's pro bono assignment sheet," Ludwig Uchitel said, "and I sent him down to Mr. Gilbert Cutter, our office manager, to arrange for his transportation to Alabama."

"When was the next time you saw Mr. Lichine?" Judy said.

"Today when I walked into this courtroom," Ludwig Uchitel said.

"Do you remember the date you initialed that pro bono assignment slip for Mr. Lichine?" Judy said.

"I checked my appointments diary before I came down here," Ludwig Uchitel said. "It was Thursday, July 27, 1978."

"Today is Tuesday, August 29, 1978," Judy said. "That means you have not seen Mr. Lichine for about a month? Thirty days to be precise?"

"That is correct," Ludwig Uchitel said.

"Then you did not see Mr. Lichine on Thursday, August 10, 1978, when he attended a meeting in Mr. Kelly's office at six-three-five Madison?" Judy said.

"No, I did not," Ludwig Uchitel said. "I repeat, I saw Mr. Lichine in my own office on Thursday, July 27, 1978, and again this morning, Tuesday, August 29, 1978. Nothing in between."

"Did you hear anything about Mr. Lichine or his activities between those two dates?" Judy said.

"I did not," Ludwig Uchitel said.

"Did you know he was fired by Mr. Kelly from his job at Isham Truitt in the afternoon of Thursday, August 10, 1978?" Judy said.

"No, I did not," Ludwig Uchitel said.

"Did you know that he was rehired the next day, Friday, August 11, 1978?" Judy said.

"Miss Cline," Ludwig Uchitel said, "I have stated that I did not see Mr. Lichine or hear anything about him or his activities from Thursday, July 27, 1978, until this morning, August 29, 1978. Shall I say it again?"

"You just have, Mr. Uchitel, thank you," Judy said. She turned to the bench. "No further questions, Your Honor." Moving toward counsels' table, she said, "Your witness, Mr. Hyatt."

"Thank you," the assistant district attorney said, getting to his feet. "I have no questions for the witness, Your Honor, but I have one for the court, if I may?"

"Certainly, Mr. Hyatt," the judge said.

"I refer to Mr. Teaman Coleridge," the assistant district attorney said. "The gentleman seated at counsels' table."

"Your witness of this morning," Judge McNally said.

"That's why I brought Mr. Coleridge up from Alabama," Mr. Hyatt said. "To testify for the defense, which he did this morning. When we came back from lunch I found him sitting at counsels' table. Since he is not sitting there at my request, I assume he was asked to do so by Miss Cline."

"Do you object to Mr. Coleridge sitting at counsels' table?" the judge said.

"So long as it is clear that he is not doing so at my request," the assistant district attorney said, "I have no objection whatsoever."

"If Your Honor please," Judy said.

"Yes, Miss Cline?" Judge McNally said.

"I apologize for what I now see was a breach of etiquette and

I hope is no more than that," Judy said. "I had a talk with Mr. Coleridge during the lunch break and asked him to sit at counsels' table so that, if it became necessary for me to check dates and place names as well as other facts about Montgomery, a city I have never visited, I could do so without wasting the time of the court by asking for adjournments. I have myself been an assistant at counsels' tables, including this one, so it didn't occur to me that what I asked Mr. Coleridge to do might be irregular, but perhaps I was wrong. If so, in addition to my apology I would now like to ask the court's permission to allow Mr. Coleridge to continue sitting at counsels' table."

"There is nothing irregular about it and there is no need to apologize," Judge McNally said. "If Mr. Hyatt has no objection the permission is granted."

"No objection, Your Honor," the assistant district attorney said. "I merely wanted the matter clarified so it would be clear that so far as the defense is concerned Mr. Coleridge has with his testimony this morning performed the service for which he was brought up from Montgomery at the expense of the district attorney's office. Any further services Mr. Coleridge renders at this hearing will be for and at the request of the plaintiff."

"Thank you," Judy said.

"If Your Honor please," Teaman Coleridge said, "I would like to add my thanks as well."

"You may, Mr. Coleridge, and they are accepted by the court," the judge said. "On that admirable note of general goodwill may I suggest, Mr. Hyatt, that you proceed with your cross-examination of Mr. Uchitel."

"I have no questions for Mr. Uchitel, Your Honor," the assistant district attorney said.

"Call your next witness, Miss Cline," Judge McNally said.

"Father Terence Danaher, please," Judy said.

The court attendant stood up.

"Father Terence Danaher come forward, please," he called.

Father Danaher started down the aisle. He seemed to have something wrong with one foot. He rocked rather than walked, somewhat like a sailor in a comedy sketch making his way along a pitching deck. Judy leaned over counsels' table and spoke quietly near Teaman Coleridge's ear.

"When Uchitel repeated what he claimed Tom said to him about why he wanted to go down to Alabama to work on *Pridemore* v. *Alabama*," Judy said, "I saw you jot down a note."

Teaman Coleridge pushed his pad toward her. He pointed with his pencil to three neatly written words: "Doesn't ring true."

"That's what I felt," Judy said. "An expression of general interest in this sort of case would have been enough. Tom had nothing to gain by getting Uchitel's back up with that kind of smart-ass remark."

"I don't believe Tom made the remark," Teaman Coleridge said. "That's why I made the note."

"Be seated, please," the court clerk said.

Judy looked up. The clerk had finished with the oath and was carrying the Bible back to his small table. Father Danaher was settling himself in the witness chair. Judy moved toward him.

"May we have your full name, please?" she said.

"Terence Danaher."

"Your clothes, your collar particularly, they seem to indicate that you are a clergyman?" Judith said.

"I am an ordained Catholic priest," Danaher said. "I am also a member of the New York Bar and a member of the Bar of the state of Alabama."

"Where do you reside, Father Danaher, if that is the correct way to address you, sir?" Judy said.

"Father Danaher, Mr. Danaher, whichever you prefer," he said.

"I would prefer to suit your preference, sir," Judy said.

"My work is now entirely secular," Danaher said. "That is to say, even though I was educated for and accepted into the priesthood, it is as a practicing lawyer that I have spent my adult life, and do so now. Perhaps, therefore, Mr. Danaher would be more appropriate, but if you call me Father Danaher I will not be offended."

"If only to avoid even the suggestion of offense," Judy said, "I will call you Father Danaher, if that's all right with you?"

"As you wish, young lady," Danaher said. "I assure you I will not be offended."

"Thank you," Judy said. "You say you are now practicing law. Is that in New York, Father Danaher, or in Alabama, or both?"

"Alabama," Danaher said.

"You are in private practice?" Judy said.

"No, I am not," Father Danaher said. "I am the executive director of the Alabama branch of the Southern Poverty Relief Legal Assistance Association."

"Were you in court this morning, Father Danaher?" Judy said.

"I was," Danaher said.

"Then you heard the testimony of Mr. Teaman Coleridge?" Judy said.

"I did," Danaher said.

"Mr. Coleridge explained the nature of your organization's work and identified himself as a member of your volunteer lawyers' pool," Judy said. "Was Mr. Coleridge correct in his statements about both, Father Danaher?"

"He was," Danaher said.

"Then I think we can dispense with a repetition of the details," Judy said. "If you agree, sir?"

"I do," Danaher said.

"Mr. Coleridge also suggested it would be less cumbersome if your organization was identified in this proceeding by its initials, namely, SPRLAA," Judy said. "For the same reason, may we with your permission continue to use the initials in this examination?"

"By all means," Danaher said.

"Thank you," Judy said. "It would make things simpler. Now, then, Father Danaher, would you tell us how you got here today?"

"I took a taxi," Danaher said.

"Of course, yes," Judy said. "I didn't mean that, Father Danaher. Let me try again. Did you come here in response to a subpoena?"

"Certainly not," Danaher said.

"What brought you here, sir?" Judy said.

"A telephone call from you, Miss Cline."

"Where did I reach you, Father Danaher?" Judy said.

"At the apartment of a friend with whom I am staying here in New York," Father Danaher said.

"How did I know you were staying there?" Judy said.

"Oh, I see what you mean," Danaher said. "Well, now, let me see. Yes. You told me that you wanted me to appear at this hearing, so you called my office down in Montgomery."

"Did I say how I got your Montgomery number?" Judy said.

"Why, yes, I believe you did," Danaher said. "You said you called Mrs. Campion and she gave you the SPRLAA office number in Montgomery."

"Mrs. Edwina Campion?" Judy said.

"Yes," Danaher said.

"Secretary to Mr. Hugh Kelly?" Judy said.

"Correct, yes," Danaher said.

"Of Isham, Truitt, Kelly, Merz, Shreve, Uchitel and Condomine?" Judy said.

"Yes, of course," Danaher said. "I don't see why we have to go through all this tedious—"

"And when I got your Montgomery office on the phone they said you were staying with a friend up here in New York and they gave me your friend's number," Judy said. "Is that right, Father Danaher?"

"If you say so, yes, I suppose it is," Danaher said.

"And when I reached you on the phone here in New York at that number," Judy said, "and I told you I wanted you to appear at this hearing, and I asked if you wanted a subpoena, you said?"

"I said a subpoena was not necessary," Father Danaher said. "Just give me the address and tell me when you want me and I'll be there. That's what I said, was it not?"

"It was," Judy said. "And here you are, Father Danaher. On behalf of the court as well as my client I want to thank you for your co-operation."

"Nonsense," Danaher said. "I am a member of the Bar. It is my duty as it is the duty of all lawyers to co-operate with the law to make things as easy as possible for the pursuit of justice. No thanks are necessary, young lady."

"By the way," Judy said, "would you give us the address of this friend with whom you are staying, Father Danaher?"

"Nine-seven-six Fifth Avenue," Danaher said.

"That lovely apartment house facing the Metropolitan Museum of Art and overlooking Central Park?" Judy said.

"I suppose so," Danaher said. "I don't pay much attention to things like that. When I come to a strange city I'm just grateful to have a bed to sleep in."

"Who owns the bed you are at present sleeping in, Father Danaher?" Judy said.

"I don't think I understand your question," Danaher said.

"What is the name of the friend with whom you are presently staying here in New York?" Judy said.

"Kelly," Father Danaher said.

"Hugh Kelly?" Judy said.

"Yes," Father Danaher said.

"The same Hugh Kelly whose secretary is named Mrs. Edwina Campion?" Judy said.

"Yes," Father Danaher said.

"Hugh Kelly of Isham, Truitt, Kelly, Merz, Shreve, Uchitel and Condomine?" Judy said.

"Yes, yes, of course," Danaher said. "Hugh Kelly and I were at Fordham Law School together. We are old friends. I always stay with Hugh and his wife when I have occasion to come to New York."

"What is the occasion for your present visit?" Judy said.

"Mr. Kelly's appointment by the President to his liaison post at the Vatican," Danaher said. "I came up to see him off to Rome."

"Any other reason?" Judy said.

"Again I don't think I understand the question," Father Danaher said.

"You say you came up to New York to see Mr. Kelly off to Rome," Judy said.

"That's right," Danaher said.

"Mr. and Mrs. Kelly flew to Rome last week," Judy said. "They've been in Rome for six days."

"Oh, I see what you mean," Danaher said. "I don't get to New

York very often. I thought so long as I'm here I'd spend a few days and make it a short holiday."

"I trust you're enjoying it," Judy said.

"I am," Danaher said.

"Seeing Mr. Kelly off," Judy said. "Did it take long?"

"Again I don't understand your question," Danaher said. "Couldn't you be more direct? Stop all the beating around the bush? Say what you mean?"

"I'll try," Judy said. "You say you came up to New York to see Mr. and Mrs. Kelly off to Rome. Today is August 29, 1978. Mr. and Mrs. Kelly flew to Rome seven days ago. That would make it August 22, 1978. Did you arrive in New York on August 22, 1978, go to a party for the Kellys, and then watch them get into the car that drove them to the airport?"

"Oh, no, nothing as hurried as that," Danaher said. "I arrived in New York the day before they flew to Rome."

"That would make it August 21, 1978?" Judy said.

"If you say so, yes," Danaher said.

"What I say is unimportant," Judy said. "You are doing the testifying, Father Danaher. If Mr. and Mrs. Kelly flew to Rome on August 22, 1978, and you arrived in New York the day before that, I say you must have arrived in New York on August 21, 1978. Now I ask what do you say?"

"I say yes, all right, I arrived in New York on August 21, 1978," Danaher said. "What about it?"

"How did you spend that day in New York?" Judy said.

"I don't really know," Danaher said. "I wasn't paying attention to my movements. I was here for a pleasant social engagement, seeing an old friend off on a trip. How am I to remember everything I did? Could anybody answer that question? Could you answer it? What did you do on August 21, 1978?"

"I went to my office," Judy said. "Six-three-five Madison Avenue. Did you?"

"What?" Danaher said.

"On that day, August 21, 1978," Judy said, "I ask you, Father Danaher, did you go to the Isham Truitt offices at six-three-five Madison Avenue?"

"As a matter of fact I did, yes," Danaher said. "Now that you mention it I remember now Hugh asked me to drop in."

"Why?" Judy said.

"Nothing special," Danaher said. "He wanted me to see the place. Yes, I remember, he's very proud of his Jo Davidson statue of St. Patrick and he wanted to show it to me."

"You mean you've known Mr. Kelly for all these years since Fordham and you never saw that statue?" Judy said.

"I suppose I have," Danaher said. "Hugh wanted me to have another look at it. Anything wrong with that?"

"Certainly not," Judy said. "It's a lovely piece of work. I've looked at it many times myself. Did you see anything else while you were in the Isham Truitt offices?"

"Anything else?" Danaher said. "No, I don't think so."

"Did Mr. Kelly introduce you to anybody in the office?" Judy said. "His partners, for instance?"

"Partners?" Danaher said. "Oh, yes, now that you mention it I remember he did. He took me down the hall to meet a Mrs. Shreve, I think her name was."

"Still is," Judy said. "Mrs. Saphira Shreve."

"Yes, that's the lady," Danaher said.

"Why did Mr. Kelly want you to meet Mrs. Shreve?" Judy said.

"No special reason," Danaher said. "Just she's a character, Mr. Kelly said, the only female senior partner, and he thought I might enjoy meeting her."

"Did you?" Judy said.

"Oh, yes," Danaher said, "I certainly did."

"What did you talk about?" Judy said.

"With Mrs. Shreve?" Danaher said.

"Yes," Judy said. "What did you talk about?"

"Why, nothing special," Danaher said. "Just hello, pleased to meet you, heard a lot about you, that sort of thing."

"What else did you do that day?" Judy said.

"What I'd come up to New York to do," Danaher said. "Drove out to the airport with Mr. and Mrs. Kelly and wished them Godspeed."

"But that was August 21, 1978," Judy said. "They didn't fly to Rome until the next day, August 22."

"If you say so, Miss Cline, okay, they did," Danaher said. "All I can say is there was nothing so memorable about those two days that I would remember them in detail."

"Let me try you on another day," Judy said. "A day that I'm sure was memorable for you, Father Danaher. May I?"

"That's what I'm here for," Danaher said.

"Do you remember calling Mr. Kelly from Montgomery on the morning of Thursday, August 10, 1978?" Judy said.

"Thursday, August 10, 1978," Danaher said with a frown that cried out to be identified as pensive. "You say that was a day you're sure was memorable for me?"

"I don't see how it could fail to be," Judy said.

"Could you refresh my recollection?" Danaher said.

"I'll try," Judy said. "You remember *Pridemore* v. *Alabama*, of course. You appeared for the defense."

"Certainly I remember," Danaher said.

"Then you will remember, of course, that the case went to the jury late in the afternoon of Wednesday, August 9, 1978," Judy said. "And the jury came back with its life-sentence verdict at about one o'clock in the afternoon on Friday, August 11, 1978. So the day in between, Thursday, August 10, 1978, that day must have been memorable for you for two reasons. First, you spent that whole day doing what any defense attorney in similar circumstances would be doing, namely, sweating out a verdict. You will agree, Father Danaher, will you not, that that's one good reason to make a day memorable for a lawyer?"

"You said there were two reasons," Danaher said. "What's the second?"

"The place where you reached Mr. Kelly," Judy said.

"What's memorable about that?" Danaher said.

"Mr. Kelly was not in his office," Judy said. "He was not due in his office for several hours. He was driving in from Quogue in his Bentley, which he intended to leave at Iggulden's for some repairs to the steering mechanism, but on the way Mr. Kelly stopped off in Queens to attend a real estate closing. For you in Montgomery, Alabama, to have traced Mr. Kelly by phone to the offices of Lightfoot and Harra in Queens, New York, is an achievement about as memorable as that of Henry Morton Stanley tracing David Livingstone in darkest Africa. Surely you remember that phone call, Father Danaher."

"Well—"

"Because Mr. Kelly remembers it clearly," Judy said.

"How do you know?" Danaher said.

"Four hours after he took the call in Queens I was in Mr. Kelly's office where I heard him describe your phone call in detail," Judy said.

"I object, Your Honor," the assistant district attorney said.

"On what ground?" Judge McNally said.

"Miss Cline is not testifying," Mr. Hyatt said.

"But she is privy to information relevant to the testimony of the witness," the judge said. "I will allow it."

"Exception," the assistant district attorney said.

"Granted," Judge McNally said. "Proceed, Miss Cline."

"Father Danaher, I repeat," Judy said. "Do you remember a phone call you made from Montgomery, Alabama, to Mr. Kelly in Queens, New York, on the morning of Thursday, August 10, 1978?"

"Not perhaps in detail," Danaher said. "The gist, though, the general content of the call, yes, I remember it, and I have a very good reason to remember it."

"What is the reason?" Judy said.

"When Mr. Lichine showed up in my office in Alabama a couple of weeks before that," Danaher said, "I remember we had a talk about the case. As Mr. Uchitel just testified, Mr. Lichine had done a very unusual thing. He had put in for this assignment. He hadn't just come down like most pro bono assignees, ready to tackle whatever the SPRLAA put on his plate. No, not a bit. Mr. Lichine had applied for the right to work on this particular case, *Pridemore* v. *Alabama*."

"You must have asked him why," Judy said.

"You bet I did," Danaher said. "He told me he'd become interested in the case when he was still a student at Harvard Law School. He'd read about it in a newspaper somewhere, and the facts intrigued him, so he did some research and dug up the reports. A year later, when he learned the case was coming up for appeal, Mr. Lichine told me he put in for it with Mr. Uchitel at Isham Truitt, and he got the assignment, and here he was, ready to join me and the rest of our SPRLAA team in our effort to save that boy's life."

"He did, didn't he?" Judy said.

"Not he—we," Danaher said. "And we did it not because of Mr. Thomas L. Lichine, Jr. We did it in spite of him."

"I didn't hear anything like that in Mr. Kelly's account of his telephone conversation with you on the morning of Thursday, August 10, 1978," Judy said.

"You didn't ask for Mr. Kelly's account," Danaher said. "You asked for mine."

"May we have it, please?" Judy said.

"Mr. Thomas L. Lichine, Jr., didn't give a damn about that black boy," Father Danaher said. *"Pridemore* v. *Alabama* was nothing more than Tom Lichine's cover story. He didn't want anybody to know his real reason for coming into the Montgomery area."

"What was his real reason?" Judy said.

"Mr. Lichine is sitting in this courtroom right now," Father Danaher said. "Why don't you ask him?"

32

"He refuses to take the stand."

Of the five heads in the room only one did not move. It belonged to the speaker. Of the four heads that did move only one was covered by a hat. From under the tricorne Saphira Shreve said, "You mean you've spoken to young Lichine?"

"No," Godfrey Condomine said. "I've spoken to his father."

"I didn't know the little twirp had a father," Walter Isham said.

Godfrey Condomine said, "Your ignorance, my dear Walter, is the penalty you pay for serving as this firm's symbol of probity. To keep our symbol if not untarnished, then at least reflecting a high polish in the pitilessly corrosive glare of a media-ridden civilization, your partners find it simpler to keep from your eyes and ears some of the seamier aspects of life as it is lived by the sweating multitudes."

Ludwig Uchitel said, "Godfrey, every time you come up from Washington I begin to worry about the English language. Do you have to talk like a character in one of your own novels?"

"Would you have Jane Austen talk like a character in one of George Gissing's novels?" Godfrey Condomine said.

Among his published works was a biography of the author of *Pride and Prejudice.* Just before his death Edmund Wilson in *The New York Review* had described it as worshipful.

"Not me," Ludwig Uchitel said. "Whoever he is, if you're against the guy, Godfrey, I'm for him. There's nothing personal in that. It's just that the way you talk reminds me of the time on our honeymoon when Eloise and I drove over from London to Hampton Court. Eloise wanted to go into the maze, and I said why not? What else does a guy say on his honeymoon? So we went in, and I'll say this for the experience. One good thing came out of it."

"What?" Godfrey Condomine said.

"By the time Eloise and I got out of that damned Hampton Court maze I understood what it is that scares me in your books, Godfrey. It's easy to get into one of your sentences, but it's hell's own job getting out."

"May I remind you, gentlemen," Saphira Shreve said, "we haven't gathered in this expensive hotel suite to discuss Godfrey's merits as a novelist. We're here to get through the annual chore of choosing our new junior partners, if any."

"Did you pick this place?" Paul Truitt said.

"Yes, why?" Saphira Shreve said.

"You've got guts, Saphira," Paul Truitt said. "It's a big improvement over that Algonquin bridal suite we've been using for years, but mainly thank God I'm not the one who has to face Gil Cutter's lecture on extravagance when he gets the bill for this annual clambake."

"I did not choose this suite because I think it's an improvement over the Algonquin," Saphira Shreve said. "I happen to like the Algonquin, especially the bridal suite. Sammy and I spent our wedding night in it. And if I have to face a lecture from Gil Cutter my conscience is clear. Our meeting in this gaudy Park Lane suite will cost Isham Truitt not one dime. Gil Cutter leased it two weeks ago for a motion picture-TV project Ken Kreel is working on, and I asked Ken to allow us to use it this afternoon."

"When I was Ken Kreel's age," Ludwig Uchitel said, "junior partners did not get the firm to rent hotel suites for them to handle the sort of projects Ken is good at. In my day you were lucky if you could bury it on your federal tax return under 'entertainment for business reasons not reimbursed by employer.'"

"I've seen some of Ken Kreel's projects," Paul Truitt said. "They remind me of something my father told me Trotsky said to the German ambassador on the first day of the Brest–Litovsk treaty sessions. The German was comparing the ease of the imperial conquests on the Eastern front with the ease of Casanova's conquests in another area. According to my father, Trotsky said if a man is willing to dine on radish tops he need never go to bed hungry."

"Unless we stick to what brought us here," Saphira Shreve said, "nobody at this table is going to do any dining today."

"Knock it off, Saphira," Ludwig Uchitel said. "You're beginning to sound like a Condomine character."

"Why not?" Godfrey Condomine said. "She's looked like one for years. Did you know that, Saphira?"

"God forbid," Saphira Shreve said. "I'd like to remind you that you were the one who injected the name of young Mr. Lichine into this meeting. Would you mind telling us why, or getting his name out of here?"

"Getting the name of young Lichine out of here," Godfrey Condomine said, "I am afraid is a task that presents difficulties not unlike those involved in what my maternal great-grandfather used to call 'bottling off the Ganges.'"

"Don't for God's sake tell us what your paternal great-grandfather called it," Ludwig Uchitel said. "Saphira promised Ken Kreel we'd be out of here by six o'clock."

"All right, Ludwig, I think we've had enough of that," Saphira Shreve said. "Go on, Godfrey, and for God's sake snap it up."

"I have gone over the material you sent along, Saphira," said the author to whom *Playboy* never failed to refer, frequently without provocation, as Jane Austen in knee pants. "I have in fact gone over the material several times. The last time on the plane coming up from Washington this morning. Repetition does not seem to improve the situation, my dear Saphira, except on one point. I note with relief, a relief I am sure is shared by everybody at this table, that this year we are spared our annual hair-shirt hour of groveling in our own inhumanity for once again passing over the name of that brilliant but dreary dim bulb Ezra Kingsley Cooper. For this happy release to whom do we owe our gratitude?"

"To Cooper himself," Ludwig Uchitel said. "He stumbled on Ken Kreel's project, or some seamy piece of it, and the damn fool marched in on Manny Merz with what amounted to a blackmail demand. Make me a partner or else. Manny did what we should have done years ago but none of us had the guts to do."

"Or the opportunity," Walter Isham said.

All heads turned to the figure at the head of the table. He could have been sitting for that Underwood & Underwood group portrait of Woodrow Wilson's Supreme Court.

"Hey, Walter," Paul Truitt said. "If you know the details of Ken Kreel's project I think it's only fair to let your partners in on it."

"Paul, I remember the days when you would not have to be reminded there is a lady present," Walter Isham said.

"She'll give you permission," Paul Truitt said. "Right, Saphira?"

"Saphira, you will disregard Paul's crude levity, and as senior partner I will apologize for it," Walter Isham said. "No, Paul, I do not know the details of Ken Kreel's project, any more than I know the details of some of yours, and I don't want to know them. I make it a policy to trust all my senior partners until their projects show up in red figures on our auditors' annual statement. I merely make the point that on the Cooper situation we were caught on the horns of a dilemma, and when Cooper presented Manny with a way of escape, Manny took it. More power to both of them."

"Neither one of them needs it," Ludwig Uchitel said. "The Fillmore board has just dropped Manny Merz into the bowl of chicken fat known as Southern Shoals Asbestos. It's the sort of bowl Manny was born to splash around in. As for Ezra Cooper, the moment Manny kicked him out on his ass Falk Prudhomme picked him up on the bounce at almost twice the salary Cooper had finally reached with us. Which ought to tell us something about the way we've been picking our partners."

"If it does," Godfrey Condomine said, "I don't think it would be wise to listen. We might hear echoes about how the people around this table were picked. Let's stick to this list of candidates with which Saphira has supplied us. I've studied it, as I'm sure you all have. What strikes me, as it does every year at this time, is that our problem is always the same. It is a matter of dollars and cents, always corrected upwards for the change in numbers caused by inflation."

Godfrey Condomine smiled. "A quick review of how we get our dollars and how we spend them might be useful at this point," he said. "We are still doing business at the same old stand, buying brains wholesale and selling them retail. An Isham Truitt associate is expected to produce for Gil Cutter's computers at least 1,600 billable hours a year. At a ball-park figure of, say, $70 an hour the associate thus brings into our coffers a gross of $120,000 per annum. Half of this disappears as overhead. Large law firms are fueled by large expenses. With $60,000 of the associate's gross earnings for the firm sent down the spout in lunches at Caravelle, we are left with $60,000 to play with. If we pay the associate $30,000 in salary that leaves $30,000 in net profits to be cut up by the likes of us. All things considered, not a bad business to be in, especially since we are in a position to pass our inflation on to the client. A junior partner, on the other hand, is expected to produce not 1,600 billable hours per year but only 1,000 hours. Why? Because partners, even juniors, must not be seen hunching over the handlebars, wearing running pants on their way around town from client to client, or in any way illustrating the cherished maxim that haste makes waste. It does nothing of the sort. Any honest lawyer will tell you what haste does. It makes big bucks. At a billing rate double that of an associate, or $150 an hour, that means the junior partner brings into the firm a gross of a mere $150,000 per annum. 'Mere' because the difference between his gross and the associate's gross is a not very impressive $30,000. Barely enough to cover the first reward of achieving junior partnership, namely, a personal drawing account. Obviously, therefore, to be worthy of becoming a junior partner the associate must demonstrate qualities other than those of a competent or even brilliant drudge capable of grinding out 1,600 billable hours a year."

"You ought to talk about money more often," Ludwig Uchitel said. "When you're dealing with dollars and cents your vocabulary goes from Jane Austen to 'Sesame Street.'"

Condomine's smile reappeared. "The writers for 'Sesame Street' get no residuals," he said. "Jane Austen is still in print.

Now, Saphira, in going over this fat mass of material I was impressed by two things. First, the large number of associates we now have on our staff, and second, only two of them seem on the record to possess those extra qualities to which I refer."

"Which two?" Walter Isham said.

"First this young man named J. C. Taunton," Godfrey Condomine said.

"Oh, yes," Paul Truitt said.

"What does that intonation mean?" Ludwig Uchitel said.

"It means I've never had anything to do with him," Paul Truitt said, "but even when he's sipping from a paper cup at the water cooler I don't like his looks."

"Why not?" Ludwig Uchitel said.

"He reminds me of my father's description of the faces he used to see around the conference table at Brest–Litovsk," Paul Truitt said.

"Which side?" Ludwig Uchitel said. "German or Russian?"

"Russian," Paul Truitt said.

"Instead of picking a partner," Ludwig Uchitel said, "I suggest we all take to the hills."

"Would it not be simpler merely to draw a line through his name on our list?" Godfrey Condomine said.

"Not so quick, please," Walter Isham said. "A talent for the law is not always draped in grace. There is a passage in one of the Holmes–Pollock letters in which Holmes describes a contemporary of John Marshall who detested the appearance of the Chief Justice so much that he had a picture of Marshall painted into the bottom of his chamber pot."

"The perfect setting for a picture of J. C. Taunton," Paul Truitt said.

"Yes, but what does he look like?" Walter Isham said.

"You remember the *Our Gang* comedies in the movies?" Paul Truitt said.

"I was raised on them," Walter Isham said.

"There was this skinny little kid always seen on the right?" Paul Truitt said. "A sort of mama's boy? He wore a Little Lord Fauntleroy suit? And he had those droopy sort of hooded eyelids? With a small twisted slimey smile on his lips?"

"The one who always stole the pennies out of the blind man's cup and then stood by looking angelic while his colleagues were berated and chased for the crime?" Walter Isham said.

"That's our J. C. Taunton," Paul Truitt said.

"He sounds promising," Walter Isham said. "Let's table a decision on Mr. Taunton. I will review his case personally. Next?"

"That leaves only one," Godfrey Condomine said.

"The recommendation by her rabbi is glowing, but we must make allowances," Saphira Shreve said. "She is a very pretty girl, Godfrey."

"And Hugh Kelly is a very, how shall I put it, a very dirty old man?" Godfrey Condomine said.

"He may be," Saphira Shreve said. "So are a lot of novelists. It has nothing to do with Hugh Kelly's enthusiasm for Miss Cline."

"What has?" Godfrey Condomine said.

"She may be a lapsed Catholic who is having second thoughts," Saphira Shreve said.

"Is that why you fired her?" Godfrey Condomine said.

"Who told you I fired her?" Saphira Shreve said.

"Hugh Kelly," Godfrey Condomine said. "I called him in Rome to check on his enthusiastic recommendation. He told me since he wrote that plug for Miss Cline he has decided to withdraw it."

"Why?" Paul Truitt said.

"Hugh is irked by Miss Cline's insistence on taking on the defense of young Mr. Lichine in the extradition hearing presently being argued in the New York Supreme Court."

"Was she asked not to defend Lichine?" Paul Truitt said.

"She was ordered not to," Saphira Shreve said.

"By whom?" Godfrey Condomine said.

"Me," Saphira Shreve said.

"Why?" Godfrey Condomine said.

"Walter can answer that better than I can," Saphira Shreve said.

"I could give you the long answer," Walter Isham said. "Or I can give you the two-word answer."

"Start with the two words," Godfrey Condomine said.

"David Fillmore," Walter Isham said.

"I'm surprised," Godfrey Condomine said. "But not astonished."

"How about giving us a break?" Ludwig Uchitel said. "Just for Lent, Godfrey, could you give up leaning on Jane Austen's syntax and lean on your own?"

"I'll be much more effective if I lean on yours," Godfrey Condomine said. "I asked Tessie to get me a transcript of your testimony at this extradition hearing. In it, Ludwig, you make two points. One, Lichine got his job with Isham Truitt at the insistence of David Fillmore. Two, Lichine got sent down to Alabama on this ill-fated pro bono assignment at his own insistence. Is my statement correct?"

"Yes," Ludwig Uchitel said. "Now all you have to do is connect that up with your statement that Miss Cline was ordered not to defend Mr. Lichine at this extradition hearing."

"I was the one who issued the order," Saphira Shreve said. "It might save time, Ludwig, if I made the connection."

"Anything that will keep Jane Austen out of this room will help," Ludwig Uchitel said. "Please take the ball, Saphira."

"The first hint we had that Mr. Lichine was trouble came from Father Danaher," Saphira Shreve said.

"Who is Father Danaher?" Godfrey Condomine said.

"Part of Hugh Kelly's Catholic Connection," Saphira Shreve said. "He's our man in Montgomery."

"Meaning what?" Godfrey Condomine said.

"He's the Isham Truitt troubleshooter on the spot in Southern Shoals Asbestos country," Saphira Shreve said. "Just as you are in Washington."

"Odd," Godfrey Condomine said. "I always thought of myself as the Fillmore National man in Washington."

"Aren't we all?" Ludwig Uchitel said.

"As I get older," Walter Isham said, "I find myself more and more frequently cautioning my partners against frivolity in serious matters. You are all aware of what the world is aware of. Isham Truitt, no matter what else it may be, is the legal arm of Fillmore National. David Fillmore is Fillmore National. Proceed, Saphira, if you please."

"About a month ago," Saphira Shreve said, "Father Danaher warned Hugh Kelly that Tom Lichine had precipitated a dangerous situation in Montgomery."

"Dangerous to whom?" Godfrey Condomine said.

"Isham Truitt," Saphira Shreve said.

"And Fillmore National, of course?" Ludwig Uchitel said.

"Of course," Saphira Shreve said.

"What sort of dangerous situation?" Godfrey Condomine said.

"Father Danaher could not quite pinpoint the trouble," Saphira Shreve said. "He knew only that Mr. Lichine was not doing the work in Montgomery he had been sent down to do as part of our pro bono program."

"According to the testimony transcript I read," Godfrey Condomine said, "Mr. Lichine was sent down to help with the defense in a murder case that was on appeal."

"That was his ostensible assignment," Saphira Shreve said. "Under the cover of working on his assignment, Mr. Lichine, according to Father Danaher, was off on a project of his own."

"What sort of project?" Godfrey Condomine said.

"Father Danaher did not know," Saphira Shreve said.

"He sounds just about as bright as most members I've met who belong to Hugh Kelly's so-called Catholic Connection," Ludwig Uchitel said. "Schmucks one and all."

"In spades," Paul Truitt said.

"Would it not help, Saphira, if we had a more precise gauge?" Godfrey Condomine said. "What, for example, did Father Danaher recommend we should do about the unidentified situation that, if I am to judge by the chain reaction he seems to have set in motion here at Isham Truitt, first Hugh Kelly and then my other colleagues believe is a dire threat to our, meaning Fillmore National, interests?"

"In plain English, Saphira," Ludwig Uchitel said, "what did this horse's ass Father Danaher recommend should be done?"

"Father Danaher recommended we stay out of it," Saphira Shreve said.

"When I was a lad 'It' meant Clara Bow," Godfrey Condomine said. "What did 'It' mean in the context of Father Danaher's recommendation?"

"Let young Lichine take the consequences," Saphira Shreve said.

"What consequences?" Godfrey Condomine said.

"In the course of this unclear activity Mr. Lichine was involved in down in Montgomery only one thing is crystal clear," Saphira Shreve said. "Young Lichine got himself in trouble with the police."

Ludwig Uchitel said, "That, Godfrey, is the Jane Austen way of saying the stupid little son of a bitch got himself indicted for murder in the second degree."

"How?" Godfrey Condomine said.

"A fight with the police," Saphira Shreve said.

"Which is why, Godfrey," Ludwig Uchitel said, "the state of Alabama is trying to extradite what Walter just called the little twirp back to Alabama."

"That is correct," Saphira Shreve said.

"And our way of staying out of it was to send our distinguished of counsel Mr. Howard Dent into the breach?" Godfrey Condomine said.

"It was not our way," Saphira Shreve said. "It was Howard's way. Hugh Kelly was shocked when he learned Howard intended to defend the young man."

"Why didn't Hugh stop him?" Godfrey Condomine said.

"Other people have tried to stop Howard Dent," Saphira Shreve said. "From Wendell Willkie and Commonwealth and Southern in the early days of TVA, to Joseph Stalin and his colleagues at Yalta in the late days of Franklin Roosevelt. Howard Dent always did what he set out to do, and he set out to defend Tom Lichine."

"Taking into court with him as his assistant Miss Judith Cline," Ludwig Uchitel said.

"That young lady seems to have a charm for older men," Godfrey Condomine said and then continued, "When Howard Dent removed himself from the scene Isham Truitt didn't just fold its tent and fade from the picture. Whose idea was it to allow Miss Cline to keep the show going?"

"Manny Merz's," Ludwig Uchitel said.

"Not quite," Saphira Shreve said. "Manny did step forward,

but it was only after Hugh Kelly called him from Rome and told him to take over."

"Manny doesn't seem to have had a very long run in the role," Godfrey Condomine said.

"He wasn't supposed to," Saphira Shreve said. "Hugh asked Manny to step in and go through the motions long enough for the Fillmore board to meet and elect him the new executive officer of Southern Shoals to succeed Sosthenes DeKalb."

"At which point," Godfrey Condomine said, "I see the plot as Miss Austen would have seen it. Manny Merz fades from the picture, and the young, distraught, left-to-her-own-devices Miss Cline proves not to have enough devices to cope. She collapses and young Mr. Lichine is left on his own. Devices, that is. They prove to be insufficient and young Mr. Lichine gets it where Father Danaher urged Hugh Kelly to let the little twirp get it. In the neck."

"I hope this won't upset you, Godfrey," Saphira Shreve said, "but Miss Cline refused to collapse."

"That, then, explains your threat," Godfrey Condomine said.

"Yes," Saphira Shreve said. "What it doesn't explain is that girl's conduct."

"She disregarded your threat?" Godfrey Condomine said.

"As well as Gil Cutter's execution of my threat," Saphira Shreve said.

"Then Hugh Kelly's orders were carried out?" Godfrey Condomine said. "Miss Cline was fired?"

"Only from Isham Truitt," Ludwig Uchitel said. "Young Lichine rehired her immediately."

"Making us all look pretty silly," Godfrey Condomine said.

"Not yet," Ludwig Uchitel said. "She's still on her feet in Special Term, Part Two. We won't start looking silly until she loses what Howard Dent started to fight for, Manny Merz pretended to continue fighting for, and Miss Cline is now apparently determined to give her all for, namely, that writ of habeas corpus for Thomas Lichine."

"What are her chances?" Godfrey Condomine said.

"We'll have to wait and see," Ludwig Uchitel said.

"We can't wait long," Walter Isham said.

Again, of the five heads in the room only one did not move. And again it belonged to the speaker. The other four stared at the senior partner whose active services had been reduced to representing Isham Truitt at all funerals important to the firm.

"Hugh Kelly did say the sums involved were potentially vast," Saphira Shreve said. "The way he put it, he said the concern of the bank is not casual."

The old man, whose family had been intermarrying with the Fillmores like Egyptian Pharaohs since Leander Fillmore established the bank in 1908, shook his head with a small, weary sigh.

"It's not only the money," Walter Isham said. "It's also more than the bank."

There was a pause.

"The girl must be stopped," Saphira Shreve said.

"It's possible she's already done that herself," Paul Truitt said. "Godfrey reported that the boy refuses to take the stand."

"Godfrey said it was the boy's father who told him," Ludwig Uchitel said. "How come, Godfrey?"

"I've known Tom Lichine Senior for years," Godfrey Condomine said. "I don't see him as often as I used to when he was a figure in the New York theater. He's more or less retired now, and I'm in Washington most of the time, but after I read that transcript this morning I called him up."

"Here in New York?" Ludwig Uchitel said.

"The Lichines live five floors above us at the Waldorf Towers," Paul Truitt said. "Been there for years. What did the boy's father say, Godfrey?"

"I told him I'd read Father Danaher's testimony," Godfrey Condomine said. "That the Cline girl asked Danaher what happened down in Montgomery, and Danaher said why don't you ask Tom Lichine?"

"Why didn't she?" Ludwig Uchitel said.

"That's as far as the transcript goes," Godfrey Condomine said. "Because I had this meeting with all of you scheduled for this afternoon, I decided not to wait until tomorrow morning. So I called Lichine's father, chatted a bit about old times, then zeroed in on his son's problem. Lichine Senior didn't seem to know much. I got the impression he doesn't see the boy very often. I asked if the boy was going to take the stand, and he knew the answer to that all right. He said absolutely not."

"Why not?" Ludwig Uchitel said.

"He didn't know," Godfrey Condomine said. "Or perhaps he didn't want to say. All I got out of him was that young Lichine will not take the stand."

"The girl must be stopped," Walter Isham said again.

"How?" Saphira Shreve said.

"I have a suggestion," Godfrey Condomine said. "All this material you gave us to read for this meeting, Saphira. It indicates that this year we have only one associate in the shop who has the qualifications for partnership. Is that correct?"

"It seems so," Saphira Shreve said.

"Why not make that one person the offer?" Godfrey Condomine said.

"Because she might give us the same answer she gave Saphira," Ludwig Uchitel said.

"The situations are totally dissimilar," Godfrey Condomine said. "Saphira issued an order. We would be making an offer."

"I don't see how that answers my question," Ludwig Uchitel said.

"My dear Ludwig," Godfrey Condomine said. "In the Mecca of the Western World, namely New York, as in the Mecca of Jane Austen's world, namely Bath, twenty-five-year-old girls just out of Harvard Law School do not turn down junior partnership offers in things called Isham, Truitt, Kelly, Shreve, Merz, Uchitel and Condomine."

33

"It's a bribe, Mother."

"Congratulations," Nellie Cline said. "I'd given up hope you'd ever be offered one."

"You didn't used to talk that way in the days when you and Pop were going to meetings in Mecca Temple to denounce the Teapot Dome gang," Judy said.

"We were young then," Nellie Cline said. "Throw the rascals out was the fashionable way for playwrights to get ahead. And you weren't born yet, so we'll strike that from the record. The lawyers in your father's plays used to call it hearsay and therefore not admissible in evidence."

"So is your information," Judy said. "You were not present."

"Godfrey Condomine was," Nellie Cline said. "He's an old beau of Amelia's. Maybe of Tom Senior's, too, for all I know. The point is Godfrey's role in life is Cholly Knickerbocker rolled into one. He's such a compulsive gossip even when he doesn't kiss he tells in relentless detail. It couldn't have been more than a couple of minutes after you'd all cleared out of this Mr. Kreel's Park Lane suite before Godfrey was on the blower to the Waldorf Towers. I happened to be having a drink with Amelia and Tom Senior at the time, so I listened in on the extension. Judging by the first draft I heard on the phone, when it emerges in one of his novels it's going to be one hell of a scene. I was interested, of course. Godfrey's stuff may not be swift but it's never dull. It wasn't until he got to the curtain line about the offer they'd decided to make to Miss Cline that I decided to invite him to dinner."

"Oh, Christ," Judy said. "Is he going to be here, too?"

"What do you mean, too?" Nellie said. "All I did was leave a message with my daughter's answering service to come have a pot-luck supper with her A.P.'s."

"I came up the rear elevator so I could sneak into my old room for a shower before I showed myself to you and Pop," Judy said. "Coming through the kitchen what was sticking out of the Gristede's bag was a dead giveaway. French bread always used to mean company for dinner."

"It still does," Nellie Cline said. "Want a hand with that?"

"Mother, I was wearing panty hose before you heard they'd been invented," Judy said. "Did you tell Pop about my bribe?"

"I haven't had a chance yet," Nellie Cline said. "When I got home from Amelia and Tom's he was still downstairs in the studio, and now he's in the shower, but you don't have to worry. I'm sure he'll be pleased."

"Because the bribe was made?" Judy said. "Or because he thinks I'm going to accept?"

"Aren't you?" Nellie said.

"It's my first experience," Judy said. "What's your advice to a daughter who is being asked to part with her virginity?"

"Never for a penny less than a price above rubies," Nellie Cline said. "Stick it to the bastards for as much as you can get, baby."

"You know what they want in return," Judy said.

"I also know you're worrying about it too much," Nellie Cline said. "If you step out Tom can always get another lawyer."

"He doesn't want another lawyer," Judy said. "He wants your daughter Judy."

"He told you that?" Nellie Cline said.

"He sent his Bianca to tell me that," Judy said.

"Aren't you and Tom talking?" Nellie Cline said.

"Not about Alabama," Judy said.

"Isn't that unusual?" Nellie Cline said.

"In what way?" Judy said.

"I always thought before a lawyer can go into court to defend someone he had to make sure he knows his client's version of what he's defending the client against," Nellie Cline said.

"I know Tom's version," Judy said. "He told it to me and Mr. Dent and Mr. Kelly. Bianca tells me Tom feels the best way to prove what he told me is to put witnesses on the stand to introduce the facts and then let the facts speak for themselves."

"According to Godfrey Condomine these particular facts have a speech difficulty," Nellie Cline said.

"How does he know?" Judy said.

"He told Amelia and Tom Senior on the phone this afternoon he'd read a transcript of the testimony that's been taken so far," Nellie Cline said. "Is that what you'll be wearing tonight?"

"I didn't have time to go back to my own apartment," Judy said. "I remembered among other things I left here in the closet when I moved, this was one I always liked."

"So do I," Nellie Cline said. "I still do. Which reminds me. Wait here. I won't be but a minute."

She disappeared from her daughter's room the way she had always moved in and out of Judy's life: like a busy teacher who had not realized until she entered the classroom and saw her favorite pupil that there was something she had been meaning to give the child, and so the entire class would now have to wait while she hurried back to her office to fetch it. As Judy grew older, and became more aware of patterns in her own as well as other people's behavior, it seemed to Judy her mother's whole life had consisted of hurrying back to earlier arenas to fetch something she had forgotten or discarded, something that now seemed indispensable to her functioning successfully in her new environment.

Nellie had dropped out of high school in Kansas City to try her luck in New York as a fashion model. She had a successful year on Seventh Avenue until she decided she really wanted to be a designer. Nellie hurried back to Kansas City to finish high school. With her diploma she returned to New York and a good job in Bonwit's custom department. Here she was spotted by a *Vogue* photographer who felt she had a much brighter future as a magazine fashion model. He was right, at least for another year, when Nellie caught the eye of a Hollywood producer who was shooting a movie on location about the life of a New York magazine model who had started as a designer. Nellie hurried back to Bonwit's for a couple of brush-up weeks at the custom-department drawing boards. The movie was not successful but Nellie attracted the attention of a rising young playwright with two successful courtroom melodramas to his credit who was casting his third. The play was described by Alexander Woollcott as "a *succès d'estime* and a flop *de fiasco*" but Nellie and the playwright fell in love during the Boston tryout. They were married the day after the New York opening but could not go on their honeymoon until the play closed six weeks later. During the honeymoon Clifford Cline wrote a new play for his bride. It was a musical. Nellie went back to Kansas City for a month of intensive voice study with her high school music teacher. The result satisfied Clifford Cline but not the director or the producer. They hired Amelia Troy. She was perfect in the part.

During the two-year run on Broadway, Amelia Troy and Nellie Cline began the long friendship from which Nellie never had to hurry back to an earlier arena to fetch something she had forgotten or discarded. Nellie Cline came from all of her past to the Amelia Troy arena the way General Grant came from Galena to the Army of the Potomac: fully prepared to take command. Nobody, it seemed to Judy Cline, could doubt that as Amelia Troy's closest friend Nellie Cline's life, like water finding its own level, had reached tranquility at last. Even in moments like the present, when she dashed out of a room in order to come dashing back with something she felt she should have remembered to bring with her in the first place.

"Here," Nellie said. "Stand up straight."

Judy stood up straight. Her mother fastened something to the dress at Judy's shoulder, then turned her to face the mirror. Judy stared at the diamond gardenia for a long moment.

"Mother, it's beautiful," she said. "Especially with this dress."

"More beautiful than it ever looked on me," Nellie Cline said. "With any dress."

"When did you get it?" Judy said.

"It was your father's wedding present," Nellie Cline said. "On the opening night of the only play I ever starred in."

"Why haven't I seen it before?" Judy said.

"It's too private to wear," Nellie Cline said. "For me it represented the one moment in my life when I'd reached whatever it is kids think they want to reach when they're still kids. After that night I wasn't a kid anymore. I kept it for the moment when my daughter wouldn't be a kid anymore. I figure that moment arrived today when Godfrey Condomine told me they'd decided to offer you a partnership. Make sure you don't lose it before your father transfers ownership to you on his insurance floater."

"Mother," Judy said, "I can't accept this."

"Why not?" Nellie Cline said.

"I'm not going to take that bribe," Judy said.

"It hasn't been offered yet," Nellie Cline said. "When it is, you may change your mind. Like a great many bad novelists, Godfrey Condomine is very persuasive."

"Is that why he's coming to dinner?" Judy said.

"I heard what he had to say this afternoon on the phone," Nellie Cline said. "With meat prices the way they are these days do you think I'd invite him to share a rack of lamb just to hear his polished second draft of a scene I already know?"

There was a tap on the door.

·"Yes?" Judy called.

"That you, Jude?"

Nellie Cline went to the door and pulled it open.

"It's both of us," she said. "Which one do you want?"

"I saw you an hour ago in my own living room," Thomas Lichine Senior said. "It's Judy I've come to see now."

"Where's Amelia?" Nellie said.

"Helping Clifford knot his tie," said Tom Lichine's father. "Why don't you go lend a hand, so I can have a few minutes alone with Judy before Jane Austen in knee pants arrives from Washington."

"Show Uncle Tom your present," Nellie Cline said as she went out.

"Where?" Tom Senior said.

Judy pointed to the diamond gardenia on her shoulder. Tom Senior leaned close and peered.

"They certainly know how to do these things better nowadays," he said.

"Do what things?" Judy said.

"Package their thirty pieces of silver," Tom Senior said.

Judy stared at the man she had known since she had begun to recognize the distinctions in appearance that could be used as guidelines for separating a single human being from the herd. In a view that must have been obtained from a perambulator or perhaps from the arms of a parent or nurse, she remembered noting first the tallness of the new image. Then came a sense of pleasure in the image. And finally, the identity of the tall, pleasant image by a name: Uncle Tom Senior.

Judy did not know then, of course, that there was a Tom Junior. When she found out she learned how to separate father and son by name as well as appearance. In her mind Tom Senior fell into the category that contained all adults, including her own parents. In this category people did not, like Judy herself and Tom Junior, grow older. They were ageless. Judy was using the meaning of the word inside her head long before she knew it existed. Now, twenty-five years later, facing Tom Lichine Senior in her old bedroom at ten-ten the word rose automatically to the surface of her mind. He was indeed ageless.

"If a person can be bought for thirty pieces of silver," Judy said, "I don't think it matters how the stuff is packaged."

"Does that mean you haven't made up your mind yet?" Tom Senior said.

"Suppose I haven't?" Judy said.

"Then I'm not too late," Tom Senior said.

He never had been, Judy felt in a moment of revelation that took her by surprise. Tom Senior had always seemed contemporary. Even now, when he was almost exactly the same age as her own father, Tom Junior's father looked like one of those people caught by the newspaper camera in a moment of attractive movement over the caption "Seen Arriving at Heathrow Airport." Not the newest teen-age rock-music multimillionaire awash in beads and hair and doxies, and not the baleful ambassador from Islam carrying in a Burlington Arcade attaché case the newest OPEC price increases, but someone in between. A survivor from an earlier time who was still capable of enjoying and even gracing the present.

"You're not too late for what?" Judy said.

"Saving the hide of the man I always thought you were going to marry," Tom Senior said.

"He's now married to somebody else," Judy said.

"He still happens to be my son," Tom Senior said. "It gives a man a protective feeling."

"You think he has to be protected from me?" Judy said.

"Of course not," Tom Senior said.

"Then what do you think?" Judy said.

"I think you have to be protected from people like my wife and your mother," Tom Senior said. "If I can help keep you out of their clutches, I might help keep Tom Junior out of the clutches of those bastards in Alabama."

"Since I started on this case," Judy said, "I've built up a list of the people who would like to fix Tom's feet. I still don't know why they want to do it, but I do know Nellie and Amelia have not surfaced on that list."

"Give them time," Tom Senior said.

"You sound like the hero in the bribery scene at the end of Act One of *I Am Dying, Little Egypt*," Judy said.

"Why not?" Tom Senior said. "I played the hero in that scene. How are you fixed for cash?"

"I never know until I get my monthly bank statement," Judy said. "When I do get it I'm usually overdrawn. Why?"

"When you're usually overdrawn you're also usually expecting your monthly salary check," Tom Senior said. "I hear there won't be any more."

"Who do you hear these things from?" Judy said.

"A girl named Sandra Behr," Tom Senior said. "Know her?"

"Only by name," Judy said. "I know her friend, though. Phoebe Pember. Why?"

"Sandra's mother and I were drama majors together at Carnegie Tech," Tom Senior said. "A month after we both got to New York she married a City College man who was just starting an electrical appliance business in Westport, where she's lived happily ever after."

"Her daughter Sandra hasn't," Judy said. "I've been trying to help her friend Phoebe Pember get Sandra to the right therapist, but no luck so far."

"Sandra told me about that when she gave me a copy of the transcript of *Pridemore* v. *Southern Shoals Asbestos,*" Tom Senior said. "She helped Phoebe Pember bootleg it for you out of the Isham Truitt steno department."

"After you retired from the stage," Judy said, "I used to wonder once in a while how you filled in your time. I didn't realize you kept busy directing clandestine operations for the Isham Truitt paratroops."

"I'm full of surprises," Tom Senior said. "Including a supply of cash to tide you over until you land another job."

"How does that differ from the bribe you're trying to talk me out of?" Judy said.

"It's a matter of numbers," Tom Senior said. "I can't offer as much as an Isham Truitt senior partner. I'm just a successful cuckold."

It was like the moment at lunch two days ago when her father had broken the news to Judy that he had never wanted her to be an actress. She wished older people would not come up with these revelations at a time in their lives when the only function the confession can possibly serve is to embarrass the confessee.

"I'm sorry," Judy said. "You didn't have to say that."

"If I'd said it long ago," Tom Senior said, "I might have prevented Tom's derailment into the Bianca Bean camp."

"You really ought to shut up about that," Judy said. "Among other things."

"I'd like to point something out to you," Tom Senior said. "A man who jumps off a bridge is in no position to say halfway down 'Oops, sorry, could I go back and rethink this?' Once you make that kind of choice you'd better learn to live with it. There's no way back. I knew about Amelia and David Fillmore when I met her. Who didn't? What I didn't know for a long time was it went on after we got married. I found out after the series of flops that forced Amelia off the stage. That made two unemployed performers in one family. Then I noticed something. There we were, both with no visible means of support, but still living at the Waldorf Towers and neither one of us suggesting maybe we'd better move. The mystery didn't take long to solve. My only problem was learning how to live with it. I'm sure it's no news to you that I managed. What may be news to you is that it's not difficult. The secret of being a successful cuckold is to treat yourself as a pimp. It works out quite well. She gets her forty-thousand-dollar Mercedes for Christmas. I get the fat bank account into which I squirrel away what I consider my fair share of her earnings. Out of it will come whatever funds you need to stay on as Tom Junior's lawyer without accepting bribes from outsiders."

Judy touched the diamond gardenia on her shoulder.

"I got into this thing without any help from insiders or outsiders," she said. "I'll get myself out in the same way."

34

Senator Pierre Prudhomme of Alabama was born Peretz Wiseman on Southern Boulevard. The day the midwife delivered the
new member of the Wiseman family the Triangle Shirtwaist
Company burst into flames. It brought to national attention the
horrors of the New York City sweat-shop scandal. The fire also
ended the successful five-year career of Peretz Wiseman's immigrant father as a manufacturer of ladies' shirtwaists. The elder
Wiseman gathered his wife, his two older children, his newborn
son, his bank books, his lares and penates, and headed south.

In Montgomery, Alabama, he bought a dry-goods store from
an immigrant Frenchman named Guinzbourg. The Frenchman
pointed out that, if his wife's health had not dictated an immediate return to their native Brittany, he would never walk away
from the store he had only recently founded: it had just begun to
prosper. Another thing the Frenchman pointed out was that Jew-
ish names like Guinzbourg were not a commercial asset in
Montgomery, Alabama. The black customers found it difficult to
pass the name along without distortion. For commercial purposes Wiseman was simpler than Guinzbourg, of course, but the
French translation of Wiseman was Prudhomme, a combination
of syllables that could not help but fall trippingly from the
American tongue on the American ear. Why not try it? The elder
Wiseman was eager to try anything that would separate him and
his family from the Triangle Shirtwaist experience. He took the
Frenchman's advice.

The modest dry-goods store grew into Prudhomme's Department Store, and Prudhomme's Department Store produced the money that fueled the family's interest in politics. By the time Pierre Prudhomme, né Peretz Wiseman, was elected to his first term as United States senator, no Democratic party move of consequence in Alabama was made without his approval. He was rounding out his third senatorial term, and beginning to lay the groundwork for his fourth campaign, on the day his secretary rang to say Mr. Godfrey Condomine had arrived to keep his eleven o'clock appointment.

"Send him in," Pierre Prudhomme said.

He stood up and came out from behind his desk to receive the visitor.

"You're late, Godfrey," he said, taking Condomine's hand.

"Am I?" Godfrey Condomine said. He glanced at his watch. "I make it one minute to eleven."

"So do I but I'm not talking about minutes," Pierre Prudhomme said. "I'm talking about days. This chair okay?"

"Perfect," Godfrey Condomine said, dropping into it. "If I understand you correctly you're saying I'm days late?"

"That's precisely what I'm saying," Pierre Prudhomme said.

"But I called for this appointment only yesterday when I got back from New York," Godfrey Condomine said.

"By which time you were already three days late," Pierre Prudhomme said.

"Which means, I suppose, if I'm to adopt your arithmetic," Godfrey Condomine said, "I'm now four days late?"

"That's correct, Godfrey," Pierre Prudhomme said.

"One would suppose," Godfrey Condomine said, "I should at this point say late for what, but a more interesting point intrudes, namely, from what point do you start counting this lateness of mine which is, I assure you, a puzzle to me."

Pierre Prudhomme laughed. He was a portly man who had lived a quarter of a century without a hair on top of his head or a distinctive feature on his face until the night he saw *The Maltese Falcon* for the first time on "The Late Show." The result was not unlike the moment when the Prince of Wales, later Edward VII, for the first time saw Lillie Langtry. It didn't exactly change his life, but it did add a touch of definition to Pierre

Prudhomme's view of himself. From that moment of contact with *The Maltese Falcon* he decided he was Sydney Greenstreet. He never told anybody about this decision, so perhaps nobody ever found out, but Pierre Prudhomme knew. He began to shape his image accordingly. He cultivated a menacing glance, a croupy chuckle, and a waddling walk. Seated behind his desk, of course, all he could use was the glance and the chuckle. He used both liberally on Godfrey Condomine.

"You know, Godfrey," he said, "I'm probably the only member of the United States Senate who has not only read your novels, some of them, anyway, but your biography of Jane Austen as well. From what you just said, I have reached an interesting conclusion about your career."

"What did I just say?" Godfrey Condomine said.

"I confirmed your estimate that I considered you four days late for this appointment you made only yesterday, and you made a reply," Pierre Prudhomme said. "Please if you will, please repeat your reply, and don't say you can't remember because I know damn well, Godfrey, you have never forgotten a line you've ever spoken until you've had time to get to your desk and set it down on paper. So please repeat your reply to my statement that yes you are four days late."

"One would suppose, I think I began, yes, that's it, one would suppose," Godfrey Condomine said, "I should at this point say late for what, but a more interesting point intrudes, namely, from what point do you start counting this lateness of mine which is, I assure you, a puzzle to me."

"And from that statement," Pierre Prudhomme said, "I have reached the conclusion after all these years that you've never quite made it as Jane Austen because your artistic subconscious is really in bondage to Henry James."

"My shrink, who has pointed this out to me several times, will be glad to learn he's got senatorial confirmation," Godfrey Condomine said. "Now tell me why I'm four days late for this appointment I made only yesterday."

"Four days ago Howard Dent died," Pierre Prudhomme said. "When I read the obituaries with my breakfast coffee I was convinced you'd be on the blower as soon as you got through the New York *Times*."

"I don't understand that," Godfrey Condomine said. "When you read about a man's death you call people who knew him. His family. His friends. His associates. I did that. Howard had no family, of course, but he had many friends. I called those I knew who had been close to him, and I called my partners, of course, but I don't see why I should have called you. I don't mean to be rude. I mean only that I never connected you with Howard. Were you and he close friends?"

"Not close, no," Pierre Prudhomme said. "He was thirty years my senior. I was still a kid in law school when Howard Dent was all over the front pages as one of FDR's hot shots trying to bring TVA to life in spite of the greed of Commonwealth and Southern and the guile of Wendell Willkie. Years later, when I got into politics, and after I was elected to the Senate, of course, I got to know him somewhat. It would have been difficult for anybody to be in public life in this country for the last half century without at least crossing Howard Dent's path. But a close friend? No, I was never that."

"Did you think I was?" Godfrey Condomine said.

"No more so than I was," Pierre Prudhomme said. "Even though I knew he was of counsel to your firm, I knew that was pretty much Walter Isham's doing. Everybody knows they were old friends, and Walter wanted to help him out of the boredom of retirement, but you and I are about the same age, so till Howard joined your firm less than a year ago, I would assume you knew him just about the way I did."

"Yet on the day you read his obituary you expected me to call you and ask to come and see you?" Godfrey Condomine said.

"I certainly did," Pierre Prudhomme said.

"I wish you'd tell me why," Godfrey Condomine said.

"I'll be glad to," Pierre Prudhomme said. "If you tell me something first."

"If I can," Godfrey Condomine said.

"What are you doing here this morning?" Pierre Prudhomme said.

"I've come to ask a favor," Godfrey Condomine said.

"Personal?" Pierre Prudhomme said.

"In a way," Godfrey Condomine said.

"What way?" Pierre Prudhomme said.

"For me and my partners," Godfrey Condomine said.

"For your firm?" Pierre Prudhomme said.

"Yes," Godfrey Condomine said.

"That's personal enough," Pierre Prudhomme said. "What would you like me to do for you?"

"One of our young associates," Godfrey Condomine said. "He's got himself into a mess, and we as a firm feel responsible, because it happened during a pro bono assignment we'd sent him out on."

"Thomas L. Lichine, Jr.?" Pierre Prudhomme said.

"How did you know?" Godfrey Condomine said.

"I'm the senior senator from Alabama," Pierre Prudhomme said. "I have been for eighteen years. It's part of my job to know everything that happens in Southern Shoals country."

"How much do you know about this?" Godfrey Condomine said.

"You came to ask a favor," Pierre Prudhomme said. "You'd better ask it before you ask questions."

"The boy is under indictment in Montgomery on a charge of murder in the second degree," Godfrey Condomine said. "We have reason to believe the indictment is a frame-up. We wondered if you'd talk to your people in Montgomery and get the indictment quashed."

"If it's a frame-up," Pierre Prudhomme said, "why not let it go to trial and have the boy exonerated by a jury of his peers?"

"There are complications," Godfrey Condomine said.

"There always are," Pierre Prudhomme said. "What kind are yours?"

"I'd rather not discuss them," Godfrey Condomine said.

"Use your head, Godfrey," Pierre Prudhomme said. "Unless you do you're asking me to walk into a blind alley."

"The firm would be embarrassed by any discussion of anything except the central fact," Godfrey Condomine said. "The indictment."

"Seems to me the firm should have used its head before they

sent Howard Dent in to defend the boy from extradition," Pierre Prudhomme said.

"We couldn't control Howard," Godfrey Condomine said.

"But you could control Manny Merz," Pierre Prudhomme said.

"Of course," Godfrey Condomine said.

"Now, however, you've discovered you can't control Miss Judith Cline," Pierre Prudhomme said. "Is that it, Godfrey?"

Godfrey Condomine's features were suddenly contorted by what the senator from Alabama apparently interpreted as a struggle for words. He stepped into the breach with a few bars of the Sydney Greenstreet chuckle.

"That's it, Godfrey, isn't it?" Pierre Prudhomme said.

"Yes," Godfrey Condomine said.

"I've never seen the girl," Pierre Prudhomme said. "I know nothing about her. What makes you think I can control her?"

"If the indictment against the boy is quashed, it won't be necessary to control her," Godfrey Condomine said. "The request for extradition will be dropped. The boy's request for a writ of habeas corpus will evaporate. The case will be over."

"Godfrey, do you know the difference between a novelist and a lawyer?" Pierre Prudhomme said.

"I've never thought about it," Godfrey Condomine said.

"Give it a minute or two now," Pierre Prudhomme said.

"You tell me the difference," Godfrey Condomine said.

"The novelist doesn't have to do a goddamn thing except plead to his muse," Pierre Prudhomme said. "The lawyer must plead to the indictment."

"What's the difference?" Godfrey Condomine said.

"The novelist can decide the case is over when he types the words 'The End,'" Pierre Prudhomme said. "The lawyer's case is never over until those words are typed by a judge or a jury."

"You're turning me down?" Godfrey Condomine said.

"Not yet," Pierre Prudhomme said. "I'm holding your favor in abeyance until you do something for me."

"What do you want?" Godfrey Condomine said.

"The favor I was going to ask you four days ago," Pierre Prudhomme said. "When I finished reading Howard Dent's obituary and I was so sure you were going to call me for an appointment."

"If I can do it, Pierre, you know all you have to do is ask," Godfrey Condomine said.

"Yes, I do know that," Pierre Prudhomme said through what was to Godfrey Condomine, who had never seen Sydney Greenstreet on the screen, merely an irritated clearing of the senatorial throat. Pierre Prudhomme said, "How well do you know David Fillmore?"

"As well as any Isham Truitt partner except Walter Isham himself," Godfrey Condomine said. "Walter is his brother-in-law, as you know."

"Yes, of course I know, but I know you better than I know Walter Isham," Pierre Prudhomme said. "So I'm making my request to you. If you need Walter Isham's help in getting it done, you won't have to call on outsiders to get that help."

"What do you want done?" Godfrey Condomine said.

"A friend of mine wants to play a round of golf with David Fillmore," Pierre Prudhomme said. "Tell Walter Isham I feel it would be in the best interest of all concerned if the game is arranged for some time tomorrow here in Washington."

35

George B. Taunton was proud of three things: his circle of friends, his son Jack, and his golf game. The first was large, the second was bright, and the third was disastrous. He rarely broke a hundred.

"One-o-six," George Taunton said, reading the total from his card. "Not bad for a dedicated hacker. How about you, Mr. Fillmore?"

"Eighty-nine," David Fillmore said. "Not good for a man who was coached privately by Bobby Jones when I was no taller than a niblick."

He stepped into the golf cart and sat down beside George Taunton.

"The most private spot in Washington is that small rise on your left just beyond the clump of maples," David Fillmore said. "It's free at the moment. If we hurry we can have the hill for our conference before Cyrus Vance arrives to hammer something out with the Russian ambassador. Step on it."

George Taunton stepped on it. He brought the golf cart to the top of the hill by combining a long looping arch with a snappy little U-turn. He flipped the power switch and leaned back. He looked out across the steering wheel and the Potomac to the Capitol dome.

"Nice view," George Taunton said.

"Not exactly the opening remark I'd expected from an old Washington hand," David Fillmore said.

"It was intended to provide you with a chance to do better," George Taunton said.

"Pierre Prudhomme told me you're a man who likes to start without skirmishing," David Fillmore said.

"If you have a better way," George Taunton said, "I'm on target for a direct hit."

"What are my chances for Senate confirmation?" David Fillmore said.

"Nil unless—" George Taunton said.

"Unless what?" David Fillmore said.

"Unless you really want to be this country's next Vice-President," George Taunton said.

"What makes you doubt it?" David Fillmore said.

"The way you and your team have been acting," George Taunton said.

"We've been doing something wrong?" David Fillmore said.

"Maybe not if your view is restricted to what can be seen from the Fillmore National Bank board room," George Taunton said.

"Yours is not," David Fillmore said.

"My view is that of a man standing at the elbow of Pierre Prudhomme and all the other members of the Senate confirmation committee," George Taunton said.

"What do my chances look like from there?" David Fillmore said.

"Either you're working very hard to get the Senate to reject your nomination," George Taunton said. "Or you don't know the nature of the work you're doing."

"By you do you mean me?" David Fillmore said.

"No," George Taunton said. "I mean your lawyers."

"They act for me," David Fillmore said.

"Unfortunately," George Taunton said, "everybody in Washington is aware of that."

Out of the corner of his eye Taunton watched the muscles harden under the skin of the long, lean face. It was as though one of those undersea creatures in a Jacques Cousteau TV special had surfaced in the trough of a wave.

"They're fucking it up?" David Fillmore said.

"That's the way it looks from down here," George Taunton said.

"Would you do something for me?" David Fillmore said.

"If I can," George Taunton said.

"You're not sitting in a golf cart on a hill overlooking the Potomac," David Fillmore said. "You're sitting at Pierre Prudhomme's elbow in that Senate Hearing Room. Okay?"

"Okay," George Taunton said.

"You're seeing what the senators are seeing," David Fillmore said.

"Okay," George Taunton said.

"What do you see?" David Fillmore said.

"I see one of the world's richest men," George Taunton said. "He owns everything, including one of the country's biggest banks, and a not inconsiderable piece of the state of Alabama called Southern Shoals Asbestos. For years there have been rumors that people who work down there in this rich man's asbestos mills have been contracting something called white lung disease. For years the rumors have been piling up that a lot of these workers are dying of lung cancer. For years the most persistent rumors have been that Southern Shoals has been suppressing and falsifying the statistics and medical reports to conceal the extent of the human damage. The reason is obvious. The damage suits against Southern Shoals could bankrupt the company. For years the rumors have been that Southern Shoals has kept the lid on the scandal by bribery. Southern Shoals is supposed to own the police, the courts, the state legislature, even the United States senators from Alabama. Is that all clear?"

"I don't know what you're talking about," David Fillmore said. "But I'm interested in every word you have to say. Don't leave any out."

"A year ago," George Taunton said, "a man down in Montgomery committed a murder during an armed robbery to get the money to pay for the oxygen his father needs to stay alive. His father can't breathe without oxygen because he contracted white lung disease during his thirty years as a Southern Shoals mill worker. The murderer and his son, who drove the getaway car, were tried and convicted and sentenced to death. For a while nothing happened because this was the period during which the whole country was waiting for the Supreme Court to make up its mind about capital punishment. When the Court finally made up its mind the state of Alabama started preparing to electrocute these two convicted murderers, father and son. An organization of do-gooder lawyers stepped in and brought an appeal for one of the convicted men on the ground that he was a minor. Among the do-gooder lawyers fighting for the boy's life a young man from New York showed up. He was assigned to the case on a pro bono basis by the New York law firm by which he was employed. The jury brought in a verdict that saved the kid from the electric chair and gave him instead a life sentence. If nothing else happened, your confirmation as this country's next Vice-President would have gone through the Senate the way Einstein went through the multiplication table. Instead the shit hit the electric fan."

"Meaning what?" David Fillmore said.

"Your lawyers panicked," George Taunton said.

"My lawyers," David Fillmore said.

George Taunton gave him a slanting look. The underseas face had split across the middle. For a moment Taunton thought Fillmore was smiling, but only for a moment. Both rows of Fillmore's strong white teeth were exposed. They were clamped together tightly, as though the owner had just stripped the meat from an artichoke leaf, and was now running a cleansing forefinger across his teeth, back and forth, back and forth. He could have been hunting a concealed lock that would if pressed snap his jaws open.

"Isham Truitt," George Taunton said. "They are your lawyers, aren't they?"

"What?" David Fillmore said. "Oh. Isham Truitt. Yes, of course. They're my lawyers. I was just trying to remember something. Please go on. My lawyers stepped in, you say."

"I say they panicked," George Taunton said.

"How?" David Fillmore said.

"They started acting like a bunch of kids in a school bus that's been sideswiped down an embankment," George Taunton said.

"Please break that down into detail," David Fillmore said.

"Everybody in Washington was watching, you understand," George Taunton said. "Everybody on Pierre Prudhomme's committee, anyway."

"Watching what?" David Fillmore said.

"The young pro bono lawyer who had come down to Alabama from New York to help with the defense turned out to be an Isham Truitt associate named Thomas Lichine," George Taunton said. "So the geniuses up at six-three-five Madison in New York to whom you pay all those fat fees, without thinking the thing through, acting like any bunch of hysterical schoolgirls on that sideswiped bus, the first thing they did was fire young Lichine."

"He was rehired immediately," David Fillmore said. "I happen to know that for a fact."

"Unfortunately so do Pierre Prudhomme and his associates in the Senate," George Taunton said.

"Why unfortunately?" David Fillmore said.

"You're one of the world's richest men," George Taunton said. "You have more flunkies, including secretaries, press agents, and lawyers than Jimmy Carter has teeth. Why should you take a personal interest in what happens to an obscure associate on the staff of a law firm that employs more than two hundred of them?"

"Couldn't it have been a simple humanitarian interest in elementary fair play?" David Fillmore said.

"Sure it could," George Taunton said. "And I am Valery Giscard d'Estang. When a Senate committee is fine-tooth-combing its way through the career of a man the President is about to nominate to be our country's Vice-President, they spend very little time hunting for examples of the man's humanitarian interests in elementary fair play. What these statesmen are interested in is headlines. Headlines are made by dirt. I regret to say that your expensive lawyers at six-three-five Madison spent the next few days working industriously to pile up for the Senate committee a small mountain of manure that as of this moment can be smelled not only in the Senate but in a far more important chamber as well."

"What are you talking about?" David Fillmore said.

"The Oval Office," George Taunton said.

Again the lips spread wide. The teeth clicked together. The forefinger started the circular trip back and forth across the gleaming enamel. After a few circuits David Fillmore again seemed to find the hidden spring lock. The teeth snapped apart.

"Assuming you're telling me the truth—" he began.

Setting one foot out of the golf cart onto the grass, George Taunton said, "You can bring this thing along anytime. I'll just walk back to the club house."

With a sharp, hard pull David Fillmore brought him back to the seat beside him.

"Don't be a melodramatic ass," he said. "Assuming you're telling me the truth as you see it, meaning as Pierre Prudhomme and the members of his committee see it, just what is the nature of what they see or smell or think they see and smell?"

"A clumsy attempt to cover up this country's white lung disease scandal that the asbestos industry and especially Southern Shoals has been sitting on for years," George Taunton said. "I must say I've never seen a major law firm put on a more brilliant performance of calculated stupidity."

"That strikes me as a pretty broad indictment," David Fillmore said.

"Judge for yourself," George Taunton said. "The way the Oval Office and Pierre Prudhomme's committee are judging. After firing and then hysterically rehiring Mr. Lichine, the Isham Truitt brain trust moved on. Their people in Montgomery, unaware that up in New York Lichine has been rehired, proceed at once to set up a fake police brawl in which a cop is alleged to be killed. They then get Lichine indicted for the cop's murder. When the Montgomery cops try to arrest him, they find Lichine has skipped to New York. Egged on by the local Isham Truitt boneheads, the Montgomery D.A. brings extradition proceedings against Lichine in New York. In New York the Isham Truitt brain trust decides the firm must not in any way be identified with the young man. They act on their decision by raising Lichine's bail in secret, and sending in the most distinguished name on their letterhead to defend the boy in court. When the distinguished name drops dead in the courtroom, Washington starts hearing rumors of foul play. Clearly floundering, Isham

Truitt now sends in one of their senior partners to bat for the man who dropped dead, but before the substitute hitter can clear the bases Isham Truitt hauls him out of the game by getting the Fillmore National board of directors to appoint him the new executive director of Southern Shoals Asbestos in Alabama. An Isham Truitt associate who happens to be a girl steps in to carry on the defense of young Lichine, at which point Isham Truitt decides they have the situation under control, but the girl doesn't seem to be aware of the confusion in the Isham Truitt command post. She takes her assignment seriously. The four-thumbed plotters decide they must get her out of the picture. First Hugh Kelly offers her a holiday in Rome, complete with hot and cold running water and color TV plus an audience with the Pope, and when she refuses to go, they decide to bribe her to get her off the case. She thumbs her nose at them because, it turns out, she is young Lichine's childhood sweetheart. In desperation, therefore, Isham Truitt sends its Washington partner to see Pierre Prudhomme and ask him to use his influence up in Alabama. All they want Pierre to do is pull down the lid on this Pandora's box by asking the Montgomery D.A. to quash the indictment against Lichine in the hope that this will terminate the extradition hearing in New York."

"What are the chances?" David Fillmore said.

"Just about the same as yours for Senate confirmation," George Taunton said. "I think I used the word 'nil.'"

"You also used the word 'unless,'" David Fillmore said.

"Yes, I did," George Taunton said.

"How does the word translate?" David Fillmore said.

"Get rid of Isham Truitt," George Taunton said.

"And hire another lawyer to defend young Lichine?" David Fillmore said.

"No, of course not," George Taunton said. "Young Lichine doesn't want another lawyer. He's in love with the one he's got and she's in love with him. It's David Fillmore who needs another lawyer. No matter how much he loves the one he's got."

"Isham Truitt?" David Fillmore said.

"Your only chance for Senate confirmation as Vice-President is to divorce yourself completely from the Southern Shoals Asbestos mess," George Taunton said. "Your only chance for such a divorce is to get rid of the law firm that has handled Southern Shoals for you and your family since the company was started."

"You are suggesting I get rid of Isham Truitt?" David Fillmore said.

"It's your only hope," George Taunton said.

"Mr. Taunton," David Fillmore said. "You are in over your head. You obviously do not understand the relationship between a family like mine and a law firm like Isham Truitt."

"You want to bet?" George Taunton said.

"No, because I don't think you know what you are talking about," David Fillmore said. "Isham Truitt has been the legal arm of the Fillmore National since my grandfather founded the bank in 1908. It is not the sort of relationship that can be terminated the way you get rid of a chauffeur or a butler."

"I've never had a butler and I drive my own car," George Taunton said. "As a result I may know a few things you don't, Mr. Fillmore. I am a lawyer and a good one. A good lawyer can do anything. If you want to be Vice-President of the United States you have to get rid of Isham Truitt. The decision is yours. If you decide you want to get rid of Isham Truitt, I can show you how."

"How?" David Fillmore said.

"The way to get rid of a law firm that represents a bank is to merge the bank with another bank," George Taunton said. "The lawyers for the new bank sit down with the lawyers for the old bank to work out the details. When the details are completed, where you had two banks you now have one. The one bank needs only one law firm. Of the two law firms that worked out the merger the head of the merged bank now chooses the law firm he wants to stay with. In this case you will be the head of the merged bank. You will choose the law firm that will now represent your new bank."

"You are suggesting the destruction of Isham Truitt," David Fillmore said.

"If a man wants to be Vice-President badly enough," George Taunton said, "I don't think he will lose much sleep over that."

"He'd have to find a bank he's willing to merge with," David Fillmore said.

"If he found the proper law firm he wants as a successor to Isham Truitt," George Taunton said, "I'd see to it that the proper bank came with the package."

"You've got such a law firm?" David Fillmore said.

"Pierre Prudhomme has," George Taunton said. "His brother Philippe is senior partner of Falk, Prudhomme and Rhodes, a name known and honored at Wall Street's blue-chip Bar. Among many other distinguished clients Falk Prudhomme represents the Montana Copper National Bank and Trust. To make the firm more palatable to you, Falk Prudhomme has recently acquired one of Isham Truitt's most prestigious men, a twenty-eight-year veteran named Ezra Kingsley Cooper, so there will be no problem about continuity of methods, and if this package can be put together you will acquire in additon a very handsome dividend."

"What's that?" David Fillmore said.

"The most brilliant young man presently on the Isham Truitt roster," George Taunton said. "He happens to be my son Jack."

"Anything you've left out?" David Fillmore said.

"Only the new name of your new law firm," George Taunton said.

"Which will be what?" David Fillmore said.

"Falk, Prudhomme, Rhodes, Taunton, Cooper and Taunton."

"Who's the second Taunton?" David Fillmore said.

"Your present golfing partner," George Taunton said. "My present firm will become the Washington branch of your new law firm. Our first task will be to see to it that you are confirmed by the Senate as our new Vice-President."

"You seem pretty confident you can do all this," David Fillmore said.

"A man who can in one afternoon make a permanent change in the golf score of a man who was trained by Bobby Jones can do anything," George Taunton said.

"My golf score?" David Fillmore said.

"Yes," George Taunton said.

"You say you can make a permanent change in my game?" David Fillmore said.

"I have already done it," George Taunton said.

"I'm afraid I'm not aware of it," David Fillmore said. He tapped his score card. "I shot an eighty-nine. An eighty-nine it remains."

"No, it does not," George Taunton said. "When we started the round I noticed at the end of the first shot you transferred a penny from your left pants pocket to the right."

"It's my way of keeping track of the number of shots I take on each hole," David Fillmore said. "At the end of each hole I count the pennies I've transferred to my right pocket, and jot down the number on my score card. I've been doing it for years."

"I noticed another thing you've obviously been doing for years," George Taunton said. "When you got to the first green and holed out you neglected to transfer a penny from your left pocket to your right. You merely counted the number of pennies already in your right-hand pocket and set that number down on your card as the score for the hole. By forgetting to transfer the last penny you obviously forgot to count the last putt. A perfectly understandable error. My guess is you've been making the error for years. As a result, for years you've always been eighteen shots short on your score card. Thus."

Taunton took the score card from David Fillmore.

"You recorded a score of eighty-nine today," Taunton said. With his pencil he made a correction on Fillmore's card. "But you forgot to count your eighteen final putts. So, you must now add eighteen to the eighty-nine you did score, which gives you your true score for the round, or one hundred and seven. That means two things. One, I beat you with my score of one hundred and six."

"What's the other thing?" David Fillmore said.

"Your old teacher Bobby Jones can at last stop spinning in his grave," George Taunton said. "He's been aware for years every golf game his pupil played was scored short on your card by eighteen shots."

David Fillmore took his score card from Taunton and stared at it.

"Assuming I accept the merger plan you have just outlined,

and you become my new lawyer," David Fillmore said, tapping his score card. "What do you suggest I do about this?"

"Switch to tennis," George Taunton said. "My son Jack is a superb teacher. Part of the service Falk, Prudhomme, Rhodes, Taunton, Cooper and Taunton provides for its favored clients."

36

On the door of Gilbert Cutter's private office, framed in teak to match the corridor woodwork, hung a headline he had clipped from a full-page advertisement that appeared in the New York *Times* shortly after Pearl Harbor: "Lucky Strike Green Has Gone to War!"

New employees and callers who had occasion to visit the Isham Truitt office manager for the first time always asked what the decoration was doing there.

"Attracting your attention and causing you to ask that question," Gil Cutter said. "Which provides me with an opportunity to make this reply. You are standing—take this chair, please, it's more comfortable—now you are sitting in what I call the engine room of what to most people is a great big important New York law firm. It's that, of course, one of the biggest and one of the most important, but to me, the man who has to keep the whole kit and caboodle sailing along smoothly, Isham Truitt is what I like to think of as a great big deluxe ocean liner with no tourist accommodations. We're strictly a one-class ship, and that class is first, for crew as well as passengers.

"Isham Truitt does not take on anything but name clients, and we do not hire anything less than the best in the way of staff to service them," Gil Cutter continued firmly. "This goes for our office boys and secretaries and computer programers as well as for our lawyers, associates, and paralegals. Through these doors, it used to say on a famous sign outside Flo Ziegfeld's office, pass the most beautiful girls in the world. Mr. Isham wouldn't tolerate anything on our front door outside the reception room except the firm name. If he ever wavered, however, he could do no better than paraphrase Mr. Ziegfeld by changing the words 'beautiful girls' to 'solvent clients.' We shoot for a look and a feel in our surroundings that matches the kind of numbers that appear on the bills we send out.

"I was only a fourteen-year-old kid from the Bronx when I started with Isham Truitt as an office boy thirty-six years ago," Gil Cutter said. "But I got the message immediately—class all the way. By the time I was promoted to the accounting department I started to get another message. Class all the way is a one-way street. If as an office boy I was sent uptown with a client who needed help carrying his or her books and records back to an office or a home, I was expected to maintain the standards of the firm by taking a taxi and putting in a petty cash slip for the cost. Having discharged my duty, I was expected to return to the office in the subway. If I put in a petty cash slip for a taxi both ways, I was taken into the then office manager's private quarters for a talking-to. It was delivered in language never heard in the Isham Truitt corridors.

"After Pearl Harbor," Gil Cutter said, "when I first saw that slogan in the newspaper ads, 'Lucky Strike Green Has Gone to War,' I knew from the gossip around the office that Lucky Strike green had done nothing of the sort. Government priorities had eliminated the green dye chemicals from civilian use for the duration. The manufacturer of Lucky Strikes was forced to discontinue his traditional green package. His advertising agency took a necessity of war and converted it into a commercial display of patriotism. When my boss in the Isham Truitt accounting department bawled out a young associate for submitting what he felt was a needlessly inflated expense account, he used to say in those days if Lucky Strike green can go to war, so can your swindle sheet. I was so impressed that I clipped the phrase out of an ad in the *Times* and years later, when I became the Isham Truitt office manager, I framed it and hung it on my door.

"It's an easy way to break the news to a new employee," Gil Cutter said, "that the tastes he acquires while wining and dining a client should not be carried over to the food he consumes for which the firm must reimburse him when he works late and dines alone. I've found it has a very salutary effect, especially now with inflation and most of our employees too young to remember the war, much less prewar prices. If, for example, what you've come to see me about is an expense you incurred in the line of duty and now feel you should be reimbursed for, I'll bet seeing that sign about Lucky Strike green going to war will cause you to revise your request downward."

"Don't make that bet," Tony Tessitore said. "You'll lose because that's not what I've come to see you about."

"Take this chair, anyway," Gil Cutter said. "It's currently the most comfortable one in my office."

"Thanks," Tony Tessitore said. "You want that side door open?"

"It gives me a nice slanting view of the door to Stenographic," Gil Cutter said. "We've got forty-six girls in there eating up salary when they should be typing briefs."

"You've also got Mrs. Merle Bethune and her eagle eye sitting in there on a raised platform," Tony Tessitore said. "I'm sure it's safe to leave the girls to her exclusive bird-dogging for a few minutes. I've come to ask you a question."

"Confidential?" Gil Cutter said.

"Top secret," Tony Tessitore said.

"I'll close it myself," Gil Cutter said.

He crossed to the side door, closed it, and pushed the lock button in the knob.

"What's on your mind?" Gil Cutter said, coming back to his desk.

"What would happen to this firm, Gil, if we lost Fillmore National?" Tony Tessitore said.

Lowering his skinny frame into the chair behind his desk, Gil Cutter seemed to pause in midair. He didn't, of course. The effect of hovering, however, was unmistakable. It was underscored when his pants touched the sponge-rubber cushion that shielded his gaunt hams from the hard wood. Gil Cutter seemed to land with an inaudible thump.

"Would you ask that again, Tessie?" he said.

"What would happen to Isham Truitt if we lost Fillmore National?" Tony Tessitore said.

"As a client, you mean?" Gil Cutter said.

"I mean as an address to which we send bills that have been paid promptly for seventy years," Tony Tessitore said. "What would happen to this firm if we lost that relationship?"

"Same thing that would happen to this country if we lost Montana," Gil Cutter said.

"Things like that don't happen," Tony Tessitore said.

"They might," Gil Cutter said.

"How?" Tony Tessitore said.

"An earthquake could remove Montana from the national scene," Gil Cutter said.

"David Fillmore's big mouth could remove Fillmore National from your programed computers," Tony Tessitore said.

He spread on the desk in front of the office manager the copy of the New York *Times* he had brought into the room.

"I've seen that," Gil Cutter said. "He's scheduled to testify before the Senate Confirmation Committee about his nomination for Vice-President. He hasn't testified yet."

"Meaning what?" Tony Tessitore said.

"Until a man answers a question under oath," Gil Cutter said, "what he might have said in his answer has not yet been said."

"This is the United States Senate," Tony Tessitore said. "When they ask a question they get an answer. If they don't, the man who was asked the question doesn't get what he wants."

"Only if the questions asked are of the kind that are often described in the media as embarrassing," Gil Cutter said.

"What sort of questions do you think those publicity hungry bastards are going to ask David Fillmore?" Tony Tessitore said. "How his golf game is going?"

"Why not?" Gil Cutter said. "The questioning in these things is pretty free-wheeling, often irrelevant, frequently deliberately so. What sort of questions do you think they'll ask David Fillmore?"

"Gil, will you stop playing dumb?" Tony Tessitore said. "The whole country is watching that circus we started and don't seem to know how to stop down in Special Term, Part Two. That Senate committee is going to ask Fillmore a lot of tough stuff about Southern Shoals Asbestos."

"Does he have to give it to them?" Gil Cutter said.

"What does that remark mean?" Tony Tessitore said.

"People in Washington have been asking Southern Shoals Asbestos tough questions since the days I was an office boy in this place," Gil Cutter said. "I don't recall once in what's getting close to being forty years that anybody at Isham Truitt or Fillmore National ever bothered to answer those questions."

"You know why, of course," Tony Tessitore said.

"So does everybody in the country," Gil Cutter said. "Because for all practical purposes Southern Shoals owns Alabama. If you own something you can always find a way not to talk about it. The best way is to hire the right mumbler to do your talking for you. Fillmore National has always considered Isham Truitt the best mumblers in the business."

"It doesn't work that way when the head man of Isham Truitt's most important client wants to be Vice-President of the United States," Tony Tessitore said.

"Then it's up to Isham Truitt to see to it that David Fillmore does not become Vice-President of the United States," Gil Cutter said.

37

When Tony Tessitore entered the courtroom the first thing that caught his eye was Judy Cline at counsels' table. She was leaning forward in a head-to-head conference with a young man sitting beside her. A moment later Tony Tessitore's eyes jumped to the man on the witness stand. Tony wondered at once why he had not noticed this man first. The man was certainly a more eye-catching spectacle that morning than anybody or anything else in Special Term, Part Two.

First, the man was not actually sitting in the witness chair. The witness chair had been removed from the witness stand. It stood to one side, empty, near the stenographer's table. The man was sitting in a wheelchair. The wheelchair had been moved into the space on the witness stand normally occupied by the witness chair. And second, the wheelchair itself was unusual. It seemed to be fitted with some sort of special equipment. At first Tony Tessitore had no luck figuring out the nature of this equipment. Then he saw the man reach down to the side of the wheelchair. He came up with a white plastic mask. It was attached to a white hose. When the man put the mask over his nose and mouth Tony Tessitore got the picture. The wheelchair was fitted with oxygen.

"May we proceed, Your Honor?"

Judy's voice brought Tony Tessitore's glance back to counsels' table. He realized at once why he had been surprised to discover that the man in the wheelchair had not been Tony's first attraction. He didn't know the man in the wheelchair. But Tony Tessitore knew Judy Cline. What had caught his eye at once was not Judy alone, but Judy and the young man seated beside her. The young man with whom Judy had been in a head-to-head conference at counsels' table was black.

"Please do, Miss Cline," the judge said.

As he moved quietly down the aisle to a seat as far forward as he could get, Tony's mind skipped back to the transcript he had read the night before. He flipped pages mentally until he reached the top sheet. McNally. That was the judge's name. John V. McNally, Jr. Judy stood up. The black young man touched her elbow. She stopped moving forward and leaned back to the young man. He whispered something in her ear. Judy nodded, straightened up, and came forward toward the witness stand.

"I apologize for the delay, Your Honor," Judy said. "In the hope of saving the court's time I was just double-checking some place names in Montgomery with Mr. Coleridge. He is, as you know, a native of that city."

"Yes, of course," Judge McNally said. "Proceed, Miss Cline."

"Your name, please," Judy said to the witness.

"Abraham L. Soybush," the man in the wheelchair said.

"'L' for Lincoln?" Judy said.

"Yes, ma'am," the witness said. "Abraham Lincoln Soybush and proud of it."

A low ripple of laughter moved across the courtroom. Tony Tessitore was not impressed. As he never missed an opportunity to remind his wife, Sylvia, Tony had spent more of his life sitting around in courtrooms than Cleopatra had spent lying around on barges. Ripples of opening laughter were meaningless. If Jack the Ripper had opened his testimony with a Gillette razor commercial he probably would have brought down the roof of the Old Bailey. The yock, however, would have done nothing to keep his neck out of the hangman's noose.

"Where do you live, Mr. Soybush?" Judy Cline said.

"Buford Lane, Jefferson Davis Junction, Montgomery, Alabama," Abraham Soybush said.

"No street number?" Judy said.

"We don't have street numbers in Jefferson Davis Junction," Abraham Soybush said. "Everybody knows it's down back of the railroad yards, and everybody goes to Jefferson Davis Junction knows how to get to Buford Lane, and anybody gets to Buford Lane knows how to reach Abraham L. Soybush."

"What do you do for a living, Mr. Soybush?" Judy said.

"I breathe pure oxygen," Abraham Soybush said.

Another ripple of laughter. Shorter this time. And definitely tentative. This was not lost on Tony Tessitore. The yahoos didn't know yet if this joker was funny.

"I meant what do you do for a living, Mr. Soybush, in the financial sense," Judy said.

"I help my wife with the operation of the Soybush Tots Home," Abraham L. Soybush said.

"A family-owned business?" Judy Cline said.

"Yes, ma'am," Abraham Soybush said. "Me and Myrtle, that's my wife, we own and run it. The whole thing."

"What is the nature of the business?" Judy said.

"A sort of nursery home for small children you could call it," Abraham Soybush said.

"How small?" Judy said.

"About kindergarten age, mostly," Abraham Soybush said. "But we take younger ones, too. Nursing infants, for example. We get one of those now and then."

"Then you and your wife provide a live-in service?" Judy Cline said.

"If we have to, yes, we do that, too," Abraham Soybush said. "When we started, that was in 1953, it was mainly for working mothers wanted a place to leave the kids during the day when they were out on their jobs. My wife, Myrtle, is very good with little ones, maybe on account of the good Lord never saw fit to bless us with more than one of our own, so the word spread, and people with special problems started coming to see us, and we took them all."

"What sort of problems?" Judy Cline said.

"Well, the first one I remember," Abraham Soybush said, "there was this young mother. She was having trouble with her husband, and a divorce was building up. She wanted the baby, a cute little girl not quite a year old, eleven months plus she was, the mother wanted the baby out of the line of fire, so to speak, and she said she'd heard so much about us and how good we were with kindergarten kids, she wondered would we take her little girl. Myrtle and I, we said sure, and we did, and it worked out so well we started getting adoptions."

"Would you explain that?" Judy Cline said.

"Well, you take a girl she's not married and she gets in the family way but the father is not what we call available," Abraham Soybush said.

Tony Tessitore graded the laugh. A bunt. He decided it was time to grade Mr. Soybush. It was a mistake, Tony had learned, to do that too soon. If you did you had a tendency to judge by appearance, and the appearance of a witness could be misleading. A kid who looked like a hood in a police lineup often turned out to be a choirboy with the most merit badges in his Scout troop. A girl who looked like the inspiration for Walt Disney's *Snow White* not infrequently turned out to be a hard-as-nails bimbo peddling her tail on Times Square under the auspices of a drug-pushing pimp. A first glimpse of Abraham L. Soybush presented all the problems of the first glimpse of any person in a wheelchair. What you saw was not a real human being but the sort of symbol that lived on March of Dimes posters: a carefully constructed tear-duct flusher. Abraham L. Soybush was no exception. A fat, shapeless lump imbedded in a mass of metal bars, leather straps, a network of tubes, clamps, oxygen tanks, and other bits and pieces of life-sustaining equipment. It took a little time, usually a few minutes of q. and a. with examining counsel, before the human being began to emerge from the fund-raising poster. In the case of Abraham L. Soybush, what brought the man out of the wheelchair for Tony Tessitore was the fat man's jokes. He didn't just make them. He monitored them. He clocked his laughs. This did not mean he was an unreliable witness. It meant he was an experienced one. He took his own readings on how he was doing. This meant also, therefore, that he had to be watched for shifts in tactics. A man who wanted more laughs might not hesitate to get them with less truth.

"I understand," Judith Cline said.

"Or say the father is available but they can't get married for one reason or another," Abraham Soybush said. "Or they don't want to get married, or they can't afford to have a baby. So an adoption is arranged. Myrtle and I, we don't have anything to do with that. We just receive the newborn infant from a doctor or whatever, perfectly legal and on the up and up, and we take care of the infant until the people who want the baby, the people who adopted it, all perfectly legal as I say, they come and pick up the infant."

"You're not then in any way part of what is known as a baby farm?" Judith Cline said.

"Not in any way, shape, form, or manner," Abraham Soybush said. He had obviously, Tony Tessitore noted, had a certain amount of experience with lawyers. "Myrtle and I never touch anything that's even remotely illegal. We never have taken an infant unless it was through a lawyer and we never will. Mostly, though, as I say, it's daytime care for working mothers, or sometimes a family has a contagious disease or something like that, say, and they want a small child away from the danger zone, you might call it, until the Board of Health says it's okay. That sort of thing."

"You say you and your wife started this Soybush Tots Home in 1953," Judy Cline said. "Is that correct?"

"Yes, ma'am, 1953," Abraham Soybush said.

"Is that just a date?" Judy said. "Or does the date have some special significance?"

"The date has tremendous significance," Abraham Soybush said.

"In what way?" Judy Cline said.

"In 1953 I could no longer leave my house to go to the plant where I worked," Abraham Soybush said. "In 1953 I started living on this."

He reached down for the white plastic mask, placed it over his nose and mouth, and took several deep breaths. This was not the first time Tony Tessitore had seen people take oxygen in public. He knew a performance when he saw one. In that particular role Mr. Soybush was neither better nor worse than most amateur actors.

"For the record," Judy Cline said, "Mr. Abraham Soybush is

seated in a wheelchair equipped with an oxygen-supplying device. Mr. Soybush has placed a mask over his nose and mouth. The mask is attached to a hose. The hose runs to a small metal tank strapped to the side of the wheelchair. Mr. Soybush is breathing through the mask."

The witness removed the mask and placed it in his lap.

"That'll hold me for about five minutes," Abraham Soybush said. "If I don't talk too loud or too fast."

"Take your time, please," Judy said. "May I continue?"

"Yes, ma'am," Abraham Soybush said.

"You say 1953 is a date of tremendous significance because in 1953 you could no longer leave your house to go to the plant where you worked," Judy Cline said. "Would you tell us, Mr. Soybush, by whom you were employed and what sort of plant you went to and what sort of work you did until you were incapacitated in 1953?"

"I worked for the Southern Shoals Asbestos Corporation," Mr. Soybush said. "In their Montgomery acoustical-ceilings plant."

"Acoustical ceilings?" Judy Cline said.

"Yes, ma'am," Mr. Soybush said. "Asbestos is used for a lot of industrial purposes. You've seen the Southern Shoals ads in the magazines and on TV. We are at the heart of more than three thousand products that affect your daily life. It sure affected my daily life except you work around asbestos it doesn't hit you in the heart, it hits you in the lungs. I started with Southern Shoals when I was a kid, right after Pearl Harbor, in the ship-insulation plant. Then, after the war, they switched me to brake linings, and for a couple of years I was in fireproof roofing shingles before I ended up in Plant Number Four, that's acoustical ceilings. Acoustical ceilings was the end of the road for me. By 1953, like I said, my lungs were so bad I couldn't breathe without oxygen, so I wasn't any good in a plant anymore, so when Southern Shoals fired me, my wife and I, we had to do something else for a living, and Myrtle came up with the Tots Home idea. Thank God she did, otherwise I wouldn't have made it these last twenty-five years into 1978. It's not a question of starving. It's a question of breathing so you can eat the food that gets on your table if you can afford to buy the food. The cost of the oxygen alone, it's more per week than I ever earned from Southern Shoals the years I worked there."

"How much oxygen do you use, Mr. Soybush?" Judy said.

"I have a big four-day tank at home, and I spend most of the day hooked up to it," Mr. Soybush said. "Then I've got a one-hour tank. I take that in the car when I go out to get groceries or something. I've also got the one I'm using now, this thing hooked up to my wheelchair. It's a four-hour job. I've got a spare out in the court clerk's office in case this hearing goes on very long, and then I've got extras in my hotel room to get me through the plane trip back home to Alabama."

"Who pays for all this oxygen?" Judy Cline said.

"Medicare takes the heat off most of it," Abraham Soybush said. "The rest comes out of what Myrtle and I make running the Tots Home."

"What about Southern Shoals?" Judy Cline said.

"Not a dime," Abraham Soybush said.

"Southern Shoals Asbestos contributes nothing toward your medical costs?" Judy Cline said.

"Like I said," Abraham Soybush said, "not one single solitary dime."

"I never heard of such a thing," Judy said.

"You ever been down in Alabama, ma'am?" Abraham Soybush said.

"No, I never have," Judy Cline said.

"If you ever spent some time down there you'd understand it," Abraham Soybush said.

"Why?" Judy said.

"Southern Shoals is Alabama," Abraham Soybush said. "They can get away with anything down there."

The district attorney stood up.

"I object, Your Honor," he said.

"On what ground?" Judge McNally said.

"Irrelevant and immaterial," Mr. Hyatt said.

"Surely not to the state of the witness' health?" the judge said.

"The health of this witness is irrelevant to the habeas corpus hearing now being argued before Your Honor," the assistant district attorney said.

"Is it, Miss Cline?" Judge McNally said.

"No, Your Honor," Judy said. "The health of this witness has a direct and crucial relevance to the plaintiff's case."

"You intend to establish that relevance?" the judge said.

"I do, Your Honor," Judy Cline said.

"Objection overruled," Judge McNally said.

"Exception," the assistant district attorney said.

"Granted," the judge said. "Proceed, Miss Cline."

"Mr. Soybush," Judy said. "Would you explain in your own words, keeping as close as you can to the subject of your own physical condition, what you meant when you said quote Southern Shoals is Alabama. They can get away with anything down there. Unquote."

"Before I got too sick to do the work," Abraham Soybush said, "I was business manager of Local Number Five of the Asbestos Workers Union, so I got to see a lot of material the average asbestos plant worker doesn't bother to go looking for. Today we're in 1978. All the way back in 1907, when Southern Shoals Asbestos built its first plant in Montgomery, that's seventy-one years ago, in 1907 the first case of asbestosis was recorded in a California asbestos plant."

"Is that the medical name for your ailment?" Judy Cline said.

"Depends on who you talk to," Abraham Soybush said. "The Southern Shoals doctor or your own private doctor."

"What's the difference?" Judy Cline said.

"The Southern Shoals doctor he's liable to say you've got a smoker's cough," Abraham Soybush said. "Give up cigarettes he'll tell you."

"Did he tell you that?" Judy Cline said.

"Yes, ma'am," Abraham Soybush said.

"Did you do it?" Judy said.

"I couldn't," Abraham Soybush said. "I never smoked cigarettes."

The laugh was solid. Tony Tessitore watched the face of the witness. Abraham Soybush's tiny lips, sunk like a slot in the fat piggy bank of his pasty face, twitched with pleasure. His next move would tell the story.

"Cigars neither," Abraham Soybush said.

The story was disappointing. Abraham Soybush should have quit while he was ahead. The follow-up laugh was a wavery little rolling dribble.

"In 1935, that's twenty-eight years after that first case of asbestosis showed up in California," the witness said, "Indiana reported the first case of asbestos lung cancer, and eleven years after that, we're now in 1946, the first reports of mesothelioma started coming out of Southern Shoals in Alabama."

"What happened?" Judy Cline said.

"Nothing you could read in your newspaper," Abraham Soybush said. "But I was still business manager of Local Number Five, so I was still reading material the average asbestos-plant employee didn't get to see, and I still read it."

"What sort of material?" Judy Cline said.

"Like a statement made last year by Dr. Herman Graffenreidt of the Mount Sinai School of Medicine," Abraham Soybush said. "I've got it right here. It's only four lines. Would you like to hear it, ma'am?"

"Yes, please," Judy Cline said.

The witness worked his hand carefully down into the nest held together around him by the metal framework of the wheelchair. He came up with a newspaper clipping.

"'The dangers of asbestos were well known in 1935,'" Abraham Soybush read. "That's Dr. Graffenreidt's words, you understand."

"I understand," Judy said.

"'It is difficult to explain the quiet of the following decades,' Dr. Graffenreidt continues," the witness said. "'Little was done. Regulations were few. Government inspections were infrequent.'"

"Were you aware of any regulations or government inspections at the Southern Shoals plant in Alabama where you worked?" Judy Cline said.

"Nary a one," Abraham Soybush said.

Tony Tessitore wondered about that "nary." The homespun touch was not uncommon, but it was jury stuff. Mr. Soybush, however, was performing before a judge. A New York judge at that.

"How did you feel about working with a product that medical research now tells us is harmful to health?" Judy Cline said. "Were you aware of any danger? Did you see or feel anything while you were on the job that might have warned you of danger?"

"Oh, sure, we all saw things," Abraham Soybush said. "You couldn't help it. The first plant I worked in, the ship-insulation plant, the asbestos was so thick all around you it looked like it was snowing all day long."

"Didn't you find that upsetting?" Judy Cline said. "Didn't it make you ask questions?"

"No," Abraham Soybush said. "We'd had no warnings. We had no fear of the stuff. In fact we'd raise as much dust as possible so the boss would think we were working real hard."

"You say your condition became so bad in 1953 that you could no longer go to work in the plant," Judy Cline said.

"Correct, ma'am," Abraham Soybush said.

"Long before 1953, however, you must have known something was wrong with your health," Judy said.

"I sure did," Abraham Soybush said. "Two, three years before that, around 1950, I began to have this shortness of breath and these pains in my chest."

"What did you do?" Judy Cline said.

"I went to the infirmary," the witness said.

"The company infirmary?" Judy Cline said. "Southern Shoals Asbestos?"

"Yes, ma'am," Abraham Soybush said.

"What did the doctors tell you?" Judy Cline said.

"What I said," the witness said. "Quit smoking cigarettes."

"And when you told the doctor you didn't smoke cigarettes?" Judy Cline said. "Or cigars or anything else? What did he say?"

"There's nothing wrong with you," Abraham Soybush said.

"The doctor told you that?" Judy Cline said.

"Yes, ma'am," the witness said.

"The company doctor of the Southern Shoals Asbestos Corporation told you there was nothing wrong with you?" Judy said.

"Not only me," Abraham Soybush said. "I wasn't the only one coughing and having these pains in the chest. Lots of men in

Local Number Five had them. They all went to the company doctor and they all got the same answer. There's nothing wrong with you. Stop smoking and that cough will clear up."

The assistant district attorney spoke from a sitting position, and he spoke slowly.

"Your Honor," he said as though he had been challenged to imitate an acceptable southern drawl, "I think it is only charitable to note that counsel surely knows better, and having noted it, I respectfully ask that counsel be instructed to refrain from any further attempts to lead the witness into telling us what quote lots of men in Local Number Five unquote or lots of men anywhere else were told by so-called company doctors for whose appearance in this hearing no preparation has been made. I am merely pointing out—"

"I know what the district attorney is pointing out," Judy said to the bench. "And I apologize to him as well as to Your Honor for a lapse that was totally uncalled for as well as completely unnecessary. I withdraw the question."

"Thank you," Mr. Hyatt said.

Tony Tessitore permitted himself an inward nod of approval. This Cline kid had stuff.

"I will ask another one," Judy Cline said. "Mr. Soybush, do you know the plaintiff in this habeas corpus hearing?"

"Yes, ma'am, I do," Abraham Soybush said.

"Do you know him personally?" Judy Cline said.

"Yes, ma'am, I do," Abraham Soybush said.

"How well do you know him?" Judy Cline said.

"Excuse me, ma'am," Abraham Soybush said.

Again he groped in his nest for the white plastic mask. He placed it over his nose and mouth and took several deep breaths. Tony Tessitore thought the performance showed more polish. Mr. Soybush was clearly growing more at ease in his role. It could mean, of course, that he might grow careless. It could also mean the scene was bringing him to his favorite moment in the play.

"I'm sorry," he said, replacing the mask in his lap.

"Quite all right," Judy said. "May I continue?"

"Yes, ma'am," Abraham Soybush said. "I'm fine now, thank you."

"Would you read back the last question, please?" Judy said to the stenographer.

The neat little man leaned forward over his machine and delicately lifted the top layer of his tape.

"Miss Cline," he read. "How well do you know him?"

"By him I refer to the plaintiff, Mr. Thomas L. Lichine, Jr.," Judy said. "How well do you know him, Mr. Soybush?"

"About as well as I reckon most fathers-in-law know their sons-in-law," Abraham Soybush said. "Mr. Lichine is married to my daughter."

38

"Why not?" Gil Cutter said. "If your name was Soybush and you wanted to be an actress, what would you do?"

"I'd go to Denmark and have one of those sex-change operations," Tony Tessitore said.

"That costs money," Gil Cutter said. "I imagine if your family runs a child-day-care operation in a place like Montgomery, Alabama, the one thing there isn't too much of lying around the house is money. What's she look like?"

"You remember when George Gershwin died?" Tony Tessitore said.

"In 1937," Gil Cutter said. "I was in my first year at Pace Institute. Why?"

"When they went through Gershwin's personal effects," Tony Tessitore said, "I remember in the *Daily News* it said they found a golden key on his key ring and it fitted the front door of that French actress who was just making a splash in Hollywood."

"Simone Simone?" Gil Cutter said.

"That's the one," Tony Tessitore said.

"This Bianca Bean, she looks like that?" Gil Cutter said.

"Dead ringer," Tony Tessitore said. "Except slightly bigger tits."

"Holy cow," Gil Cutter said. "How does a stuffy little asshole like this Tom Lichine land a number like that?"

"Maybe he's got something bigger than an asshole and it could even be he knows how to use it unstuffily," Tony Tessitore said. "Me, I'd turn the question around. How did a kid from the

Alabama boondocks land the *Harvard Law Review* son of the great Amelia Troy?"

"Theater stuff," Gil Cutter said. "A very weird scene, believe me. You ought to see some of the crap that shows up on Ken Kreel's expense accounts. I query them, of course, but he's always got one of those answers like national security no-can-talk. Once I refused to okay a medical expense that turned out to be an abortion, and I got a call from Walter Isham, personally no less, saying he admired my diligence as the office financial watch dog but would I for Christ's sake pay Kreel's voucher and keep my big mouth shut about it. Just guessing I'd say Lichine being the son of the once big star Amelia Troy, meeting young actresses is about as tough for him as it is for you to meet young night law students like Ira Bodmer. How did the Cline broad react to the news?"

"I found that pretty nearly more interesting than anything that happened down there this morning in Special Term, Part Two," Tony Tessitore said.

"How come?" Gil Cutter said.

"You know the rumors about her," Tony Tessitore said.

"About her and Hugh Kelly, that's a lot of shit," Gil Cutter said. "That old kocker just can't stop trying to lasso one more harp for the cardinal's band."

"No, I don't mean Hugh Kelly," Tony Tessitore said. "And I don't mean Cline and Howard Dent, either. Cheryl Marvin says if the old fucker hadn't dropped dead in a courtroom it would have been in a sack he'd needed a ladder to get into. She says Dent couldn't get it up anymore, and she said she knows whereof she speaks."

"I don't doubt it," Gil Cutter said. "What rumors about Cline are you talking about?"

"How she got herself adopted before she was born because her parents and the Lichine family are so close the childless Clines just had to dig up a playmate for the Lichine kid," Tony Tessitore said. "They grew up together, kid sweethearts and all that, and both families assumed they were going to get married as soon as they graduated from Harvard Law, together naturally, when young Lichine knocked everybody on their ass, including his childhood sweetheart, by a surprise marriage to this totally unknown kid, this Bianca Bean."

"Yeah, I know," Gil Cutter said. "I got all that from Saphira Shreve two days ago when she ordered me to terminate Cline, which I did. Unfortunately it looks as though the young lady hasn't got the news yet because there she is, down in Special Term, Part Two, still battling for the Lichine habeas corpus writ that's already knocked Howard Dent out of the box and sent Mandamus Manny into Sosthenes DeKalb's spot, and where it will all end, if the damn thing ever does end, God alone knows."

"I think He's not alone anymore," Tony Tessitore said.

"You also know?" Gil Cutter said.

"I didn't say I know," Tony Tessitore said. "I said I think."

"Do a little thinking out loud, for Christ's sake," Gil Cutter said. "If I'd sent one of my computer clerks downtown and let her kill a morning in court she'd have come back with more than I've got out of you so far."

"Yes, but would it stop David Fillmore from becoming Vice-President of the United States?" Tony Tessitore said.

"How should I know?" Gil Cutter said. "These computers, Christ, they're like my wife's poodles. They can do everything but talk."

"So can David Fillmore," Tony Tessitore said. "As long as he can talk there's always a chance he'll do it from a witness chair, and if he does that either in Washington or on Centre Street you know what we both agreed that would do to the future of Isham Truitt."

"Don't remind me," Gil Cutter said. "Just tell me how we can keep him out of those witness chairs."

"I don't know how to do that," Tony Tessitore said. "But after watching this Cline girl in action this morning, I'm prepared to shift my ground a little."

"In what way?" Gil Cutter said.

"Maybe it wouldn't be the end of the world if Fillmore got into a witness chair," Tony Tessitore said. "If he could be briefed on how to answer the questions about Southern Shoals without blowing the ball game."

"Who's going to do the briefing?" Gil Cutter said.

"I repeat again I didn't say I know," Tony Tessitore said.

"I repeat again you also said you think you know," Gil Cutter said.

"I think from watching her work this morning that's what this Cline broad has in mind," Tony Tessitore said.

"To tell Fillmore what to say when they get him on the witness stand?" Gil Cutter said.

"Stop screaming," Tony Tessitore said. "All I said was I think that's what she has in mind. I couldn't actually walk up to her and ask, could I?"

"No, but you could stop acting like a dumb managing clerk," Gil Cutter said. "A bright one knows more than docket dates and where to serve a subpoena. I tell you what I told you yesterday. If they get Fillmore on the stand we're dead. The only hope is to keep him out of a witness chair."

"You're so smart," Tony Tessitore said, "I don't see why you don't stop the bullshit and just come up with the answer to that one."

"Okay, smart-ass, I will do just that," Gil Cutter said. "I didn't piss away my morning listening to a lot of hot air down in Special Term, Part Two. I did a morning's work. From what you brought back, your report on what happened down there this morning, I will now tell you why David Fillmore will never, repeat never, sit down in a witness chair."

"Speak up," Tony Tessitore said. "I'm ready."

Gil Cutter stood up, came out from behind his desk, and crossed to the side door. He closed it gently, shutting off his slanting view of the entrance to Stenographic and Mrs. Merle Bethune's forty-six typists.

"David Fillmore will never sit down in a witness chair," Gil Cutter said, "because in 1953 in Montgomery, Alabama, I was the one who put Abraham Lincoln Soybush into the Tots Home business."

39

Standing in the doorway of 25 West Forty-third Street, Judy could keep an eye on her wristwatch as well as on the traffic coming up toward her from Fifth Avenue. When the small black Mercedes turned into Forty-third Street her watch showed twelve minutes after eleven. Judy's mother had said Amelia Troy usually made the turn somewhere between ten minutes after and a quarter after. On schedule, then, was the phrase for this morning's performance.

Judy waited just long enough to identify the silhouette of the woman behind the wheel of the approaching vehicle. It was Tom Lichine's mother all right. Then Judy turned and walked into the lobby of 25 West Forty-third.

She went briskly down the long marble tunnel to the rectangle of sunlight at the far end. When she stepped out of the building onto the Forty-fourth Street sidewalk the big black limousine was waiting at the curb. The rear door opened as Judy came across the sidewalk. She stepped into the car and sat down beside David Fillmore. The door slammed shut. The limousine got under way.

"Hello, sweetie," David Fillmore said, turning toward her. He did not turn very far. When his eyes apparently brought Judy into focus David Fillmore swung away toward a small silver grille on the limousine wall at his left. He pressed a button and spoke into the grille.

"Stop the car, Hess."

"No, don't," Judy said. "Mrs. Lichine asked me to come tell you she won't be able to make it this morning."

Smoothly, without hesitation, Fillmore turned back to the silver grille. He pressed the button again.

"Sorry, Hess," he said. "Keep going."

The car started moving again.

"What are you doing here?" David Fillmore said.

"Speaking for Mrs. Lichine," Judy said.

"She's always managed to make an adequate job of it for herself," David Fillmore said.

"This is a subject I know more about than she does," Judy said.

David Fillmore glanced at his wristwatch.

"How long do you need?" he said.

"That depends on you," Judy said.

"Five minutes?" David Fillmore said. "Five hours?"

"No longer than your usual rides with Mrs. Lichine," Judy said.

The sharp face grew sharper. It was the narrowing of the eyes. The process seemed to help him see Judy more clearly. Again David Fillmore turned to the small silver grille and pressed the button.

"Hess, go up the West Side Highway only as far as Ninety-sixth," he said. "Then cut over east and take me to the UN." Fillmore's hand dropped from the grille. "That give us enough time?"

"Probably," Judy said. "I am Tom Lichine's lawyer."

"He doesn't need one anymore," David Fillmore said. "That extradition hearing was a mistake. The Alabama indictment has been quashed."

"No, it has not," Judy said.

"Young lady," David Fillmore said, "I ordered my attorneys yesterday to take care of it."

"They followed your orders," Judy said. "Unfortunately, the Montgomery district attorney was unable to comply."

"Why not?" David Fillmore said.

"Tom Lichine does not want the indictment quashed," Judy said.

"Has he gone crazy?" David Fillmore said.

"Possibly," Judy said.

"What the hell does he want?" David Fillmore said.

"Vindication," Judy said.

"Oh, God," David Fillmore said. He slumped back on the rear seat, ran a hand caressingly across his hair, and sighed deeply. "All right, young lady, give it to me."

"Tom Lichine feels he was sent down to Alabama to do a job, and he did it," Judy said. "In the course of doing it he seems to have annoyed certain people. They took action against him in a way he considers outrageous. In defending himself Tom managed to put his hands on certain documents that he sees now were what caused these certain people to become annoyed with him. He understands their annoyance but he will not forgive their action against him. He wants his name cleared. He feels the only way he can accomplish that is to have these documents presented in the court action that these certain people brought on themselves when they cooked up that fake indictment. They forced Tom to defend himself by bringing this action for a writ of habeas corpus. He intends to get it."

"Do these certain people have a name?" David Fillmore said.

"Of course," Judy said.

"If we're going to get this thing settled before I get to the UN," David Fillmore said, "I suggest we use it."

"Southern Shoals Asbestos," Judy said.

"What have they got to do with me?" David Fillmore said.

"Nothing," Judy said. "If you put your hands on Tom's documents before he presents them in court."

"How do I do that?" David Fillmore said.

"You testify in Tom's habeas corpus hearing tomorrow morning," Judy said.

"If I don't?" David Fillmore said.

"The documents Tom presents in court tomorrow morning will become the basis for the only crucial questions you will be asked when you appear before the Senate committee that will decide whether or not to confirm your nomination as the next Vice-President of the United States."

"Aren't you a little young for blackmail?" David Fillmore said.

"I'm only two months younger than Tom Lichine," Judy said.

"You didn't think that made him too young to be framed on a fake murder charge."

"I had nothing to do with that," David Fillmore said.

"Only one thing," Judy said. "Your direct intervention to try and call it off when it backfired."

"I withdraw the word 'blackmail,'" David Fillmore said. "You are asking me to make a deal."

"Tom Lichine is asking you to make a deal," Judy said.

"In this car you are the one who is doing the asking," David Fillmore said.

"All right," Judy said. "I am."

"State it clearly," David Fillmore said. "In the first person singular, if you please."

"I want you to appear as a witness tomorrow morning at Tom Lichine's hearing in the New York State Supreme Court, Special Term, Part Two," Judy said.

"If I don't?" David Fillmore said.

"The President will have to send up to the Senate another nomination for Vice-President," Judy said.

"I would rather pass up that honor than submit to pressure from the kindergarten," David Fillmore said. He pressed the button under the silver grille. "Hess, you can skip Ninety-sixth Street," David Fillmore said. "Take me direct to the UN."

"You haven't asked the nature of the documents Tom Lichine has in his possession," Judy said.

"I don't have to," David Fillmore said. "I know what they are."

"Not all of them," Judy said.

"What have I overlooked?" David Fillmore said.

"A memorandum indicating that in 1953 Isham Truitt, your attorneys, received instructions from you to make an investment in something called the Soybush Tots Home in Montgomery, Alabama."

"Young lady," David Fillmore said, "who the hell are you?"

"Meet me in court tomorrow," Judy said. "I'll see you get a chance to find out."

40

Judge McNally set the rimless pince-nez on the thinnest part of his nose. The bits of glass shivered slightly as he dipped his head to open the file folder on the bench in front of him. While he studied something in the file, the assistant district attorney came out from behind the bench on the court stenographer's side, and the young black lawyer came out from the other side, back of the witness stand.

Ira Bodmer, watching from a seat on the aisle, knew what that meant: a conference in chambers. It had obviously started before Ira arrived in court. The judge had come out first and the lawyers had waited offstage until he was settled on the bench.

The judge now waited until the assistant district attorney and the young black lawyer were seated at counsels' table. Then Judge McNally looked up. He stared out at the courtroom on what seemed a puzzled quest. It would not have surprised Ira Bodmer if what was going through the mind of His Honor was the same question that had raced through Ira's mind when he entered the courtroom: "Where the hell is Judy Cline?"

"For the record," Judge McNally said, sending his words in the general direction of the stenographer. "After a conference in chambers attended by the presiding judge, Mr. Hyatt, the district attorney, and Mr. Teaman Coleridge of plaintiff's counsel, it was agreed that in the temporary absence of Miss Judith Cline, this hearing will proceed with Mr. Coleridge examining for Miss Cline."

The pince-nez shivered again as the supporting nose changed direction.

"Is that correct, gentlemen?" Judge McNally said.

"It is, Your Honor," Mr. Hyatt said.

"That is correct, sir," Teaman Coleridge said.

"Proceed, Mr. Coleridge," the judge said.

"I will recall Mr. Thomas L. Lichine, Jr.," Teaman Coleridge said.

The uniformed attendant stood up.

"Thomas L. Lichine, Jr., please come forward."

Watching Lichine come down the aisle, Ira Bodmer had the odd feeling that the past two weeks, almost three, had been erased from the calendar. Once again it could have been the morning when, after filing the Grantham Estates 1977 federal return with the night clerk at the Tillary Street IRS facility in Brooklyn, Ira had entered the Isham Truitt offices at eight minutes after seven and heard Tom Lichine snoring away in his locked room. More accurately, it could have been a couple of hours later, at nine-thirty, when Lichine had walked in on Ira and Sal Giudice in Tony Tessitore's command post to inquire about his lost key case.

Coming down the aisle of Special Term, Part Two toward the witness stand, the handsome young man looked as though he had not even changed his clothes since that morning two or three weeks ago. Or, to annoy Ira Bodmer, he had put on the same clothes he had worn that morning. Lichine was draped in the same blue blazer, the same white button-down oxford shirt, the same black knitted tie, and the same snotty look.

It wasn't the clothing, of course, that annoyed Ira Bodmer. It was the look. Many people had that look. Most of these people did not bother Ira Bodmer. It was the look of a man who felt he was better than anybody else. Ira Bodmer understood that feeling. There were times, at night in his classes at Alexander Hamilton Law School, for example, when Ira himself had that feeling. What burned his ass about this Lichine character was the way he used the look. As though he had a special pair of telescopic sights through which he sent it out and zeroed it in. So that when you were in Lichine's presence you had the feeling it wasn't only that he believed he was better than anybody else. He gave you the feeling he believed he was better than, say, Joe Smith if you were Joe Smith, or Harry Jones if you were Harry Jones.

Ira Bodmer was not Joe Smith or Harry Jones. He was Ira Bodmer and it killed him that even here, in a courtroom full of people, where Ira Bodmer was practically invisible, he should feel all the time Thomas L. Lichine, Jr., was walking to the witness stand, and getting himself sworn in, the stuck-up bastard was actually doing those things on the surface, with only a part of his mind. The real business of his mind, what he was giving his serious attention to, was making it clear to Ira Bodmer that he believed he was better than Ira Bodmer.

"Mr. Lichine," Teaman Coleridge said. "Were you in this courtroom four days ago when Mr. Uchitel was on the stand and Miss Cline was questioning him?"

"I was," Tom Lichine said.

"Do you recall Mr. Uchitel's statement that you came to him and specifically asked, as your pro bono tour of duty, that you be assigned to *Pridemore* v. *Alabama* down in Montgomery, Alabama?"

"Yes," Tom Lichine said, "I recall Mr. Uchitel's statement."

"Do you recall, further, Mr. Lichine, when Miss Cline asked Mr. Uchitel if he asked you why you wanted to be assigned to *Pridemore* v. *Alabama*, Mr. Uchitel said you made a certain reply?" Teaman Coleridge said.

"Yes," Tom Lichine said, "I also recall that statement by Mr. Uchitel."

"Do you recall Miss Cline asking Mr. Uchitel to repeat your alleged reply to him?" Teaman Coleridge said.

"Yes, I do," Tom Lichine said.

"Do you recall Mr. Uchitel's claim that you told him 'I suggest you ask Mr. Fillmore'?" Teaman Coleridge said.

"Mr. Uchitel's claim was justified," Tom Lichine said. "I did tell him quote I suggest you ask David Fillmore unquote."

Ira Bodmer had never before seen Teaman Coleridge. Tony Tessitore had told Ira, of course, that a black lawyer from Alabama had joined Miss Cline in the courtroom as assistant in the defense of Mr. Lichine, but Tessie had said nothing more. So it was on the face of a total stranger that Ira Bodmer had now seen, or thought he had seen, a reaction that puzzled him: Tom Lichine's admission that he had told Ludwig Uchitel "I suggest you ask Mr. Fillmore" had clearly been a zetz to Mr. Coleridge. For a moment the young black man seemed rattled. The way a court clerk, asking a witness if he would tell the truth, the whole truth, and nothing but the truth, might be rattled if the witness had replied "I certainly will not." Mr. Coleridge, like the court clerk, had expected the expected. Instead, he had received the unexpected. It took him a moment or two to recover his balance. Mr. Coleridge did it smoothly enough to earn a plus mark in Ira Bodmer's assessment of his performance.

"And finally, Mr. Lichine," Teaman Coleridge said, "did you hear Miss Cline's question about whether Mr. Uchitel had followed your advice to ask Mr. Fillmore, and Mr. Uchitel's reply that he had not?"

"Yes," Tom Lichine said, "I heard that."

"As a prelude to my next question," Teaman Coleridge said, "I would like to state, Mr. Lichine, that Miss Cline and I have discussed the thrust of my present examination. She knows exactly what I am about to ask you. If she had not been unavoidably detained this morning, Miss Cline and not I would be asking my next question. Is that clear, Mr. Lichine?"

"Perfectly," Tom Lichine said.

"Would you tell us now, Mr. Lichine, why you made that statement to Mr. Uchitel?" Teaman Coleridge said. "The statement quote I suggest you ask Mr. Fillmore unquote."

"Because Mr. Fillmore knew why I would ask to be assigned to *Pridemore* v. *Alabama*," Tom Lichine said.

"You mean you consulted Mr. Fillmore before you made the request to Mr. Uchitel?" Teaman Coleridge said.

"No, I don't mean that," Tom Lichine said. "I have never consulted Mr. Fillmore about anything. I have never spoken a word to Mr. Fillmore and he has never spoken a word to me. I have never seen Mr. Fillmore in person, although I suppose if I saw him I would recognize him from seeing his picture in the papers and on TV. I've never had my picture in the papers and I've never been on television, so I'm certain if Mr. Fillmore saw me in person he would not recognize me. In the phrase 'total strangers,' Mr. Fillmore and I are about as total as you can get."

"And yet you say Mr. Fillmore knew or would know why you asked Mr. Uchitel to be assigned to *Pridemore* v. *Alabama*," Teaman Coleridge said.

"Yes, I do say that," Tom Lichine said.

Ira Bodmer, who in the past had wondered about it often, now found himself wondering again about something Mr. Teaman Coleridge did next. What could lawyers expect to gain from pausing in the heat of an examination to stare in scowling silence down at their shoes? Ira was sitting close enough to see that Mr. Coleridge's feet were encased in a pair of very nice shoes. They had the look of coming from a good shop. They were clearly expensive. They were beautifully polished. When the lawyer looked up, and Ira saw his face, he concluded that perhaps to a man who worked on his feet in public the reassurance obtained from a reminder that, what he was standing up in was at least as good as what his opponent stood up in, was in moments of stress worth the pause. It was probably not unlike refilling a fountain pen before embarking on a long, difficult letter.

"Mr. Lichine," Teaman Coleridge said finally, "I don't know Mr. David Fillmore, either. He is just a name to me. Also, as in your case, he is an occasional newspaper picture or TV image. So I cannot ask him what you told Mr. Uchitel to ask him. I can, however, ask you. Would you tell the court, Mr. Lichine, why you asked Mr. Uchitel to assign you to work on Virgil Pridemore's appeal from a death sentence in Montgomery, Alabama?"

"I had never before visited Montgomery," Tom Lichine said. "It happens to be my wife's home town. We were married not quite four months ago. At the time of the wedding we couldn't go off on a honeymoon because my wife was working in a play and I was involved in a couple of complicated matters for my boss at Isham Truitt. Just about the time my name came up on Mr. Uchitel's pro bono assignment schedule, my wife's play closed and I more or less wrapped up my contribution to the two matters my boss at Isham Truitt had me working on for several weeks. It seemed a good time for me and my wife to take our delayed honeymoon. It also seemed a good time for me to meet my in-laws. They had not been able to come to New York for the wedding because my father-in-law is an invalid. Travel is a difficult and expensive business for him. This way, by getting myself assigned to Montgomery, Alabama, a whole series of birds could be killed with one stone. My expenses would be paid, and my wife's expenses could be kept pretty nearly to little more than her fare, because we would be staying with her parents. I would have a chance to get to know my in-laws, they would get to know me, and it would be a pleasant interlude for my wife, who is fond of her parents and vice versa."

"Am I to understand, then," Teaman Coleridge said, "that you chose *Pridemore* v. *Alabama* for your pro bono assignment only because the case was being tried in Montgomery, Alabama?"

"Not exactly," Tom Lichine said. "I'd heard about the case about a year ago, just before I graduated from Harvard Law School. In fact, it was the case that brought me and my wife together."

"Could you expand on that, please?" Teaman Coleridge said.

"I met my wife at a party here in New York," Tom Lichine said. "I was down from Cambridge for the weekend. After we were introduced, and I told her I was at Harvard Law School, she started telling me about this case in Montgomery, Alabama. I became interested at once, perhaps because I became interested in her, and one thing led to another."

"What was it about this case in Montgomery, Alabama, that attracted your wife's interest?" Teaman Coleridge said.

"It dealt, as you know, with a murder that occurred because a man whose father suffered from white lung disease was trying to put his hands on the money to pay for the oxygen his father needed to stay alive," Tom Lichine said. "My wife, who was of course at that time not yet my wife, knew a great deal about the problem. Her father was a sufferer from the same disease. He still is, as you obviously must have noticed when he testified in this courtroom yesterday."

"Abraham Lincoln Soybush?" Teaman Coleridge said.

"Yes," Tom Lichine said. "When Miss Cline asked him if he knew the plaintiff in this habeas corpus proceeding, you may recall Mr. Soybush said he knew the plaintiff about as well as most fathers-in-law know their sons-in-law. That's me."

"Yes, I do recall that, of course," Teaman Coleridge said. "Just to pull the threads together, then, you knew about the Pridemore case for almost a year. Then, a month or so ago, when you learned it was coming up for appeal in Montgomery and the SPRLAA needed pro bono legal help, you volunteered."

"That's about the size of it," Tom Lichine said.

"We know, of course, the outcome of the appeal," Teaman Coleridge said. "From the standpoint of what happened to young Virgil Pridemore, therefore, I would guess you derived a great deal of satisfaction from the work you did in Montgomery."

"I did, yes," Tom Lichine said.

"In spite of the unforeseen consequences?" Teaman Coleridge said.

"Which ones?" Tom Lichine said.

"There were several, then?" Teaman Coleridge said.

"Certainly more than one," Tom Lichine said.

"Well, then, let's take them one at a time," Teaman Coleridge said. "Let's look for a moment at the discrepancy in the date on the warrant on which you were detained here in New York for extradition to Alabama, and the date on the indictment brought by the district attorney in Montgomery. The former states that the alleged murder for which you were indicted took place in Alabama on Thursday, August 10, 1978. The testimony adduced by the district attorney here in this courtroom indicates that the alleged murder took place on Friday, August 11, 1978, after the jury came in with its verdict. I think it would help clear this up if we began with the place where you were staying in Montgomery. You have testified that you and your wife were staying with her parents, Mr. and Mrs. Abraham Soybush. Is that correct?"

"It is," Tom Lichine said.

"You also testified to the fact that after you addressed the jury in *Pridemore* v. *Alabama* you returned to your hotel in Montgomery," Teaman Coleridge said. "Is that correct?"

"It is," Tom Lichine said.

"You were staying in two places?" Teaman Coleridge said.

"I was," Tom Lichine said.

"Would you explain that, please?" Teaman Coleridge said.

"When my wife and I arrived in Montgomery we moved into her parents' home," Tom Lichine said. "After the trial got under way, especially when I started digging for the material I later used in court, my hours became irregular. In order not to disturb the Soybush household, I checked into the Montgomery Lee Hotel around the corner from the courthouse."

"And it was in the Montgomery Lee Hotel that you had your meeting with Father Danaher?" Teaman Coleridge said. "The meeting that ended with his ordering you out of town? Late on Wednesday, August 9, 1978?"

"That is correct," Tom Lichine said.

"Would you fill us in, then," Teaman Coleridge said, "on your movements between late Wednesday, August 9, 1978, and early afternoon on Friday, August 11, 1978, when you were seated in the courtroom in Montgomery and heard the jury bring in its life-imprisonment verdict?"

"As I stated yesterday," Tom Lichine said, "I arrived in New York at three-thirty in the morning. That was Thursday morning, August 10, 1978. I took a taxi from the airport to my apartment. My boss, Mr. Kenneth Kreel, was staying in our apartment while my wife and I were in Alabama because his own place was being repainted. I had given him my wife's key. When I tried to let myself into the apartment with my own key, I found the security lock had been fastened on the inside. I rang the bell and knocked but there was no answer. I went downstairs to an all-night drugstore and called the apartment. For a while there was no answer but finally Mr. Kreel came on the wire. He said he'd been in a small accident, and if it was at all possible would I spend the night or what was left of it somewhere else. I asked if there was anything I could do for him, but he said no, he was all right, he just didn't want anybody in the apartment at the moment.

"I could have gone over to the Waldorf Towers," Tom Lichine continued, "where my parents live, but it was after four in the morning by now, so I taxied over to the Isham Truitt office and I went to sleep on the couch in my room. At seven-thirty I was awakened by Mr. Tessitore and his assistant Ira Bodmer, so I taxied over to the apartment of a friend of mine. I shaved and showered and came back to the office at nine-thirty, where I went to Mr. Tessitore's office to ask about my key case, which I seemed to have lost. I spent the next few hours in the Isham Truitt office. After a meeting with Mr. Dent and Miss Cline and Mr. Kelly in Mr. Kelly's office I went back to my friend's apartment, and called my wife in Alabama. She said the jury was still out. So I flew back to Montgomery on a late-afternoon plane. I was back in time for dinner with my wife and her parents. The next morning I went to the courthouse and waited for the jury to come in, which it did about one-thirty, as I recall."

"So that you were in New York, as you testified in your first appearance on the stand, on Thursday, August 10, 1978, for that meeting in Mr. Kelly's office," Teaman Coleridge said.

"I was," Tom Lichine said.

"In your first appearance on the stand in this hearing," Teaman Coleridge said, "you were questioned by your then attorney Mr. Howard Dent."

"Yes," Tom Lichine said.

"In the course of his questioning," Teaman Coleridge said, "Mr. Dent asked you about that meeting that took place on Thursday, August 10, 1978, in the private office of Mr. Hugh Kelly, a senior partner in Isham Truitt, the firm by which you were then employed here in New York and by which you had been assigned on a pro bono basis to the SPRLAA in Montgomery, Alabama. Present at that meeting were Mr. Kelly himself, Mr. Howard Dent, Miss Judith Cline, and yourself. Do you recall what took place at that meeting?"

"I do," Tom Lichine said.

"On cross-examination by the district attorney," Teaman Coleridge said, "Mr. Hyatt asked you to describe what took place at that meeting. Is that correct?"

"It is," Tom Lichine said.

"Do you recall your reply?" Teaman Coleridge said.

"I invoked the Fifth Amendment," Tom Lichine said. "I refused to answer Mr. Hyatt's question on the ground that it might incriminate or degrade me."

"I want to be very careful about my next question," Teaman Coleridge said. "I am not asking you to tell me what you refused to tell Mr. Hyatt. I am asking why you refused to tell him. Perhaps I am asking the impossible. In my mind, however, I see a distinction between a man's refusal to say something that he feels might incriminate or degrade him, and the same man's refusal to say the same thing because he feels it may incriminate or degrade somebody else. In one case the man is shielding himself. In the other case he is shielding somebody else. I don't think you can answer my question, Mr. Lichine, unless such a distinction exists."

"It does," Tom Lichine said.

"There is such a distinction?" Teaman Coleridge said.

"Yes," Tom Lichine said.

"Could you tell us, then—" Teaman Coleridge said, and paused. "No, let me rephrase that," he said. "Would you be willing, then, to tell us why you refused to answer Mr. Hyatt's question?"

"I did it to save Mr. Howard Dent from public disgrace," Tom Lichine said.

Ira Bodmer could feel rather than hear or see what was suddenly happening all around him. People whose chests did not move were catching their breaths. Arms and legs that remained visibly motionless were easing into more comfortable positions.

"Would you expand on that, Mr. Lichine?" Teaman Coleridge said.

"In the course of the work I did with the other SPRLAA lawyers who were working on Virgil Pridemore's defense," Tom Lichine said, "I found myself turning up material that was denied to others. As the son-in-law of Abraham Soybush I was shown certain evidence he had been accumulating for years not only as the business manager of Local Number Five of the Asbestos Workers Union but also, beginning twenty-five years ago in 1953, as a victim of the white lung disease. Much of this sort of evidence is always a matter of statistics. The damaged workers say their employers did nothing. The plant owners say they did everything humanly possible. The number of people who got sick, when they got sick, and what was done about their sickness, these are matters of constant dispute. In the case of white lung disease the manufacturers of asbestos, especially Southern Shoals, which is the largest in the country, maintain they have from the very beginning tried to minimize the danger to workers in their plants. They claim they have set up research centers to study the problem and find cures. They insist they have on a regular basis conducted physical examinations of their employees, prescribed treatment, and kept records that are useful to researchers hunting for a cure. All this may or may not be true. It depends on whose evidence you are hearing. What happened while I was down in Montgomery working on *Pridemore* v. *Alabama* is something about which there can be no argument."

"What is that?" Teaman Coleridge said.

"A piece of paper," Tom Lichine said. "A memorandum. A secret memorandum. Written in 1938, that's forty years ago, a secret memorandum written forty years ago by Sosthenes DeKalb, at that time chief executive officer of Southern Shoals Asbestos."

"To whom was this memorandum addressed?" Teaman Coleridge said.

"To all Southern Shoals executives," Tom Lichine said.

"What was the subject matter of this secret memorandum?" Teaman Coleridge said.

"The physical examinations that Southern Shoals' doctors were giving their own employees in Southern Shoals infirmaries throughout the country, including Montgomery, Alabama," Tom Lichine said. "They had been giving these examinations to Southern Shoals employees for several years. In 1938 the Southern Shoals' doctors became disturbed. Their reports to the top brass were upsetting. In these situations what scares top brass, of course, is financial liability. If the trend that was already becoming clear in 1938 continued, and the liability for the spread of white lung disease in the Southern Shoals plants could be nailed down to the way those plants were run, the financial damage to Southern Shoals could be so large that it might bankrupt the company."

"Did this secret memorandum recommend any course of action?" Teaman Coleridge said.

"It did," Tom Lichine said.

"What was the recommendation?" Teaman Coleridge said.

"It was not a recommendation," Tom Lichine said. "It was an order."

"From Sosthenes DeKalb?" Teaman Coleridge said.

"To all Southern Shoals executives," Tom Lichine said. "Ordering them to suppress or destroy all reports of company-given physical examinations that showed lung contamination in any Southern Shoals employee."

"This was in 1938?" Teaman Coleridge said.

"Yes," Tom Lichine said. "And a month ago, in 1978, I managed to put my hands on a copy of this memorandum."

"How?" Teaman Coleridge said.

"The business manager of Local Number Five of the Asbestos Workers Union gave me a Xerox of the original," Tom Lichine said. "He has kept the original in a safe-deposit box in a Montgomery, Alabama, bank since 1953."

"Why the delay?" Teaman Coleridge said.

"He was afraid of reprisals," Tom Lichine said. "He was waiting for an appropriate moment. Meaning a moment when he could make the revelation in safety."

"Safety to his physical person?" Teaman Coleridge said.

"Yes," Tom Lichine said.

"You were the appropriate moment?" Teaman Coleridge said.

"I as his new son-in-law was the appropriate moment," Tom Lichine said. "For the first time in twenty-five years, since he dug up the memorandum after he was himself incapacitated by white lung disease, Mr. Soybush felt they would not dare move against him physically for making the revelation."

"What does all this have to do with Howard Dent?" Teaman Coleridge said.

"Mr. Dent drafted that memorandum for Sosthenes DeKalb in 1938," Tom Lichine said.

"As a lawyer employed by Southern Shoals?" Teaman Coleridge said.

"No," Tom Lichine said. "As a major stockholder protecting his holdings."

"In 1938?" Teaman Coleridge said.

"Mr. Dent became familiar with the area in the early days of the New Deal," Tom Lichine said. "He was one of Franklin Roosevelt's chief lieutenants in the fight to establish the TVA. During the course of that fight Howard Dent came to know the Southern Shoals people, and they came to know Howard Dent. The friendship turned out to be a mutual assistance pact. Howard Dent took his reward in the form of Southern Shoals common stock. As a major stockholder it was in his personal interest to mastermind the white lung disease cover-up."

"Yet I understood from Miss Cline that Mr. Dent volunteered to serve without a fee as your counsel in this habeas corpus matter," Teaman Coleridge said.

"He was ninety-one years old," Tom Lichine said. "Rich and full of honors. A legal fee, especially the small one he could expect from a client like me, meant nothing to Howard Dent. The evidence I was in a position to reveal at a hearing of this kind meant everything to him."

"In what way?" Teaman Coleridge said.

"It could destroy his reputation," Tom Lichine said.

"You are saying Howard Dent wanted to serve as your counsel because it would provide him with an opportunity to suppress the memorandum you have just described to us?"

"As well as his long, secret involvement with Southern Shoals," Tom Lichine said.

"It doesn't seem to have turned out that way, does it?" Teaman Coleridge said.

"No," Tom Lichine said. "My taking the Fifth was a shock to him. It was a signal. It told him for the first time that I had not been fooled by his offer to defend me. He grasped that there was another reason why I had consented to let him act as my counsel in this hearing. A reason that would set in motion forces he could neither control nor suppress."

"What was your reason?"

"I wanted to save Miss Cline from learning the truth about

the man she had believed for years she was going to marry," Tom Lichine said.

"What man?" Teaman Coleridge said.

"Me," Tom Lichine said.

41

"Oh, my God," Tony Tessitore said.

"I know," Ira Bodmer said. "That's what I thought, too, when I heard Lichine say it. Hold it a second, Mr. Tessitore. One second."

Ira opened the phone-booth door and looked out. The crowd shoving and pushing around the entrance to the courtroom had grown larger. Ira pulled his head back in and pushed the door shut.

"It's all right," he said into the phone.

"Are you crazy?" Tony Tessitore said.

"I'm sorry, Mr. Tessitore," Ira Bodmer said. "I didn't mean it's all right like in everything is okay. I mean the noise and the shoving out in the hall, the crowd's bigger, that's all. I mean the word seems to be spreading through the building. But nothing's happening in the courtroom. I mean the recess is still on. I can keep talking till I hear the bell."

"Well, then, talk, for Christ's sake," Tony Tessitore said at the other end of the wire. "Don't you realize what this means?"

"Sure I do," Ira Bodmer said. Then: "No, I don't. I mean let me just tell what happened, and you can tell me later what it means."

"All right, all right," Tony Tessitore said. "Talk."

When Ira Bodmer finished talking about the 1938 secret memorandum, Tony Tessitore said, "Oh, Jesus. How did all that work its way around to Lichine's father?"

"His father-in-law," Ira Bodmer said. "Lichine's. When Mr.

Soybush got too sick to work in the plant, he and his wife started this Tots Home, and one day the plant lawyer came to see him and asked if they could take a pregnant mother who was about to give birth. Soybush said they could do anything if the price was right. So one day a woman showed up with a doctor and a private nurse. They kept her under wraps. After a few days the woman had the baby. A few days after that she disappeared. And a few days after that they came for the baby."

"They?" Tony Tessitore said. "How many theys are we dealing with?"

"The first they, the doctor and the pregnant woman," Ira Bodmer said. "She was the famous actress Amelia Troy. The second they, the ones who came after the baby was born, they were Amelia Troy's husband and another nurse. They took the newborn baby and they went away."

"How did Lichine on the stand tie all this to us?" Tony Tessitore said.

"He testified his father-in-law, Mr. Soybush, he got paid for the whole thing by Mr. David Fillmore's lawyers," Ira Bodmer said.

"Oy!" Tony Tessitore said.

"I know," Ira Bodmer said.

"What else do you know?" Tony Tessitore said.

"Like what?" Ira Bodmer said.

"Like why did Lichine Junior want to spill this stuff right now?" Tony Tessitore said. "It's been twenty-five years."

"I don't know yet," Ira Bodmer said. "It was at this point that young black lawyer, he asked for the recess. There goes the bell, Mr. Tessitore. I better get in there. I'll call you back."

42

"Your full name, please," Judy Cline said.

"David Fillmore."

"Your address?" Judy said.

"One Rockefeller Plaza," David Fillmore said. "New York one-o-o-two-o."

"Your occupation, please?" Judy said.

"I am the chairman of the board of the Fillmore National Bank," David Fillmore said.

"According to this morning's New York *Times*," Judy said, "you were scheduled to testify today before a United States Senate committee examining your qualifications for the job of Vice-President to which you were recently nominated by the President."

"That is correct," David Fillmore said. "I requested and received a postponement."

"Why?" Judy said.

"My Washington appearance was in conflict with this one," David Fillmore said. "This one seemed to me more important."

"No further questions," Judy said. She turned to the assistant district attorney. "Your witness, Mr. Hyatt."

The assistant district attorney came toward the witness stand.

"Mr. Fillmore," he said. "You are aware of the nature of this hearing?"

"I am," David Fillmore said.

"You are aware that some of the testimony adduced here is

of an extremely damaging nature to the Southern Shoals Asbestos Corporation?" Mr. Hyatt said.

"So the press would seem to indicate," David Fillmore said.

"What happens here today could militate against your confirmation by the Senate for the post of Vice-President, could it not?" the assistant district attorney said.

"Without any doubt," David Fillmore said.

"To my knowledge, Mr. Fillmore, you were not subpoenaed to appear here today," Mr. Hyatt said. "Is that correct?"

"It is," David Fillmore said.

"Who asked you to come here and testify?" the assistant district attorney said.

"The young lady now seated at counsels' table," David Fillmore said. "Miss Judith Cline."

"If you know the risks involved in your appearance here," Mr. Hyatt said, "why did you agree to testify?"

"I could not say no to the lawyer for my own son," David Fillmore said.

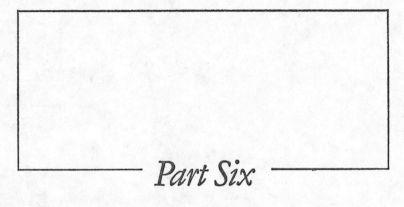

Part Six

"Religion has done love
a great service by making
it a sin."

ANATOLE FRANCE

43

"It looks like my husband has finally found his wife," Bianca Bean said.

Teaman Coleridge turned to the girl standing by his side at the far end of counsels' table. They were waiting for the courtroom to empty and for Judy Cline and Tom Lichine to finish their private talk at the other end of the long table.

"What took him so long?" Teaman Coleridge said.

"They're both from up north," Bianca Bean said. "About some things northerners are not as swift as southern folk."

"Where does that leave you?" Teaman Coleridge said.

"On a line in the unemployment insurance office," Bianca Bean said.

"I somehow don't think that's your style," Teaman Coleridge said.

She touched him lightly with a short, slanting smile.

"Southerners are always swift about each other," Bianca Bean said.

"There's always such a thing as a civilized, inexpensive no-contest divorce," Teaman Coleridge said.

"If I found the right lawyer," Bianca Bean said, "I don't think the expense would be any problem."

Teaman Coleridge gave her a short, slanting smile of his own. She had a street-smart look. When he was a boy in Montgomery all the girls he used to find himself turning to catch another glimpse of had that look. Bianca Bean reminded him of an actress his grandfather had admired deeply.

"Simone is a lovely name," Schermerhorn Coleridge had said. "It is a rare girl indeed who deserves to wear it twice."

Teaman Coleridge remembered Simone Simone only from newspaper photographs. Faded ones, at that. His recollection, however, was vivid. He took another look at Bianca Bean. She had bigger tits, of course, but nowadays what girl didn't?

"I'll bet I know what you're thinking," she said.

"I hate to lose," Teaman Coleridge said. "Tell me without betting, and I'll tell you something in exchange."

"You're thinking when Tom and I met a few months ago," Bianca Bean said, "why didn't he just go to Miss Cline and say I've just learned something about myself that I must check out before I feel I have the right to marry you."

"Why didn't he?" Teaman Coleridge said.

"A few years from now he might have," Bianca Bean said. "Today, however, he's still trapped in one of those stifling moral dilemmas in which honky has not yet learned how to breathe."

This time the smile was only in her eyes, but it was still slanting.

"All right," Teaman Coleridge said. "I owe you something. What would you like to know?"

"Are you personally unhappy with the way it came out?" Bianca Bean said.

For Teaman Coleridge it was not a new thought. He had been thinking about the future. It would be built, of course, around the break-up of Isham, Truitt, Kelly, Shreve, Merz, Uchitel and Condomine. Rising from the wreckage, Teaman Coleridge could see two clear possibilities. One, the almost inevitable formation of a Washington-based firm: Falk, Prudhomme, Rhodes, Taunton, Cooper and Taunton. Two, a brand-new firm called either Lichine, Cline and Coleridge, or Cline, Lichine and Coleridge.

Whether the billing led off with Lichine or with Cline would depend, of course, on the degree of commitment by the partners to something called chivalry. The white partners, that is. Teaman's grandfather Schermerhorn, who had been one of Howard Dent's classmates at Harvard Law School, would without doubt have made it Cline Lichine. But that was in another time, if not in another country, and besides that particular wench was dead.

Today, in 1978, chivalry would have to contend with Millet and Friedan and Abzug. What was being assembled was, after all, a law firm not a lifeboat. So it would probably be Lichine first and Cline second. As for Teaman Coleridge, he knew his place, whether in a lifeboat or on a letterhead. The time was not yet ripe, however, for him to assume it. When the ripened moment arrived the grandson of Schermerhorn Coleridge would be squatting solidly in position behind home plate, ready to make the catch. In the meantime he would without discomfort make do with third place.

"I guess they're finished," Bianca Bean said.

Teaman Coleridge looked more closely at the heads bent toward one another at the far end of counsels' table. If Judy Cline and Tom Lichine were not finished, there was something touchingly reassuring about the two attractive youngsters bowed gropingly toward each other, uncertain about how to resume a relationship that had never really ended. They would have a joined lifetime to work on the details.

"I think it's my job to speak first," Bianca Bean said as she moved along beside Teaman Coleridge toward the far end of counsels' table. "I don't want to leave them in any doubt."

"About what?" Teaman Coleridge said.

"That I have no intention of standing in their way," Bianca Bean said. "That I'm glad they finally made it, and I wish them nothing but luck."

"Why don't you say just that?" Teaman Coleridge said.

"Because they're a couple of lawyers," Bianca Bean said. "So are you. You all speak that funny 'in' language. How about lending your new client a few of your billable words?"

"*Res ipsa loquitur,*" Teaman Coleridge said.

About the Author

JEROME WEIDMAN, who won a Pulitzer Prize for FIORELLO!, has long been a distinguished novelist, short story writer, essayist, and playwright. Among Mr. Weidman's twenty-two novels are I CAN GET IT FOR YOU WHOLESALE, THE ENEMY CAMP, THE SOUND OF BOW BELLS, the so-called Benny Kramer Sequence (FOURTH STREET EAST, LAST RESPECTS, TIFFANY STREET), and A FAMILY FORTUNE. His short stories—which have appeared in *The New Yorker, Harper's Magazine, Esquire,* and every other major magazine in this country and abroad—have been collected in eight volumes, and his books and plays have been translated into ten languages.